About the author: Alastair McIver

Alastair is a Christian writer and journalist. He has been widely published in both tennis and Christian publications over a career spanning three decades. After many visits to central and south Asia, hearing testimonies from women about the widespread injustices perpetrated on them in their lives, he determined to expose some of the wrongdoing he observed on his travels in a revelatory but fictional format.

The Daily News is a political conspiracy thriller, the first in the *Roza Beshimov Investigates* series.

Disclaimer

The names, characters and incidents portrayed in this novel are the work of the author's imagination. Any resemblance to actual persons or events are purely coincidental.

Dedication

I would like to dedicate this book to all those who have prayed with me on the journey to publication, especially my family, my prayer partner and my church friends.

The Daily News

There is nothing hidden that will not be revealed...

Reading notes

There is a ten-hour time difference between Bishkek (ahead) and Washington (behind)

The seats of political power in both Bishkek (capital of Kyrgyzstan) and Washington DC, are called the same – The White House

Kyrgyz words used throughout the book:

Marshrutka – bus

Ala Kachuu – bride kidnapping

Kyrgyz Characters:

Feliks Ormanbekov, President of Kyrgyzstan

Kadrjvan Akayev, Prime Minister

Alexander Kulov, Foreign Affairs Minister

Shirin Kurmanbek, Proprietor of the Bishkek Daily News (BDN)

Ednan Askar, Editor of BDN

Temir Batyrov, Olga Kola and **Roza Beshimov,** journalists at BDN

Kamil Joroev – nomadic background dweller now working for the Kyrgyz government

American Characters:

Robert de Layney, Secretary of State, US Administration

Stoski Ocean, Press Officer to the Secretary of State

Miriam Serenatti, President of the United States

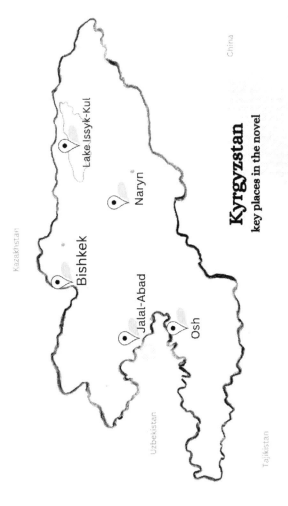

Kyrgyzstan
key places in the novel

China

Lake Issyk-Kul

Naryn

Kazakhstan

Bishkek

Jalal-Abad

Osh

Uzbekistan

Tajikistan

Part 1

Literary Tongues

Prologue

And so it came to pass, with autumn leaves falling to the ground outside of his small barber's business on Akbura Street, that Azimbek Beshimov, razor blade in hand, looked down at the unsuspecting Mr Kurmanbek. The proprietor's media sized bulk, swelled by too many generous lunches with government officials, press personnel and businessmen, fitted snugly into the arch of the black faux leather barber's chair. It had been angled back to a horizontal position, parallel to the floor, with only a blistered white ceiling for unsuspecting customers to view. His scalp rested on the black head rest, his gravelly neck exposed to the mercy of the razor-wielding barber of Bishkek. Trapped. A captive. A victim?

Azimbek's daughter, Roza may have taken three years to achieve her degree in media studies, and been able to proudly hold the proof closely to her chest, but that didn't guarantee her a job in 21st century Kyrgyzstan. She still needed the help of her father to get her on to the first rung of the media ladder. She pestered him to speak with the unsuspecting Kurmanbek, not only an established newspaper proprietor but a loyal and long-standing patron of Azimbek's modest parlour.

The executioner's razor blade was just millimetres from its target, ready to draw blood.

'She's keen, she's bright and she'll do anything to work in journalism, if she could only get her foot in the door," he said, with no hint of malice.

This has to be done well, thought Azimbek.

"Local barber slits newspaper tycoon's throat" would not be a good look on the news stands, even if the headline was depicting an unfortunate accident.

He needn't have worried. In an amazingly nerveless action, born of nearly 30 years' experience, the barber of Bishkek executed a smooth upward motion, tracing around the contours of the proprietor's protruding Adam's apple, and removing in one slick movement a perfect line of rich white lather that had, just seconds before, covered his neck and lower face. No blood.

A few minutes later, the deed was done. The proprietor, delighted with his shave, promised Azimbek that he would speak with his editor to see if a meeting could be arranged.

Azimbek, for his part, was so happy to have won over his client for his daughter, that he declined payment.

The deal was secured on a warm handshake between the two men.

The rotund Mr Kurmanbek, a little spring in his step, squeezed his way through the single, glazed door of the little barber's shop, and into the early morning brightness of another hot and sunny

11

Bishkek day. A contented Azimbek, wiping his blade with a towel, a broad smile on his face, watched him go on his way.

1

Friday evening – Bishkek, Kyrgyzstan

Batyrov's mobile phone lit up. He stretched over to his bedside table and pressed the green icon.

"Temir, it's Erik, Erik Sidarov. I'm sorry to call you on a Friday evening. I need to talk with you. Are you free at all this weekend?"

Batyrov was taken aback. Like the rest of Bishkek's workers, he was unwinding at home after a long week, but he knew that Sidarov, a veteran of Kyrgyz political life who had survived three Presidential coups and five elections over 15 years, would not be calling unless it was something important.

Before he could splutter out a response, Sidarov assumed Batyrov's acceptance.

"Let's meet tomorrow morning. But not at Chuy. Can you come to my apartment?"

Batyrov was both curious and excited. Phone to ear, he lay his weary head on to the pillow and anticipated the possibilities. Why me? Why now? Why Sidarov?

Invitations like this one had, over the years, always made Batyrov's heart skip a beat. They usually meant political misdemeanour, something Batyrov never liked to ignore. It was for calls like this that he existed.

As he stretched out his 6 foot 2 inch frame on his bed, his toes pressing into the footboard slat, he stared up at a small crack in the ceiling. It had appeared last winter. He had intended to fill it and repaint it. But he never got round to it. There were always more important things to attend to, like planning his retirement. And why not?

At 66 years of age, and like most seasoned political journalists of similar vintage, he had earned it. He had dreamed of moving away from the capital, putting his feet up at his little holiday home on the east side of Lake Issy Kul. He had said as much to his editor and there was even talk of a leaving meal at the end of the year.

As much as he might be ready for it, though, the inevitability of retirement did not sit well with him. In fact he dreaded it. Cutting the umbilical cord of investigative political journalism from his life might be the sensible option. But a life of fishing for trout and pikeperch every morning and reading ghost-written autobiographical memoirs about corrupt politicians, a glass of *Moskovskaya Osobayam* to hand, into the late evening, would leave him bereft of that which had driven him for 40 years!

And now, tonight. This autumnal Friday night. Sidarov.   Sidarov, one of the few Kyrgyz politicians he had any respect for. Why had he called? What was so important? What was on his mind?

He pondered his dilemma for a few moments before making his decision. His inevitable decision. He would meet Sidarov in the morning, and take it from there.

"Of course, Erik. Of course. 9.30am?"

The small crack in the ceiling would have to wait....again. So might retirement.

2

Friday morning – White House, Washington

6,000 miles away, Washington was waking up to its coffee and bagels. White House staff, sporting heavy coats, scarves wrapped tightly around their necks, were entering the estate's leafy grounds, showing their security passes to smartly suited personnel, some of them armed. Another political day on Pennsylvania Avenue was about to begin.

Stoski Ocean walked in to Secretary of State Robert de Layney's office with purpose. He picked up a remote control and pointed it at one of the three television screens which hung from the office wall.

"Good morning, sir. This doesn't look good."

"Yes, I did have a good trip Stos," de Layney responded, a hint of good natured sarcasm in his voice.

He had only been at his desk for a few minutes, back in his office following his short visit to the South Americas. It had been successful, but exhausting and the two hours difference between time zones didn't aid any recovery his sleep deprived body was crying out for. His trusty alarm clock didn't help either. He had never really asked his teenage daughter why she had chosen the chorus of Miley Cyrus' *Party in the USA* as his ringtone. Perhaps it was because it never failed to jolt him from his slumber.

"I'm sorry, sir. But you need to see this."

De Layney averted his tired eyes from his morning batch of order papers and peered at the monitor attentively studied by his Press Secretary. It was telling its latest story, in graphic detail.

Drought. Death. Corpses.

"What does this have to do with us?" muttered de Layney, his tone dismissive.

"Sir, in a few days time we will be flying right into the eye of that storm, just north of where these pictures are coming from. It could turn out to be a major distraction if we're not careful."

De Layney shrugged his shoulders, dismissively.

"It might all be sorted by then. The world moves on, you know, Stos."

Ocean didn't look convinced.

"And it might not…sir. Be sorted, I mean."

De Layney acknowledged Ocean's concern.

"OK, so we might need to address it somehow with words of sympathy in the region, but our only agenda item is to get our agreement signed. Other than that, we ignore it. Don't we?"

"Of course, but it's still an unfortunate coincidence. We happen to be heading into central Asia to sign a multi-million dollar military deal when the number one news item in the world is about people dying of thirst in the region. The media will want to know why we are pumping millions of dollars into Kyrgyzstan for a military deal at a time of drought!"

"Dammit, Stos, we are not responsible for monitoring the world's rainfall, or lack of it!"

"Yes, but…."

"And anyway, as far as the media is concerned, this is just a trade deal. And it is. Airspace for dollars. That's a trade off. No one needs to know any more at this stage. We can't risk any security leaks on this one."

Ocean didn't want to appear to be contradicting his increasingly animated Secretary of State. But he needed to make his point. After an extended pause, he changed tack.

"The environmentalists will be all over it, sir. Some already are. *Death by Drought*, they're calling it in the Post! *Climate Genocide*. That's the Globe. We may have to fight for the moral high ground here."

De Layney slumped back into his leather chair.

"Mmmm. Eco nutters. I forgot about them. You may be right. We don't want to be in their line of fire. They'll milk it for all it's worth, promoting their ridiculous agendas and asking stupid questions, just as they did after Brazil last year. Why the media gives them so much airtime, I'll never know?"

The two men looked each other in the eye, a pregnant, elongated stand off between them. Ocean awaited the Secretary of State's next move.

"OK, Stos, I hear you. But the airspace agreement is what we are going there for, and that has to take priority. It's by far the biggest military deal we've made in a decade and we need to focus on getting it done. If the Middle East blows up again, no one's going to care about the environment. We have the opportunity to bring stability to the region, even if we have to work with back-alley Kyzik dictators to do it…."

"Kyrgyz, sir. We're going to Kyrgyzstan."

"And…," continued the animated Secretary of State, "by placing our aircraft just a few hours away from Israel, we get to re-order the region back in our favour. That's big. We are about to put one over on the Russians and Chinese. Drought or no drought, we mustn't be deflected from the task in hand."

Ocean knew that the Secretary of State was right. The signing of an agreement which would reinstate an American military presence in central

Asia for the first time since their unceremonious eviction from the Kyrgyz capital eleven years before, was ground-breaking. It would bolster the Americans *'Agenda for Peace and Stability'* initiative in the Middle East and swing the global pendulum of influence, both militarily and politically, in their favour. Israel was positively purring at an American military presence on its doorstep.

"If you pull this off, Robert, our enemies will have to think twice before targeting Tel Aviv with their bombs," Israel's President had told de Layney three months earlier. The two men nodded agreement across continents. But they also knew that this would be a hard sell. The covertly negotiated 'trade' deal would come as a major shock, not least to Kyrgyzstan's oblivious neighbouring superpowers. But once signed, a US long-term presence on central Asian soil would be secured, and irreversible.

De Layney sought to reassure his always apprehensive Press Secretary.

"Stos, look at me."

The two men made eye contact.

"Focus on the bigger picture. Militarily, this is unsurpassed in our life time. We both know it's win win for us. There can be no negatives coming out of this...."

De Layney picked up a White House pen, a thick red and white stripe along its side.

"….not even drought."

3

Friday evening, White House, Bishkek

The panoramic view from President Ormanbekov's 7th floor vantage point never disappointed. The White House's neighbouring landmarks, the Philharmonia building and the Monument to the Martyrs of the Revolution, dominated the periphery. The minaret of the Central Mosque in the distance stretched itself majestically upwards, touching the underbelly of the capital's greying horizon. It was a sight that he and his two trusted allies, Prime Minister, Kadrjvan Akayev and the Foreign Affairs Minister, Alexander Kulov, never grew tired of. Bishkek at its finest.

Ormanbekov was in buoyant mood. His *'Grand plan for the Republic,'* as he liked to call it, was about to be birthed. A celebratory mood was in the air. Ormanbekov, Akayev and Kulov, the three most powerful men in Kyrgyzstan, sensed it. The President knew it.

"Our destiny is at the arrivals desk," he joked, a glint in his eye. "The Americans are arriving shortly with a very large satchel of dollars. And we, only we, the Republic of Kyrgyzstan, have what they want."

The three men lay their brief cases and bags on to the large, polished algumwood table, at the centre of which was placed a carafe of water and an unopened packet of *Khortitsya Krasnaya Originalnye* Russian cigarettes.

A small drinks cabinet sat unobtrusively at the far end of the room. A round, silver tray, with three cut glass decanters on it, was placed at the centre. One was filled with Gorilka vodka, one of Ukraine's finest, another with Stolichnaya Elit, a similar Russian tipple, and the third with Ararat cognac. Akayev poured three drinks and distributed them.

Ormanbekov turned to face his colleagues.

"Gentlemen, a toast. *Kyrgyzstandyn erkindigi uchun.*"

"Freedom for Kyrgyzstan," they repeated in unison, before raising large measures of Stolichnaya Elit to their lips.

Ormanbekov walked back towards the window and took in the view, reflecting momentarily on his journey. His eyes began to moisten. It had been a long one, two decades of sweat and tears. He didn't like to think too much about the blood!

"Are we sure they will buy into our plans?" querled Akayev.

"They will do anything to set their feet back on Kyrgyz soil. You know, comrades, we could bankroll Kyrgyzstan with roubles or yuan, but those currencies don't come with an American accent. And they want easy access to the Middle East. Only we can give it to them. They will not decline our offer. For all their deficiencies, they want to see the world a better place, but only if it is built in their image. Their arrogance won't allow them to fail."

Their meeting concluded as it had begun, with a toast 'to success.'

"*Iygilik uchun*," they harmonised before picking up their bags and exiting the room.

There was little more to be said. The finishing line was drawing near. Victory beckoned.

4

Friday evening, Vefa

Ormanbekov's driver returned him to his guarded, gated private residence located in the Vefa sector of the capital. It was empty. His wife Yelena had picked up their twelve year old daughter, Rosaria, after school that afternoon and was on her way to the family's weekend retreat in Issy Kul. Ormanbekov, with an American Secretary of State arriving on Tuesday evening, was going nowhere.

He took off his shoes, slipped into his comfy, felt *tapoçkalars* and switched on the TV. He slouched back on to the sofa, resting his weary feet on the tan, velvet coated Ottaman pouffe and clicked on to the sports channel. 'Replay.' The Austrian Open. Semi-finals. Live.

He turned up the volume. The latest Kazakh tennis sensation was serving for the first set against his seeded French opponent when the phone rang. It was Kulov.

"Have you seen the news?"

Ormanbekov knew that he wasn't talking tennis.

He switched to the Asia 1 Channel just in time to see an image of an awkwardly shaped individual, lying by the side of the road, being sniffed at by a Chippiparai dog and pecked at by passing birds.

"....this is Jane Morley, reporting for CBN News, Peshawar, northern Pakistan."

"What's this all about, Alexander?"

"Drought. On the Tajik Afghan border. Thirst. And cholera. It's killing thousands. The media is on to it."

Ormanbekov's delayed response didn't match Kulov's obvious concern.

"How interesting, Alexander. The south Tajik border, you say."

"And north east Afghanistan. Afghans are pouring north in their thousands, seeking refuge, water, anything."

"So, the much anticipated drought has finally arrived. How very timely."

Kulov hadn't expected any sympathy from his President. Compassion wasn't his strong suit but even *he* was excelling himself this evening. But what did Ormanbekov mean by 'timely'? Kulov didn't have long to wait for an answer.

"This may well work in our favour, Alexander. We always knew that drought would come but now that it has arrived, we can make it work for us. This really is very good news."

"But the agreement is already finalised?"

"But not signed," responded the President. "I'm sure that the Americans won't object to us tweaking it a little. Maybe we could add a little environmental clause before they put pen to paper. After all, they wouldn't want to be seen to be signing a 10 year military deal in the very same week that thousands of our neighbours are dying of thirst. The environmentalists would be all over it, calling them callous, heartless. And they'd be right. No Alexander, this timely drought might help us push forward our water project. I don't know how we will do this, but it's possible. And….and, we might even be able to extract a few additional dollars from our American friends to drive it forward. It's all very convenient."

Kulov had to admire the President's attempts to turn a tragic event into an opportunity for financial gain. Regional dominance, using Kyrgyzstan's abundant fresh water supplies, had been discussed over several months, but only as phase two of the region's ongoing power play. It was to be discussed after the Americans had put pen to paper on the lucrative airspace agreement they were coming to sign. Now, it seemed to Kulov, that because of the drought, Ormanbekov was minded to bring phase two forward. He wanted to know more.

"So Feliks, you want to amend the agreement to garner American support for our environmental agenda."

"Financial support, Alexander. Financial support."

"On top of the millions which they are already paying us."

"Indeed, Alexander. That's going to be significant enough, but now, for a few extra dollars, we can add some icing on to the cake."

"You sound confident, Feliks."

"I am. If we bring forward our water project…."

"Whatever that will look like," interjected Kulov.

"….*if* we bring forward our water project," Ormanbekov continued, undeterred by Kulov's intervention, "and support our thirsty neighbours, it will diffuse those hostile environmental voices that are constantly on our backs. No one will be able to say that we, or the Americans for that matter, are putting military needs before humanitarian needs."

Kulov sensed that the President was thinking fast, on his feet. It was impressive, but he had no way of knowing where his thoughts were heading. The water project was no more than just a name, a political aspiration. There had been no planning meetings, no strategy papers written about how Kyrgyzstan could turn its formidable natural asset into an income stream. Perhaps it was because most of Kyrgyzstan's political strategy was firmly entrenched in Ormanbekov's mind until it was ready to be released.

Or maybe, thought Kulov, it was because no one had ever come up with an answer to the question, 'how can Kyrgyzstan stay on the right side of international law when it comes to its utilisation of a national asset like fresh water?' Was that the one big hurdle that had kept this ideological aspiration on the back burner?

Right now, it didn't matter. Drought was afoot, and moving Ormanbekov's thinking forward. It was his opportunity to mastermind a plan that, on the surface would appear to benefit the region's needs, while at the same time bring financial gain to his country?

Could he couch it in a way that would see the Kyrgyzstan Republic stay on the right side of international protocols and agreements, the global environment lobby and the financially supportive European Union?

What he had in mind would all be unethical. Yes. Unscrupulous. Certainly. Illegal. Probably. But that was Ormanbekov. Ever the opportunist. Ever the ambitious politician with a lust for national power, regional recognition, global status.

"Are you there Alexander?"

Kulov had been lost in his thoughts, but quickly returned to the call.

"Yes, yes, Feliks. So what are you thinking?"

"The Americans may be desperate to get a foothold back in our country but even they wouldn't want to be seen to be ignoring the crisis in the region they are about to set foot in. That would be embarrassing for them. And given that this crisis has just blown up in our faces, I am perfectly at liberty to raise it with them, do you not think, Alexander? They may need a little persuading but they won't reject us. They wouldn't dare. Just focusing on their military needs at a time like this would make them look very bad in the eyes of the world. And don't forget Alexander. We hold the trump card. If they won't play ball, I'll threaten to pull the military deal."

Ormanbekov laughed loudly down the phone, causing Kulov to take his mobile from his ear.

"Anyway, think on Alexander. I still haven't worked out how we can turn our abundant water assets to our financial advantage, but maybe, just maybe, this drought is our opportunity."

Without waiting for Kulov to respond, Ormanbekov ended the call and sat back on the sofa.

He picked up the remote, and switched back to the sports channel. The Kazakh had held serve to take the first set 6-4."

"Bravo, bravo."

Ormanbekov laid back on the sofa, and nodded off.

At midnight, the clock in the hallway struck 12 times. On the 8th chime, he stirred. He adjusted his eyes to the brightness of the TV, the only light in the room. The Kazakh was being interviewed on court after a victory which had seen him defeat the French No 4 seed in a final set tie-break.

Ormanbekov shrugged his shoulders. He would have preferred a Kyrgys player in the final, but if it had to be a neighbouring Kazakh, so be it.

He went to the polished cabinet that housed his alcohol portfolio and stood in front of the beautifully carved Schneider mirror that hung on the wall, a gift from the Swiss Prime Minister during a previous visit to Geneva.

He took out a cut glass tumbler, into which he poured a large brandy, his third of the evening. He raised it to eye level.

'*Za zdorovye,*' he said to the face staring back at him from the mirror, before swallowing his drink down in a single motion.

The President switched off the TV, and took to his bed, a contented man.

5

Saturday morning, Sidarov's apartment, Bishkek

The following morning, having not enjoyed as much sleep as his tired body and mind needed, Temir Batyrov made his way up Yakov Logvinenko Street towards the junction of Manas and Sovietskaya before taking a sharp left into Toktogul Street.

Sidarov's apartment was plush and the coffee was strong.

"Thank you for coming over, Temir."

The two men walked into the living room. Batyrov sat down on the maroon and brown, reverse applique designed sofa. Sidarov stood by the window. He didn't hang about.

"Temir, I'm told by one of the 7th floor guards at the White House that Ormanbekov, Kulov and Akayev have been meeting covertly for months, every Friday evening apparently, without fail. I don't know what it's about, but with the Americans due next week, I fear that Ormanbekov may be up to something. Ormanbekov isn't a time waster. Anything he does out of hours with those two isn't going to be for the greater good."

Ormanbekov was not known for his transparency and had a track record of making duplicitous deals, not usually for the benefit of the country he was President of. It was something that Batyrov had written about many times over the years. So this wasn't news to him, but he respectfully pondered Sidarov's words.

"Mmmm. Sounds a bit suspicious, Erik."

Sidarov nodded his agreement.

"They've been meeting for at least three months....*three months*," Sidarov emphasised. "Maybe more, just the three of them, every week. That's out of character for Ormanbekov. He likes to keep his hours in check."

"And the meetings are just with Akayev and Kulov, you say. His closest political allies?"

"His *only* political allies," interrupted Sidarov again, with a sly grin. "And Joroev is involved."

"Joroev?" enquired Batyrov.

"He's a government runner, one of their fixers on the ground. Akayev's used him before for minor jobs. Rough, nomadic type, from the mountains."

Batyrov sat back and sipped on his coffee. Over the years, he had never asked politicians like Sidarov about their motives for passing on such information to journalists like him, even if this particular piece of intelligence did seem a little speculative. But the timing of the information was curious, coming on the eve of a what was being trailed as the signing of a major trade agreement between the Kyrgyz government and the United States. Batyrov himself had been covering the proposed deal for several days, even though there was not much to write about. The government was keeping the details close to its chest, though its media release did refer to it as *'historic – a diplomatic first between Kyrgyzstan and the United States and one that will seal relations between the two countries for years to come.'*

Bold words, especially coming from such a small republic as Kyrgyzstan.

Batyrov's mind was working overtime. He had often wondered why the Americans would send their Secretary of State merely to sign off a trade agreement. It may have been hailed as 'historic' but what could the Kyrgyz possibly have to offer the Americans that would justify such hyperbole? And now there was Sidarov's intel about the covert meetings every Friday to consider.

"I'm sorry there's not much to go on, Temir, and it may be nothing, but I'm going to dig around a bit in the White House, maybe press the guard a bit more, if you can look at it from the American angle. Ask Askar if he knows anything."

Batyrov finished his coffee and looked at his watch. It was 10.15am. Sidarov's information was sparse, but Batyrov promised to follow it up with his editor on Monday. If anyone knew anything, it would be Ednan Askar.

"And Temir..." said Sidarov as the two men exchanged a warm handshake on the marble floored hallway of the apartment. "Total discretion." "Of course, Erik. Of course."

6

Saturday morning, Ala Too Square, Bishkek

Batyrov headed back towards his apartment, Sidarov's words ringing in his ears. Despite the early hour, he could feel the sun's warmth beginning to demand its inevitable attention. His cheeks began to burn up.

He crossed over the road into the shade of the Ministry of Defence building, and headed south, towards Moskovskaya Street. But as he approached the National Hospital, he changed his mind. He turned round and began the journey back up Toktogul and towards Chuy Avenue.

He needed time to think. He had a choice to make. One last political scoop, possibly, or retirement. And what better place for him to make that decision than the White House, Bishkek's imposing legislative parliament building? It had been the source of so many of his stories over the years. Was this to be one final one?

Within minutes, it came into view. He stopped on the south corner of Ala Too Square, leaning his shoulder against the dry bark of one of the many poplar trees which lined its perimeter, and breathed in the view. So familiar. So beautiful.

Elderly Kyrgyz women, dressed in their colourful *keynek* dresses, some with *elecheks* on their heads to protect their wrinkled faces from the blistering sun, were tending the grandiose flower bed arrangements that decked either side of the walkways leading up to the White House steps.

The fragrance of alyssum, coleus and sedum, planted in the shape of two giant Markhor goats, filled the air. Every now and then, a revolving spray would emerge from an undersoil sprinkler system keeping the carefully manicured flower beds moist and fresh.

Amidst the colourful sea of red and white flora and Wimbledon-green lawns, Saturday traders were selling their wares. To Batyrov's thoughtful gaze, business wasn't looking good. Freshly made bread, already hardened by the increasing heat of the day, looked forlornly for a home. Limp lettuces withered in the late morning sunshine. Huge, ripe tomatoes, seemingly undaunted by the relentless procession of visiting flies to the warmth of their shiny red skins, sat motionless, unmoved, as they had done since 7am. Small, individual bouquets of 'good fortune' mountain herbs, crudely tied together with flaxen yarn, competed for visitor attention. Beggars, sitting cross legged on their worn *Shyrdaks,* could intermittently be seen gathering up any loose *som* that passing folk might have thrown their way.

And all around, tourists gathered at regular intervals to snap the precisely timed and militarily executed shift changes of White House guards, their white *kalpaks* resplendent like crowns on the tops of their heads, their ceremonial SKS7 rifles to their shoulders.

The scene was always spectacular, and for once, Batyrov was taking time to enjoy it. There hadn't been many such opportunities during his time in political journalism. He savoured the moment, the seductive beckoning of one more story to complete his political portfolio before retirement, playing on his mind. The calm before the storm?

Beyond the Square, Batyrov raised his eyes towards the majestic grandeur of the Republic's neo-classically designed Presidential building, his second home. He knew it so well having spent much of his working life walking its corridors, back and forth to its media briefing rooms and ministerial offices.

Inside or out, the White House never failed to impress. He first entered it as a cub reporter in the aftermath of the break up of the Soviet Union in 1991. For six years he had just been another freelance hack, searching for stories to fill the pages of any national newspaper or magazine which would take his copy.

But in 2005, his big break came. Revolution. And when the people began to fill Ala Too Square, it would mean only one thing. Bloodshed.

The Tulip revolution didn't disappoint in that regard. Shots fired, blood shed, scores dead. Presidential change was the inevitable consequence. It would also mark a change for Batyrov.

A few days after the uprising, when things were beginning to settle, an email dropped into his inbox. It was signed off by Shirin Kurmanbek, owner and proprietor, Bishkek Daily News.

Kurmanbek, always on the lookout for fresh talent, had been alerted to Batyrov's fiercely independent freelance offerings during the revolution. Indeed, he had even predicted it, citing a rural uprising days before the outlying villagers and urban poor began to gather in the Square.

And so it came to pass, that in the late spring of 2005, Temir Batyrov was plucked from obscurity and into political deputy-editorship. By the summer of that year, the Square had regathered its pre-revolution beauty, just in time for him to report on Ormanbekov's first, failed bid to become a member of the State legislature. Twenty years later, Ormanbekov was not only a member of parliament. He was its President. And Batyrov had followed his murky political journey every step of the way. Corrupt practice and political intrigue was never far from view. It became a regular talking point among political media journos in the bars of Chuy Avenue.

Batyrov had a nose for it. It didn't endear him to the political elite. Successive Presidents and their media officials had always been wary of the independent press, a hangover from their communist days, but they could not silence it. Batyrov himself had often wondered why he, with his pointed and direct questions, was still allowed into government press conferences. He liked to believe that it might have something to do with his relationship with Senate members, political survivors, people like Sidarov who may have respected and even sympathised with his constant search for truth and justice but were too fearful for their jobs, or their political lives, to do anything about it. Or maybe they just wanted to adhere to the mob motto: *'keep your friends close, but your enemies closer'*. Who could know? Certainly not Batyrov.

As he stared at the White House, he wondered why anyone would want to make it their political home. Yes, power, yes, money, yes ego. But since 1991, all it had really seen was conflict. Yesterday's revolutionaries, many of whom had fallen on the capital's battlefield on which Batyrov stood, were not afraid to rise up and effect change.

Would a new generation of radicals be back? Was another uprising on the way?

He had no answers but he was curious. If only it hadn't been the respected Sidarov who had called him last night, he would be a free man! But it *was* Sidarov, and if *he* suspected something untoward was taking place, then Batyrov knew that retirement would have to go on pause.

7

Saturday morning, Vefa and White House, Bishkek

Before he had even showered and dressed himself, Ormanbekov turned on the Asia 1 news channel, hoping that the drought which Kulov had told him about the previous evening, would dominate the headlines in the run up to the American visit. It did.

He brewed some coffee, opened his laptop on the kitchen table and set up a *Poly* video call. Yelena came into view.

"A stroke of good luck, for sure," he said. "De Layney may be coming for airspace, but now we can bargain for more. The drought is quite timely, and then last night…."

"What do you mean?" interrupted Yelena. "I thought the Americans were just coming to sign it off."

"Indeed, my dear. But as I was saying, after Kulov's call last night, I had a dream, a strange dream."

"A dream? Ha. What dream?"

"It gave me the solution, the answer to the problem we have, right here and now in our midst."

"My dear, I think you must have had a little too much *Uglichsky* with your wine last evening. You know how you always struggle with your thoughts when you eat cheese late at night."

"Not this time, Yelena. I have the answer. We've always had the answer, here in Kyrgyzstan, right under our noses. Under our feet. I just didn't see it coming. Until last night."

"You've lost me."

"It's about our water project. It's stalled but the drought has set me thinking about it once again."

"Yes, ok. Keep speaking. I'm just going to let Rosaria in."

"So, we have water," continued Ormanbekov, speaking to a blank screen for a moment. "Fresh water. We have had it for centuries. The Aral may have dried up but the Tien Shen mountains give it to us in abundance, year on year. The problem is that it's all up here in the north. If we could transport it south, easily and quickly, we could solve the drought issue overnight. And resolve decades of water shortage for our neighbours. And now, with the Americans arriving this week...." Ormanbekov paused, a menacing tone to his voice, "....they can help us to pay for it."

"Is that legal? Ethical?" enquired Yelena, back in view.

"Ha, you jest, my dear. We're a former Soviet republic. Ethics is not something that we do."

"And your dream told you all this?"

"Don't mock Yelena, please."

Feliks put his half eaten *zhupka* back on to his plate and wiped his mouth with his serviette and stared at the screen. Yelena knew that look. He was about to elucidate.

"In my dream, I was taken into the celestial mountains. Naryn to the west, Tuyuk Botomoymok to the north. From my vantage point at Kol Suu, I looked southwards over Kyrgyzstan. I saw it in all its glory. The land I love. The land I rule. I felt so *alive* Yelena. And then as I looked down, I saw trickles of water, rivulets, tributaries, many of them, running down the mountain, fast, away from my gaze. They were heading southwards towards the Pamir and as they travelled, their banks expanded and the flow increased until they arrived at the Chon Alai Range. By which time the water was running freely. Millions of litres. Fresh water. Kyrgyz water. And then I woke up, sat up. I knew immediately that it was for a purpose. The water we own is our future, our inheritance. We must use it for gain. For our benefit."

"But the drought."

"indeed. The drought Yelena. If we can offer a *krujka* of water to our neighbours, we will. But it is *our* water. They will have to pay."

Yelena returned her husband's look across the screen. She knew he was ruthless, but this was politics. And power. And maybe he was right. Using water as a commodity was genius, even if it went against regional protocols. International law. She stared out from the monitor at him, and with a little shrug of the shoulders, delivered her conclusion.

"Well, I suppose that if we can solve the drought crisis, it will put Kyrgyzstan on the map, that is for sure."

Yelena was no politician but she had a knack for citing the bigger picture.

"Precisely, Yelena. The airspace agreement *and* this will send a powerful statement to our neighbours, and to Russia, that we have arrived. We will become the primary republic in central Asia, leapfrogging those arrogant Kazakhs and Uzbeks."

There was excitement in Ormanbekov's voice.

Yelena looked unmoved, as was her way. She sprinkled some dried fruits on to her bowl of steaming hot buckwheat porridge. She was used to her husband's geo-political machinations and his poetic musings, but this morning he was excelling himself.

"So, your dream. Did it tell you how we can move it, north to south?"

"No but I have thought of that."

"Oh...?"

"Underground."

"Underground," Yelena repeated.

"We have the cold war pipes. It is these that will transport the water to where the need is greatest. And where there is need, people will pay."

"And the drought has created need."

"The drought in the south is a gift which will generate revenues to Kyrgyzstan beyond even that which even our finest economists could predict. And the Americans will help us. I will make sure of it. It will be the *haskap* berry on top of the cake."

Yelena put her cup down.

"So dreams can come true, Feliks?"

"I am sure of it," he responded. "Water has always been a part of my longer term plan after the airspace deal was signed. But until last night, it was for the future. Now, though, I see it. Clearly. We can move it to where it is needed and we get the Americans to pay. My dream has brought forward my plans."

A bell rang in the hallway and a black and white image of his chauffeur and security detail flashed onto the camera beside the front door.

"My car has arrived. I need to go."

"Good luck with it all, Feliks. The Americans can be quite stubborn."

"Ha. Tell me about it."

She blew him a kiss across the mountains.

"Rosaria and I will be back tomorrow evening, or maybe Monday morning, depending on the weather. I will make sure she does her homework."

"Say 'hello' to her. Right now, I need to get going. I need to follow my dream."

He closed the laptop down, picked up his pristine, Egyptian cotton serviette and ran it across his mouth, making sure that he captured any hidden food excess. He put on his coat, unlocked the front door using the pre-set code, and stepped out into the sunlight. It may be Saturday morning, but there was work to do.

8

Monday morning, Bishkek Daily News office

Batyrov turned into Razzakov Street. The Star Building came into view. Another week at the Bishkek Daily News beckoned.

As he crossed the road towards the office, he saw a young, smartly attired Kyrgyz woman standing outside, looking around nervously. She offered a smile.

"You must be Miss Beshimov," Batyrov stated warmly. "But you're early. It's only 7.25am. The office doesn't usually open until 8."

"I know. I'm sorry. I just wanted to be on time on my first day."

He pressed four buttons on the security key pad and held out his hand.

"Batyrov. Temir Batyrov."

"Roza...please call me Roza....if....." she paused, as if cautioning herself against being too familiar with someone she didn't know "....If that's what you do here."

Batyrov acknowledged her courtesy without responding verbally.

"Come, I'll take you up. We're on the third floor. The first floor is real estate and the second is some sort of finance company, insurance I think...."

He pushed the button marked 3, before leaning in towards her.

"....but we're the one that matters," he whispered, an impish smile on his face.

They stepped into the lift. Roza smiled back at Batyrov. Her debut journey into the world of journalism was about to begin.

Ednan Askar was busy filling his attache case with several buff folders when Batyrov knocked on his open door.

"Come in Temir. How was your weekend?"

Askar was a man of few words.

"Good, thank you. What time is your flight?"

"11.15....so....I got your text. You went to see Sidarov. What's it all about?"

"Well, it may be nothing, but he's suspicious....of Ormanbekov...."

"Ha, who isn't?" interrupted Askar.

"....particularly with the Americans coming," continued Batyrov. "He seems to think that

Ormanbekov is cooking up something with Akayev and Kulov. Have you heard anything?"

"Nothing, but Akayev is heading to the Dushanbe summit. He might even be on the same flight as me. If not I'll just have to invite myself for supper with him this evening and do a bit of probing."

"If he'll have you, Ednan," joked Batyrov. "He's quite particular who he eats with these days, ha! Anyway, have a good trip."

"Are you kidding me? This is a two day regional aviation summit. Not a World Trade Organisation Ministerial Conference. I'm not expecting too much excitement!"

Batyrov laughed and headed for the door.

"Oh, by the way, Miss Beshimov has arrived."

"Yes, I've briefed Olga. She's going to look after her but if you could keep an eye on her too, that would be good. I need to get to Manas. Let's speak again on Wednesday morning when I get back."

Ednan Askar made his way out of the office just as the wall clock struck 7.45am. Three chimes.

Olga Kola, her head peering round the door of the kitchenette, caught a glimpse of her boss as he headed out. She was holding up a mug which sported the image of a black and white football on one side, and on the other, the crest of *FC Ekolog Bishkek*.

"Coffee, Roza?"

"Actually, do you have any green tea?"

"Oooh. Very healthy," she responded with a grin.

"And…." continued Roza a little shyly, "a different mug? My father is a *FC Dordoi* man. He would never forgive me if I drank out of that."

"And fussy too."

Batyrov entered the main office just as his female colleagues burst into laughter.

"Glad to see you two getting along well," he said, before hanging his jacket up on the coat rack by the front door. "I see you've found your desk, Roza, and Olga will set you up with a password on your laptop and show you how to access our system."

Olga returned from the kitchenette.

"Here we are. Green tea for you. And coffee for me. Sorry no *Dordoi* mugs to hand. You'll have to make do with a Bishkek Daily News mug for now."

Roza gathered in the cup with both hands and smiled at her colleague.

"Welcome to the Daily News family."

Roza offered a slightly nervous grin in response.

"Thank you."

9

Monday morning, White House, Washington

Back in Washington, De Layney was seething and Ocean was the recipient of his loud anger.

"Last week it was climate change. Now it's drought," he shouted. "A week in and all the US news media can talk about is what's going down three continents away."

Ocean discreetly closed the door to avoid de Layney's outburst travelling down the beige carpeted corridor to the President's suite. Ocean's discretion did little to suppress his Secretary of State's mood, however.

"Isn't anything else going on out there, Ocean? Can't we change the news agenda? Can't you do something about it? Dammit, that's what we pay you for isn't it?"

De Layney brought his fist down hard to his desk. It hurt....the desk.

Stoski Ocean had seen it all before but remained calm, as he always did.

"Sir, I don't make the news, I can only try to manage it. The UN is reporting 40,000 dead, and more than two hundred thousand on the move. It's a refugee crisis like no other. I know it's bad timing for us, sir, but it's a really big deal."

"Yes, yes, it's a big deal. Until, that is, we sign off our agreement. That will be next week's headline Stos. Stos?"

Ocean left the question unanswered. But he knew that he had a job on his hands.

'*An insensitive US prioritising its own military ambitions over and above that of the world's thirsty nations*' was a narrative that the Americans wanted to avoid at all costs. It was Ocean's job to see that it didn't happen. He topped up his Secretary of State's coffee cup.

De Layney sat back in his chair, breathing hard. His reddened face betrayed his calmer demeanour. After a few minutes, he sat forward, head in hands, and spoke softly, to no one in particular.

"It used to be that drought only happened in Africa, to Africans. Now they've sent it to Asia. Not one of their finest exports."

Ocean topped up his own coffee cup and sat down to make some notes.

After a few minutes, an agitated de Layney, unable to ignore the muffled background noise emanating from the TV, slammed his buff folder on his desk and picked up the remote.

He stood in front of the monitor and increased the volume.

"Where is this?" demanded de Layney.

"Pakistan, sir, on the Pakistan Afghan border. Afghanistan borders Tajikistan and to the north is...."

"Kyzikstan, I know," interrupted de Layney.

"Kyrgyzstan, sir, it's Kyrgyzstan."

"Can't we put the Disney channel on for a change?"

De Layney didn't like what he was seeing. Understandably. Images of dried up rivers and reservoirs, dead bodies lining pockmarked streets filled the screen. Pictures like these didn't need an accompanying commentary to fire up the global warming debate. But they had one.

CBN's seasoned reporter, Jane Morley, was in full flow once again, enhancing the graphic images with her own powerful narrative. As an experienced pro, a veteran correspondent who made her name reporting on the Iraq conflict, she knew how to maximise public attention.

An elderly couple, lying side by side on the ground under a beech tree on the edge of one of northern Pakistan's deciduous forests, deserved some sort of respectful acknowledgement. Miss Morley delivered it, her hushed tone emphasising the gravity of the image set before the world's eyes.

"They died of thirst, needlessly, their hands clasped together in death, as much as they had been in life. The question is, who is responsible?"

Text book journalism.

In seconds, the bodies of this anonymous, elderly, wrinkled, post-mortem couple would be seen and shared widely on social media. Its visual impact would be far greater than any words that a mid-career CBN journalist, even a good one like Miss Morley, could utter.

Despite his dismissive attitude, de Layney knew in his heart that these images had the power to distract public focus away from Middle East security and towards global environmental issues. It was already happening. In real time. Not only were they being beamed into his own office for the fifth consecutive day. They were, on this breezy, autumnal Monday morning, being watched by millions of cereal-eating US citizens across America in the comfort of their own kitchens.

Good morning America!!

De Layney stood motionless, looking thoughtful.

"OK, so it's grim. But it's got nothing to do with us. It's an Afghan problem. A UN problem. And I can't let it detract from the job in hand."

Ocean watched de Layney retreat to the safety of his maroon, leather clad chair. Perhaps, he mused, his Secretary of State thinks that the problem will simply disappear if he continues to deny its relevance out loud.

"….this is Jane Morley, reporting for CBN News, Peshawar, northern Pakistan."

De Layney reduced the volume. He couldn't deny that Miss Morley's narrative had got to him. An old adversary from the days when he was a Senator and she wrote for the Wall Street Journal, they had locked horns often. This morning, she was getting under his skin once again.

10

Monday lunchtime, White House, Bishkek

"Maybe one for the future, Feliks," Japarov had told the President over their light lunch of *samsa* and *shorpo*. "Access will be hard, of course, as indications are they are very deep. But we will excavate carefully and report back in three months."

Ormanbekov was meeting with central Asia's head of emerging markets, Ulan Japarov. The President had summoned him after the discovery of diamond deposits in the far north-eastern corner of the Republic. Such a discovery probably didn't warrant bringing Japarov all the way from Cholpon-Ata by ministerial car, but then, Ormanbekov had never let cost and time get in the way of having a good lunch with one of his own in Arzu, his favourite local restaurant.

And, he was keen to have a follow up initiative in place to succeed the airspace agreement and now, the water project that was forming in his mind. And if diamonds were it, it would be the perfect trifecta for Ormanbekov's regional power grab, if he could pull it off. And who would bet against it?

Two cars were waiting as the men, their individual security details in tow, emerged from the Arzu's flower decked entrance. With a rotund restaurant manager looking on, Ormanbekov bid farewell to his guest and Japarov was despatched back to Cholpon-Ata.

Ormanbekov headed back to the White House. He emerged from behind the blackened windows of his *Auras Senat Limousine* and headed up the familiar steps towards the officials' door marked *'Slujebniy vhod.'*

As he made his way towards his office, he glanced at the framed photographs of former Presidents which hung on either side of the corridor.

"One day, my own photograph will hang here," he whispered.

He had justification for his optimism. After all, he had come a long way.

Sixteen years of incarceration might not, to many a political prisoner, seem something to be revisited in a hurry. But as he paused to look at the photograph of Askar Akaev, Kyrgyzstan's first post-Russian President, he acknowledged that being locked up had its benefits. Akayev himself had managed to avoid jail after his political downfall, but it had taken him 20 years for all of the corruption charges against him to be dropped. Maybe, Ormanbekov mused, his predecessor should just have pleaded guilty. After all, where better to plot a political comeback than in the isolation of a prison cell? Ormanbekov would know.

When he entered the Lefortovo Correction Unit on the outskirts of Moscow in 2005, Feliks Ormanbekov was an angry man, with pent up frustration in his bones. He understood the ways of central Asian politics but he felt that he had been unjustifiably singled out by his enemies after his bid for power. However, he soon came to realise that time in jail, despite only having a concrete bench to sit on by day and folded towels as a pillow on which to rest his head at night, at least allowed him the space to plan revenge on his political opponents. During daylight hours, he was his own boss, master of his own thoughts. He enjoyed the opportunity to plot without the threat of ideological interference, away from prying eyes and media intrusion. But most of all, he enjoyed being free from politburo 'minders' constantly breathing down his neck. He used the time wisely. His carefully thought-through plans had led him to many conclusions, but only one outcome. Regional power.

To achieve it, Ormanbekov knew that he would need money, lots of it. That would have to come from another nation. He would choose the United States. He didn't trust the Russians, and he didn't like the Chinese. The Turks had their own agenda of aligning themselves with the EU and the other Stans all had self-interest at their core – and no money, besides. Ormanbekov was self-interested also, but was prepared to do something more than pontificate over his ambitious goals. This was no pipe dream. He had formulated a plan.

And then one day, a Tuesday, 16 years on, the key turned in the lock and he stepped out into the dazzling Bishkek sunlight. He was a free man once again. And he was ready. He didn't waste any time in setting up news media interviews to launch his campaign. He took every opportunity he could to speak one message of economic growth and prosperity to the electorate, while nodding subservience, even forgiveness, to those who had campaigned for his downfall.

For Ormanbekov, it was a win-win strategy. Moscow quickly welcomed its repentant son back into the fold, while Kyrgyzstan's six million residents lapped up talk of a prosperous future, with investment in farming and industry, free from political corruption.

It was wholly deceptive, but deception was Ormanbekov's strong suit. And it worked.

He was elected to the Supreme Council in 2022 and three years later he was its President, the country's most powerful politician. He called his new ministers to office on a Thursday and held his first cabinet meeting on a Friday. The following Friday, desperate to begin the process of bringing his plans, formulated in Lefortovo, into being, he instigated his early evening, covert meetings with Akayev and Kulov, his two most trusted and loyal political allies. The path towards a greater Kyrgyzstan and regional primacy was underway. It would take courage. Ormanbekov knew he had to be ruthless. And that he would need help. It was to the welcoming arms of the Americans that he turned.

And they would shortly be on their way to Bishkek, about to be taken in by the gospel according to Feliks Ormanbekov.

11

Three months earlier, White House, Bishkek

"Put yourself in my shoes, Robert. How would you feel?"

Ormanbekov's question, delivered calmly towards the end of their first trans-continental telephone call three months earlier, was a calculated nod to de Layney that the Kyrgyz government, even in independence, was fed up with Moscow continually breathing down its neck, casting its menacing shadow over the Republic, and was ready to do business with the Americans. And he had the ultimate carrot by which to achieve his aims. It was radical diplomacy. There was no precedent for a minor central Asian Republic approaching the world's leading superpower with an initiative of its own. But with what the Kyrgyz President had to offer, how could it fail?

An agreement was drawn up and a date was put in the diary for the signing under the guise of a 'trade' agreement. Despite any lack of detail, the Washington Post's International Business Supplement, picking up on the fact that this deal completely sidelined Kyrgyzstan's neighbours, including Russia, headlined it *'Diplomatic Dynamite'.*

'How would Moscow and the other *Stans* react?' it asked its readers.

Even with such momentous political ramifications on the horizon, the Kyrgyz President's negotiating style was eloquent, a sagely warmth to his rhetoric. His delivery was poetic, influenced, as one political feature writer on the Los Angeles Times described it, 'by his childhood years surrounded by books.'

The Californian journalist's research would be proved right. As a schoolboy, Feliks' father would often take him on a literary tour of some of the Muscovite homes and museums of Russia's finest literary scribes. Those visits consummated his love of his father's *kitep dukonu* with his love of books. The shop, in the literary quarter of Moscow, carried the works of all of the great Russian writers, Dostoevsky, Turgenev, Golgol, Pushkin and the romantic poet, Mikhail Lermontov.

Lermontov's abode on Molchanovka Street was the nearest to the book shop and therefore one to which he would become most frequently acquainted, but his personal favourite was Chekhov's Moscow home, on Sadovaya-Kudrinskaya. He would often reminisce to his latter day colleagues of his excitement, as a child, at walking up from Arbatskaya metro and viewing, for the first time, the early 18th century, classico-Russian building. He even carried an old, faded photograph of the house in his wallet.

It was these writers who, in part, shaped Ormanbekov's politics. It was only natural that he would press his father into taking him to visit the homes.

Such a literary upbringing didn't only serve as an educational indulgence, however. It also gave him, according to one journalist who profiled him favourably in Russia's *Komsomolskaya Pravda* newspaper, the ability to speak 'in literary tongues', a gift that could make even his most ardent political opponents listen attentively, even if they had little sympathy for his position.

The journalist, like the Kremlin he represented, was himself seduced with Ormanbekov's glowing talk of Moscow as *'the crutch which supports the Kyrgyz people in their drive for independent economic stability.'*

Ormanbekov used all of his oratorial experience to woo the Americans into partnership with him. He was ready.

Unlike the learned President, however, it took the Americans a few days to grasp the significance of the political carrot that Ormanbekov was dangling in front of them.

"What can they possibly offer us that we need?" de Layney shouted dismissively at Ocean as he placed the handset back in its unit following their initial call.

Ocean, his alert press aide, had already worked out the answer.

"That which we had up until 2014. Sir."

De Layney put his coffee cup down on its saucer, slowly, his mind swiftly casting itself back into history.

"Dammit, Stos. Of course. You're right. Why didn't I think of it?"

"My guess is that he's resurrecting the Manas air base. And he's about to offer it to us. We want air access in the region and he needs dollars. It's so simple. This could be our route back into Manas and more importantly...."

"....yes, Stos. Fast access into the Middle East. Israel and Palestine."

The two men eyed each other. De Layney sipped at his coffee again.

"OK. Let's sound him out a bit more. If we're right, we negotiate. If we're wrong, we initiate it....as our idea."

"Oh I think we're right sir. It's the only thing he has which we would be remotely interested in, and he knows it. Manas is his bargaining chip. I suggest, sir, if I may, that we let Ormanbekov take the lead. He's smart, thoughtful, very persuasive. And he likes to be in control. Let him make the first move."

The Americans had underestimated the President. He knew what he was doing and was about to bring his seductive plan, the Lefortovo plan, into reality.

"Trust me. We are on solid ground," he told Kulov at the start of negotiations. "They will jump at the chance of a deal with us. They've never got over the humiliation of eviction in 2014. They are still hurt and embarrassed and that is why they've ignored us for so long. Their temporary military base in Romania has never worked for them and why would it? I wouldn't wish Bucharest on my worst enemy."

The two men laughed out loud.

"But now, Alexander, I believe that the time is right. Manas is ripe for resurrection. The Russians and Chinese may make their overtures. They all want to set foot again on this uninhabited piece of Bishkek real estate, *our* piece of real estate. But I know that it is the Americans who will grasp the nettle. They will move heaven and earth to reclaim a military presence in our region."

And so it was, that during their next communication, Ormanbekov uttered the words that the Americans never thought they would hear again.

'Let's talk Manas.'

12

Tuesday morning, Bishkek Daily News office

It was Roza's second day at the Bishkek Daily News. She and Olga were contemplating a trip out to Social Coffee. A lunchtime sandwich beckoned. Ednan Askar was still in Dushanbe. Roza hadn't seen him since yesterday and then only briefly before his swift departure. In his absence, the seasoned Temir Batyrov was in charge. He walked in, a briefcase and bottle of sparkling water in his left hand and a coat draped over his right arm. Sticking out from underneath the coat was a folder.

Roza put her mug down but before she could offer to relieve him of his load, Batyrov, in a juggling masterclass, bent his knees and half threw, half placed the folder on to Roza's desk. The folder avoided her mug by inches and landed, face up, its title page looming large in front over her eyes.

Media briefing.

"Would you like to cover this, Roza?" he asked with rhetorical authority. He continued his journey to his office without missing a step. It was clear that he wasn't expecting anything other than affirmative response to his question.

Roza couldn't disguise her joy. Her first commissioned assignment. And so soon. And then she opened the folder:

'Kök börü ulak-tartış sporttuk iş-çarası'

'Ak-Kula ippodromunda.'

In a fleeting moment, she went from ecstatic expectation to inner conflict. Her head dropped.

Despite being a 21st century journalist in training, Roza was realistic enough to know that she would have to come into contact with some of Kyrgyzstan's more unpalatable historic customs. But she hadn't anticipated that her very first assignments would be to cover what had colloquially become known as *'the struggle for the goat.'*

She had grown up knowing about the barbaric, testosterone-fuelled Kok Boru *ulak-tartysh* sporting event. Her father was a fan. But she had never desired attendance.

"Who in their right mind would want to watch men on horseback and sticks knocking the headless carcass of an animal around a field, for pleasure?" she had often asked him.

"It's our history," he would lamely tell her in response to her protestations.

She knew that he had a point. It *was* part of Kyrgyz history. Central Asian culture was conceived on the back of nomadic travellers, those who had made their way along the Silk Road over the centuries. Roza had them to thank for this ancient practice. It didn't help her mood, however. In the first throes of her career in journalism, she was being asked to write up the grisly outcomes of this brutal, bloody festival.

As she stared at the document before her, her horror at what she was being asked to cover had not gone unnoticed by Olga, who promptly walked over to her desk and, with an empathetic tone, whispered in her ear, "Don't worry. Not all of the assignments are like that. It's just part of something that we all have to do."

Roza nodded and smiled back at her.

Olga spoke sympathetically, as one who had been through the same induction process. Not for the first time, the two women looked at each other before bursting out laughing. A lunchtime visit to Social Coffee was looking more appealing by the minute.

xxx

Despite the misgivings about her first assignment, Roza was powered by adrenalin, thrilled to finally call herself a journalist. She was already enjoying the unpredictability of her role.

"I don't think I'm going to be bored here," she told Olga. Even as she put her cup of *Rose Elaichi* tea to her lips, she would be proved right.

69

'Ah, a text from Batyrov. Would I like to cover Dordoi Bishkek FC's fixture with FC Kaganat this evening?'

Although she had passed it many times, Roza had never been inside the Dolen Omurzakov Stadium. So she was tempted, of course. It would have been her first 'proper' commission and would precede the *Kök Börü* media briefing on the Friday. But football wasn't one of her passions, and she didn't want to deny Askar's regular sports' freelancers, an old friend of hers from university, the opportunity to cover one of his.

"Do you think he'll mind if I decline?" Roza asked Olga, a little sheepishly.

"Of course not. He'll let you know if an assignment is compulsory."

"Like 'Kök Börü.'"

The two women giggled as they headed back to the Star Building, arm in arm. The afternoon news desk beckoned.

xxx

That evening, Roza, her second day completed, decided to head out to celebrate. She took a shower, changed her clothes, checked her social media, and then headed off towards the Metro Bar, taking her usual route eastwards on Ryskulov Street.

She had always preferred the Metro because of its more central location, conveniently situated nearby to her rented apartment. It also had a better choice of beers.

As she turned into Turusbekov Street, she was confronted with barriers which had been erected in preparation for the State visit. Security arrangements around the White House had begun early.

She double-backed along Turusbekov Street and jumped on to a passing *mashrutka* which would take her the long way round to her destination.

As it trundled along in the fading evening light, Roza took note of the geography of her city. Its dull but imposing buildings. The sound of drills and the relentless rolling of heavy machinery along the capital's streets had been the backing track to her early teenage years. She could still taste the dust of her youth. And, as she looked outwards through the *mashrutka's* grimy windows, she wondered what had changed?

Cosmetic improvement, yes, she thought, but most of Bishkek's offices and shops, even the new ones, remained a darker shade of grey. Apart from Chuy.

As the *mashrutka* turned into Bishkek's main thoroughfare, she began to appreciate the efforts of planners who had sought to modernise the city. The shopfronts were brighter. Some even had a splash of colour about them. The lighting inside had improved, making them more welcoming to shoppers. Mobile phone and computer shops, many of them stocking the latest models that China and the United States had to offer, were beginning to appear, alongside international banks and supermarkets. Best of all, though, were the growing number of up-market boutiques which were springing up in Malls along Manas Avenue, the likes of Burberry, Luis Vitton and her favourite perfumery, Versace. She could dream.

Roza leaned back for a moment and smiled at her weak reflection in the window. Bishkek was changing, slowly, and for the better, but she knew that with Mother Russia's menacing shadow still hovering oppressively over all of the central Asian Republics, like a giant umbrella, modernisation would always be a slow process. The Metro Bar came into view.

She pushed open the stiff, glass door and looked around. Her neighbour, Alya, who she had arranged to meet, hadn't arrived yet from her work. As she took out her mobile phone to check the football score, a text message arrived.

'Darling Roza. Delayed at factory. Production problem. It's overtime so I need to take it. Maybe we can meet up later in the week. So sorry. Sweet kisses to you. Alya xxx'

Roza was despondent but she knew that Alya worked hard at the image pressing factory and needed to take every opportunity to earn. After all, she had her mother and young son to support.

'C'est la vie," she sighed.

Roza reverted back to the sports app. Twenty six minutes gone. No goals. She didn't regret her decision not to cover it.

A young waitress, dressed in grey jeans and a red t-shirt, approached the table. Roza ordered a bottle of *Nashe Pivo*. Her favourite beer.

She would be drinking alone this Tuesday evening.

13

Two months earlier, White House, Bishkek

Negotiations between Ormanbekov and de Layney had continued throughout early spring but the President remained calm. He wasn't in a rush. He knew the value of the prize that awaited his patient approach.

And he was superstitious. He was a man who preferred to make some of his biggest decisions by the changing seasons. By them, from his office window, he formulated his plans. Akayev and Kulov were not impressed.

"What a way to run a country," Akayev had whispered to his colleague as the took the stairs to Ormanbekov's office suite.

And there he was, stood at the window, binoculars in hand, surveying the continuing meltdown of snow from the high peaks of the Tien Shen mountain range, something he had been doing for several weeks.

"Akiri. Akiri. Bravo," he spoke out.

He handed the binoculars to Kulov but he didn't need them to see what the President was getting excited about.

"Look, Alexander, look. It's gone. Melted away."

It had.

In its place was the bucolic beauty of springtime.

At last, Ormanbekov could look forward to the glorious re-emergence of flocks of Argali wild sheep, Ibex, birds of prey, including the Lammergeier vulture, one of Ormanbekov's favourites when out on an ornithological weekend trek.

As both men observed the mountainous beauty before them, the morning mist began to lift, revealing lush green summits, rich in glory.

"The miracle of nature," said Kulov, trying to look impressed.

The President stared into the distance before declaring, "Now, is the moment."

Kulov assumed that the President was referring to his ongoing negotiations with the United States, but he couldn't be sure until Ormanbekov asked him, "What is the time in Washington?"

Kulov looked at the clock on the wall and made his calculation.

"2145 hours. Quarter to ten in the evening."

"Perfect. I'll catch him at home."

The President strode purposely towards his desk and picked up his phone.

Kulov wondered what Ormanbekov was up to. He had already played his trump card. Manas was on the table. Negotiations were going well. What could be so important? At this time of the morning. Or evening, US time?

"Robert, my friend. I'm so sorry to call you late in the day but...."

"I was just heading for the sack, Feliks. Can it wait until tomorrow morning?"

"Well, that will be *my* evening, and....well, I have a meeting today with my Financial Secretary and he's a bit of....well, you know. He's an accountant. Need I say more?"

Ormanbekov belched out a vulgar laugh.

De Layney offered a cautious acknowledgement. He never liked talking money, especially late at night. But the impending deal that they were negotiating was so important that he sensed he had little option but to hear him out.

"So, Robert, now that we have a ten year proposal with a further three year option on the table, we need to talk money. I wonder, did you receive the draft calculations I sent you yesterday. I know they are based on the agreement pre 2014 but I adjusted them a little to reflect inflation, currency adjustments and so on. Have you had a chance to look at them?"

He had. And he wasn't pleased. He was not a number cruncher, but, in anticipation of the over inflated financial demands he anticipated the Kyrgyz President would bring forward, he had managed to agree a counter offer with the US Treasury for a long term dollar commitment based more on American expectations than Kyrgyz greed. It was generous, based on the previous lease value that the Americans had paid for the multi-acre space more than a decade earlier. It took inflation into account and even placed a cap on the numbers of aircraft flying into and out of Manas. Further contingency options were set out in case of a major conflict erupting and the final agreement would ensure continuity for a decade even if the American Administration changed.

"I have a counter proposal. It's the best we can offer, Feliks. It's generous and long term. I trust that it will find favour with you and your colleagues in government? I'll have it sent over to you in the morning."

Ormanbekov was secretly delighted, but he wasn't about to show it.

"I hope that it is closely aligned to the calculations from my own Exchequer. But let me study it, Robert, and get back to you."

"Don't take too long, Feliks. We need to discuss the timetable. Our Department of Defence is itching to get started and are already planning operations. They want to liaise with your State Defence Committee on criteria. Ideally, they'd like preliminary preparations to be taking place by the summer with the first of our aircraft on site by September."

"I am sure that we can work to that timetable. Also, we, you and I, Robert, need to come up with an official, formalised, joint statement. My neighbours, especially the more volatile ones, are not going to be happy when we announce this to the world, especially as all they are expecting is a trade deal. Our agreement must carry the weight of partnership within its parameters."

"We can work on that. But no leaking of our intentions, Feliks. No one can get a sniff of what we are planning."

"Indeed, Robert. This must remain strictly private, between us and other collateral parties. I wouldn't want my neighbours, big or small, to get wind of our initiative. Better to surprise them, don't you think? I am assuming that you will come here personally to sign the agreement. That way, the whole world will know of our joint intentions."

"Of course, Feliks," de Layney responded, trying to sound calm. "Thank you for your gracious invitation, which I am pleased to accept."

"And all this assumes that we can sign off on the finance, Robert...."

"....which I am sure we can," he hurriedly replied.

Ormanbekov concluded the call and smiled at Kulov.

"As predicted, Alexander, the Americans, for all of their closed doors diplomacy, are enthusiastic. We have them in our pockets. Their determination to re-establish their presence at Manas has a cost, but they will meet it."

"He didn't mind being called so late?"

"Look out there, Alexander."

The President motioned Kulov's eyes back towards the Tien Shen range.

"The snow has departed. Spring is here. It is our time. I always act in a timely fashion."

Kulov, staring out of the window, tried his best to rationalise Ormanbekov's superstitious eccentricities, but as always, he failed. Past experience had taught him that trying to logicalize any of the President's political calculations was futile. So he just nodded his head, as he aways did, secure in the knowledge that at least Ormanbeokov, for all his behavioural oddities, usually made the right call.

"And he wants this deal so badly he will speak at any time. Did I tell you how we began our negotiations, Alexander?"

Kulov was attentive.

"Even *I* was surprised at the length the Secretary of State would go to secure exclusive negotiating rights with us."

"What do you mean?"

"He was so desperate to ensure a bilateral approach that he offered us an 'in good faith' deposit, up front. Can you believe it? At that point, I knew we had him."

"How stupid are these Americans?" Kulov jested.

"Of course, I told him there was no need, that we wouldn't be talking to anyone else, but he insisted."

Kulov brought over a percolated coffee from the cabinet and placed it in front of the President.

"It would have been discourteous to reject his kind offer, don't you think, Alexander?"

14

Tuesday evening, White House, Bishkek

Akayev knocked on the door.

"Ah, come and join us Kadrjvan. A drink."

A bottle of water was placed in front of the empty chair. But it was from the bottle of Ararat cognac that the President poured the drinks.

"Gentlemen. In twenty four hours time, the American Secretary of State will be standing on Kyrgyz soil. We have reached the mountain top. Tomorrow, the Stars and Stripes will stand alongside the state flag of the Kyrgyz Republic. It has been a long journey but the end is in sight. And beyond that, a new beginning. I give you a toast. The future prosperity of Kyrgyzstan."

"Keleçektegi güldöp-önügüü," they echoed before downing their brandies in unison.

There was only one thing on the agenda. Security.

"Everything is in order," reported Akayev. "We arc roady."

"Remind me."

"We are responsible for all internal White House security while the Americans will take charge of security at the Hyatt and between the two."

"Ha."

Ormanbekov put his glass on the table forcefully.

"The Americans like to think that nobody can do security like them. How amusing!"

"Yes, Feliks. Their official line was that our police would need assistance with security for the visit. It was insulting."

"They need to feel important, Kadrjvan. Let them be. Are their security people here yet?"

"They arrived a few days ago, working with Officer Joe Ramirez, their senior agent on the ground here in Bishkek. He's made all the White House arrangements."

"I know him. He's the US Ambassador's man, Head of Politics at the AUCA. He doesn't usually cause us any trouble. Let's make sure we keep it that way. What about the sewer?"

"It's all in place, Feliks. I am speaking with my contact right after this meeting."

"Good. Very good," said Ormanbekov, standing up. "If there is nothing else, this meeting is concluded. Until tomorrow, gentlemen."

The three men left the room, the President to his car that would take him home to Vefa, Kulov to the main elevator, and Akayev in the direction of the east wing lifts and to the exit closest to his destination. He had travelled this particular corridor many times, but had rarely paused to study its collection of framed photographs of Kyrgyz National cultural and sporting figures that hung on its beige painted walls. He slowed his pace along the *shyrdak* felt-carpeted 'walk of fame,' taking in the portraiture, each representing a piece of Kyrgyzs history.

Author Chinghiz Aitmatov, ballet dancer Bubusara Beishenalieva, musician Abdylas Maldybaev and lightweight boxing champion, Orzubek Nazarov, all famous for being a part of Kyrgyzstan's modern day cultural image, followed his pedestrian stroll towards the east wing lifts, now coming into view.

He pressed the button marked *'jer'* and waited. The ground floor where he would step out would offer him a choice of exit, front and back, to the eastern corners of the White House perimeter gates. He chose back, taking the corridor which would lead him past another set of framed photographs, these ones of Kyrgyz political heroes, Kasim Tynystanov, Askar Akayev and Roza Otunbayeva, Kyrgyzstan's first three Presidents and Nasirdin Isanov, Otunbayeva's first Prime Minister.

Pictorially, wall by wall, and floor by floor, this former Communist Headquarters proudly displayed the Republic's short history both culturally and politically. Perhaps, Akayev fantasised, his own picture would hang on these walls one day, alongside that of his President.

But who could tell? Not one Kyrgyz politician since 1991 had really known their destiny. Life at the top was deemed fragile. A sharp blade between the shoulders had always been a distinct possibility for anyone who sought political power.

Ormanbekov, however, was a different proposition. He had secured his position carefully, thoughtfully and intentionally over many years. And he ruled by fear. Akayev knew that being one of his deputies had its risks, but if he survived, it would have its benefits too.

He passed the final framed print on his right, that of Kyrgyzstan's first Education Minister, Boris Bakiyev, before stepping past the security desk, manned by two upright National guardsmen, and out into the Tuesday evening dusk.

He crossed the road into Panfilov Street before turning right into Silk Road Avenue, where he had arranged to meet Joroev.

Spotting Akayev approaching, Kamil Joroev dropped his cigarette on to the floor and walked towards his paymaster, his first step crushing the cigarette. Akayev took a beige envelope from his case and gave it to him.

"It's all in here, exact timings, requirements and distractions. Do you have the boy?"

"It's a girl, Mr Akayev."

"A girl!"

"She wanted to do it."

"Can you trust her?"

"She has 250 *som*. She will get the other 250 when the job is done."

"Don't let me down," Akayev said, before turning to walk back towards the White House estate.

15

Tuesday evening, Vefa

Yelena could tell that her husband was in a celebratory mood when he called her before heading home. She chose a vintage red to go with the meal she had prepared.

"You are in good cheer this evening, Feliks," Yelena said as she served their starter.

"With good reason, my dear. I had Japarov in yesterday. He tells me there is diamond potential in the north. And, diplomatic consummation with de Layney is imminent. It will be complete this time tomorrow."

"Are you leaving me for another man?" she asked playfully. "Is this what the English call a bromance?"

Yelena raised a glass to her lips, a loving smile on her face, her cheeks glowing. The *Tchotiashvili Saperavi Reserve 2015 was* doing its job well.

"Of course not my dear. De Layney may have the US Treasury to fall back on, but I have you. How could de Layney's bank account compare with your beauty and brains?"

"Ha, you *are* in a very good mood this evening, Feliks."

"Why wouldn't I be? I have the Americans in my pocket and you in my arms. You are 'more precious than silver, more costly than gold; and more beautiful than diamonds,' even those in your jewellery box my dear."

Yelena blushed a little, surprised at such joyful candour. Literary tongues.

"I didn't know that you were familiar with *bibleyskaya proza*."

"Ah, yes, Bibliya. My father kept one, not for sale you understand, but hidden in a cupboard under the stairs of his little bookshop. When he went out, he would leave me in charge. I would be reading Sholokhov, or Solzhenitsyn if I wanted to impress him when he exited. But by the time he returned, I would have read a chapter from Torah. It became a habit. I would read by the window, keeping my eyes on the road and when I spotted him by the Brusnika bakery on the corner of *Boshoy Rzhevskiy Pereulok*, I would be tucking *Bibliya* safely back in its resting place, under the stairs and I would retake my place behind the counter. He never knew."

Yelena leaned back in her chair.

"My husband and the Word of God," Yelena joked. "Whatever next?"

Yelena's rhetorical question was left to hang for a few moments.

"So not all of your secrets are dark ones, my dear. Is there anything else that I need to know?"

"Ha, no. I have no more secrets, Yelena. I am just content. I have all that I want right now, with more to come. But this evening is for celebration. Tomorrow, we bankroll Kyrgyzstan."

Yelena didn't hesitate. The glass broached her lips again.

"*Iygilikke*," she declared triumphantly.

"Indeed my dear. To my success."

For once, she didn't check his pride. After all, credit where credit was due. This *was* his success. It would be *his* success.

16

Tuesday evening, Metro Bar, Bishkek

Roza sat alone, observing the clientele as it came and went. She sipped at her sweet tasting beer and began to reflect upon her new life, all two days of it. She had a job she enjoyed, colleagues she liked and some *som* in her pocket. Life was good.

The cafe was dimly lit, intimate even, but it didn't take her long to notice two men sitting two tables away. With so few people in, it was easy for her to pick up on their conversation, despite it being delivered in relatively hushed tones. Her naturally enquiring mind was always alert to other languages and this conversation, spoken in English, but with American and Kyrgyz accents, was no exception.

The Kyrgyz national had his back towards Roza. His companion, the American, wore an untidy beard and had unkempt hair. Maybe that was his 'Tuesday look', she thought to herself as she sipped her beer.

She wondered who they might be. Not tourists, for sure. Maybe they were academics, discussing their academia in riddles, searching for solutions to the issues of the day. Or political fixers, or maybe even journalists, like her? Ha, surely not.

She took another sip of beer, before draining the bottle into her glass. Her journalistic antennae were reaching out inquisitively, her eyes and ears straining for a hint of an unusual story. It came.

"I've been contacted," said the Kyrgyz. "They want me to help set some things up before your Secretary of State arrives. The President has plans for partnership with the US. They assure me it will be mutually beneficial. But the word on the street is that the deal is more than just a trade agreement."

"What do you mean?" asked the American. "De Layney is coming to sign off a trade agreement. That's all. What more is there to know?"

"That's just it, Joe. There *is* more. I don't know the details but it's something to do with water. It's confidential, but the President is plotting something. Something big. Something to favour the Americans. I know it."

"Ormanbekov. Favour the Americans? Ha. Not unless there is something in it for him."

Roza knew that these two men in her midst, the American, Joe, and the unnamed Kyrgyz, were speaking about the US State visit, but she couldn't work out who they were or why they were so interested in it. More than a trade deal? What did that mean? And why the talk of water all of a sudden?

She glimpsed at the American out of the corner of her eye. She sensed his displeasure that a Kyrgyz was telling him some seemingly important American state information? Roza's curiosity was aroused. She picked up her glass again and listened in.

"Anyway, what could your President possibly offer us?" asked the American, demonstrating an arrogance that his younger companion ignored "And why would Ormanbekov want to help us anyway?"

"Money....dollars," shot back the national. "It's all about the money."

Roza observed the increasing intensity of their interaction.

The big American repositioned himself in his chair. It creaked with his weight, sending off three or four crackling sounds across the bar room.

"So, what do you want me to do?" he asked.

"Akayev wants us, you and me, to be alert to things as they happen. I'm told things could move fast once the Americans get here."

"I don't take orders from Akayev. I report to my Ambassador," retorted Joe frostily.

"I know, I know, but listen, Joe. Whatever agreement is signed, they want us to keep in contact. Akayev needs your man in Mira to be onside."

At the word 'Mira', Roza took her pen and notebook from her bag and began to make notes. She knew Akayev as Ormanbekov's Prime Minister and she knew Mira as the location of the American Ambassador's residence. She jotted it all down, including the name of the American, 'Joe' who picked up the conversation as she wrote.

"But why wouldn't he be onside? Surely de Layney will keep my Ambassador in the loop? What is so secret?"

The same question was bothering Roza. What *was* so secret here? And who was this Kyrgyz national? An informer, perhaps, or a fixer. Kyrgyzstan's murky underworld where shady deals and corrupt practices take place worked on the well oiled actions of such people. Perhaps the Kyrgyz national was some sort of government spy. Batyrov would know, surely. But he wasn't there.

The Kyrgyz national took a deep breath and leaned forward. He spoke in hushed tones, a sense of urgency in his demeanour.

"I don't know, Joe. But there *is* more. It's not only about money. It's about power, regional power. I've heard that the President has plans for Kyrgyz water. He's fed up with failed EU programmes and interventions when it is us who owns it. According to him, Kyrgyzstan has always been suppressed, the poor relation of the five Stans. Well not anymore. That will change. He believes that the Americans can help us to deliver water parity in the region, using the drought crisis as an excuse to act out his plan. If he can pull it off, you Yanks will be seen as the good guys, helping us to win the war on drought. But his real prize is primacy in the region. He thinks that he can adjust the agreement to help him achieve that. Our neighbours may have the ear of Moscow, and industrial muscle, but we have water. It's ours. Ormanbekov thinks we can make it work for us."

"Primacy! That's preposterous," retorted the red faced American, a little too loudly. "Change the agreement? He can't possibly succeed."

"He can succeed, and he believes he will. The signing of the trade deal is just the first step. The drought that is happening in Pakistan and parts of Afghanistan's northern border with Tajikistan has brought Ormanbekov's plans for regional control of water forward. Ormanbekov thinks that the trade deal offers him an opportunity. The deal is due to be signed later this week, but keep an eye out for one or two late amendments."

The Kyrgyzs national suddenly paused and sat back on his chair. He looked around the virtually empty bar, conscious that in his enthusiasm to convey the information he, too, might have spoken a little too loudly. He had, although Roza was the only one who seemed to be paying any attention. And she was absorbing every word, covertly writing down some of the detail in her notebook.

She studied the national from the back. All she could see was his brown leather jacket and dark mountain boots. His attire was smart, but rural, and his accent was uncultured, a strong, southern Kyrgyz slant to his speech. He wasn't from the city, though his voice seemed vaguely familiar.

Her journalistic mind was working overtime, creating a story where none might exist. Though that seemed unlikely given what she was hearing.

An American in Bishkek and a Kyrgyz from the mountains. An odd couple, certainly. But who were they? What were they talking about? And why?

17

Tuesday morning, White House, Washington

Ocean walked towards the window overlooking the gates he had just entered five minutes before. He paused as he saw in the distance a group of around 100 eco-protesters being ushered towards a designated space away from the outer confines of the White House estate.

He poured himself his usual coffee, black, and sat down opposite a tense de Layney.

"What's the latest, Stos?"

"People are on the move, in all directions. Southern Tajiks are heading north and the Afghans are moving east. Pakistan is looking to close its borders today or tomorrow. Its government has called for emergency shelters. The UN has already set up makeshift camps along Afghanistan's northern territories but access is a problem. They're airlifting food, water and medical supplies by helicopter to the region. But they need a tsunami of aid to slow down the death rate."

Stoski's words were delivered clinically but with a solemnity which suggested worse to come. It didn't impress de Layney, however.

"And we're heading there tonight," he said dismissively. "Where are the annual floods when you need them?" he joked, devoid of any compassion.

Ocean ignored him.

De Layney sighed, loudly.

"What's to be our official line, Stos?"

It had been a question that had been occupying the Press Secretary's mind for days.

"I think we have two choices, and two only. We either stand our ground and separate it off from the agreement, which might make us look callous, or we adjust a clause in the agreement to reference our commitment to environmental issues in the region."

An aide knocked on the open door and awaited his invitation to enter.

"Yes."

The aide walked towards de Layney and presented him with a piece of paper. It was a message from his out-of-town Secretary of Defence, Jim Powell, who, by order of the President, had headed back to Ft Lauderdale to be with his dying mother.

"Thank you," said the Secretary of State as he unfolded the cream-coloured bond notepaper.

"It's from Jim. He must be listening in. He's suggesting that we add a clause into the agreement to reference that some of the money provided for in our trade deal be channelled towards aid. 'BUT NO EXTRA MONEY,' he writes in caps. And I agree. That way, we kill two birds with one stone and get the media and the environmentalists off our backs."

"That's good, but it might still cost us," retorted Ocean.

"How? No extra money means no extra money. We make it a condition of our agreement that some of the money we are allocating for Manas be used by them for environmental support in the region. It's a late change but Kyrgyzstan....do I have that right this time. Stos?" smiled de Layney.... "Kyrgyzstan is getting enough of our dollars. They won't turn us down!"

"What about Ormanbekov though?" Ocean asked. "We can't be seen to be interfering in how an ex-Soviet state spends its money."

"Our money, Stoski, our money. The deal has not been signed yet. Until they sign the deal, the ball remains in our court."

De Layney sipped his coffee in silence, knowing that not signing would was not an option.

"Kyrgyzstan might see it a little differently," countered Ocean. "They are not going to want to alter an agreement that has been months in the making. The chances of that happening are surely zero."

"If he wants the deal badly enough, and he'd be crazy to turn it down, he will agree to our terms. And not a cent more. It's the Kyrgyz who will look crass if they don't use some of that money to support their own. I've raided so many departmental budgets to make this deal happen and increased my enemy count in the process. I'm not prepared to do more from this end but…." he paused to make sure that Ocean was attentive, "…we have to ensure that the media knows that we are insisting on some of that money being used to provide aid in the region. That will get us off the hook. Then we can look the eco-nutters in the eye and tell them that we have done our bit. And Ormanbekov needs to know that any bad press coming out of Kyrgyzstan once the deal is signed will not be acceptable."

"Well, he controls the media, or most of it, so that shouldn't be a problem," retorted Ocean.

The two men were confident of their position.

De Layney was gambling that Ormanbekov would never threaten a multi-million dollar deal that would offer a massive boost to the always floundering Kyrgyz economy. De Layney was determined not to threaten the agreement either. The prize was simply too great. De Layney knew it and his President, Miriam Serennati, knew it. That is why she demanded such secrecy from the outset. Only she and her team, de Layney and his team, her Chief of Staff and the Chief of Defence, plus the Israelis, had been included in the negotiations.

"It's a deal which will shift the balance of power in the region away from Russia and China, and towards the United States of America," Serenatti had told the assembled group at its inaugural meeting, perhaps eyeing up her own Presidential legacy, something to write her memoirs by. "If we can pull it off, it will be a momentous, once in a generation diplomatic coup. We have to succeed. Secretary of State de Layney has my 100% support and I expect him to receive the same level support from all of you."

He had. And now the eve of signing was in sight. The global hand of northern hemisphere history was on his shoulders.

18

Tuesday evening, Metro Bar, Bishkek

The Metro Bar door opened just as the large clock on the wall behind the counter showed the time edging towards 10.05pm. Two young men entered, casually dressed in open neck shirts, jackets and chinos. One had a yellow and blue scarf around his neck. They were talking loudly about the game.

Instinctively, Roza took her mobile phone from her bag and clicked on the sport icon. She thought that she ought to know the score of the match she had been invited to report on even if she hadn't been there.

"Two sent off as Dordoi Bishkek score injury time winner to go top," read the headline.

FC Kaganat's journey back to Osh was going to be a long one, she mused. But her father would be pleased.

Despite the loud entry of the two football fans, observed by everyone in the bar, Roza's attention quickly returned back to the two men sitting at the table next to her.

The American continued to listen in disbelief to the national's words.

Joe knew from his Ambassador that the so called 'trade agreement' was actually all about airspace for American dollars, but he wasn't going to let on. He, like everyone else, was sworn to secrecy. But water? What was that about? Could it be something to do with the late amendments the Kyrgyz national was referring to?

The American looked perturbed, distressed even, that the person he considered his subordinate would be feeding him top secret information such as this, if it was true, of course. He couldn't be sure of its voracity, but he sensed elements of plausibility in what he was hearing. The Kyrgyz national leaned forward again. There was more.

"Ormanbekov is using the drought to pressure the Americans into some sort of environmental adjustment to the agreement. He knows that they are fed up with the global *Fair Water* movement always criticising them, its constant haranguing and demands for more and more US investment in the drought regions of the world. And….well, I think he may be proposing something to help de Layney out. Maybe giving him something to get the US electorate and the American green lobby on his side. Ormanbekov wants to offer him a solution to that problem. Not sure how though."

Joe looked aghast.

"What? That's crazy. Ormanbekov couldn't care less about the US electorate."

"You're right, of course. But he's clever. Smart. He's looking at it from their point of view and making them think he's helping them out. Maybe he's after more money. I don't know."

"He won't get that. The agreement is ready for signing."

The American, looking humbled, drained his drink, implanting an additional circular white rim around his mouth. Roza thought he looked faintly ridiculous. She would like to have taken a photograph, but such an intervention would be too risky.

She took the winter edition of *Cosmopolitan* from her bag, a purchase from earlier that evening. A glossy picture of a woman in a beige, thick knitted jumper filled the front cover.

'Kraski Zimy – 2025' read the headline. She turned the pages which flipped over to the *'Autumn colours'* cover story, featuring a photo-shoot on the steps of St Petersburg's Winter Palace. It was a spectacular spread.

She glanced over the top of the magazine she was pretending to read. She was still none the wiser as to what their conversation was about but she had heard enough to know that a whiff of misdemeanour was in the air. If only Batyrov was there with her. He would know what was going on. And what to do.

She looked at the back of the head of the Kyrgyz national, his black swept back hair, his neckline, his slim shoulders leaning forward towards the table. His posture was intense, as it had been all evening.

The American had become less animated but still looked agitated. He, like the national, spoke fairly quietly, and was focused, never taking his eyes away from his companion. It allowed Roza the opportunity to observe his features more closely. Behind the beard was a kindly face, eyes that focused, lips that protruded. Glimmers of white enamel shone from his mouth when he opened it. His hair sat to one side, though his beard was unkempt. It was as if he'd rushed out from his home having brushed his teeth but forgotten to trim his facial hair.

Was there a woman in his life, wondered Roza? One that might smarten him up a little.

Just as she was thinking about ordering another glass of *Nashe Pivo,* the two men stood up. One of them – the Kyrgyz national - rose so abruptly that he knocked over the chair he had been sitting on, causing everyone in the bar to turn their heads. Embarrassed, he picked up the chair and put both of his hands up towards the bar, acknowledging the owner with a gestured smile.

"*Kechiringiz, kechiringiz,*" he said, and with his apologies accepted, he made for the door closely followed by the American.

The elongated exit from the bar allowed Roza her first look at the national.

He was handsome at first sight but, like the American, could do with some smartening up. A hair wash would be a good start. He was tanned, with rugged facial features, the type usually associated with film stars. He looked familiar. Perhaps she had seen a Russian movie with him in it, or his double?

As he moved closer to her table towards the door though, her eyes were drawn elsewhere, to his right hand, the one he had used to pick up the chair he had just knocked over and then gestured his apology with.

As she fixed her gaze on it, she froze, numb with terror.

She had spotted a gap where an index finger should be, a mutilated stump.

Surely not? It couldn't be, not after all this time.

As he approached her table on his way to the exit, she looked to the side of her magazine and glanced upwards, hoping to catch another look at his face. To her horror, she saw several scars. These weren't any old scars, however. These were scars that she recognised, scars that she herself had inflicted on the Kyrgyz national in her attempts to escape his clutches almost 10 years before. This was a man from a past she was trying to forget, a man she had hoped she would never see again.

As he clumsily walked past her chair, the bottom of his black, leathery jacket brushing against her shoulder, she knew that it was him. It was Kamil Joroev.

19

Tuesday evening, Metro Bar, Bishkek

Roza heard the glass doors close behind her, but remained glued to her seat. Statuesque. She wondered what she would do next. She was in shock. What *could* she do?

She averted her eyes towards the high shelves behind the bar. Bottles of regional wines, their labels faded, some decorated with dried wax which had been allowed to overflow, their burnt, black wicks protruding out of several of them, took her attention for a few moments.

Acting as naturally as she could, she turned her head towards the door, taking care not to draw any undue attention to herself. She needn't have worried. It was business as usual in the bar; couples, a few students, workers, the two football fans, all in deep in conversation. And laughter. Not so Roza. She remained numb.

Had he noticed her, glanced at her? Had he recognised her?

Yes, she was now a fully grown woman and yes, she was not dressed in a school uniform, but she was the same person. Her facial features and demeanour hadn't changed that much. She was still the same Roza Beshimov today as she had been nine years ago.

Despite being in the company of the Metro Bar's friendly patrons, she began to feel naked and alone, exposed by her own, horrific discovery. She momentarily lowered her head back down into her magazine, desperately hoping that no one had noticed her demeanour. No one was looking.

Finally, she forced herself to look again towards the exit door. Her peripheral vision took her eyes to the street outside. To her surprise, the two men, who she now knew to be an American called Joe, and a Kyrgyz national from her past called Kamil Joroev, were standing beside the same *marshrutka* stop from which she had alighted earlier. They were deep in animated conversation, Joe doing most of the talking. She watched as a small group of boys, begging for a few som, interrupted them. Joe dismissed them before shaking hands with Joroev. That hand. She watched them go their separate ways, into the darkness.

Roza, her heart pumping, hurriedly paid her bill, left the bar, pausing briefly at the entrance to make sure that Joroev hadn't doubled backed on himself. He hadn't. She spotted him on the other side of the road and crossed, following him at a distance, always keeping close to the shop fronts. He walked at a brisk pace westbound along Chuy, past the computer and bicycle shop fronts, before taking a left on to Jash Gvardiya Boulevard.

Joroev crossed the road and walked the few yards to a wide alleyway, making his way towards some metal steps, with what looked from a distance like a rusty handrail on each side.

The fire escape. She watched his ascent, step by step, one U bend after another. There were five floors altogether, but at the third, Joroev took a key from his jacket pocket and entered in to what Roza thought must be the back door to his apartment. If the block had a lift, it must be broken, she thought, not an uncommon occurrence, even in the plusher parts of Bishkek.

Approaching cautiously, she drew to within fifty metres of the dimly lit building, edging herself closer and closer to the metal outer steps taken by Joroev. The street, practically deserted and a far cry from the bustle and bright lights of Chuy, had several lamp posts but only one was working. Her heart was thumping, and sweat was on her brow, despite the fast diminishing evening temperature.

About 20 yards from the staircase, she paused before stepping into a door well. Her head was full of questions. What was Joroev doing living here in Bishkek, and in such a plush area of the capital? How could a horse trader afford such accommodation? Was he still a horse trader? Who was Joe, the American? What were they involved in? And what did Joroev mean when he spoke of 'water' in the context of the American trade agreement? Why would he even *know* about it? Who, what had Joroev become?

As she speculated on the answers to her own questions, her worst nightmare played out before her eyes. The third-floor door, the one which only moments earlier Joroev had entered, opened.

Instantly, Roza leaned back into the door well. Had he spotted her? Even if he had, surely he wouldn't recognise her from that distance, after almost ten years. She was just being paranoid, surely?

Roza comforted herself with what she wanted to believe. She reassured herself that she had remained hidden and anonymous from the man she was stalking.

She was not going to take any risks, though. She had to act, and act quickly if she didn't want him to walk straight past her. Head down, she immediately stepped from the door well and walked briskly away from the apartment block back down Jash Gvardiya Boulevard. She knew she had a few seconds head start. He was still coming down the fire stairs when she made her move. If he was going to pursue her, he would have to run to catch her up. She tried not to look over her shoulder as she turned back into Chuy, with its evening bustle and busyness, even at this late hour. There was safety in numbers, and at that moment in time, she just wanted to make herself invisible in the crowds of one of Bishkek's main streets.

She stepped into the first doorway that she came to, a bread shop. Closed. She was breathing heavily, unsure whether Joroev had seen her, or worse still, followed her. These were terrifying moments.

She watched and waited, looking at passers by, couples heading home after their evening out, young men, some a bit worse for wear from drink, exiting bars and taverns. Some older folk were coming out of the many restaurants of Jobek Jelu. But no sign of Kamil Joroev.

After what seemed like an age, Roza stepped back on to the sidewalk and headed east along Chuy to the *marshrutka* stop. She walked speedily, occasionally looking over her shoulder, making sure that there were people around her. Despite the late hour, she was pleased to see several people waiting at the stop. She squeezed her way on to the next humid and noisy *marshrutka*, standing near to the driver and a couple of women who were discussing the new tax that the government was proposing on rail travel.

Arriving at her flat, Roza managed to put the key into the front door lock first time, despite her hand shaking. She closed the door firmly behind her and threaded the internal chain to its lock. Relief.

She took her shoes off and slipped her snug, felt *tapockalar* on to her feet, boiled up some hot water, added some lemon, and sat at the kitchen table, shaking.

She had no idea what to do next. She headed into her living room and slumped on to the sofa, fully clothed, and in emotional shock, she rested her head on a cushion, and fell asleep.

20

Tuesday evening, Roza's apartment

Just after 11pm, there was a knock on the door. Roza awoke from her slumber with a start. The television was showing highlights of the football game, though she couldn't remember switching it on.

Who on earth could be visiting her so late in the evening? She shuddered. Surely not? Fearfully, she walked towards the door, lifted the metal swing cover of the fortified glass peep hole, and peered through. Roza breathed a sigh of relief and unlocked the door enthusiastically.

"Olga."

She beckoned her in. Roza relocked the door from the inside, making sure that the chain slide mechanism was secured.

They both stood there for a moment, in the hallway, staring at each other. Olga apologised for turning up unannounced and so late, before bursting into tears. Roza embraced her, and after a few moments, began to shed tears of her own.

Roza stood back, her hands on Olga's shoulders. A smile crossed her face.

"Am I pleased to see you. Come in. I could do with a friend right now," Roza said, anticipating that the news of her ordeal that evening could never be trumped by whatever her colleague had come to share.

Olga took a bottle of red wine from her bag, and what turned out to be *Bliny* with jam, one of Roza's favourite sweet snacks.

"Kazakh. Nice," Roza said taking the bottle from her friend.

The two women sat down.

It was late, but never too late for a sip of *Lagyl Arba Old Tradition Saperaviis*. And they both had stories to tell.

Roza would share hers with Olga in due course, but it was Olga who started the conversation. She spoke speedily.

"It's my mother. She called tonight. She sounded really unwell and has to visit the hospital tomorrow. She needs money, which I will have to send her because my brother, Nurlan, who usually supports her, has just lost his job at the print factory. It's the second time my mother has had a relapse."

Roza took her hand.

"Oh, I'm so sorry, Olga, both for your mother and brother."

Olga relayed stories of previous cancer scares within the family, and how Nurlan had been so supportive of his parents and siblings over the years.

"He was my rock, Roza. When my husband, Kylich died, my parents didn't really understand what was happening, or why it happened. Neither did I. Nurlan was just there for me, listening. And now he's lost his job…."

Olga's tears reappeared. She sobbed uncontrollably for a few seconds. Roza poured them both another glass of wine and the two of them talked about their families.

By 11.40pm, Roza had relayed her own story.

Olga had listened in complete silence. Shocked. If anything was going to take her mind off her own family circumstances, then Roza's story was it. It was as if it was their destiny to hear each other out, to support each other, on the same evening. They had both needed a distraction, if just for a short while. The re-telling of their respective situations gave them that. Each had a shoulder to cry upon. It was timely.

Olga stood up.

"You must tell Ednan. You can't keep this to yourself."

"You're right," said Roza. "I'll tell him in the morning. It's too late now."

"He won't be there first thing tomorrow. He's going to a media briefing at the White House with Mr Kurmanbek."

Roza was deflated. What could be more important than sharing her own devastating story with her editor?

Olga got up and walked to the window. It was approaching midnight. She surveyed the night lights which illuminated the capital, making it look much prettier than it really was. She took out her phone.

"Who are you calling?" Roza asked.

Olga's eyes remained focused on the city. She spoke softly.

"When I lost Kylich, Ednan was the first person I told. My parents were back in Russia and had never really liked my husband, or understood him. I asked Nurlan if he would tell them, which he did. But Ednan was there for me. He arrived at my apartment the very next morning with a huge bunch of flowers. He offered me compassionate leave. He came to the funeral. He even paid for it. And he was there to welcome me on my return to work."

She turned to face Roza.

"Ednan looks after his own. He would only mind if you didn't call him. You can't leave this."

A reluctant Roza looked at the clock. Five minutes to midnight. She took another sip of her wine and slumped back in the sofa. A few seconds passed by. Roza looked up from her daze and was shocked to see Olga tapping away on her phone.

"Mr Askar, I'm very sorry to bother you so late…."

Two minutes later, the call was concluded.

"That's settled. Ednan will meet us at the office at seven o'clock tomorrow morning, before he heads to the White House."

Roza was startled.

"Don't worry, Roza. He may be my boss, but we go back a long way." Olga went to pick up her beige jacket which she had thrown on to the edge of the sofa an hour earlier.

"And now I must be going. It's late and we have an early start in the morning."

"No, no" exclaimed Roza with some urgency and too much volume.

"No, Olga, please stay."

Sensing the anxiety in Roza's voice, Olga put her jacket down again.

"I don't want to be alone tonight," she whispered. "The sofa is very comfortable. Please."

The two women smiled at each other

"Do you have a toothbrush I can borrow?"

21

Tuesday lunchtime, White House, Washington

With drought and death on all of the news casts, the last person Ocean need to bump into in the corridor leading to de Layney's office was Rhey Adams, US Secretary of State for the Environment. De Layney's Press Secretary wasn't an admirer, preferring his predecessor who didn't use hyperbole to state the blatantly obvious to everyone.

"It's been coming for years. But rainfall in the last two years has been really sparse. Even the monsoons are like autumn showers. And that affects hydro-electric power supply and agricultural yield. Everything's been knocked off course."

Ocean knew it had been a mistake to engage Adams in conversation. But he wasn't finished.

"We've done our best, water sharing and management agreements are in place, the EU has contributed funding and the UN has tried to knock heads together in the region. But those nationalistic neighbours. They just don't want to work together. And now they're paying the price."

"Drought is no respecter of borders, sir," was the best that Ocean could offer in response, before he continued his journey along the corridor.

"Safe travels, Stoski."

The Environment Secretary went on his way to pontificate, but Ocean had work to do. He was under increasing pressure from journalists who wanted to know more substantial information about the trade agreement due to be signed.

"Why the secrecy?" one had asked pointedly.

It was a fair question and one that would be answered later that week. But not yet. De Layney and Ocean would have to conclude their White House meetings and head to Dulles International airport before all would be revealed.

Meanwhile, there was no sign of the crisis abating. Pakistanis and Afghans were out on the streets, desperately seeking the final drops from communal taps. In rural areas, whole families would congregate beside drying streams and sparsely filled rivers, attempting to bathe themselves in depleted waters, using the same muddy liquid to wash their clothes in as to drink from. Thirst and hunger were in full public view. Asian communities were under threat. Lives, thousands upon thousands of them, were being lost.

Ocean walked in to hear CBN's Jane Morley wrapping up another of her reports. She was on good form.

"And now, as I look around me, all I see is death, death of Afghans, death of Pakistanis, primarily. Yes, aid is slowly arriving here in Peshawar and being distributed to nearby border camps set up by the UN, but the death count continues to rise. The western world is finally waking up from its slumber, opening its eyes to perhaps its greatest ever challenge. Maybe it's a good thing that the Americans are due here in the region in a couple of days time to sign off a trade agreement. They can see for themselves first hand what is going on here."

De Layney exploded with rage.

"Why does she have to mention our agreement in a report about drought? She's trying to discredit us. They are two completely separate things. We have to keep them apart Stos."

"In fairness, sir, she is only reflecting the lack of information we have put out to the media. And she's saying what many are thinking, especially the environmentalists. Maybe, sir, we *should* consider the unthinkable."

"What, postpone it? No. Absolutely not. We've come too far to turn back now. Dammit Stos, the plane is on the tarmac. This is not a time for turning back. We press ahead."

Ocean was sympathetic with de Layney's position. The military deal had dominated his agenda and occupied his thoughts for weeks. In the past month alone, he had had high level meetings with the US Department of Defence, the

Israelis and US military generals. Things were moving towards a conclusion, fast.

But the drought….

Ocean and de Layney both knew that questions about why this crisis was happening were being asked by moms at every school gate from Montana to Michigan, by factory workers in the great car plants of the deep south and by mid-west farmers, who knew a thing or two about water shortage. He knew that leaders of the developed world – and eco-advocates – would be heading to his door on his return. He would need answers.

Europe would not be immune from its own responsibilities, but de Layney knew that he would have to take a stand, if only to protect America's reputation as a world leader. His problem was that no one, not he, not the Environment Minister, nor any other silver haired White House politicians, responded well to crises especially when their focus was on other matters. And de Layney and his colleagues weren't the only ones feeling the heat. US President Serenatti herself had been grilled relentlessly about America's policy on overseas aid for southern hemisphere countries, something which didn't feature prominently in her election manifesto. She knew though, that as long as pictures of dying families, clinging to each other in their risible, bone visible state, were being unashamedly beamed into the homes of millions of people around the developed world, environmental questions would need to be answered. Soon.

De Layney was becoming anxious about the task ahead of him. A humanitarian catastrophe in a region being lived out in northern hemisphere living rooms was a toxic combination for any visiting politician, let alone a US Secretary of State.

And then there was that picture, now an iconic image for the crisis, with Jane Morley's accompanying words alongside: '*Joined in life - inseparable in death.*'

The wider press, ahead of the game as ever, were sensing a story. They had been led to believe that a simple, long term trade deal, involving Kyrgyz raw materials, was in the offing, no more, no less. They knew nothing of its military intentions. But the Secretary of State's decision to attend himself, instead of sending an under-Secretary to sign it off, had heightened interest.

And now, wherever they looked, drought.

What should have been a regional crisis was now an international one. The larger US media networks, heavily criticised for their lack of coverage of previous droughts, weren't going to repeat the mistakes of the past. This time round, news editors were dripping a relentless diet of images and 'on the ground reports' into American homes.

Current Affairs programmes were bringing 'experts' together on a daily basis to discuss the catastrophe, while politicians willing to comment offered cautiously platitudinal solutions which they themselves didn't believe in.

Wherever you lived in the world, whatever screen you looked at, no one was going to be able to escape the south Asian drought.

22

Wednesday morning, Bishkek Daily News office

A pink sunrise hovered over Bishkek. Morning was breaking. The Americans were in the air. Olga was asleep.

Roza opened the shutter windows to her third-floor apartment and gazed out across the city and beyond to the Tian Shen mountains. She held her cup of peppermint tea close to her chest.

"My country, my people," she uttered. "My city."

She looked down. Bishkek was waking up in slow motion. People were on the move. Roza observed the comings and goings of early Wednesday morning municipal workers. From the safety of her upper window, she found herself thinking about the events of the previous evening. Her heart pumped quicker than it ought for such an early hour. Surely he hadn't followed her? Of course not. She was being paranoid, again! Anyway, it was only 6am.

She looked back towards the ever-growing concrete landscape, a mix of urban Soviet decay and new build, tree-lined boulevards and Turkish funded stores. The Central mosque call to prayer could be heard in the distance.

Olga, stretched out full length on the sofa, her feet sticking out under the purple duvet which had so snugly covered them during the night, began to stir. She opened her eyes in time to see Roza heading towards the kitchen.

"Coffee?"

"Please. May I use your shower?"

An hour later, the two women were walking arm in arm towards the office.

Roza had intended to apologise to Olga that her own problems had dominated their encounter the previous evening but in the time it took them to walk to Razzakov St, she hadn't managed to. Her mind was on other things, not least how she would explain her own discovery to her boss?

The women arrived on time.

Ednan Askar, alert, awake and already at his desk, greeted both women warmly, and invited Roza to take her coat off and sit down opposite him.

As she was about to speak, there was a knock at the door. The tall Batyrov, his tanned and friendly face, lined with history and experience, walked in.

"I hope you don't mind. I asked Temir to join us," said Askar, who had taken control of the meeting. "Thank you all for coming in early."

"No, no, I'm so sorry to inconvenience everyone" Roza interrupted. "Thank you for seeing me. I know it's a big day for you."

Askar nodded.

"Olga has been discreet but she told me last night that what you have to say is very important. She tells me that you have had quite a fright. So tell us what has happened and we will see if we can help at all."

Roza, her lips conjoined, her hands clasped together, began her story with the same words that she had spoken to Olga the evening before.

"Nine years ago, I was a victim of *Ala Kachuu*."

Having delivered her opening line, she slowly looked up to observe the wide-eyed group sat around her. She had their attention.

"You were bride kidnapped," said a surprised Batyrov. There were few things left in the world that would shock the man who had covered most of Kyrgyzstan's less palatable anti-social and illegal behaviours in his thirty year journalistic career. But this was one of them. He knew about *Ala Kachuu*, of course, but had never met one of its survivors.

Equally, Roza had never shared her ordeal with anyone since that fateful day and its aftermath. But here she was, unexpectedly brought to this pivotal point in her life.

Roza's eyes were fixed downwards, almost in embarrassment. The shame. She was visibly shaken by what she was about to reveal and still wondered about the wisdom of sharing something she had been trying to leave behind her for almost a decade.

Then, she had been forced to share her ordeal in all of its gory detail if only so that the police could write their report and file it away in the draw marked 'unresolved kidnappings,' which in the event, was what happened. The Bishkek police must have a filing cabinet full of 'unresolved bride-kidnapping' cases, thought Roza several years later.

Today, the re-telling of her story would be a voluntary act, brought about by extenuating circumstances. And there were no police, just trusted colleagues. Even so, she was nervous.

The sagely Temir Batyrov, under whose mentorship Roza's early tenure at the newspaper office had been put, placed a reassuring hand on her shoulder.

"Take your time," he said gently. "There's no rush."

Roza lifted her shoulders and let out a sigh, puffing her cheeks out as she did so. She began to speak again, this time with clarity and coherence.

"Yes, I was kidnapped, nine years ago. And last night, I saw the man who did it."

Askar sat back in his chair. He wanted to tread cautiously but was not a man to waste time, time he didn't have that day. A little reluctantly, and not wishing to be seen to doubt her testimony, he cut to the chase.

"Before you tell us more, Roza, I have a question for you, if I may. How do you know it was him, after nearly a decade? I am not doubting that the man you saw is your captor, but the police will want proof. Without it, it would be your word against his."

Askar's instincts were always to question things before coming to a conclusion. As the editor of Kyrgyzstan's leading independent newspaper, he had little choice. The buck stopped with him. His meticulous, probing methods had always stood him in good stead. And they would again today.

Roza sat up in her chair.

"Actually, I do have proof."

Batyrov, who was pouring himself a black coffee from the cafetiere, paused and turned to look across at Roza. Both men were attentive. Olga looked on.

"If I can explain how I escaped you will see how I have the proof that the man I saw last night in the Metro Bar and whose conversation I overheard is the same man who kidnapped me in 2016."

"To cut a long story short, I….."

"It's ok," interrupted Askar, feeling a little chastened by his own scepticism. "Take your time. That is why we came in early, to give you space. It's important that we know the full facts."

He didn't have time, of course, but he sensed that this was becoming more important than he had originally anticipated.

Roza took a swig of water, and sat back in her chair. For the first time in a very long time, she was about to relive her experience of *Ala Kachuu*.

23

Wednesday morning, Bishkek Daily News office

"The man's name is Kamil Joroev. He and his family kidnapped me when I was 15. I was held in the mountains for two days. It was terrifying."

"Did they force you to marry? Was there a ceremony?" Olga asked impatiently.

It was the right question, a journalist's question, a question they all wanted to know the answer to, but maybe it came too early in the day. Roza composed herself before answering.

"No, no, I managed to escape. It's ok."

Askar, glancing at the clock, moved the conversation on.

"Tell us about your capture and how you escaped. And your proof about this man."

"It was a school day, a Wednesday, like today. I was walking home with two friends when a car pulled up just ahead of us. I remember it was an old, faded-green Gaz M21. I was between the car and a newly painted tree. I remember one of my friends pointing out its shiny white trunk gleaming in the afternoon sunshine. All of a sudden, two men jumped out from the back of the car and ran towards us. They grabbed me and forced me into the car. It all happened so fast, before I could even understand what was going on. One minute I was walking home with my friends; the next, I was in the car, screaming. History lessons at school didn't tell us about *Ala Kachuu* but we all knew it existed. But I was shocked when I realised I was becoming one of its victims."

"Go on…"

"I fought hard but the men were too strong for me. My two school friends were shouting at the men and banging on the closed window, but they were powerless to intervene. I remember being overcome by the sheer physical violence of my attackers who kept on forcing my head downwards."

Roza paused, perhaps wanting to check on her audience again. She was in unfamiliar territory here, having to offload something that had remained with her for so long. They were attentive.

"They bore down on me with imposing strength. My neck was pressed into the torn upholstery. I couldn't breathe and just wanted to faint….then one of the men shouted out, 'kettnk….kettnk'….'go….go….' and the car just took off at speed."

She paused again, as if re-living the moment in real time. Her three colleagues, their hearts beating in unison, remained composed.

Olga Kola, sitting next to Roza, took her hands in hers, and squeezed them gently. Surely this was not the same, bright and breezy media graduate who had joined the Bishkek Daily News team at the start of the week? Was it?

Ednan Askar, experienced, wise and thoughtful, had been observing the mood of the group as Roza spoke. He knew what she was talking about. He had heard it all before, but never from the mouth of a survivor. Under his editorship, the Bishkek Daily News had played its part in keeping this ancient wrongdoing, which he had colloquially dubbed 'take and flee,' in the public eye. And with some success.

The readership always soared when such a campaign was run, sales boosted by parents who knew of someone who had experienced *Ala Kachuu* for themselves, fearful perhaps for their own daughters or grand-daughters.

Askar, an honourable man of few words, had sat opposite dozens of Kyrgyz parents over the years, all with tears in their eyes, who told him of their tales of loss, of their beloved children, girls, who simply disappeared from urban sight, never to return. It was always assumed that they had ended up in the mountains south of the capital, but no one could ever locate them, and the police never seemed to try that hard.

Perhaps that wasn't so surprising, given the remoteness of the vast area that they would have to search in order to recover a kidnapped bride. And anyway, Askar always knew that even if his editorial team were ever to get close enough to a potential bride-kidnapper, the nomadic community that surrounded the perpetrator would rally round, denying all knowledge of their neighbour's wrongdoing.

Had any of his campaigns been worthwhile, he wondered to himself?

Once a victim had been snatched from the city, there was little more that could be done. Dozens, maybe hundreds of kidnapped brides continued to live a nomadic life in a family they didn't know with a husband they didn't love. It was to be their lot.

Roza, though, wasn't one of them.

Askar studied the striking 24-year-old closely. With his journalist's hat on, he recognised in her something that was special.

Apart from her talent and ambition, revealed to him at her interview three weeks earlier, here sat not a prisoner, but an escapee. What an accidental coup for the newspaper. Another campaign waiting to happen, perhaps. Told by one of its survivors, a journalist.

Roza, for her part, seemed visibly relieved to have begun the process of getting it off her chest. Her grandmother had once told her that sometimes, it is easier to open up to people you hardly know than to those you are close to.

These were not just people though. These were her new colleagues, adults, professionals. Life had moved on. She was a grown up now. This would be her journey from now on.

24

Wednesday morning, Bishkek Daily News office

"I was driven eastwards out of Bishkek towards Lake Issyl Kul and then south on the Naryn-Torugart road. I don't think it had seen any repairs for thirty years. It was a very rough journey. Despite my head being held down for much of the journey, I instinctively knew the direction I was being taken. When I was allowed up for air, I would catch sight of a place name or a landmark which I recognised from previous childhood holidays with my family. I marked these places in my mind. Eventually, after what seemed like several hours, the car drew to a stop. I sensed I must be the Naryn region but I wasn't sure."

"That's incredible, Roza. You must have been terrified."

"I was, but I was more fearful of what might lie ahead for me."

She reminded Olga that while Naryn may have been an important focal point for the three regions that surrounded it, her overriding feeling was that she was about to become a totally anonymous stranger among its 250,000 inhabitants.

"And I was cold. I was dragged from the car by my loud captors, and my sense of isolation was immediate. Geographically, climactically and emotionally, I was lost. But I also sensed that openly resisting captivity would have been futile to my cause and so I decided to show acquiescence to my primitive captors to see what would happen. It seemed to work. As soon as I was removed from the car, I could detect a change of mood. The 'family' quietened their voices and welcomed me to my new surroundings. An elderly, maternal figure put a blanket around my shoulders and ushered me towards an open, outdoor fire which offered some light as well as heat. It was eerie. I sensed that I was being softened up, being prepared for some sort of marriage ceremony. The family needed and wanted me to comply and turning the harsh and physical into the gentle and engaging was their way of doing it. In that situation, there was only one thing for me to do, and that was to play along with it. If I was going to outsmart my captors then demonstrating a little acceptance of my situation, even if it was faked, was a good starting point."

Olga listened in awe to her colleague as she continued her eloquent monologue. Askar glanced at his watch. Roza continued.

"It was all a bit surreal. People, maybe friends of the family all came to look at me, but no one spoke directly. They simply wanted to eye me up and down. I was really cold but tried to get my bearings. There was a snow-capped fence which encircled the family 'estate' which comprised a compound of three *gers*, two larger ones and a smaller one. I was put into the smaller one which housed two makeshift wooden beds, a corrugated bath tub and a kerosene stove on which to heat up water from the nearby stream. The stove helped to warm my *ger*. It had dark brown, felt cladded walls, which offered some insulation but not enough to counter the night-time Naryn chill."

Roza began to tense up. Olga noticed her shiver, and affectionately rubbed her back up and down a couple of times.

"Apart from the brief exchange between myself and Kamil Joroev on the first night following my kidnap, very little else was spoken in the period between capture and escape. Kamil's mother Elnura had several times tried to place a white scarf onto my head…."

"It's a sign of marital intention, I think," Olga interrupted, looking at Batyrov and Askar, making the wrong assumption that neither of them knew of this custom.

Undeterred, Roza warmed to her theme.

"I fought her off each time. I remember being so thankful that I hadn't been raped by her sons on my first night. But it didn't stop her haranguing me at every opportunity, trying to make me feel guilty about not accepting this opportunity of marriage to her youngest."

Askar and Batyrov were transfixed as Roza went on to explain how the Joroev family, horse traders for generations and led by Kamil's grossly unkind mother, had secured her with a rope tied around her wrist and ankle. And how, during every meal, she would work to loosen the ropes. It would make her skin red raw and her body weary. She wondered, she said, about the futility of escape. After all, these were seasoned equine traders, expert in the art of racking up horses. There was surely no escaping these knots.

"The only exercise I had in her two days of captivity," she continued, "was the short walk to the hole in the ground, some 20 yards from the *ger*, where I would relieve myself. Kamil had proudly announced to me on my first evening that he had dug it specially for me, in the hope that this would endear me to him. It revolted me. On the second evening, the family's conversations were becoming increasingly animated, and I sensed that they wouldn't wait much longer in their quest to enforce matrimony. So my escape had to be that night, or never."

"What did you do?" asked an animated Olga.

"I knew that the knife that Kamil used to shoe the wild horses that grazed downstream towards the lake was always left embedded in the fertile mountain soil next to his *ger*, nearby to where the hole in the ground was located. As darkness fell on my second night in captivity, I put my plan into action. Before supper was cooked, I called Kamil to tell him that I wanted to relieve myself. Kamil, as was his way, came over and slackened the ropes which were wrapped around the tree outside my *ger*, enough for me to reach my makeshift toilet…."

She paused, looking down to the floor.

"Sorry, this is all so embarrassing."

"You're among friends, Roza," Olga reassured her.

"He had the courtesy to withdraw while I relieved myself, but he always returned to take me back to her *ger* and re-tie the rope so tightly that my ability to move around remained severely restricted. But on this occasion, before I called him to let him know that I was finished, I managed to edge myself towards his *ger*, trying hard not to tread on any branches or stones that would alert the family to my movements. I don't know how but I managed to reach and extract the hunting knife from the ground. I fell backwards but managed to recover quickly enough to reposition myself into my squatting position above the hole in the ground. I know, it's gross but that is what happened. I hid the knife beneath the elasticated waistline of my *beldemchi*, which the family had made me wear on my first night of captivity, and hoped that Kamil wouldn't notice its absence from the ground. He didn't. This was it, I thought. I was ready. This was my chance to escape."

The group of journalists were captivated by Roza's story. None of them moved. Roza carried on.

"I called Kamil who came out wearing just a vest and trousers held up by a corded *gashnik*.

He walked me back to my ger and re-tied the rope that held me to the tree. My heart was racing. I was fearful that he would notice something unusual, something hard, protruding from my overgarment. Thankfully, he didn't. 'I'm going to get changed and then I will bring you your supper. We can talk this evening,' he said. I was frightened. His tone was sinister. His mother must have been nagging him to move things along. Maybe she wanted the enforced ceremony to happen the next morning. It only made me more determined to carry out my plan. I remember thinking, the next half hour is going to define my future."

25

Tuesday/Wednesday overnight, Europe

US Air Force 2, flight 313 from Washington DC, was making good time.

The Americans were flying over the eastern Irish coast, their flight path taking them south towards their short refuelling stop-over in Germany. Nine hours later, they would be touching down on Kyrgyz soil. Talks would commence in the State room in Bishkek's White House first thing on Thursday.

The Secretary of State and his press officer spent much of their time on board in the President's suite, away from US officials and an American government photographer. De Layney and Ocean needed to finalise their detailed responses to any media questions that might arise about the drought. De Layney was confident that the bigger story, the shift in the balance of power in the region, would prevail, but Ocean liked to prepare for all eventualities.

"How long until we land in Munich?"

"Less than 45 minutes," retorted Ocean, checking his watch.

"I'm having a shower. When I get back we'll work on a final strategy to make war and water into a compatible and compassionate message."

And with that, de Layney walked over to the mini-shower cubicle, passing his white ironed shirt, dark jacket and immaculately pressed trousers along the way. He turned on the water tap.

Ocean's brain went into overdrive. He had been appointed to the post because of his quick mind and ability to think on his feet. Many a time he had batted away probing, hostile media questions from US journalists, questions which required the government to deflect attention away from itself. That was his job. But this time, flying into a crisis ridden region plagued by death to sign off on a military deal which journalists weren't expecting, his job was going to be that bit harder.

De Layney emerged from the shower and dressed himself. As he straightened his angled, striped, navy and maroon tie in front of the mirror, his mind flashed back to the image of the elderly Nepali couple. He dismissed it as mere mind games.

"What have we got, Stos?"

"Well," offered Ocean, "we are about to touch down in a region where people are dying of thirst and sickness. It's for the Asians to sort out but we need to be sensitive…."

"....and appear compassionate," interrupted de Layney. "So, our strategy needs to be one that diverts responsibility for dealing with the crisis back to the region. We also need a narrative that will be acceptable back home. So we fall back on our tried and trusted line."

"Global security for American citizens. A presence in central Asia is essential for peace in the Midde East."

Ocean was well versed in political speak.

"Never fails."

"Yes, we can't be seen to be ignoring the crisis, but...."

"....but it's not for Americans to solve. We are sympathetic but we are here to strengthen security for American citizens around the world, especially in the Middle East, as well as wider security in the region. That's good Stos. We're getting somewhere now."

A few minutes later, de Layney felt he had a settled position. He relaxed his head back into the head rest and shut his eyes.

Fifteen minutes later, he was woken by the airline tannoy.

"Preparing to land at Munich International Airport; please turn off all personal computers and mobile phones, extinguish all cigarettes, fasten seat belts."

The live TV feed in the President's suite, which also included a bed, a bar and a running buffet, was shut off. The screens went blank.

He swivelled his passenger seat. It clicked into a locked frontal position. A few minutes later, the plane touched down, with barely a bump.

De Layney looked through the small, oval aircraft window. The distant terminal travel ways were bustling with airport personnel, overalled technicians, ground staff and luggage transporters. De Layney watched as the aircraft slowly turned away from it all, towards a refuelling bay in the south western corner of the airfield. Two fuel tankers stood by, ready for action. The autumnal night sky was cloudless. Its stars shone brightly. Silent night. Ninety minutes later, the 'plane slowly and smoothly taxied its way along the runway to its take off position.

'Ladies and gentlemen. Please make sure that your seats are in the upright position and your seatbelts are fastened. We are now preparing for take off.'

Next Stop Bishkek Manas. And history.

26

Wednesday morning, Bishkek Daily News office

Roza had scarcely paused for breath as she articulated a story which, despite its age, had not grown weary. She had kept it tucked inside her memory for such a long time that she spoke it out with a sense of relief.

This was her moment. And she was in full flow.

"I watched through the turned-up canvas of the ger entrance as the makeshift fire pit exploded into life. One thing that these mountain people certainly understood was how to cook above the flame. Elnura, the mother, brought out some steaming bread from the large *ger* and placed it at one end of the family table. I didn't waste any time. As soon as I was alone, I hacked at the rope with the knife; backwards and forwards, forwards and backwards."

Roza became animated, sawing her hand back and forth, demonstrating the ferocity of her actions.

"I remember thinking how grubby the blade was but it was extremely sharp and thankfully, it did its work. Within seconds, my hand and foot were free. I hacked away at the canvas behind me and managed to create a small, triangular hole just behind my mattress. I put my hand through it and felt around on the icy ground for the biggest rock I could find. I was very scared but consumed with anticipation about the possibility of escape. Of course, I had no idea where I would escape to or what direction I would go, but it didn't matter. I just had to get out from the clutches of the Joroev family. I held on to the rock and gripped the knife. My heart was pounding, but I waited patiently for Kamil to come back with my food. As soon as he entered the tent and bent over, I hit him full in the face with the rock. He dropped the plate, much of the steaming food landing on me. It burnt my legs. I only had on a light cotton *beldemchi*. He fell to his knees, and I lashed out with the knife. I was terrified but my attack took him completely by surprise, so much so that a piece of his torn vest attached itself to the knife's blade. After that, he was unable to offer much resistance. He lay on his back, semi-conscious, motionless. I ripped at the small hole I had made in the canvas, and squeezed myself through it. It was not as easy as I thought it would be. I managed to get half my body out and just needed to bring my legs through. Just as freedom beckoned, though, there was a strong hand on my ankle. I twisted myself back round and slashed away at the canvas which began to tear open with each strike. I got the knife back into the ger and thrust it towards Kamil's bloody hand and leg. In the struggle, he tried to wrestle the knife from me. He grabbed for the handle but…."

Suddenly, Roza stopped. She had spoken for so long, the swell of her brown skinned decolletage rising and falling with every revelatory utterance. Silence came as something of a relief to the gathered group. It wasn't that they weren't absorbed, more that they were trying to come to terms with her story. In the continuing silence, only Roza's breathing could be heard.

Olga leaned over and placed her arm around her. The burden that she had carried for such a long time was finally falling from her shoulders. Roza's head was bowed as she began to sob. Olga drew her in, but Roza resisted. Olga withdrew her arm. She understood. This was a big moment. Roza was about to conclude her story. And she needed space.

"As I slashed away at him with the knife, he tried to snatch it from me, but in doing so, he grabbed the blade. It had blood and a fragment of his vest around it and maybe he thought that would protect his hand. But as he tried to wrestle it from my grasp, he….it sliced off one of his fingers. It was disgusting. He fell backwards, screaming out in pain. It must have been agonising. I'll never forget that scream. Or the sight of his finger hanging there, about to drop off, blood pouring from the wound. I pulled at the knife and vest and it all became intertwined with the blade. For a split second, I can't explain it, but I remember that I wanted to help him, to bind it up. But I knew there was no time to lose. I squeezed myself out of the ger. I was shaking, dirty, bloodied and bedraggled. I ran."

Temir's softly spoken tone interrupted her animated flow.

147

"And you ran....to where?"

"I ran for the trees. I was terrified that they would catch me but I had a head start on the family and I instinctively knew from my visits to the hole in the ground that the terrain I headed towards was downward, so that is where I decided to run. And although I was breathless I was young and easily able to outrun my older pursuers. After I had been running for two or three minutes, I remember I could still hear Kamil's mother shrieking to her sons, '*srocno kuuo kotorulgan!*'......*quick, catch her, catch her...*' It said much about her that she cared more about recapturing me than for her own son, who must have been in agony. Anyway, I ran until I could run no more. As the shouts and screams from the family grew fainter, I knew that separation from it was mine. I remember falling into the uncomfortable safety of some wild and crackly bracken by the side of the road. I lay on my back looking at the clear dark sky above. It seemed further away from me than I wanted it to be, but its blue-grey glow, decorated with numerous stars, helped my exhausted body and mind to sleep. It was my first, deep sleep for two days."

Ednan Askar, Temir Batyrov and Olga Kola allowed Roza the silent space to recover her emotions. And theirs. This was a story that they hadn't been expecting to hear, certainly not on a Wednesday morning before the sun had fully risen.

Olga gestured towards Roza. This time, there was no resistance. Roza turned to face her, and in the relief of the moment, buried her head into her colleague's shoulder.

27

Wednesday morning, Bishkek Daily News office

The clock on the wall in Askar's office struck three cords. 7.45am. Askar would have to leave soon. Batyrov asked the next question.

"What happened next? How did you get back to Bishkek?

"I woke very early. It was not fully light. I remember my limbs ached and I was very cold. There were cuts and bruises on my arms and legs. I tried hard to get my bearings. I looked at the knife. There was a piece of bloody material still wrapped around the blade. I didn't know what to do, whether to discard it or keep it. I decided I would keep it until I could get home. I remember breathing in the cool, mountain-scented, morning air. I was experiencing freedom once again and I was thankful. I savoured the moment. I heard a rippling sound and followed it to its origin, a freshwater stream. I watched it make its slow journey downwards and observed how it negotiated its pathway around the rocks and foliage. I noticed how the water took its directional lead from broken branches and wayward logs which sought to deflect its journey at every turn. I remember putting my hand into the shallow but freezing cold water, enjoying the tingling sensation on my fingers. I splashed it liberally over myself, my face, my arms and legs, cleaning my wounds as best I could. I remember they stung as water met dried blood. But I felt clean - no, not clean. Free."

She spoke like a seasoned journalist, as if she was writing her own story in prose, in real time. She stared out of the window behind Ednan Askar's desk, before continuing.

"And then I heard the sound of horses. I looked upwards to the grassy slopes. Half a dozen wild, feral Mongolian Dzungarian horses were galloping along aimlessly. I watched them into the distance and remember whispering to myself, 'my country, my beautiful country.' And for the first time in two days, I felt safe once again. Helped by a couple of kindly farmers along the way, I began the long journey home."

The re-telling of her ordeal was complete. It was shocking, but authentic; eloquently told by one who had experienced its horrors. Silence filled the room. It fell to Askar to break it.

"Thank you, Roza," he said gently. "Thank you for telling us, for trusting us with your story."

Batyrov, who had been leaning against the wall on which hung an old black and white photograph of the newspaper's founder, Sukhrab Kurmanbek, sat down. The four of them sat in a circle with only a desk between them, like an addiction therapy group coming together to hear each others stories.

Askar cut to the chase.

"So, you kept the knife?"

Roza nodded.

"The knife, the remains of the torn vest, the blood, I have it all. I didn't tell the police or my parents about the knife. I was scared. I wrapped it in an old newspaper and have kept it hidden for all these years. If you want proof of who my attacker was then, and who I saw in the bar last night, it's hidden under my bed, under a floorboard, at my parent's house."

Askar looked up at Batyrov and then returned his gaze back towards Roza.

"It's your proof that he did this to you."

Roza nodded again before her journalistic nous began to kick in.

"But I understand there's a bigger story going on here, isn't there?"

Askar nodded agreement.

"Joroev and the American," said Batyrov. "And the conversation you overheard."

"You're right Temir," Askar responded, returning his gaze back towards Roza, "and if you are willing…."

Askar was trying to choose his words carefully.

"….if you are willing Roza, we can use your evidence to find out what that story is."

Roza looked at Batyrov, a faint smile crossing her face. Unexpected as it was, could this convoluted reunification of captor and captured be her opportunity for some sort of greater justice, whatever that might be?

The clock on the wall struck 8.00am. Askar was due to meet the proprietor outside the office for the short walk to the White House for the press briefing which was scheduled for 8.30am. He had to leave.

"Ok, we go this alone," said Askar, with an authority which reassured Roza. "There's no point in involving the police at this stage. From now on, this will become a newspaper investigation, the American, the conversation you overheard, and we need to find out what this man….what is his name….?"

"Kamil Joroev…."

"….what he's doing here in Bishkek because from what Olga was telling me about what you told her, it's something dubious. What's his involvement with the American? Why would Joroev be here anyway, in the city, hundreds of miles from the family home?"

These were good questions.

Roza looked at her editor. He was a leader. His strength made her proud to be in his team. Ednan Askar looked back at Roza. His voice softened.

"There is also your wellbeing to consider. I will explain everything to Mr Kurmanbek. Even though we had no idea what you were going to tell us, Roza, Temir and I agreed this morning, before you came in, that we will do whatever we can to help. And given what you have told us, I think that there is a lot to be investigated. But Roza, it's your call. If you don't want to do it, you don't have to. Temir can work with Olga if you prefer. If you decide to go with it, you will need to work it alongside your day-to-day stories. Your by-line must be seen to be above the mundane stories, a cover, if you like, for the *real* story."

Roza looked at Askar, then at Batyrov. Olga gave her a little smile.

"I started it, albeit unintentionally, and I'd like to finish it, whatever 'it' turns out to be."

A nodding agreement in the room confirmed Roza's willingness to be involved.

Batyrov broke in.

"Mundane stories, eh. Maybe you should have covered the match last night after all, Roza."

The irony of Batyrov's observation was not lost on her. If she had accepted Askar's invitation to cover the football, she would not have ended up at the Metro Bar, identified Joroev, overheard his conversation with Joe the American, or shared her tale of Ala Kachuu with her colleagues this very morning.

Roza acknowledged Batyrov with a grin.

Askar headed for the door.

"I have to go, but concentrate on Joroev," he said, looking at Batyrov. "He's the key. Let's get to the bottom of this."

Roza stood up.

"Thank you, Mr Askar. I'm grateful."

"We look after our own," said Askar, confirming what Olga had told Roza the night before. Askar eyed the clock again before heading out.

"Keep me informed," he shouted over his shoulder.

The outer office door closed behind him.

"We need a strategy," Batyrov said, determinedly, "and a place to work other than our desks."

"The store-room is fairly empty," said Olga. "There's a trestle table in there....and a white board behind the stationary cupboard."

Batyrov went to check it out.

Roza went to the bathroom and returned just as Olga was putting a piece of paper next to her laptop. It was an incident report called in the evening before; a young lady who had been involved in a motoring incident on Beyshenalieva Street, when a dog ran out in front of her car and was killed.

"Can you follow this up please Roza?

Roza scanned the incident sheet. She looked up at Olga.

"Back to the day job," Roza replied, a hint of a smile on her lips.

28

Wednesday afternoon, Bishkek Daily News office

It was 3pm. The meeting with Ednan Askar that morning seemed like a distant memory.

Roza had spoken to the distraught owner of the dead dog and the driver who had inadvertently killed it. The police had been informed and were looking into the circumstances surrounding the accident, or so they said. No one was holding their breath over any charges that might be brought, either against the owner of the dog, who had let if off its leash, or the distraught driver, who may or may not have been driving without due care and attention, or worse still, under the influence of alcohol or drugs. As always, there were more questions than answers, probably too many for the police to be bothered about. Finding out the truth and administering justice wasn't really their thing, unless money was involved. But at least for Roza, the story, such as it was, represented another by-line even if it was relegated to a miniscule 250 words in the community news on page nine. But that didn't matter. It would be behind such by-lines that Roza and Batyrov could investigate Joroev further.

Roza sat in the store cupboard which had been converted by Temir and Olga into a makeshift nerve centre for the investigation they were about to embark upon. Her PC was on her lap.

Using brightly coloured marker pens which were scattered at one end of the long trestle table in their shared workspace, Batyrov had drawn some circles on to a white board which sat at an angle on a two drawer filing cabinet, leaning against the wall.

Inside one of them was the name 'Feliks Ormanbekov'. Another said 'Water'. A third said 'Kamil Joroev'. Above them all was a photograph, a grainy, photocopied picture of the bearded American with his name underneath: 'Joe Ramirez'.

"There aren't many overweight bearded Americans called Joe in Bishkek. It didn't take long for me to identify him," said Batyrov, tapping a thick marker against the white board. "I found this photo on the internet. He's a political lecturer. His profile is on the staff tab at the AUCA. I've printed it off. We need to know more about him. I have a friend who works in student admissions. I've known her and her brother for years. I'm overdue a coffee with her."

Then he tapped on the picture of Joroev.

"We know where he lives thanks to you Roza, but we need to get close to him. He may still remember you, so don't go anywhere near him. And you can't frequent the Metro Bar for a while. I will go there and talk to the proprietor to see if he is a regular there. I'll do that today. Then we'll approach him."

"What would you like me to do," asked Roza?

"Could you bring the knife in? We need to get the fingerprints off it and analyse the blood. Maybe use a towel when you handle it or just put it in a box to protect it. There will be traces of DNA on the blade and the T shirt. I have a contact at the government forensics lab. Once we have it, we can make our move on Joroev."

Batyrov and Roza smiled at each other.

"Can you get hold of the knife without your parents knowing?"

Roza nodded.

"It's payback time, Roza."

"Why is Ormanbekov up there?"

"I don't know. I really don't know, Roza. But we need to know more about what Joroev was talking to Ramirez about. Something to do with the trade agreement. And water, you say? Maybe if you could write up what you can remember of their conversation?"

Roza typed into her laptop while Batyrov paused, watching on.

"Are you ok, Roza?"

Roza nodded.

"OK, I'll see you later."

Batyrov exited, a reassuring hand placed upon her shoulder as he passed by.

29

Wednesday early evening, Metro Bar, Bishkek

There was hardly anyone around when Batyrov turned up at the Metro Bar. The early evening rush wouldn't begin for another hour or more.

A middle aged man was behind the counter, drying glasses.

"Shoro, please."

Betyrov looked around at the handful of folk in the bar. He didn't expect Joroev to be there, and he wasn't.

Batyrov placed a grainy looking, photo-shopped image on to the bar, the only picture he was able to find online of Joroev, who somehow had managed to get himself into the background of a photograph with Akayev while visiting an abattoir in Jyrgalan a couple of years ago.

"Do you recognise this man?" Batyrov asked pointing to the man standing behind the Prime Minister.

The bar tender picked it up.

He looked at it, then at the journalist.

"Are you the police?"

Batyrov smiled.

"Just an old friend."

The bartender looked back at the photograph.

"He comes by, usually on Tuesdays and Saturdays," responded the bartender. "They were in last night."

"They?"

"He meets up with a friend, an American. They always arrive separately. He always drinks *Bozo*. The American, root beer. They usually sit at that table over there."

He went back to his drying of an already well wiped glass.

Batyrov took a sip of his Shoro.

"Do you know where he lives?" Batyrov asked, trying not to draw too much attention to his enquiry. He already knew the name of the road and the apartment from Roza, but Batyrov, his journalistic antennae working overtime, wanted to find out how well the bartender knew him, whether he might even know what they talked about.

"I want to surprise him....for old times sake."

"No. Sorry."

Batyrov finished his drink, thanked the bartender, and made for the exit.

As he approached the door, the bar tender called out.

"Even if I did, you wouldn't find him there. I heard he was involved in a road accident this morning. Hit by a motor bike, I think."

Batyrov returned to the bar.

"Do you know where he is now?"

"Well, I'm told it happened on *Aytmatova* so I expect they took him to the Memorial Hospital."

"Poor guy," said Batyrov with a wry smile. "I'll go visit. Thank you for your help."

The barman went back to drying his glass.

Batyrov took a *mashrutka* heading to Aytmatova and alighted at the hospital's greying, arched entrance. He was on a mission to speak to a bride kidnapper. It would be a first for him.

Batyrov made his way to the casualty ward. A nurse told him that Joroev had some lacerations, some bruising and concussion but would only be kept in the hospital overnight and released first thing Thursday morning.

Batyrov peered through the rounded glass windows of the ward. Four patients were lying motionless in the four beds to the right, all men. A woman was in one of the beds to the left.

Another campaign for Roza to get her teeth into one day, thought Batyrov.

Roza arrived. Batryov had called her as soon as he had left the bar. She approached the swing door somewhat sheepishly.

Standing on tip toe to see through a circular window, she scanned the room. She looked away, then at Batyrov.

"First bed on the right," said Roza. Batyrov looked inside again, this time at Joroev.

His arm was attached to a tube, which was attached to a drip. He wasn't moving. One leg was heavily bandaged, but not with a plaster cast. His face was badly bruised.

"Mmmm. He doesn't look too bad," joked Batyrov.

Roza stood behind him. She wasn't smiling. Batyrov sensed the rawness of the situation. She needed some reassurance.

"It's OK Roza. I'll do the talking."

The two journalists approached Joroev's bed, Roza a cautious step behind her male colleague. Batyrov drew the plain, cream coloured vinyl curtains around the bed.

Joroev's eyes remained closed.

"What happened to you, then," asked Batyrov quietly, bending menacingly over towards the patient?

Joroev looked startled and made as if to sit up, before quickly realising his inability to do so. Wincing in pain, he looked up at his two visitors.

"Who are you?"

"This is Roza, my friend. Do you remember her?"

Joroev tried to sit up again, again unsuccessfully.

"Who are you," he repeated?

"You must remember Roza, the schoolgirl you tried to kidnap a few years ago."

The colour drained from Joroev's face. He turned his head away.

"I don't know what you are you talking about? You've got the wrong man. I've never seen…."

Before he could continue, Batyrov interrupted. "Kamil Joroev. We know who you are. We have your knife, we have your vest, we have your blood. We have your DNA. And we know where you live."

Batyrov let that sink in.

165

"But we're not here for that, not for now at any rate."

Joroev looked scared but turned his eyes defiantly back toward his visitors.

"Who are you?" he repeated.

"Never mind that. We want to have a little chat with you about your friendship with Mr Ramirez. The nurse says you will be out first thing tomorrow. Maybe we'll come and collect you. Take you home. What do you say?"

"Tomorrow."

"Tomorrow. 8.00am. Don't you be going anywhere overnight," said Batyrov, a sinister half smile on his lips.

Batyrov and Roza turned away.

"Oh, and by the way…." Batyrov turned back on himself as Roza left the ward ahead of him. He leaned over the bed to whisper in Joroev's ear.

"….not a word to anyone, especially Mr Ramirez. We don't want the police getting involved with your previous misdemeanour, do we?"

30

Wednesday evening, Vefa and Manas airport, Bishkek

As he pondered which suit to wear to greet his American guests at Manas, a lightweight striped black or an Italian charcoal grey, Ormanbekov reflected on this pivotal moment in Kyrgyz political history. The culmination of plans he had so meticulously crafted in secret whilst confined in Moscow's notorious Lefortovo Correction prison, were about to be realised. Those plans were never about dollars, although that would be a major boost to the always struggling Kyrgyz economy. They were about power, status, respect. He was tired of Kyrgyzstan being the 'fifth' republic, always thought of as the poor relation to its neighbours. He was hungry for change, for elevated status in the region, and for autonomy from Russia.

"It's a high stakes game," he had once told his deputy, "but one which I am willing to participate in."

As he straightened his tie and put his jacket on, the Italian charcoal grey, he considered what the international reaction might be to tomorrow's announcement.

The Chinese would be outraged. After years of investment in the Stans, they would expect to be in pole position for any agreement that would increase their influence in the region. That was never an option for Ormanbekov, however. He calculated that geographically, their need was not as great as the needs of those located on a different continent. If nothing else, American need would trump Chinese aspiration.

Equally, the Russians would have thought that Kyrgyzstan, like its neighbours Uzbekistan, Kazakhstan, Tajikistan and Turkmenistan would, as they had done so dutifully for so many years, simply fall into line, continuing Moscow's mission for them to be post-independence conduits for Russia's messaging to the Americans. They, too, would be as outraged as the Chinese at the deal which had been negotiated behind their back.

Ormanbekov had strung the Chinese and the Russians along. He would not allow the final details of the agreement to be announced until high level American political figures were standing on Kyrgyz soil. And very shortly they would be.

"The region will be changed overnight," he had told his two trusted political allies at their final preparatory meeting the evening before. "And, my friends, we will not only benefit from millions of American dollars, we will also gain a collateral military advantage, a border security which would far outweigh anything that the Russians can offer us. That alone is worth de Layney's signature on our agreement. What is there to lose?"

It was a fair question.

American air personnel stationed on foreign soil, central Asian soil, was a game changer, a military objective which only a few minor republics around the world could pull off. Kyrgyzstan, it would seem, was about to become one of them.

Midnight was drawing near. At Manas, three black Mercedes G-Class government official cars, security checked and driven by American military personnel, were waiting on the floodlit runway at the northeast corner of the airbase, ready to transport and escort the Americans to the Hyatt.

President Ormanbekov, Prime Minister Akayev and Foreign Affairs minister Alexander Kulov were on runway 21B, waiting to greet the Secretary of State and his party. TV cameras were set up at the end of a red carpet.

The cabin door opened. Robert de Layney and his press aide, Stoski Ocean stepped out into the midnight chill.

Warm handshakes and flash bulbs preceded the short walk down the red carpet towards two microphones. Ormanbekov spoke first.

"We warmly welcome our American friends to the Republic of Kyrgyzstan, the first, may I say, by a senior American diplomat for almost a decade. This in itself, is cause for great celebration as we look to increase our trading links with the United States of America."

He looked towards Robert de Layney.

"Thank you, sir, for taking the time to visit with us here in Kyrgyzstan. I look forward to strengthening relations between our two countries in the days ahead."

De Layney, surrounded by American Secret Service personnel, responded in kind.

The two men shook hands, smiling towards the cameras for pictures that would be beamed around Asia and the US before their official cars had even reached the airport perimeter. They would reconvene in the morning.

As Ormanbekov's car sped its way back to the capital, he gazed out into the darkness of the Bishkek night, tracking the journey's signposts, something he had done many times before. He noted the sparsely lit industrial centres of Jerkindik and Kalyka Akieva and the lights of Zavodskaya. Each minute that ticked by marked a minute closer to his goal.

Despite his calm demeanour, Ormanbekov's heart was racing.

How would things go, he wondered? What would the American response be to the additional elements that he planned to introduce into the agreement? Controlling the water supply for his own economic purposes would, over and above that which was represented in the agreement, guarantee him increased influence in the region. But he needed additional dollars. Would the Americans fall for a new amendment they know nothing about? Questions. Questions.

By the time his entourage drew towards the Zavodskaya, he had answered those questions, in his mind, at least. He concluded that American determination to achieve their military objectives in his region would far outweigh their reluctance to veto any amendment to the agreement, however late in the day its introduction.

His car entered the Bishkek City boundary, turning into Isakov Street, where it pulled up at Kulov's apartment. His Minister for Foreign Affairs was about to get out of the car when Ormanbekov grabbed his arm.

"Money talks," he whispered to Kulov, "….and when our agreement is signed, we will have all the power we need. It's taken more than three decades, but now, Kyrgyzstan is about to become the lead player in the region. There can be no turning back," he chuckled. "Go and get a good night's sleep, Alexander. Tomorrow we will dangle an environmental carrot in front of American noses. They can't resist carrots."

The two men laughed out loud before Kulov got out and the car continued its journey into the city back towards Vefa.

Would the President's judgment be right, Kulov wondered as he buzzed himself through the security gates of his apartment block? One more sleep, and they would find out.

31

Thursday morning, Memorial Hospital / Jash Gvardiya

Batyrov arrived at the hospital before 8am.

Ten minutes later, he and Joroev were leaving, medical discharge papers in hand.

"Where to?" asked the taxi driver.

"Jash Gvardiya," answered Batyrov, confirming Joroev's worst fears. The taxi driver threw his cigarette butt from the window and started the engine. Ten minutes later, Joroev was limping up the fire escape steps to his third floor apartment. Batyrov followed him in.

"You and I are going to have a little talk."

The apartment was basic but adequate. It had a large living room, a bedroom, a kitchen and a bathroom. Clothes were strewn around, on the floor, on window hooks and there was a shirt hanging over the kitchen chair. On the small balcony, with its rusty blue surround, there was a small fold-out clothes stand on which hung some socks and underwear. The place smelled of stale alcohol.

Without asking, Joroev hobbled to his kitchen where he poured some *syuzmo* into two glasses and motioned Batyrov to put a jug of water on the table.

Two chairs stood alongside each other to the far side of the circular, hardwood dining room table. Batyrov pulled them round.

"What do want from me?" asked Joroev, wincing in pain as he sat down.

Batyrov did not have time to be patient. He needed answers now.

"Who do you work for?"

"If I tell you, will you leave me alone?"

"Right now, you are not in a position to ask me any favours, Joroev...."

Batyrov picked up his drink and brought it slowly to his mouth.

"....but I'll think about it."

"I work for Akayev. I'm his eyes and ears on the ground. I helped him with some intel about the American visit."

"Who is the American?"

Another test question for Joroev.

"That's Joe, Joe Ramirez. He works at the AUCA but is also the US Ambassador's right hand man. He is my contact. But Akayev doesn't know that I feed some intel back to him. Joe pays me well. But please don't tell Akayev. Please. If he finds out, it's the end of me."

"Sounds like you have quite a few secrets, Joroev...."

Batyrov had a kindly face and a softly spoken voice but could be extremely menacing when he needed to be.

"....and now I know two of them," he said.

A short silence ensued. Joroev looked down at his hands, tightly clasped together. He was perspiring. Batyrov sensed the pressure he was feeling. Joroev still didn't know who he was. Batyrov hadn't told him. A friend? Roza's father, perhaps? But why was Batyrov asking him about who *he* was, who he worked for, and Ramirez? He was scared. And confused. It was time to come clean about his past.

"You have no idea what it is like being born into a nomadic clan," he began, quietly. "We don't have the comforts you urban dwellers have. We sleep on horsehair mattresses, we don't have running water from a tap, or electric fires in the winter. If we want to eat, we have to kill. And women are scarce. Marriage is scarce. We have different rules for women."

"So you decide to come to the city for your brides."

Joroev ignored Batyorv's sarcastic intervention. His eyes were still transfixed on to his conjoined hands, his head bowed. An elongated silence ensued before Joroev spoke again.

"I remember growing up. I hardly saw my mother. Before I would get up in the morning, she would be out, turning the cattle out from our shed on to pastureland, or feeding the horses. Then she would return home to heat the ger we lived in. In the winter, I would wake up to see her cleaning the woodstove of ashes having already fetched logs from the store. Then she would get breakfast ready, eggs, always eggs, and pancakes. After breakfast I would go to the village school where all the local children went. In the day she would serge carpets to sell on the roadside for any passing trade that came along. I would come home at 4 and she would have some outdoor work for me to do. Then we would eat together and as soon as it was dark, I would be sent to bed. That was my day, my life."

Batyrov listened, intently.

"My father died of alcohol poisoning when I was young, 8, or 9. My mother told me that he beat her, but I already knew. I heard it, often, and saw it occasionally. She seemed to accept it as part of her life, but I was frightened of him. When I was eight, she told me that one day I would have a wife to look after me. But I didn't understand. When I was twelve, my brother went to Bishkek and came home with a bride. I'd never seen her before. My mother told me that acquiring a bride from the city was how we land-dwellers married. I believed her though it didn't seem right to me. On my eighteenth birthday, she said that I needed a wife. She sent me here with my older brother. His marriage had never been happy so I didn't know why we would do this. I didn't want to go. But I had no choice."

He looked up at Batyrov, his eyes moistening before looking downwards again. What Joroev said next surprised him.

"It was Roza who showed me how wrong it was. Her determination to escape and the ferocity she employed to achieve it made me think."

He held up his hand to show Batyrov his severed finger.

"My mother was furious with me for letting her escape. But I was glad she escaped. After that, I knew I had to get away too. As soon as my wounds were healed, I did what Roza did. I ran away, and came here, to the city. I haven't had contact with my family since. My mother, my brother or his wife. I used to beg for food at the monument on Molodaya Gvardiya Boulevard, hoping that someone might offer me work."

"Ramirez lived on Beyshenalieava Street. One day, he stopped and asked me what I was doing there. I said I was looking for work. He said he headed up the Politics faculty at the University and that he did a bit of work for the American government too. He said he had heard that the Kyrgyz were looking for an unofficial government contact 'on the ground' a local 'fixer', a national. Paid work. He introduced me to Akayev and I have been working for him ever since."

Joroev's hands were back around his glass, the stub of his missing finger black with ingrained dirt. His head remained fixed downwards. He may have been tearful at that moment but Batyrov couldn't see his eyes. It was clearly the first time that Joroev had shared his background with anyone. It was also the first time that Batyrov had heard such a story, from the mouth of a perpetrator. In the same way that Roza had found it within her to share her ordeal, so this was Joroev's time. Batyrov found himself unexpectedly feeling some sympathy for him.

Joroev glanced up at the journalist.

"Please tell your friend I never meant her any harm. I'm sorry for what happened to her. Please tell her."

Joroev looked up at Batyrov. Their eyes met, and when they did the journalist offered him the briefest acknowledgment.

32

Thursday morning, White House, Bishkek

Right on schedule, three black, diplomatic cars approached the hotel's semi-circular periphery to the front of its glass doored entrance. The convoy awaited its American VIPs for their short journey to the White House. It would be an historic five minute ride.

At every turn, de Layney and Ocean passed news vending booths which showed pictures of the President and the Secretary of State shaking hands on the Manas airport tarmac just nine hours earlier. Each billboarded photograph was accompanied by a familiar headline.

'Jıluu kol Alışuu' was the bold offering from Bishkek Daily News.

"Is that my hand?" enquired de Layney jokingly, as their car headed towards Chuy.

"Yours and Ormanbekov's, sir."

The convoy turned into Chuy. National Guardsmen were already in their places, standing to attention on the White House steps.

Ormanbekov, Akayev and Kulov, all wearing long black woollen coats, a defence against the autumn chill which in recent days had produced some early morning snowflakes, milled around in the White House reception area, awaiting their guests.

A dark suited Kyrgyz woman approached the three men and addressed Akayev.

"Sir, the US Secretary of State has left the Hyatt. They will be here in three minutes."

Ormanbekov picked up the itinerary and turned towards Akayev.

"This all looks satisfactory, does it not, Kvradjan?"

"Perfectly, especially those parts of it that are not written down," he grinned.

"Ah, the little distraction before lunch."

"And the presentation."

"The presentation. Of course. My specially commissioned artwork by my dear friend Alnara Abdulova."

"We are indeed fortunate that one of Kyrgyzstan's most prominent artists favours our mission."

"She has created such a stunning piece. Linking the Fergana steppes with the blue waters of Songkol Lake is a creative work of genius and will be a reminder to the Secretary of State of the investment he is about to make into Kyrgyzstan's most natural of assets."

The American convoy turned into Abdumomunova Street. Ocean was studying the day's programme too. He waved his hand across the carded itinerary, adorned at its head by the striking red and yellow colours of the Kyrgyz flag.

"This all seems pretty straightforward. Take a look."

He passed it to de Layney who scanned it briefly.

9am - Informal working breakfast (*blinis*, pastries and coffee)

10am - Official talks commence

In addition to trade, America and Kyrgyzstan to commit to work together to counter regional terrorism and south Asian drug trafficking

12.15pm – Adjourn for lunch - Arzu Restaurant

2pm - Official talks reconvene, White House

4pm – US delegation departs for Hyatt Hotel

6pm – Press conference and trade agreement signing

7pm - Formal state dinner, White House lounge

With traditional Kara Jorgo folk dancing.

Manaschi singers and hamuz players will perform songs taken from historic Kyrgyz literature and put to music.

9.15pm – Exchange of gifts between the President and the Secretary of State

9.30pm - US delegation departs for Hyatt Hotel

"Let's hope there are no hidden agendas in here," said de Layney, a wry smile on his face.

The convoy turned into Chuy.

"What gift did we bring for the President, Stos?"

"Here it is. A framed and signed photograph of your handshake from last night, with our respective flags to the fore. Titled, 'An historic moment.'"

"That's impressive; how did you get it turned around so quickly?"

"The hotel has been very accommodating. You just need to sign it today, sir."

"I wonder what we can expect from Ormanbekov?"

"Probably a book of poems by one of Kyrgyzstan's folklore heroes. I'm told it is common for foreign dignitaries to be given such gifts. Whatever it is, do try to look grateful. Sir."

"Will it be in English?"

"Kyrgyz or Russian, I'm afraid, sir."

"It's ok, either is fine. I won't know the difference."

Both men smiled at each other. They felt at ease passing the time of day but neither were complacent. De Layney was known at home for always being one step ahead of his political opponents. He wasn't so good with unknown quantities though. Despite months of dealings with the Kyrgyz in order to bring the agreement to the table for signature, he remained sceptical. He was always suspicious, especially of Russian politicians. His car pulled up at the bottom of the White House steps.

A Kyrgyz official stepped forward to open the door. De Layney gripped Ocean's arm and leaned in.

"Never trust the Soviets, Stos," he said softly. "My predecessor told me that when I took over from her. Never trust the Soviets."

"It will be ok, sir. These are former Soviets, after all."

De Layney smiled as his door was opened. He turned to face Ocean before setting foot on the pavement where Ormanbekov, Akayev and Kulov awaited.

"Once a Soviet, Stos, always a Soviet," he whispered back at him.

33

Thursday morning, White House, Bishkek

Morning talks began on time, 10am. Six men and three women sat around a rectangular table, with Ormanbekov and de Layney at the centre, facing each other. Copies of the agreement were placed in front of each delegate. There was a sense of optimism on both sides of the table. It didn't last long.

"What's this? Page four. We didn't agree this, Feliks. Mention of the drought is not pertinent to our discussions. Never has been. What is it doing in here? I thought our agreement was final."

The softening up process had begun. The American camp was confused, as Ormanbekov had predicted it would be.

"There is no need to be concerned, Robert. Yes, we have our agreement." insisted Ormanbekov, calmly. "But now, as you know, just in recent days, an unexpected crisis has emerged, right here on our doorstep. And I have been wondering, Secretary of State, how we can make our agreement a little bit more....how can I say....palatable, especially to those who would seek to criticise us for signing a military agreement while a drought is claiming so many Asian lives. My slightly amended agreement gives us the chance to offer the world a unified response, which takes into account the crisis and sees us address it, together. Secretary of State....Robert....please, take a closer look at my amendment, and you will see that we can make this work to our mutual advantage."

All the time Ormanbekov was talking, de Layney, Ocean and his officials were scanning the pages of the agreement, seeking out any further amendments. There were none.

De Layney turned back to page four. He looked distraught. Perhaps Ocean had been right all along. Maybe he should have anticipated the wider impact of signing a military agreement on a continent where an environmental catastrophe was taking place. He had dismissed Ocean's concerns at the time as irrelevant, secondary to the military win he had negotiated.

Had he been too hasty?

Ormanbekov, on the other hand, was taking a more pragmatic approach. He was making a bold suggestion, one that, even if his motives were dubious, had the appearance of political gravitas. He was suggesting to the Americans that if they would consider amending the deal *'for a few dollars more'*, it would be them, the perceived leader of the free world, who would, *'in close co-operation with the Kyrgyz government'*, emerge triumphant. It was a point Ormanbekov was keen to make to de Layney, now sat back in his chair, a look of despair on his face.

"Come now Robert. Take a look and you will see very clearly that it will be the Americans, yes, you, the Americans who will be seen as the knight on a white stallion riding in to tackle the crisis and offer some ecological stability to the region….for years to come."

Literary tongues.

Ormanbekov wasn't explaining how extra American money would solve the drought crisis in south Asia or how he himself would be party to it. His plan for regional power remained his best kept secret. And even some of America's finest diplomatic advisers sitting around the table could not be expected to guess at Ormanbekov's real intentions.

All that they were hearing from Ormanbekov was about the potential plaudits that would await the Americans once news got out that they were not only entering into a military partnership with the Kyrgyz, but an environmental one too.

De Layney wasn't convinced. He was nervous. Very nervous. He looked at Ormanbekov, steely eyed. He was adamant that there wouldn't be any last minute changes to a long term, multi-million dollar agreement thrashed out over many months. Any such changes, especially financial, had to protect the American tax payer, not to mention his own credibility. These amendments would damage both. And what was it that Jim Powell's note had said prior to him leaving?

No additional money.

His mind was made up. He wasn't going to have anything to do with Ormanbekov's amendments.

"No. I can't and won't agree to any adjustments, especially financial ones, at this late stage. In any case, why does the bill for this crisis fall to us. Can't you just allocate some of the financial package already agreed to do what you say you want to do, to counter the drought? Why do *we* have to contribute?"

The two teams looked across the table at each other. An awkward silence prevailed. Ormanbekov had his answer ready.

"Well, sadly, in anticipation of the agreement being signed and your extremely generous up front goodwill deposit, my Finance Ministry has already set up a monitoring committee to manage income and expenditure. It's the way our legal processes work. Assuming that we sign the agreement, and I hope that we do, it will all be out of my hands after that. And of course, this crisis has only just come to light, at such a bad time. We don't want to look bad in the eyes of the watching world, signing a military agreement while lives are being lost here in our region. You do understand that, Secretary of State?"

De Layney had experienced enough diplomatic dialogue in his time to know the difference between fabrication and fact. And this wasn't the latter. He wasn't the only one to be baffled. Ormanbekov's own colleagues looked incredulous at what they were hearing. But it didn't stop them from nodding, sagely as the President's words. And it had completely stunned the Secretary of State. He looked deflated. Having stepped into the ring as the favourite, he had been flawed by a sucker punch. Below the belt. It took the wind out of his sails. It drained him of inspiration. He puffed out his cheeks and sighed. No poker face.

"I agree the timing isn't great, but these are two separate issues, surely?"

"I don't think so, Robert. The timing links them, sadly. So I think that the best way of dealing with the situation that we as a government find ourselves in, is to add in some additional American support which will deliver a satisfactory environmental message to the world. If we supplement our message of increased military benefits within the region with an environmental one, it will be win win for you, and us. We can then speed through our environmental response to the crisis."

'Mmmm. Whatever that might be,' a sceptical Ocean thought to himself. Up to then, there had been no mention of Kyrgyzstan's 'environmental response' to the drought in any of their conversations. And why should there be? It was their problem. Nothing to do with the Americans.

De Layney remained silent, trying to assess the situation he found himself in. He was in a diplomatic 'no man's land' and he didn't know which way to turn.

After a minute or so, Kulov signalled to one of the women sat to the side of the room and more coffee and pastries were produced.

It created an opportunity for Ormanbekov to add more soothing words into the mix, albeit with a menacing edge to them.

"I understand, Secretary of State that this may seem like a problem for you. I really do. Neither of us wish to lose the agreement that we have all worked so hard to achieve. But believe me, things have changed in the last week or so. None of us could have anticipated the devastating drought that has led to the loss of so many lives. And while we know that this drought will not continue indefinitely, we also know that one day, it will return. We, you and I, have a once in a lifetime opportunity to stop these disasters in the future. Indeed, we have been working on a plan for many months now to counter such environmental disasters in the future. I wonder, what is important to us, sitting around this table, in this room, today? Regional security, yes, but helping tackle the drought too. We, you and I, can achieve great things, together? And, sir, may I respectfully say, the eyes of the world are upon us, right now."

Ormanbekov paused, not wishing to overplay his hand. If the Americans cottoned on that this whole charade had been staged to extract even more money from the US Exchequer, that might just be enough for them to walk out of the talks, humiliating as that would be. Ormanbekov was smart enough to know that the Americans don't like being played and, even for de Layney, humiliation has its price.

Ocean, aware of the impasse and the importance of the agreement due to be signed later that day in the glare of an international media spotlight, leaned forward and laid his hand gently on the agreement in front of de Layney.

"It's approaching midday. How about we adjourn for lunch and reflect on our options before our afternoon session?"

The Kyrgyz delegates nodded in agreement. The Americans shifted in their seats. De Layney was crimson faced and uncharacteristically speechless. Not being in control was something he wasn't used to. Ocean, on the other hand was, as always, at his best at such moments. He stood up, a signal for both delegations to stand in unison.

The entourages exited the stuffy meeting room and headed to their respective quarters to freshen up for lunch, Ormanbekov, his National Security and Foreign Affairs Ministers to the President's private office, the Americans back to the Lenin suite.

De Layney went straight to its private washroom. He leaned over one of the spotlessly clean white ceramic sinks, placing his hands either side of it, and stared into the mirror. His tie was loose, the wrinkles on his brow emitting beads of sweat. His look was one of weariness.

He was desperate not to lose the Manas airspace agreement but was becoming suspicious of Ormanbekov's real motives. Was it just more money he wanted, or was there something else going on? And what would he use any additional money for? An environmental response to the crisis? What does that even mean? The drought was genuine enough, but was there something more to Ormanbekov's amendment than he was telling?

He cupped his hands with cold water and threw it over his face. At once he felt refreshed. Ocean walked in, catching de Layney wiping himself with a jasmine perfumed hand towel. They paused and looked at each other.

"We've been ambushed, Stos. Played for fools."

"Let's see what they come back with after lunch," said Ocean, his softly spoken demeanour a calming influence on his superior.

34

Thursday late morning, Jash Gvardiya, Bishkek

Batyrov was beginning to realise that Joroev may well have a lot more journalistic value to the newspaper than he first thought. Merely exposing his past misdemeanour would not really achieve anything, but using it as leverage against him to gain some advantageous political intelligence could be beneficial.

More to the point, he felt he could work with him. He had admired the way that he had bared his soul. He felt some sympathy for his plight, his upbringing, not that he would let on to Roza.

Batyrov took another drink and decided to come clean.

"Joroev, I am a journalist, and I need your help."

"What do you want? What can *I* do?"

"This state visit. What do you know about it?"

Joroev's sense of relief at having unburdened himself of his guilt, to a sympathetic ear seemed to perk him up.

"I don't know much, but I know that it's happening now, right now, today, and a trade agreement is being signed this evening, six pm. But I also understand that the agreement may not be all that it seems. They've been planning it for months but Ormanbekov is looking to dupe the Americans somehow. It's something big. I have a contact in the White House who told me how Ormanbekov, Akayev and Kulov have been meeting unofficially every Friday evening in one of the empty rooms on the 7th floor to plot something."

So Sidarov was right.

"Go on?"

"It's to do with the agreement. What has been trailed in the media as a trade deal is not what is being presented to the Americans. There's a late amendment, something to do with water. And Akayev had asked me to arrange a distraction for when the delegates go out for lunch today, which I have already done. It's a small thing, happening at lunchtime. He wants to draw attention to the underground pipe system that we have here in Kyrgyzstan. Ormanbekov wants to open them up again to transport fresh water across the country, but I don't know why."

Joroev's information seemed incoherent to Batyrov, but it was enough for him to know that something wasn't right. He needed to act quickly.

"OK. I need you to do something for me, Kamil. I need you to get hold of the President's agreement. The President's agreement," he emphasised. "The original is no good. We need to see the amended one."

Joroev looked shocked.

"You are asking a lot."

"Do you have a security pass to the White House?"

"Only Akayev can arrange a pass for me. But I would need a very good reason for one."

Batyrov looked away. He was trying to think quickly. Time was not on his side. He needed another idea. It was Joroev who came up with one.

"There is one other option. But it would be very dangerous….for me and for my colleague in the White House."

Batyrov looked at Joroev.

"How much?" he asked.

Batyrov had him over a barrel but he felt under pressure. And maybe this was Joroev's first opportunity to be on the right side of justice for once in his life. But Batyrov needed him to deliver.

They struck a deal; 2000 *som* to Joroev to make the call to his White House contact, and another 7,000 *som* after the amended agreement was in Batyrov's hand. But it had to be immediate. Joroev picked up his mobile.

Joroev had several contacts in White House security, having dealt with many of them on discreet assignments over time. He was particularly friendly with one of the White House desk guards, Azamat Taalay, who was not a fan of Ormanbekov. Of old communist stock, Taalay didn't approve of his President's populist rhetoric which he knew was without foundation and merely a device to attract the votes of Kyrgyzstan's six million citizens.

It was to Taalay that he made the call.

Joroev told him that he had to obtain a copy of the amended agreement that day, while the two entourages and their security details were at lunch.

"It will be easy. The place will be virtually empty," Joroev said in a bland attempt to reassure Taalay.

Joroev was right. The place would be virtually empty. The irony was not lost on Batyrov, who had read the security brief in his media folder. By agreeing to the excessive American demand that non-essential White House personnel be stood down for the duration of the Secretary of State's visit, the President had inadvertently opened the way for the very security breach that he and US security personnel had sought to avoid.

Taalay took some convincing but 7,000 *som* was a lot of money to a White House security guard. It outweighed the risks, even if they were considerable. And he trusted Joroev and relished the chance to help expose any wrongdoing by his President. So he agreed. He would get hold of a copy of the amended agreement while the Americans lunched.

35

Thursday lunchtime, Arzu Restaurant, Bishkek

The Arzu restaurant, just a stone's throw from the White House, ten minutes walk at most, was ready to receive its guests. It had been chosen not only because of its proximity to the Square, "....but," as Ormanbekov had told de Layney over coffee and *blinis* that morning, "to offer you and our other American guests a wonderful opportunity to experience some traditional Kyrgyz fare."

He wasn't about to mention his real motive.

The paranoid Americans were initially reluctant, expressing their doubts about their Secretary of State *"....wandering the back streets of a liberal Islamic capital in broad daylight."*

They had been assured, however, by Ormanbekov's team that the restaurant was near enough to parliament not to pose any threat to the Secretary of State.

"And anyway, they insisted, "Kyrgyz national security personnel would patrol the surrounding streets during the short walk to and from the restaurant."

That was what worried them!

The two entourages began their short journey to the restaurant,

It was 12.35pm. The mid day heat was oppressive, but the restaurant would have air conditioning. A generator had been installed at the restaurant in case Bishkek suffered one of its regular power cuts. The President was adamant that there would be no distractions, other than that which was pre-arranged.

Secret service personnel made up four of the American group. Apart from de Layney and Ocean and an official US photographer, the rest were US government workers, mainly female, who clasped official documents to their chests as if their lives depended on them. Copies of the agreement under discussion, however, remained back in the White House. They couldn't risk losing those in a public place.

Ormanbekov and de Layney ambled along, a little awkwardness in their body language. Both the President and the Secretary of State wore open necked shirts in deference to the norms of central Asian political attire. The American security guards, resplendent in their tailored black suits, dark wraparound sunglasses, and even darker ties, remained in close proximity to their man. They all wore earpieces, wired for sound.

It was a strange sight, comical even, the two primary actors in a political drama, surrounded both closely and at a distance by two groups of wary secret service personnel, each eying the other up, no one really knowing what the other might do in the unlikely event of an incident taking place.

An official Kyrgyz government photographer and his American counterpart took pictures of the two diplomats and their entourages as they made their way to the restaurant. It was 12.39pm.

They had walked for about 250 metres. The restaurant came into view. And then it happened. Distraction.

In the immediate footsteps of where the group had been walking, a young, a dark haired girl, dressed in grubby, knee length khaki shorts and sporting a white T shirt with a red, star logo on the chest, appeared out of a manhole located to the side of the road, and ran towards a pale brown, cracked refuse bin. She peered inside, grabbed a couple of what seemed like half full plastic bags, before running back to the manhole, dropping one of them along the way.

"Hey. Stop. Stop"

The whole group turned around as one to see what the commotion was, especially after one of the American security detail had drawn his gun and shouted at the child. But by the time he had started running towards the fleet footed girl, she was gone, back down the manhole from which she had emerged.

The whole incident was over, it seemed, before it had begun. There was nothing more to be seen or heard. The American Head of Security certainly wasn't planning on following the girl down the manhole, and he would not be giving orders to that effect to any of his subordinates.

The two primary actors stood side by side, watching the commotion, both appearing a little uneasy. The Kyrgyz President showed some manufactured embarrassment at having naked poverty and homelessness displayed in front of his important guests, while de Layney was somewhat taken aback, not least that such a breach of security could be allowed to happen just a few yards from where he was standing.

The two official photographers captured the whole incident in glorious technicolour.

De Layney, trying to demonstrate statesmanship, remained calm.

"All ok?" he shouted to his Head of Security, who was standing over the manhole, pointing his firearm into the empty black hole below.

"Yes, sir, all good. It's just a kid disappearing down a manhole," came the indifferent response.

The group continued its short journey to the restaurant steps.

"My sincere apologies Secretary of State. We have a little problem with a few children living in our underground tunnels, but we are dealing with it. We are walking above a small, renovated section of tunnel which, it seems, is preferred by some over the living accommodation which is on offer above ground."

It was a brief but clinical intervention which would, hoped Ormanbekov, achieve its objective. On the one hand, the incident was so small that he could downplay it to his surprised, illustrious guest, while at the same time it would serve to draw attention to the myriad of active, underground sewer pipes that lay beneath the surface, a throwback to the Soviet era, and critical to Ormanbekov's secret plans for the control of fresh water in the region. And eventual power.

Nothing more was said between the two men during the final 50 metres of their journey. As they arrived at the timber steps leading up to the restaurant doors, two young ladies appeared, suitably attired in traditional Kyrgyz *beldemchi*, with ruffled sleeves and wearing white *elechek* headware. They wore broad smiles on their rounded faces.

They greeted the two men in unison.

"Jakşı kün jana salamdaşuu."

A long, well prepared, and welcoming table ahead of them beckoned and the group sat down at their allocated places. De Layney sat directly opposite Ormanbekov once again. Their aides, weighted numerically in favour of the Americans, sat either side.

Visibly shaken by what he had just witnessed, Stoski Ocean took his seat beside the

Secretary of State. He stared into his broth, which, upon studying the untranslated menu before him,

must be something called *Ashlyam-fu,* before leaning over, and whispering into de Layney's ear. "It may be just a manhole to the rest of us, sir, but to that little girl, it's her home."

36

Thursday lunchtime, White House, Bishkek

After the incident with the sewer girl, the American security detail left the restaurant early to inspect the route back. One of them, Louis, went on ahead to the White House itself to check for any discrepancies.

Taalay had come on duty at 1.00 pm. At 1.10 pm, he left his post at the back desk, complaining to his colleague that he had a stomach upset and was going to the rest room. He needed to buy as much time as he could.

Once out of sight, he took the elevator to the 6th floor. He stepped out and headed towards the negotiating room. Apart from the usual security to the front, back and delivery section of the White House, the building, and its offices, were virtually clear of staff. Emptying the office of non-essential staff while the Americans were in town was paying dividends.

Surrounding the coffee cups and water jugs that had been left behind were fifteen A4 grey, hard-backed folders, arrayed around the oval work top, each one with the Kyrgyz flag embossed at the top.

Taalay went straight to them, scanning the labels, in Kyrgyz and English.

Prezidenttin kensesi – 'Jasirunn Dokumentter. President's Office – Classified documentation'

This was it, thought Taalay. He flipped open the pages of one of the purple covered documents while walking towards the door. He knew the layout of the whole floor, indeed, the building. There were several offices along this particular corridor including one which had a photocopier in it.

The corridor was empty, as he expected. He rushed down to the office where the photocopier was housed. He hurriedly slapped the document he was carrying on to the top of the copier, flipped past the pages headed *'Abstraktluu'*, before arriving at three light blue coloured sheets headed *'Agreement.'*

He placed the first sheet downward on to the copier and pressed the button. Nothing. On the floor beside the copier was a card on which was scribbled the word *'istebeyt'.*

Taalay panicked. Time was moving on. He hadn't anticipated that the copier would be out of order. He had to think quickly. Alternatives. The second floor. He rushed out of the office, past the lifts, and took the stairs to the floor below, taking two at a time. As he turned the second corner, he collided with Louis, the American agent, knocking him spectacularly backwards and down into the swing doors at the bottom of the stairs.

"What the fu…."

Before Louis could finish his expletive, he winced in pain, placing his hand to his lower back.

Taalay froze for a second. He shouted out his apology to the American,"Keçir meni, keçir meni. şaşıp jatam Men bir azdan kiyin kayra kelem. kütö turuŋuz. Bul jerde küt."

("I'm sorry, I'm sorry. I'm in a hurry. I will come back in a moment. please wait. Wait here.")

The American, in shock and completely ignorant of what had been said, tried to slide himself up against the wall. Taalay gestured with his hands for the agent to stay calm and not move. He would return very soon.

He climbed over the protruding legs of the slumped body in front of him, slammed himself through the double doors, and turned left towards the office which housed another photocopier. He turned straight to the pages headed *Kelisim* and copied them.

He kept looking towards the door, his heart pounding. What if someone had heard the commotion? He could feel the sweat on his upper body. His hands were shaking. Should he be discovered, he would not only lose his job. He could lose his life.

He snatched the third sheet from the side of the copier and, as he rushed back along the corridor, he folded them in half, stuffing them into his uniform pocket. He hid the folder under his jacket. He planned to call for medical assistance for the US agent once he returned the document originals to the 6th floor, but as he pushed back through the double doors to the stairs, he stared in horror at the empty space where minutes earlier, the American had been sprawled out.

Taalay continued his speedy ascent to the 6th floor, cautiously pushing the doors ajar to see if the corridor was clear. It was. He went back into the negotiating room and placed the folder back on to the table.

Weary and perspiring from the emotional and physical energy he had expended he made his way back along the corridor to the elevator and repeatedly pressed the down button. He arrived on the ground floor, the three copied sheets of classified documents, now creased and moist, pushed tightly between his left arm and his chest.

His colleague looked him up and down.

"Are you feeling ok?"

Before Taalay could respond, they both heard voices coming from the stairs. Seconds later, he was horrified to see Louis, the American agent talking with one of Taalay's Kyrgyz colleague's who spoke English.

Taalay composed himself as the two men approached him. The American was shouting something at him, which didn't sound complimentary. Taalay didn't wait to find out what he was saying, preferring to counter his immediate anger with profuse apology.

"Men abdan ökünöm. Keçirip koygula dep aytkıla jana anın jakşı ekenin suragıla."

"My colleague says he is very sorry. And he asks me to ask if you are ok?"

Taalay was frightened. So was his desk colleague. They had good reason. Too many Kyrgyz guards had 'disappeared' from their workplaces for seemingly minor misdemeanours. The military was unsympathetic to any hint of malpractice in its ranks. For them, zero tolerance meant dismissal - or death. If his own 'misdemeanour' was ever to be found out, Taalay knew that his fate would be the latter.

"I am, just about, but ask him what the hell was that all about? What was he doing up there? And why was he in such a rush?"

Taalay had thought about his excuse during his elevator descent back to his work station. He explained, via his colleague, that he had had been feeling unwell and needed to visit the bathroom. The rest rooms on the ground floor only had urinals so he went to those located on the sixth floor. When he got out of the lift, he thought he saw someone in one of the meeting rooms, and went to investigate, but found nothing.

"By then," concluded Taalay in apologetic Kyrgyz, "I knew I had to get to the toilet urgently which I did and then was rushing back down to my post when I ran into you."

His colleague did his best to translate Taalay's convoluted story but it didn't seem to be impressing the American.

"Yeah, whatever. Take more care next time," said the unsympathetic Louis, rubbing his lower back and walking slowly towards the rear doors to where the Secretary of State and the President would be returning.

"He's lucky I didn't pull my Luger on him," he mumbled as he made his way out of the building, slowly rotating his shoulder along the way.

As soon as Louis had stepped outside, the English speaking Kyrgyz guard had some heated words for Taalay. Taalay, however, deflected his colleague away from the incident, placating him with gratitude and plaudits for his translation skills.

He was relieved, sensing that he had dodged a bullet, possibly quite literally.

He put his hand to his left breast pocket and felt the soft crumple of damp paper within. He needed to get rid of it as soon as possible. When his desk colleague went to the bathroom, he called Joroev.

37

Thursday early afternoon, White House, Bishkek

Despite the exquisite preparation by the restaurant's chefs, a lot of discarded food was left on American plates.

It wasn't the fare that was on de Layney's mind, however. All he wanted to know was why Ormanbekov would suddenly be introducing an additional element into the talks at this late stage, a question both men skilfully avoided during lunch.

As the entourages walked back, Ocean glanced attentively at the manhole from which the young girl had appeared before lunch. He paused to let his colleagues walk ahead. Standing alone, directly above the open manhole, he whispered a short prayer.

He was a Christian first. A federal civil servant second.

"Ocean, Ocean. Are you coming? We have work to do."

Back at the White House, Ormanbekov requested that he speak in private with de Layney.

The two men sat in the Presidential lounge which adjoined his office.

"Coffee?"

"Yes….yes."

De Layney had to be cautious. He didn't want to show too much anger. He didn't want to lose the deal. But he wanted answers. He remained standing, facing his counterpart across the table. Now that lunch courtesies were over, he was ready once again to confront the President.

But it was Ormanbekov, ever the diplomat, who took the initiative, choosing his words with care, delivering them with gentle aplomb.

"Secretary of State de Layney. Robert. We have something that you badly need. I am not simply welcoming you into our country because you are the highest bidder. I came to you because I think you will be good for our region going forward. So, I am simply suggesting to you that we work together to add value to our agreement. And that can only benefit you."

De Layney was rarely one to be impressed by flattery. He shot back at Ormanbekov.

"You are pulling the rug from under our feet, Feliks. I need to know why you….."

"No, no, no. No such thing. We are friends. I would not do such a thing."

"Then what?"

De Layney was willing to push Ormanbekov to his limits of patience. Ormanbekov, on the other hand, knew that de Layney would not back away from *his* primary purpose, however provoked he might feel. But he needed to change tack a little to save the two men going round in circles.

"It's all about the pipes, Robert. It's the pipes."

De Layney responded to Ormanbekov's arm gesture, and sat down.

"What do you mean, the pipes?"

"I have long been thinking about a simple answer to a difficult problem. And the drought has crystallised my thoughts."

"De Layney looked directly at Ormanbekov. What mumbo jumbo was going to come out of the President's mouth this time, he wondered?

"It's simple, Robert. We have the water. We have the pipes. And there is a drought. It happens in south Asia every other year. And true to form, it is happening again, right now, as we sit here. We, you and I, can be the answer. The response. If we can move millions of litres of fresh water, which we have here in the north, to where it is needed, we can solve the annual drought crisis. It is a logistical challenge, but it is feasible."

De Layney sat back in his chair in disbelief. When he left Washington, the last thing he expected to be talking about in such detail was the environment.

It was 2.50pm. There was a knock on the door and Ocean stepped in.

"Please join us," Ormanbekov gestured.

The President knew that de Layney and Ocean came as a team, and that he had already said his piece. He was happy now to respond to American objections.

"When was the last time that your pipes were active in any meaningful way?" asked de Layney dismissively.

"The pipes *are* active. We have assessed them and had them flushed and disinfected, all 400 kilometres, north to south."

Ormanbekov was the master of disguising his lies. De Layney was beginning to realise it but the President continued.

"We anticipated the drought. We acted quickly. Preparations have been going on for many weeks. No one knew about them apart from my two close colleagues and a few workers we recruited from the water company in Osh to treat them and create aquifer facilities for storage. We now have the capacity to transport and store enough water to supply the whole region, rather than see it end up in the ground, year after year. Don't you see, Robert. Our pipes are the answer. They can give us the prize. We don't have to build them. They are there. They *are* the prize. You yourself have seen them….even today!"

The President offered a wry smile to his guests before continuing.

"With your support and our expertise, we can manage the water supply efficiently for the long term, for the benefit of the whole region. No more thirst. No more deaths. And here is the good bit. If we include my amendment in our agreement, you, the Americans, will get the credit. You will be helping to solve a water crisis in *our* region. You can finally get those *Fair Water* activists off your backs and American eco voters on your side."

Ocean had picked up the thread of what was being said. De Layney sat next to him, in silence. They were dumbfounded by what they were hearing. Both men had been warned by colleagues that corruption was rife in central Asian politics, but neither of them had expected to be drawn into its murky waters.

Everything that Ormanbekov was saying sounded compelling to de Layney but was far removed from the purpose of his visit. It seemed to him like an eco-ultimatum. And he smelt subversion.

De Layney stood up and walked towards the window that overlooked Ala-Too Square. He absolutely did not want to threaten the air space deal. His immediate thought turned to what additional funding might be expected in order for him to secure the agreement. Despite the presence of his trusted Press Secretary, he felt alone, his facial expression exhibiting a deep sense of unease. He was thinking dollars. And failure.

Ocean, on the other hand, was thinking humanity.

"And the girl. What about the girl in the sewer. And her family?"

Ormanbekov was taken aback by Ocean's unexpected question. It was a complete change of tack. And it was clever. Compassion was not Ormanbekov's strong suit. Ocean thought that it might catch the President off guard.

He looked Ocean in the eye, perhaps for the first time that day.

"As I say, it's surprising what people, even young girls, will do for money. And ok. I admit it. The little girl was just a decoy to bring your attention to the possibilities that the underground pipe system holds for my country. But she will be fine. We will look after her."

De Layney turned and looked at Ocean. He wasn't convinced.

38

Thursday pm, Bishkek Daily News office

Batyrov was a man in a hurry. Joroev passed him the agreement that Taalay had obtained which could, if his instincts were right, expose an illicit deal between two sovereign nations.

He went straight to his office to scan it but was shocked to see that the agreement was far more expansive than a mere trade deal. It wasn't *even* a trade deal, as the media had been led to believe. He was looking at a ten year, multi million dollar military agreement. And there was an amendment showing in red on page four.

Askar walked in.

"You got it?"

"Yes. It's not a trade agreement at all. It's a military agreement. Long term and high value. The Americans are back on our soil. This is huge. Ormanbekov has pulled off something very big. Russia is going to push back on this. And also, there's this little paragraph here, page four, something to do with environmental costs."

Batyrov put the agreement on Askar's desk.

There. Batyrov's finger pointed to *Clause 11b.*

'In addition to the agreed per annum payment for use of Manas airport, the Americans agree to provide a once only $250 million payment towards environmental costs relating to the air space deal, to offset any environmental concerns that may arise from carbon emissions in the capital. In light of recent events, these funds may also be used by the Kyrgyz government at its discretion to help tackle water poverty in the region."

Askar looked at Batyrov. His suspicions were aroused.

"Why add environmental costs into what is in effect a military agreement?"

"And there was nothing about a military deal in any press handouts."

"Precisely," said Batyrov. "We thought it was a trade agreement. You got to hand it to him. And the Americans. How they kept this from leaking, I will never know."

"I don't get this amendment, though. I don't buy the Americans adding 250k to an agreement for discretionary use by Ormanbekov. It doesn't make sense."

"Or it could be genuine," responded Batyrov. "Maybe Feliks threw in an additional cost to offset the criticism that might come his way for allowing the Americans to pollute our skies."

"But it says, *'to be used by the government at its discretion...'* The Americans would be nuts to sign that off. It could leave them vulnerable to any crazy thing Ormanbekov might do."

"Yes, but the Americans *are* nuts. And they don't know Feliks like we do."

The two men paused. Maybe they were over-reacting, but Askar was nothing if not diligent in wanting to get to the truth, and Batyrov was shrewd. They were a formidable investigative team.

Askar spoke first.

"Can you find out anything else, either from Ramirez or from that security guard inside the White House? The military deal is big enough. But if there is more to this, then we need to know. In the meantime, I have to get ready to go to the White House for the announcement. It's set for 6pm."

xxx

Batyrov and Roza headed for the Metro Bar to meet with Joroev again.

He was waiting for them at his usual table, his head bowed. Batyrov ordered two coffees.

Pleasantries were sparse. Every time Joroev tried to engage with Roza, she would withdraw, her eyes dropping to the floor. Having begun the process of her own healing through the telling of her ordeal to her colleagues, it seemed now like she was moving to a second stage, that of needing to contemplate forgiveness to her captor so that she wouldn't have to carry the burden of his actions around with her for the rest of her life.

Batyrov had already told Roza of his conversation with Joroev, and his regret at what he had put her through. Whatever Joroev felt now, Roza would need time to get used to the unexpected idea of her captor's regret. That would be for another day.

Batyrov had plans for Joroev. Following their heart to heart in Joroev's apartment, he had determined that he could be a useful source of information to the newspaper going forward. He recognised the benefits of developing some sort of relationship between the Bishkek Daily News and the Kyrgyz national. But he also wanted to protect Roza from any emotional distress going forward.

The bar tender brought the drinks and set them down.

"I take it you haven't read the agreement, Kamil?"

Batyrov didn't want Joroev blabbing about it being more than just a trade deal.

Joroev shook his head.

"Good. You don't need to."

"Do you have my money?" Joroev enquired.

"I need you to do a bit more digging first Kamil," said Batyrov, ignoring Joroev's question. "There is an environmental clause in this agreement with an additional cost attached to it. I need to know how it links in any way to the airspace….sorry, the trade deal, as it implies. Or does it have something to do with the water crisis. Can you do that?"

Joroev looked uncomfortable. He immediately went on to the defensive.

"How can I find that out. It's impossible."

Batryov softened his harsh, south Kyrgyz tone, born of his parental upbringing in the valleys just north of Osh.

"Nothing is impossible, Kamil….and you will be well rewarded."

Roza nodded minimally, offering a hint of a smile to a nervous looking Joroev.

"Look," continued Batyrov, "I don't care how you do it. But we need to know what is going on. The deal is due to be signed at 6pm. We can't stop it now. But there is something not right about it. I want to know what it is."

Joroev looked at Batyrov.

"I'll speak to Ramirez to see if he knows anything."

"When can you do that?" interrupted Roza, surprising herself with her intervention.

Chillingly, she realised that these were the first words she had spoken to Joroev since her first encounter with him somewhere in the Naryn mountains, ten years previously.

"This evening. I will speak with him this evening," he told her.

"Try him now," ordered Batyrov. "We don't have much time. I will call you again at 5.30pm."

Batyrov got up from the table, closely followed by Roza. They left their half-drunk coffees on the table.

As soon as the two journalists had exited the bar, Joroev was on his phone arranging an urgent liaison with Ramirez. His panicked tone prompted Ramirez to leave his Heads of Department meeting early and come straight from the University to the bar.

Within five minutes, he was there, sitting opposite Joroev.

"What so important?" he enquired tetchily.

"I don't know. A couple of media hacks cornered me and suggested that Ormanbekov was not being straight with the Americans, maybe pulling a stunt, and they wanted to know more. Do you know what is going on?"

"A stunt? What are you talking about? Look, all I know from my Ambassador is that the US is being squeezed for more money before the Kyrgyz will sign off on the agreement, and supposedly it's for environmental reasons. My information tells me that the last-minute addition will put the trade deal, whatever it is, in a more favourable light with the international media. Though it won't do anything to improve relations with the Russians and Chinese, of course. That's all I know."

"The journalists seem to think that there could be a stitch up."

"With Ormanbekov, anything is possible," responded Ramirez.

"But he wouldn't be so stupid as to stitch up the Americans, would he?" asked Joroev.

"He's ambitious, and ruthless. I wouldn't put anything past him."

Ramirez was sceptical about Joroev's claims but recognised that if there was any truth in them, this could be an opportunity for him to facilitate his long overdue return to his homeland. If he found out that the Kyrgyz government might be planning something that would harm the United States, exposure of it would be a feather in his cap, giving him leverage with his bosses in Washington, and maybe help him to secure his passage home. He was loyal to the American flag but he was also frustrated, and tired. His estranged family lived in Texas and he craved an official post back home, preferably sanctioned and paid for by his government. This could be his ticket out. He stood up, his mind spinning with possibilities.

"Let me make a couple of calls and I'll get back to you. Wait here"

"Hurry, the deal is being signed at 6pm," said Joroev.

"There's nothing we can do about that," said Ramirez, as he walked out of the bar, dialling his phone as he exited. "Wait here," he repeated.

Ten minutes later, Ramirez re-entered the bar and sat down.

"I've spoken to the Ambassador. My people will sign at 6pm because they have to. But he says they're not happy. Ormanbekov has added another $250 million to the agreement but for Kyrgyz discretion only. That could mean anything."

"It could be to line his pocket, or it could be something more sinister," interrupted Joroev.

"The Ambassador will look into it in due course. I can't do any more now. Let's sit tight and see what happens. Let me know if you hear anything."

And with that, Ramirez left the bar.

39

Thursday pm, White House, Bishkek

Ormanbekov was becoming impatient. The impasse between the two leaders had gone on long enough. And the clock was ticking. He sought to bring the discussion back on message.

"Secretary of State. We need to conclude. Let me explain further. I am proposing a two-step plan to manage our water supply. Phase One would see the Kyrgyz government, aided by my good friends the United States of America, develop our existing water processing plant in Fergana to filter and cleanse the water as it goes through the pipes. Second, again with your help, we progress our water storage facility based on aquifer technology to build up supplies in the south and service the whole region. We can work with our regional neighbours to assist their needs. But to do that, we need funds, right now. So we included this environmental benefit clause for, as it says in our amended agreement, an additional $250 million to bring this forward."

De Layney's heart skipped a beat but it didn't stop Ormanbekov from concluding his gambit.

"You don't need to get involved in the detail, of course, Robert, but we will make sure that you, your delegation, and your Administration, take all of the credit for this generous financial gesture."

De Layney made his way from the window to the chair, and sat down. He was on the back foot, a place he rarely found himself. He was thinking quickly, calculating the political and financial implications of what the President was saying. The money wasn't huge in itself, at least in an American context. But it was in Kyrgyz terms and might well be enough to fund a water project in central Asia. But in the back of his mind were Jim Powell's words.

The agreement, however. It was his absolute imperative to get it signed off. Pen to paper. After all, that is why he had come to Kyrgyzstan. The embarrassment of coming away from a pre-agreed negotiation on the losing side did not bear thinking about, even if it had to cost him. He had to succeed. There was no other option. But the money, unauthorised. And on top of the huge cost of what was already on the table. It bothered him. He would try one last gambit to avoid the financial hit.

"Actually, I know all about your pipes, Feliks," said de Layney, regathering himself. "Don't underestimate the benefits of a cold war education."

For the second time in a few minutes, Ormonbekov looked a little surprised. De Layney had been impressed by Ocean's distraction tactic a few minutes earlier, which had brought some breathing space. It was time for de Layney to try it for himself, if only to embarrass his counterpart.

"You are well informed, Robert?"

"I know that they are there," continued de Layney, "and that they run the length and width of the country; north to south and east to west. That was quite a feat by the Russians back then. They could move any artillery, not to mention troops, around the country, without fear of exposure. You gotta hand it to them Moscow boys."

Both men, momentarily united in opposition to their mutual adversary, managed an enforced smile.

"Yes, quite a feat indeed. But that was a long, long time ago."

De Layney paused, before delivering a killer blow.

"I also know that they haven't been used since the 1950s."

De Layney found himself back in the driving seat, an Ormanbekov lie exposed.

The President drew hard on his Sobranie Black Russian cigarette.

How did de Layney know that the pipes existed, let alone that they were dormant? Infra red thermal imaging perhaps? The world had moved on.

Ormanbekov *was* embarrassed, and a little nervous. It wouldn't take long for the Secretary of State and his team to work out why additional funding was needed at all. Restoring and cleansing 400 kilometres of obsolete pipeline between Songkol, where the excess water was stored, to the filtering plant in Fergana, from where Ormanbekov planned to exploit his south Asian neighbours, was never going to be cheap. Now he had revealed its cost, even if it was a fantasy figure, plucked from the sky. Ormanbekov wondered whether the American delegation would suspect him of trying to defraud them for a restorative engineering project he had been found to be lying about. And if they did, would they punish him for it?

In a fleeting moment, the aura of invincibility that he had enjoyed ever since he had been catapulted into his Presidency eighteen months before, departed him.

Then, he had achieved 85% of the popular vote, a democratic success for the region but like most, if not all elections since 1991, one based on behind the scenes deals and unachievable promises, including the inevitable vow to root out the very same corruption that kept him in power.

A year and a half on, Moscow remained supportive of the silver tongued politician. He had favour and was one of the weapons of choice deployed by the Kremlin to keep its diplomatic links with its international adversaries, open. But now, in the here and now, the preferred Russian strategy of keeping your friends close, and your enemies even closer, would be tested to the limit.

Ormanbekov garnered a smile, before throwing his hands up in a gesture of mock submission.

"You are right, Robert. I have been found out."

It was a brazen Ormanbekov who delivered his defence, looking to recover his position.

"What can I say? The pipes *are* old, they *are* decrepit and unusable in their present state. No one has been down there for years. The only thing down there these days are Russian rats."

The mood around the table lightened a little. Ormanbekov had learnt from many past experiences that an admission of guilt to cover his tracks was a more reliable way of restoring credibility, certainly more reliable than progressing a lie. It was a tactic that would seem to work once again.

"Even the rats have to live somewhere," quipped de Layney, knowing that this small victory was only ego thick, his ego, and wouldn't alter the wider outcome.

A visibly relieved Ormanbekov embraced the warmth of de Layney's response and with a stern face and a softened tone, he leaned forward to try to enforce his advantage.

"Indeed, Robert. Indeed. But it is sad, is it not, that these Russian rats are depriving the good people of Tajikistan, Pakistan and Afghanistan, our friends and neighbours, the very nourishment that they need, and that we have, right now."

Ormanbekov's logic was persuasive, if incredible. De Layney looked at Ocean, trying to work out the President's negotiating strategy. He didn't have to wait long for another brazen lie from the President.

"But despite their age, Robert, let me assure you that the pipes *are* retrievable. I have had water engineers down there to look at them. They are repairable. I just didn't want to bother you with the detail of it all. I know you will understand."

He stubbed his cigarette into the glass ashtray in front of him and sat forward, hunched in his chair, his elbows resting on the table. He had been compromised, but he still held the Ace. And with a soft, sinister tone in his voice, he was about to deliver it.

"And we don't want to threaten the main purpose of our agreement, Robert, do we?"

The knife had been turned. The threat, albeit unlikely, of a last minute withdrawal by the Kyrgyz was enough for de Layney to experience a sharp intake of breath.

De Layney's position might have momentarily been strengthened by Ormanbekov's attempted deception over the pipes. But now he felt compromised once again. He was being asked to finance an infrastructure project on the other side of the world for a relatively small amount of money. But it was way beyond his brief. And totally unexpected. What appeared on the surface to be a worthy Kyrgyz cause had become, without the authority of the US Treasury to support it, a major stumbling block to getting the agreement signed off.

And then there was a further question that bothered de Layney. Why did Ormanbekov even need more dollars in addition to those already guaranteed within the agreement? Was it just greed? Exploitation?

Ormanbekov, like a poker player with the winning hand awaiting the capitulation of his opponent, had regained his composure. He was on home territory, the home run. All of the cards were now on the table. He just needed the Americans to agree to Clause 11b to achieve his ambitions.

"You will have to give me a little time to convene with my colleagues back home, Mr President," said de Layney. "I suggest that we adjourn for a short while and return here at 4pm."

"Sir, it's well past four now," interrupted Ocean. "The timetable is already jeopardised. We are due to sign in just under an hour. Fifty three minutes, to be precise."

"Give me half an hour," de Layney said to his host and with that, he left the room closely followed by Ocean, whose thoughts were still with the young decoy girl.

40

Thursday pm, White House, Bishkek

Miriam Serenatti was busy with her own agenda and not to be disturbed. She wasn't expecting to hear from her Secretary of State. After all, why would he need to call her? He was only putting pen to paper on an agreement already confirmed. Wasn't he?

"I'm sorry sir. She's getting ready to host an African trade delegation and has given strict instructions not to be disturbed."

The gathering of African leaders to discuss oil and natural resources had been weeks in the making. Serenatti's preparatory breakfast meeting with US Secretary of State for the Treasury, Stephen Green, was already underway. The first of the African delegates were due at the Pennsylvania Conference Centre at 8am. Serenatti was not to be deflected from the task in hand.

The two people in Washington that de Layney needed to speak with were locked in a meeting, together. De Layney threw his mobile phone on the desk in front of him. It slid off the polished surface on to the floor.

"Damn it. Damn it."

De Layney was on his own. He had a decision to make. Failure to sign was not an option.

"That's a non-negotiable," he would tell Ocean over and over again.

The internal phone rang. It was Ormanbekov.

"Perhaps he's having a rethink," offered his Press Secretary.

De Layney dismissed the likelihood with a shake of the head. He was right. Ormanbekov was bullish.

"Robert, when we reconvene, let us, you and I, come to a little arrangement, something that would not only benefit our two countries, but also you and I. If we could solve the water crisis together, you and I will go down in history as, well, the saviours of the Asian world, the two men who rescued south Asia from its thirst. That would look good on your CV, very good."

De Layney acknowledged the President's offer and put the phone down.

"He's playing the legacy card."

His mind was racing. He was happy to sup with the devil when he wasn't paying the bill, but the gradual progress of the day which resulted in this amended agreement had the hint of corruption written all over it. He may be wrong, but he was suspicious. And with good reason.

It was not in Ormanbekov's DNA to tell the truth. His own intelligence had told him that in the 400 kilometres of pipeline that he wanted to utilise in order to transport fresh water to the south of the Republic, there could be as many as 650 Kyrgyz nationals, most of whom had ignored requests from government intermediaries to re-locate above ground to a 'social housing compound.'

Ormanbekov had no intention of rescuing them if they refused his offer. If it came to it, he would, as he had chillingly whispered into Kulov's ear on more than one occasion, simply consider their loss 'collateral damage' on the road to a greater Kyrgyzstan. He wasn't going to divulge that to de Layney, though.

Whatever the extent of Ormanbekov's deception, the weight of expectation now sat heavy on the American Secretary of State's shoulders. He needed a steer, even if it was to be the wrong one.

It was Ocean who gave it to him.

"I don't think that what Ormanbekov is suggesting is that outrageous."

De Layney looked at his Press Secretary in astonishment.

"But he's asking for another 250 million. He's holding us to ransom."

"Yes, its unorthodox," countered Ocean, "but in the big picture, his position sounds plausible. As long as we don't compromise on our military requirements, we should hear him out. At the end of the day, he is right about one thing. South Asia *is* thirsty. The drought couldn't have been foreseen when we first embarked on this agreement. Maybe we can be a part of the solution."

Ocean's compassionate, Christian logic rang true, but it didn't make de Layney feel any better. He sensed that his Press Officer was clutching at straws. And he felt used. If only he could get hold of Serenatti or Green and secure their authorisation on the additional $250 million, he would feel a lot more confident about putting his signature to the agreement.

"How long have we got?

"We are due to sign in precisely....25 minutes."

Try Serenatti one more time. And Green. If we can't get hold of them, we proceed as planned...."

"And go with Ormanbeov's terms, sir?"

"Yes. But I'll hold him to his promise of making sure that we receive any international credit that is going, and you, Stos, need to come up with a media strategy that credits us back home. If I'm going to take political flak, I need to counter that with public support. I'll even take credit from the eco brigade, much as it will pain me to do so. Understood?"

"Yes, sir."

"OK. Make the calls. If we can't get through, we go and do this."

Ormanbekov and de Layney reconvened in the Presidential office at 5.40pm.

The Kyrgyz President looked at his watch.

"Our timetable seems to have slipped a little," he said, a little sarcasm in his voice.

The two men sat at either end of a three-seater, velvet lined Ludovika sofa. Ocean sat in an accompanying armchair.

"Well, Mr President, we hadn't expected to be presented with an amended agreement. It isn't what we agreed."

Ormanbekov wasn't fazed.

"Secretary of State. Sir. In the twenty hours that it took for you to fly here, the world changed. What the *Fair Water* people and government detractors around the world have been warning about for more than two decades has arrived. Don't you see, I am offering you a one-time only deal to act in a way that will see the United States lead the world's response to this regrettable situation we find ourselves in? You, the United States of America, can be the nation that counters the eco-pioneers' negative narrative. We can silence them once and for all, at least in our own respective parts of the world. If you sign this agreement, it will put the great name of the United States of America, and your own name, if I may, into the history books. And not only for the military benefits that will come to you. But also for the environmental favour that will be credited to you. You. Our water programme is ready for rollout. I need money for technical support, manpower, aquifiers, and so on. My only way of getting it now – because now is the hour – is through your good offices via this agreement. And before you ask me about the annual payments within our pre-amended deal, I can confirm that it will be invested in industry, rural projects, and jobs. But as I say, my region doesn't have any contingency to tackle the water crisis. It was anticipated, but not confirmed, until now. We have tried to secure funds from the EU but it is too bureaucratic and frankly, they are quite useless. Your good friends the British are well out of it, if you ask me. But I digress. If you sign off the additional $250 million, we can solve the Asian water shortage practically overnight. And Robert, think about it. It's not such a high price to pay for your lasting legacy, is it?"

Ormanbekov paused, with intention.

"And you, sir, I promise, will get the credit, particularly from the whole of Asia. That's a lot of credit going forward."

De Layney pretended to ponder the President's prepared speech. It was all hyperbole, of course. Nonsense, surely? He struggled to believe there was any truth in what he was hearing, but Ormanbekov, as always, spoke with persuasive passion. Literary tongues, even if it was uninterpretable?

The US Secretary of State sat back, his elbow on the arm rest. He paused, reflecting back to 2021 when the UK government had first initiated climate change language within its post-Brexit trading deals with the rest of the world. Maybe, just maybe, he could pioneer a similar US diplomatic narrative within this 'trade' agreement. Maybe. De Layney had been buoyed by his discussion with Ocean, who had suggested that this could be turned to American advantage.

Meanwhile, the clock continued to tick. He had entered the room having made his decision. But he wasn't going to let Ormanbekov know that the outcome wouldn't have strings attached.

"Cards on the table," said de Layney. "We came here for a 10-year deal for air access into and out of Manas. We agreed up front the down payment and the annual dollars. And now you want us to save the planet at an additional, unbudgeted cost to the US exchequer? If we are to do that....if....then I need your signature on a document that Mr Ocean here will draw up, affirming full credit for the initiative to the US, in the way that you have just outlined. By all means take some local credit for the roll out of whatever programme you have come up with, but internationally, our one-time investment has to be acknowledged."

"Ah, that will be so, Secretary of State," whispered Ormanbekov.

De Layney's words in defeat were like Rachmaninov's *Elegie* to Ormanbekov's ears. The President sat back in his chair, trying not too look to smug. His gamble that the rewards of the air space agreement in Middle East security terms would far outweigh any environmental amendments, had worked.

"Gentlemen, I think we have a deal."

The President leaned across the sofa and offered his hand. De Layney took it, as he was always going to do.

The President had won the diplomatic arm wrestle. David had triumphed over Goliath. De Layney had been outflanked. Ormanbekov had wooed the Secretary of State, making the seemingly expensive sound affordable. He had got de Layney to sanction, unilaterally, a financial bonus in order to secure the agreement he had travelled 6,000 miles for. Negotiations were complete.

De Laynety and Ocean leaned forward in their seats. Surely his own President, Serenatti, would understand. After all, from the outset, de Layney knew he only had one choice. And he had made it.

There was a knock at the door. It was Kulov.

"Gentlemen, we need to go now. The media awaits."

"And we have an agreement to sign," added Ormanbekov, ushering his guests from the room."

Kulov offered a faint smile. Ormanbekov a wink in his direction.

41

Thursday pm, Metro Bar and White House, Bishkek

While Ormanbekov and de Layney were sparring in the White House, Joroev was reflecting om his conversation with Ramirez. He was disappointed with the American, not for the first time in their long friendship. The arrogance he exhibited when not in control of the information flow had resurfaced. Ramirez may well be a patriot, but so was Joroev.

As soon as Ramirez had left, he dialled Batyrov's number.

Joroev had grown to like him. He had been fairer to him than he deserved. He was also warming to Roza, admiring not only the beautiful woman she had become, but also her dignity in the face of his presence, her assailant.

"Yes, what did he say?"

"Nothing. He knows nothing. The Americans just have suspicions."

"Wait there, we'll be back with you in a few minutos. I have an idea."

And they were.

Before Joroev could order another drink, a strong one this time, the two journalists were sat down next to him. Without saying a word, Batyrov produced a small, padded brown envelope from his inside jacket pocket and held it upside down, shaking its contents out into his hand before putting it on to the table.

"Get this into Ormanbekov's 7th floor meeting room as soon as you can. He meets Kulov and Akayev there on Fridays, always at 6pm. I think he'll be celebrating tomorrow evening once the Americans are gone."

Joroev stared at what looked like a tiny audio device, Chinese writing on its cover.

He looked at Batyrov, a look of incredulity on his face. How could he possibly be expected to bug one of the President's offices….and by tomorrow evening?

Roza could see that Joroev was struggling.

"Get that security guard to do it for you," she said boldly. "Do it as soon as you can, right now, while the press conference is on. There won't be anyone in the offices then. It's important. We have to know what Ormanbekov is up to."

"And we'll pay," added Batyrov.

Roza and Batyrov didn't leave any time for Joroev to respond. They were up and on their way out once again, leaving Joroev with one hand round a cup, the dregs of a Turkish coffee in its well, and the other holding a Chinese bugging device.

Ten minutes later, Joroev had told the reluctant Taalay that he had another job for him, and that it needed to be carried out 'with haste.' The stress of Taalay's previous encounter with Louis, the American security guard, prompted a swift rejection of Joroev's offer, but the incentive of another 4,000 *som* soon changed his mind.

"Meet me on Panfilov as usual at 6pm. I'll be there with the device."

Taalay waited until 5.55pm before stepping out of his booth, telling his colleague that his stomach was still feeling unsettled and he needed to visit the bathroom again. When he was out of sight, he double backed and headed for the back door of the White House, walking swiftly towards an exclusion zone guard post. He knew the guard on duty, another drinking friend of his. All he needed to do now was persuade him why he needed to absent himself from his post for a few minutes.

"It's my mother in law's birthday and if I don't get her a gift for this evening, my wife will kill me," he joked. "I just need to get to *Tabylka* before it closes at 7."

"On your head be it," retorted his fellow guard.

Taalay didn't know whether his response was aimed at his possible failure to get his mother in law a birthday gift, or worse, being discovered away from his White House post by the acting *Polkovnik*, while on duty.

Taalay hurried to meet Joroev at the park on Panfilov Street and took the device from him.

"Do it immediately," was the simple instruction from Joroev. "But you must do it. Remember, there's another 4,000 *som* for you when it is done."

And it *was* done. The corridors were empty and Taalay gained easy access to the 7th floor meeting room. He peeled off the glued back of the bugging device and secured it to the underneath corner of the table. He was back at his post by 6.15pm.

He messaged Joroev who immediately texted Batyrov to confirm 'mission accomplished,' informing him that he would need the money for his White House contact that same evening.

Batyrov had pre-activated the listening device and linked it to his mobile phone before handing it over to Joroev. Everything was in place. All he had to do now, was to wait patiently for an automated alert. He believed that Ormanbekov, Akayev and Kulov would gleefully celebrate the fruits of their labours as soon as the Americans were back in the air. He also knew that they were creatures of habit, so if he had to wait until Friday 6pm, so be it. Either way, exposure of whatever was going on in Ormanbekov's mind, was, he hoped, imminent. Yes, it was a gamble but one worth taking.

42

Thursday 6pm. White House, Bishkek

The Grand State room was decked out with Kyrgyz and American flags, ready for the announcement. The Karelian style antique desk, on which were laid two identical blotters, sat grandly to the fore. A pen sat at an angle in its holder.

Four television crews were setting up their gear. Technicians mingled with US security personnel, and photographers sat on the front row and to the side of the thirty or so chairs that had been assembled for the regional and international written media.

A young Kyrgyz woman, dressed in a western style two-piece black suit and flower print silk scarf hosted a welcome desk and issued pre-prepared lanyards. Two guards stood behind the desk, each holding Kalashnikov assault rifles. To the rear of the Grand State room sat two Kyrgyz secret service personnel, their bulky black suited jackets hardly disguising the Makarov pistols securely attached to their chests.

The media chairs, with a summary of the agreement placed on each one, were filling up. Journalists devoured its content. Animated conversations began between them. The rumours about what they could expect were becoming reality, written down in black and white in their press packs. Far from announcing a major trade agreement between the two countries, they were staring at a geo-political moment in history, a military deal that would change the regional landscape, the world order, for a generation.

"How did they manage it, Shirin?" Askar asked his proprietor. "They kept that well and truly behind closed doors."

"Maybe that is what their covert Friday evening meetings have been all about."

"I'm sure of it."

At just after 6pm, six men walked into the Grand State room. Flash lights lit up the room as two of the men, President Feliks Ormanbekov and a nervous looking Secretary of State Robert de Layney, sat down.

"It's for the greater good," whispered Ocean to de Layney on their brief walk from the Presidential office. His attempt at reassuring his Secretary of State only marginally improved the mood. The possibility that the Americans were being duped was anathema to de Layney, but nagging doubts prevailed.

Ormanbekov, on the other hand, approached the signing ceremony with confidence. His signature would deliver a bloody nose to his immediate neighbours, the Stans, as well as the Russians and Chinese. It was an unashamed power grab, it would happen overnight, and, as he proudly liked to remind his two political associates, the Americans would be complicit in its delivery.

A hush descended on the gathered attendees.

A Kyrgyz aide set one of the decoratively adorned folios in front of the President, while Ocean set down another copy in front of the Secretary of State, who was trying hard to still his shaking hand that was about to put pen to paper. His nervousness wasn't about money. It was about trust, or lack of it.

As he scribbled his signature on the agreement, he tried to think only about the long-awaited re-instatement of US Air Force planes and personnel on central Asian soil.

The strategic foothold that the Americans had in Kyrgyzstan until 2014 would be re-established from midnight tonight. They would once more have the presence in central Asia that they had never wanted to relinquish, a presence which allowed them easy and quick access to the Middle East. That was the prize, thought de Layney as he tried to block out the negotiating challenges of the day from his mind.

A secretary carefully laid blotting paper over the signatures and padded them down, before exchanging the documents for repeat signing, the trigger for another spectacular display of flashlight activity.

The two men stood up, clasping hands and smiling warmly for the cameras.

A technician placed two microphone stands next to each other, and adjusted them to their required height.

Ormanbekov spoke first.

"Media friends from around the world. You will appreciate the sensitivities involved in keeping this agreement secret over our many months of negotiation. I know that you will understand why we had to do so. But today we can reveal to you and to the world this historic partnership between the Republic of Kyrgyzstan and the United States of America. The agreement is, if I may say, '*of its generation*', and one that I am confident will bring stability to our region and beyond. I want to thank the United States and in particular its representative here today, Secretary of State de Layney, for its progressive thinking and willingness to engage with Kyrgyzstan in its drive for peace and harmony for central Asia, as well as supporting us in other areas of need at this challenging time for our region."

The Secretary of State shivered at the President's final words. Little did he know that they were uttered in an attempt to cover himself against any future media accusations of a 'cover up.'

At least he didn't go into detail, thought de Layney as he stepped up to respond. His primary hope was that the magnitude of the primary subject matter would override any interest there might be in the environmental crisis and any reference to it within the agreement. Maybe he was being paranoid, but the last thing he wanted was for his own President to find out about the additional, unsanctioned money, over the internet or in a tweet.

He needn't have worried about that, for today at least.

Little did he know, that in a final, duplicitous act, one which he would retrospectively blame on incompetent administrators, Ormanbekov had ordered that the agreements on the media chairs should not include the amendment just signed off by de Layney. There was no mention of water, or of the additional dollars agreed just half an hour earlier. If journalists had known that it was included in the agreement signed by the two leaders, they too, like de Layney, might well want to question the purpose of such an agreement. The absence of the amendment meant that a relaxed looking President wasn't expecting any difficult questions, about environmental issues at least.

And de Layney was happy to promote accord.

"Thank you Mr President for inviting us to participate with you in this historic, strategic, military and trade partnership. I want to acknowledge your willingness to stretch out your hand across continents into order to embrace American ideals, that of freedom, democracy, justice and security. I look forward to a long and prosperous relationship with Kyrgyzstan and your neighbours in the region, going forward."

Ormanbekov and de Layney's words were making history. Despite no mention of Israel, they were being analysed globally, in Washington, in central Asia, and in Jerusalem. Tel Aviv, surely, would be reassured by events.

But they would be heard with anger in Moscow and Beijing, Kabul and Tehran. Israel's Arab neighbours would be furious. And Ormanbekov's immediate political neighbours, watching in Dushanbe, Nur-Sultan, Tashkent and Ashgabat would be apoplectic.

Kyrgyzstan had unashamedly become a traitor state in their midst. The enemy within had dealt a death blow to regional unity, such as it was. Ormanbekov's secretly negotiated deal with the Americans would have unprecedented consequences for the region, and beyond.

Ormanbekov, however, would not be losing any sleep over his neighbours' anger. He knew that he had pulled off a coup. Kyrgyz security to its own southern borders would be bolstered, while the huge influx of millions of American dollars over ten years would bring jobs in the cities, support for rural land-dwellers and a boost the economy.

He had gambled that the global and regional implications of the agreement, when the corrected version was published with great apology, would far outweigh any talk of collusion or corruption. It was high risk but the media wouldn't be alerted to the amended version until the Americans were back in the air. And Ormanbekov would feign embarrassment with an apology, and threaten White House sackings.

He was happy. He had made his bed, chosen his sleeping partner, and was getting ready to lie in it.

And as he invited question from the assembled media, it became apparent that his gamble would pay off. All they wanted to know was how many American service personnel would be based at Manas; how many aircraft; how many flights per day; the revenue generated by the American presence, not to mention what impact this agreement might have on relations with Russia, China, and the European Union? What were the wider implications for such an agreement? Israel wasn't even mentioned, even though everyone suspected that this was the reason Ormanbekov had allowed a US presence back on to Kyrgyz soil. Neither were the other Stans.

"There is nothing to fear from this agreement," said Robert de Layney. "Today, Kyrgyzstan, and I would hope, her neighbours, will become closer allies in the fight for a more secure future in this region."

Talk of closer alignment between regional Republics was all political speak, and no one who had lived through decades of border disputes and political rivalries, would buy it. He wasn't saying it for local media, though. He was saying it for consumption at home.

Ormanbekov, on the other hand would be guaranteed local public support for his bold, nationalistic initiative, especially as it had been achieved with the West. His only problem now would be to fend off Russian and Chinese criticism. He could expect sanctions, but, he calculated, they would easily be offset by the income from the ten year agreement.

Stage one of Ormanbekov's plan was complete. The Americans would shortly be on their way home and he could soon begin to activate stage two of his plan, the exploitation of water resources to drought ridden south Asian countries.

"And all paid for by the yanks," Ormanbekov would whisper in Kulov's ear as they departed the Grand State room together.

43

Friday morning, Hyatt Hotel, Bishkek

The American departure on the steps of the Hyatt early the following morning was only covered by a few media outlets. The main story had already left town and was now being pored over on newspaper front pages, global newsrooms and online. The early morning chill preceded what was expected to be a glorious day, fresh, but with a clear blue sky. Four military guards stood either side of the hotel steps, alongside a resplendent line of Kyrgyz and US flags.

The two delegations shook hands warmly, a beaming Ormanbekov grasping the Secretary of State's right arm. He knew how to work the official photographers for his benefit, even at this early hour.

"You won't regret it, Robert," he would whisper in his ear. "Go home and enjoy the headlines. We will speak again, soon. And safe travels."

Kulov echoed his President's sentiment, placing Ocean's hand between both of his.

"Koopsuz sayakat üygö Mr Ocean."

"You will have to enlighten me Alexander," responded Ocean.

"Safe travels home, Stoski. Safe travels home."

Despite a smile as he got into the back of his limousine, the Secretary of State wore the face of a battle weary boxer, a man who looked as if he had arrived at the weigh-in as the overwhelming favourite, expecting to land the knockout blow in five rounds, only to find himself battling to stay in the fight. He may have stayed with his 'lighter' opponent over the full twelve rounds, but any victory he might claim seemed pyrrhic.

What price he might pay for his profligate success would only become evident on his return to the US. It might find favour with the American public, but then, as Jim Powell had suggested in a phone call to Ocean, it would only be fleeting.

"Most of them don't care a hoot about a water crisis on the other side of the world."

Whatever positive political reaction he would receive on returning to the US would surely be countered by having to explain to President Serenatti and the US Treasury what justified the additional, unauthorised expenditure.

Ormanbekov, on the other hand, had every right to be cheerful on his early morning journey back to Chuy. He had manoeuvred the Americans into parting with thousands of additional dollars against its will and set himself up as the power broker for the region. He had even manipulated the message to the media, something he would get his media office to correct that morning with an 'official apology.'

It was with a spring in his step that he and Kulov entered the White House elevator. In the privacy of the lift, he gloated about his success.

"They thought it would be easy, but we are not fools. They wanted access and their pride wouldn't allow them to fail. And we know that they will do anything to boost their own image around the world. Let them crow about the environmental investment they think they have made. Let them take the credit. But we know otherwise, Alexander, do we not? They think that their air space deal has given them one small step towards peace in the Middle East, and it may well do that. But for us, its one giant leap on our journey to take control of our region."

"And for that, we have their dollars to thank," chipped in a grinning Kulov.

"Indeed, Alexander. Indeed."

Ping!

The elevator came to a shuddering halt. The doors opened to the sound of their laughter. They exited past a couple of surprised early morning cleaners, who stepped back to allow them access to their respective corridors, corridors that very soon would be filled, once again, with the buzz of a full White House staff complement, portfolio holders, state workers and secretaries. Things would be getting back to normal. The Americans had departed. Another parliamentary day in Bishkek was about to begin.

44

Friday early afternoon, Bishkek Daily News office; Friday morning, White House, Washington

Ednan Askar arrived at the Star Building just after lunch and switched the regional *Asian News* channel on the TV in his office. A reporter was live from Paris. The American delegation to Kyrgyzstan were currently delayed at Orly during a re-fuelling stopover. Grainy mobile phone pictures showed around 30 eco-activists from *Fair Water*, in a perfectly timed stunt, breaching security fences at the airport's north-east corner. They sprinted towards the runway as the plane was taxi-ing for its stopover. French security police were seen dragging protesters away from the strip; armed National Gendarmerie surrounded the aeroplane, and the French Foreign minister, according to the reporter, was being sent to the airport to apologise to the American Secretary of State for this breach of security.

'Ha. A French farce,' thought Askar as he switched the monitor off again. He didn't know whether to laugh or cry at the turn of events. The secret 'airspace for dollars' deal was big enough, but the White House's own administrative mistake, acknowledged with the apology sitting in his inbox, was farcical. And it got him wondering.

How had the protesters got wind of it in Paris so quickly. The apology email had only dropped into his inbox at 7am. Maybe some sharp news outlet had read between the lines. Or maybe it was just a protest and he was overthinking it. That must be it, thought Askar, otherwise why would the eco nutters complain about something that would benefit their cause?

xxx

The delay in Paris did little to improve de Layney's mood. He was already weary, physically and emotionally. And as soon as he touched down in DC, he knew that he would be summoned to see the President to justify his unilateral actions. She would not care that he had been in transit for more than 24 hours, even if it was thanks to the delaying tactics of the very protesters who he thought ought to be thanking him!

And so it was. A weary de Layney arrived back in Pennsylvania Avenue to be met by President Serenetti's private secretary who had scheduled a meeting in her office for 6.45pm.

Jim Powell was already there, looking uncomfortable.

"Welcome back Robert."

"Thank you Jim."

De Layney looked at the President.

"Madame President. Miriam. We have the airspace agreement."

"Yes, we have the agreement, but at a price? Who and what gave you the right to amend it and sign off on another $250 million? The US Treasury is not happy. I am not happy. We are not a charity."

De Layney looked exasperated.

"I *had* to secure the agreement. I tried to get through to you but you had the Africans here. I had no option. It was the only way. If I hadn't, Ormanbekov would have pulled the plug!"

"No, he wouldn't. He needs it as much as we want it," countered Serenatti.

"I…."

De Layney paused, feeling lost for words.

"And anyway, I didn't amend the agreement. Ormanbekov did."

It was the best he could come up with.

"You should have called his bluff. If it gets out, we'll be a laughing stock. The Republicans will love it when they scrutinise it in detail."

"If it's the money, Miriam, I've allocated it to 'overseas contingency.'"

"It's not the money," retorted the President. "That's irrelevant to the bigger picture. This is the biggest defence deal we've struck this century. It needs to be watertight and above scrutiny. We need to be accountable. How do we know that Ormanbekov won't pocket the money or run drugs. Or people? You can bet your life that the Russians and Chinese will be asking those same questions. Rumours are already circulating about misuse of funds. American funds."

De Layney grimaced at this new information but remained silent. Serenatti continued her loud rant.

"You went above my head to change a previously agreed settlement. Don't you think we're paying enough? Isn't $85 million 'golden hello' plus $125 million a year, plus $8,000 for each landing and take off in the next 10 years enough of a carrot for a bankrupt Russian outpost? And then you give them another $250 million on top of that. For what? A few drought victims in Pakistan and Afghanistan. We're done with Afghanistan ever since the Taliban moved back in '21. Deaths on their watch are their problem, not ours. You should have checked with me first."

De Layney was taken aback by the force of her complaint. He hadn't expected such anger from his President. He needed to dampen down the fire.

"Miriam, there wasn't time. And I agree. There may be scrutiny but $250 million is not that much to account for in such a huge and important deal. And as I say, we should be able to lose that in our Defence contingency budget."

The President stared at de Layney. She was angry but had said her piece.

"Look, I'm sorry," continued de Layney. "Let me make a call to Ormanbekov and tell him we need some accountability, a supplementary statement, or something for the file, for the media. Something that will cover us."

Serenatti sat back in her chair, her hands clasped with her index fingers pointing upwards, her chin resting on them. She nodded.

"It needs to say that he will use it for humanitarian water aid and support for the region. And he needs to acknowledge it as *our* contribution. Do it today, this evening. I'll announce it as a humanitarian response to the drought at my media briefing tomorrow if it comes up."

"I'll book a call for this evening, 9pm. Bishkek should be awake by then!"

Powell got up and left the room. De Layney acknowledge Serenatti and followed him out.

"Jim. Jim."

Powell turned round to face de Layney in the corridor.

"I was surprised to see you back so soon. How is your mom?"

"My sister is there and I am on call. I'm afraid that there's very little that can be done for her now, Robert...."

De Layney said nothing but put a hand on Powell's shoulder as they walked down the corridor together.

"....but thanks for asking."

45

Saturday morning, Vefa, Bishkek; Friday evening, White House, Washington

An exhausted de Layney swiped his pass card which triggered a tiny green light. He pushed through the door marked *Secure18 Communications*. He showed his pass to a security guard sitting behind a glass canopy and continued through an automated door to his destination.

He sat down and stared at the three telephones on the table in front of him. One was lit up with a small yellow cross. He had no idea which phone related to which category of country he was calling, but international technical support did. He referred to their categorisation listing on the wall. The yellow cross phone related to Category C countries but, as he lifted the receiver, de Layney did wonder whether, in the light of this new agreement, Kyrgyzstan might be re-categorised to Category B at some time in the future. Not that it would matter to him. As far as he was concerned, all categories were landline secure, voice encrypted and neutralised from mobile tracking, not to mention alert-sensitive to outside compromise. They were also fitted with delayed speakers, which allowed the conversation to take place in real time. If the monitoring software alerted the system to any suspicious security breach, the conversation would immediately be delayed by 12 seconds to allow the automatic external lockdown option to activate.

Only a handful of US government officials had security access to this group of phones; the President

herself, Office of State Secretaries and their under-secretaries, and others at the President's discretion. High level vetted, pass-holding technicians were always on hand to set up and monitor any calls made from *Secure 18 Communications*. Technologically, US State security, the best that Silicon Valley could offer, was surely unbreachable.

The yellow cross turned green and de Layney picked up the phone.

"Sizdi azır ötkörüp jatam, mırza," came a stern sounding female Russian voice from the other end.

The accent made him shiver.

Brought up in the aftermath of the cold war, de Layney had struggled to dismiss the notion that someone was always listening in to his every word. Despite building his reputation and career on the successful management of several overseas portfolios, he had always felt a nervousness about his dealings with Moscow and its related regions

Now in high office, he continued to suspect cold war espionage, even if there was no evidence that it existed. Russia's invasion of Ukraine hadn't helped. Yet in his ten years in overseas diplomacy, no tapped phone calls had come to light; no meetings had been sabotaged and certainly no unwelcome media coverage for his overseas policies had been leaked, as far as he could tell. When he was appointed Secretary of State, he finally came to the probable conclusion that his fears may be unwarranted.

It didn't stop his nervousness at the words he knew translated simply as "…putting you through now, sir," were spoken.

"Robert, you are back home safely. That is good news."

Ormanbekov seemed cheerful and wide awake despite the early Bishkek hour.

"Mr President, greetings to you from Washington."

"And to you also, Secretary of State, from the peoples of the Kyrgyz Republic. But so soon. Did you leave your toothbrush behind…?"

The two men chuckled across continents.

"I'm calling to thank you for your hospitality for myself and my team and for our time in your beautiful capital, the perfect backdrop in which to make good our military deal, I think."

"Our pleasure, Robert, our pleasure, and I can confirm that even as we speak, my people are working on the renovation of Manas as an airbase fit for United States Air Force personnel."

De Layney knew that it was just past 7.00am Bishkek time, so the likelihood of any construction work going on at the airbase in a city that didn't wake up until after eight, was zero. He had become used to Ormanbekov's exaggerations. And in any case, it would be incoming American military personnel who would manage the restructuring of the base, not local Kyrgyz contractors.

"Thank you, Mr President. My team too are working on the deployment of service personnel and will be in touch with your Defence ministry in due course."

There was a pause before de Layney picked it up again.

"So, I want to talk to you about, well, you will know…."

He paused again, wanting to choose his words carefully.

"….you will know of the situation that evolved during our talks, and which still confronts us."

"Ah, the water problem, of course. A great tragedy for so many," President Ormanbekov responded, his voice softening. "But don't worry, we are taking care of that, thanks to you and the extremely generous support of the United States Administration."

"Well, that is the real reason I am calling. I would like…."

Again, there was another pause. Both men, aware of each other's frailties and faults, knew that what was about to be suggested may not be as diplomatic as their two countries, or the wider world, would expect from them.

De Layney started again.

"The agreement includes a clause which adds $250 million to the original package for, if I recall correctly, 'environmental benefits pertaining to fresh water supply from Kyrgyzstan in support of the region's environmental needs, at the discretion of the President of the Kyrgyz Republic.' My President wants me to expand what that means in reality. President Serenatti would like us to add some detail into that clause. For our own accountability, you understand."

"I see," retorted Feliks, after a few seconds. "I wonder, what does she have in mind? You and I know that that clause in the agreement is already signed, in response to the tragedy in Afghanistan and northern Pakistan. It blew up in our faces and we agreed that it would be good for both of our countries to be seen to be addressing the crisis. A military agreement alone being signed during an environmental catastrophe would have brought all kinds of criticism our way. The amendment was, if I may say, a clever addition to our primary deal. I must remember to congratulate Mr Kulov for suggesting it. And you for agreeing to it."

Those final words twisted the knife into an already open wound. De Layney knew that he had been compromised. Ormanbekov knew it too.

The only thing that de Layney could do now was to try to appeal to Ormanbekov's better nature. Not that he had one.

"Feliks, let me be frank with you. I am in a hole, here. My President is not happy that we....I.....changed a pre-arranged deal. I need something credible to be added into the clause to reassure her about how you will use the additional money to tackle the regional crisis. I am asking your considered response here, Feliks."

"Robert, Robert. Do not worry. Leave it with me. I am sure that we can come up with some wording, a minor amendment, that will satisfy your President. I will see what we can do."

"Can you look at this urgently Feliks? As well as Miriam we will have the media on our backs here."

"Well, Robert, it is very early in the morning here in Bishkek, and my city is only just waking up. So am I. I will see what we can do later today. For now, though, I need to have a shave and brush my teeth. And you, my dear friend, need to get some sleep."

"We are in agreement about that Feliks. Good day to you and please let me see the revised wording that you come up with when you have it ready."

Feliks ended the call abruptly. His smooth but clinical ability to pull the wool over the eyes of his international counterparts had succeeded once more. He would have no intention of dealing with de Layney's request in the way he wanted. He had other things on his mind, like his own, more deadly agenda.

In Washington, a subdued De Layney replaced the phone in its closet. The cross turned from green, back to yellow, and then to red. There was no more he could do.

The clock on the wall ahead of him read 9.07pm. He had been awake for what seemed like 36 hours. Ormanbekov was right about one thing. It was time to go home and get some rest.

‹

Part 2

... there is nothing hidden that will not be revealed

13 hours earlier - 6pm Friday evening, Jash Gvardiya, Bishkek

Batyrov had woken up on Friday morning expectant but not hopeful. The Americans had left that morning and he was desperate to get through the day for what he hoped would be Ormanbekov's political downfall, spoken in the President's own words. He would have to wait until 6pm that evening for such a political scoop. The clock was ticking.

If it didn't happen, if there was a no self congratulatory drink with the President's two colleagues, then the story was over. No admittance of wrongdoing, no revelations about water transfer. No proof of anything untoward.

Injustice would prevail.

Batyrov had his Friday meetings and spent the afternoon writing up a story for the Saturday edition of the paper, based on a portfolio interview that he did with Sidarov on the back of his recent dealings with the veteran politician. But this would be no scoop. No expose. Just talk about policy, in particular border security. It was Sidarov's speciality.

As the deadline approached, Batyrov became increasingly nervous about the prospect of silence, of failure. He allowed himself to consider the implications of a no-show, but quickly dismissed it from his mind. He had to think positively.

Surely Ormanbekov, Akayev and Kulov couldn't resist meeting up for one final celebratory toast? They were too arrogant not to. But would it be tonight? And would they meet in the same room as they had been for months, where the listening device had been placed? Would the device even work? These were questions he was too nervous to seek hypothetical answers to.

But of one thing he was sure. If nothing materialised at 6pm there would be very little chance of him finding out the reasons behind Ormanbekov's late amendment to the agreement. Or his motives for seducing the Americans out of $250 million.

He just had to wait, and trust his instincts.

Phone in hand, Batyrov approached Joroev's apartment block, tapping lightly on the door. It was 5.55pm. There were two full bottles of *Bozo* on the table, ready for consumption. Conversation was minimal. The two men waited in silence. Seconds passed. Minutes. And then, out of Batyrov's device, a small, crackled noise.

Not for the first time that day, Batyrov's heart rhythm lifted. He moved his ear closer to the phone to hear the sound of an opening door and Kyrgyz voices.

"Yes. Yes," he whispered, excitedly.

The bug was doing its work, picking up every sound clearly. He adjusted the volume control, being careful not to allow his chunky fingers to touch any of the other adjacent buttons. Then he checked that his phone was switched to record before looking at Joroev expectantly. The Kyrgyz national was animated, nodding excitedly. But what were they about to hear?

"The Chinese sure know how to make a good listening device," Batyrov said, a broad grin on his face. Joroev looked relieved that his dangerous work, not to mention that of his friend, Taalay, had not been in vain.

The two men listened intently. They heard drinks being poured, and glasses clinking. Ormanbekov, never one to shy away from grandstanding, spoke first.

"Gentlemen, it has been a long week, an historic week for our beloved Kyrgyzstan. Mother Russia has owned us for centuries. Not anymore. The umbilical cord between us has been severed. This week marks the beginning of a new era of Kyrgyz power and prosperity. The airspace agreement with the Americans has been signed. And is irreversible. Now, by good fortune, we are ready to implement the second phase of our plan, control of regional water supply. Our offer to supply fresh water through Tajikistan to drought countries will make us even richer than the Americans have done, not to mention save thousands of Afghan and Pakistani lives of course. Our southern neighbours will not be able to resist my humanitarian offer, my generosity...."

"....at a good price," interjected Kulov."

"Indeed, Alexander, of course. Water, for the first time in our history, is to become a regional trading asset. Our fresh water will bring the dead back to life, and make the poor rich. And who do we have to thank for raising our status in the region? Our good friends *amerikalıktar.*"

"*Americkaliktar*," the three men repeated in unison, before downing their drinks.

"Our neighbouring Republics have looked down on us since 1991. Now, they won't be able to look down on us ever again."

"*Kırgızstandın keleçegine bravo,*" chorused the group, accompanied by another clink of glasses.

Joroev was focused, but not understanding what he was hearing. Batyrov, with a nose for the unlikely, was fast getting the impression that the agreement was more, much more than that which had so slickly been presented to the media just 24 hours ago, to the hour. He would be proved right. Ormanbekov was about to reveal the true extent of his genocidal plan to his colleagues. Batyrov took out a small notepad from his inside jacket pocket.

"Alexander, I want you to manage the final stages of the fresh water project. You will oversee the transportation of water from north to south. It's a long journey. Let's make sure there are no problems along the way. Kadrjvan, I want you to start negotiations through our networks in Kabul and Peshawar for the immediate supply of fresh water to Afghanistan, emphasising their urgent need for our water to save Afghan lives. Tell them about our plans to supply water from our mountains to support their irrigation projects and feed their people. Stress to them that we can deliver fresh water from the mountains and lakes of central Kyrgyzstan, to their greatest areas of need within 48 hours and then ongoing as required. Of course, remind them that there would be a price to pay but suggest that we include that in our existing negotiations over the import deal for their dried fruits. We have already talked with the Tajik President about safe access through his territory. Make sure that we have our agreed secure access corridor in place. We don't want any dissident interference getting in our way. Any questions?"

There was a pause. The as yet unspoken question had to be asked. It was Kadrjvan who asked it.

"When do we release the water?"

"Have the families moved out?" enquired Feliks.

Again, another pause before Akayev responded.

273

"There has been reluctance, resistance. We have spoken with representatives of the families, but they don't want to move. They won't move. They say they are happier living underground. And they don't believe we will go through with enforced evacuation. They are stubborn."

"Mmmm…"

"And there is another problem. We can't locate many of them. There is a lot of underground pipe to monitor, over 400 kilometres, and their representatives won't let us anywhere near them."

Ormanbekov sounded unmoved.

"But some have moved, yes?" he asked.

"Yes, we have brought up around 400 people who are being held at our centre near Uzgen."

"How many does that leave?"

"We think about 600 or more. It's hard to know. They have lived down there a long time."

"Good, pay the willing ones to say how we rescued them and get hold of our man at Bishkek News 24 to record some interviews."

"Aktamov?"

"Yes, Akmatov. The line will be that we are rehousing all of the sewer families in government hostels."

"All of them?"

"Well, those who have come. The others? Well, that's up to them. But that is the line. Tell him he will be rewarded."

Kulov and Akayev were stunned at Ormanbekov's callous words. He was ruthless, moving the conversation on quickly.

"Is the Manimex filter in place?"

"Yes Feliks. It was installed three weeks ago at our southernmost point and now its being technically checked for its ability to filter the water and deliver purity. We will run a trial this weekend."

"No, no trial. We are ready," interjected Ormanbekov. "No more delays. We have been working on this for months and we warned them a month ago of our plans to disinfect and cleanse the pipes. Millions of gallons of clean, fresh water, is stored in our aquifer locations and dams here in the north, ready for release. We need to transfer it to the south with immediate effect so that it is ready for distribution once the Afghans and the Pakistani foreign ministers have agreed to our terms, which they will."

"So.....when," asked Alexander again. "We will need to mobilise the work force."

"We do it this weekend, tomorrow, overnight. Quietly and quickly. They have ignored our warnings. If the sewer families won't leave their home, then they will have to die in their home. And anyway," Ormanbekov concluded chillingly, "they could do with a decent bath."

The chilling silence that followed Ormanbekov's pronouncement encompassed the mood of the moment and echoed across the city's airwaves, all the way to Jash Gvardiya.

It was bad enough for Batyrov and Joroev, listening of this declaration to murder from afar, but Akayev and Kulov were actually in the room. They had always acquiesced with their President, partly in admiration and partly in fear. They were Ormanbekov's chosen, two of his oldest colleagues, and he had constantly persuaded them of the rewards he would bestow on them in return for their loyalty. But they knew that behind the clever rhetoric, he had a maniacal mind.

Today, they were seeing it in action.

47

6.20pm Friday evening, Jash Gvardiya

There wasn't much that shocked Batyrov these days, but the President's ice cold pronouncement, delivered *'on the rocks'*, shook him rigid.

He knew that Ormanbekov had always had a reputation for mistreatment of his political opponents. Some were known to have been imprisoned, tortured even. But these were civilians. Innocents. This was surely a new low, even for Ormanbekov.

He looked up at Joroev. The national was shaking, tears welling up in his eyes.

Batyrov put his hand on Joroev's arm.

"Is this the government I work for?" he asked.

"It's ok, Kamil," Batyrov said reassuringly but without much conviction. "It's ok. Now we know, we can act."

He knew that they were words without meaning. What could he possibly do to avert such an imminent plan?

After a long pause, Joroev looked up, his moist eyes meeting with Batyrov's.

"Some of my friends live underground. How can I warn them in time? I don't even know how or where or...."

Kamil broke down, heaving his tears out into a grubby handkerchief.

Batyrov placed his hand on his back and strengthened his grip on his arm. He rarely felt helpless, but on this occasion, he had no words of comfort for his unlikely accomplice, a nomadic dweller whom he had only met a few days before.

Batyrov's thoughts turned to two men, perhaps the only two men in the country who had the power to act and expose political malpractice at short notice; Shirin Kurmanbek and Ednan Askar. He wanted to call them but as soon as that thought entered his mind, he remembered that they had taken off together that morning for a weekend fishing trip to Karakol, to the Kekemeren river, their favoured place for their annual 'boys' outing, where they hoped to catch some *Amu-Darya* trout. Worse still, Batyrov knew that there was no internet access at Kurmanbek's shack, which had running water and little else.

Batyrov recalled Kurmanbek's words to him and Askar when he purchased the shack back in 2014.

"It's the perfect hideaway. No TV, no internet, no phone signal. The place for me to get away from it all when time permits."

That memory was no help to Batyrov, or Joroev, right now. For the first time in his journalistic life, Batyrov felt impotent, unable to comprehend a way forward. A fog of emotion clouded his thinking. A sense of hopelessness overwhelmed him.

He considered Joroev's situation. If the planned drowning, the sweeping away, the underground tsunami of hundreds of sewer families was exposed, Ormanbekov's allies and hatchet men would run for their lives. But they wouldn't forget. They would want to find out who leaked the plan to the media. Corrupt, central Asian politicians have long memories and could be clinical in their ruthless retaliation against those who are disloyal to their cause. Joroev, as one of the very few people who could possibly have gained access to the plot, would, at best be a fall guy, at worst a prime suspect. Either way, he would disappear. Batyrov knew at that moment that he had to protect him. But how?

Sitting there together in isolation on a Friday evening, there was little either one of them could do but grieve the imminent loss of their fellow countrymen.

The two men sat in prolonged silence.

Suddenly, without warning, Joroev jumped up from the table, knocking over the chair he was sitting on, the same careless motion which had exposed him to Roza in the Metro Bar a few days earlier. He rushed out of the door, leaving a startled Batyrov looking over his shoulder, wondering where his tearful accomplice was heading.

He followed him out, spotting him limping painfully down the stairs to street level.

"Kamil, Kamil," shouted Batyrov.

Kamil hobbled as quickly as his strapped up body would allow, up Jash Gvardiya towards Ryskulov Street. But after a few minutes, with the ageing Batyrov trying to keep up, he slowed to a stop, bending over, his hands on his knees, out of breath, and exhausted.

He turned round to see the journalist walking slowly towards him. The two men fell into a natural embrace, the distressed Joroev weeping loudly on Batyrov's shoulder.

"I don't know what to do...." he wailed. "I don't know what to do."

As the two men walked aimlessly back to Joroev's apartment, their heads bowed, Batyrov called Roza.

Roza was enjoying a shower when her mobile phone rang. It was placed on a towel on a chair, out of reach of her wet hands. Having lost one phone a year earlier by dropping it in the bath tub, she was not going to lose another! Seeing Temir's name light up the screen, she quickly stepped out of the cubicle, dried her hands and answered it.

She listened to Batyrov in silence. He was apologetic, but said he needed to see her urgently. Very urgently.

"And try to get through to Ednan. It's a long shot, but try. Get him to call me. Meet me at the office in 30 minutes. And bring Olga."

It was the last thing she wanted to do on a Friday evening, but there was urgency in Batyrov's orders. She dried and dressed herself, tried calling Askar, without success, and then called Olga.

Even without a plan, Batyrov felt that he needed to do something. Consulting his junior colleagues was the first step to formulating some sort of response to what he had just been listening to. He knew that contacting the new Chief of Police would have no effect. He was in Ormanbekov's pocket and letting him know that he was on to the President's plan would endanger Batyrov's life, not to mention those of his sources. Apart from that, he, as a mere journalist, wouldn't be believed.

Batyrov took Joroev back to his apartment and told him not to leave.

"And don't contact anyone. Wait for me to call you."

He headed for the Star Building. Olga arrived at the same time as he did and the two of them went in together. They sat in Askar's office, Batyrov in the bosses chair.

"Let's wait for Roza."

Olga knew that something serious was going on. She would have to wait a few minutes more to find out what it was.

48

6.45pm Friday evening, Jash Gvardiya

Despite Batyrov's strict orders, Joroev decided to call Ramirez. It wasn't a good time.

Three times he called. Three times he heard the engaged signal.

Ramirez was on the phone to Sandie, his ex-wife, from her home in Massachusetts. It was always a long call. This time, there was a good reason.

Canning, their 17 year old son, an only child, had got into some sort of trouble at college, and they were talking about what to do about it. Despite the couple being divorced for ten years and living 6,000 miles apart, Sandie would always turn to her ex-husband in matters that involved their son.

Ramirez hadn't been home to see Canning for several years. He had planned a visit 5 years ago, in 2019, but, much to his shock, his exit visa had been denied by the Kyrgyz authorities. In theory, it had been granted, but the complexities of Kyrgyz bureaucracy had determined that if he left, he probably wouldn't be allowed back into to the country on his return. Despite getting the US Embassy to put pressure on the Kyrgyz Ministry of Foreign and Internal Affairs, his request for guaranteed re-entry was turned down, much to his disgust.

A year later, the Covid-19 crisis was making its mark across the world. It would be the Americans now who wouldn't entertain his application.

Two applications, two rejections. He felt let down by the very two countries he had served for much of his professional life. There was little else he could do but continue his role in Bishkek, estranged from his family, without dissension and in silence.

So Sandie complaining that he 'hadn't seen his son in five years,' and 'was it any wonder he was getting into trouble' was not something Ramirez wanted to hear at the end of a long week.

He felt guilt and as an absent father living on another continent, he also lived his life with a sense of failure. Sandie never missed an opportunity to remind him of his dereliction of parental duty that had affected their son throughout his teens.

Ramirez was relieved when the call finished but it hadn't ended well. It concluded with him saying, "....there's not much that I can do from 6,000 miles away! You'll have to sort it."

And with that, he touched the red cross icon on his screen, threw the phone on to a chair and headed to the kitchen. The last thing he wanted that evening was to speak to anyone else, especially as he hadn't eaten anything. Fat chance.

Ramirez offered a loud expletive before heading back to the living area to see who was calling him.

"It had better not be *her* again," he shouted out in anger.

It wasn't.

"Kamil. It's not a good time."

Even though Joroev himself was full of anxiety, he sensed Ramirez's stress and tried to speak calmly.

"Joe. Joe, don't hang up. Listen, please hear me out. It's important. Very important. It appears as if the deal which you guys signed yesterday is not all that it seems. It's corrupt. And Ormanbekov is evil. He's planning to control fresh water supply in the region using American money from the deal. He aims to pump it through the Songol to Fergana pipeline this weekend. He's planning to murder hundreds of sewer families living underground by drowning them tomorrow. Saturday. Overnight. In secret. It's a massacre. And the Americans are paying for it. We have to stop it, Joe. We have to stop it. Are you listening? We have to…."

Ramirez's Friday evening was quickly turning from bad to worse. He tried to compute all that Joroev was saying, but was struggling. It was a lot to take in. He initially dismissed it in his mind as the rantings of an emotional national out of his depth. But, what if there was some truth in it? And did he 'really say 'the Americans are paying for it?' What did it mean? And what might it mean for him? He had known Joroev long enough to recognise exaggeration. This tearful rant was no exaggeration. He needed to know more.

"Yes, yes, Kamil, I hear you," he interrupted. "But slow down. And calm down. How do you know all this?"

Joroev went on to describe how he and Batyrov had overheard the President's conversation from the White House's 7th floor meeting room earlier that evening. How Ormanbekov had been working on his secret water plan for months. How an extra $250 million had been added into the agreement. How he was pressing ahead with his plan for regional power. And worst of all, how he planned to achieve it. Joroev was beginning to shout down the phone at Ramirez.

Ramirez sat down, trying to take it all in. The White House bugged. The Americans duped. Joroev's relationship with a journalist. Listening in on the President's conversations. He knew absolutely nothing of this.

"Genocide, this weekend," he whispered back at Joroev. "I can't believe it."

"You need to tell your Ambassador. You must act now to stop this....tonight!"

Ramirez listened, hard. He had long forgotten his call with Sandie. It was all about Joroev now. Was he credible? If he was, what could Ramirez do? It was Friday evening. No one at the Embassy would be contactable. Even if they were, what could *they* do? And then there was that mention of Batyrov. He knew of him by reputation but hadn't known that Joroev knew him. Now that the media was involved, there would be scrutiny, implications, exposure even. But of what? Ramirez knew that Ormanbekov was a rogue, a loose cannon, and ruthless. But the idea that he would murder hundreds of his own people in an act of genocide was surely not a viable one, was it?

If Joroev was telling the truth - and it was still a big if as far as Ramirez was concerned - and Ormanbekov's underlying plot was exposed, the Americans would have to deny all knowledge of it.

Surely, Ramirez had a duty to take it further, to report it to the Ambassador, if only to unburden himself of the responsibility that now rested on his shoulders. How could he ever forgive himself if he had information that could implicate the American government, his government, in some sort of murderous, international collusion?

"Let me think for a moment, Kamil. I'll call you back."

There was no time for Joroev to respond. Ramirez ended the call and sat back on the sofa, He tilted his head upwards. Despair. A spider, a dead one, seemed to be stuck to the canvas lamp

shade which rested itself on the single bulb
hanging from the centre of the ceiling. Burnt alive.

49

6.55pm Friday evening, Ramirez's apartment and Mira

Ramirez poured himself a vodka, a large measure and sat down again to think. And there was a lot to think about.

If Joroev was to be believed, then death by water was imminent. Hundreds of nameless, innocent men, women and children would be swept away underground, drowned, perhaps just metres below where he was sitting. They would never be seen or heard of again. What would become of their corpses? Ormanbekov couldn't risk just leaving them to decompose at the end of a pipeline. They would surely be removed, maybe buried deeply in one of the many, dense woods in the south of the Republic.

His mind momentarily drifted back to the late 1990s when, having secured a post working for the US State Department, he was sent to Bosnia after the Balkan conflict. His job was to observe the UN's grim task in trying to locate the many mass graves which were scattered across the country.

He recalled one UN colonel saying to him, "If you want a mass grave to be found, make it wide and long. But if you want to erase it from history, dig it deep."

Ramirez had never fully grasped the significance of the colonel's words. Until now. If Ormanbekov wanted to hide his wrongdoing from history, he could. All he had to do was to bury the dead in a deep and remote grave.

He shuddered. Doubt turned to numbness, a feeling of helplessness, an inability to impact what might be going on around him. Beneath him.

He had no option.

He called the Ambassador. The phone rang. And rang. Where was he? Panic set in. The clock was ticking on sewer lives. If Ramirez didn't forewarn the Ambassador about the situation, then he himself might be held partially responsible for the grisly outcome. He shuddered at the thought.

He called for a third time. He wasn't expecting an answer. Even if there was one, what would he say? Would he re-tell the story with vigour, or would he downplay it as the hallucinatory rantings of a frightened Kyrgyz national?

In a fleeting moment, he wondered whether the lives, the deaths, of Kyrgyz sewer families would even matter, if no one found out about them.

He immediately regretted it, ashamed that for a millisecond, he had allowed himself to align his thinking to that of the President.

Ramirez knew how he operated. If he was about to murder his own, Ormanbekov would pay handsomely for the silence of the perpetrators, anyone who might be in on the impending horror. If they refused to be paid off, then they would have to pay with their lives. The whole matter would remain hidden in history. Ramirez couldn't allow that to happen. He ended his futile attempts to contact the Ambassador and called Joroev back.

"Get down to Mira now. The Ambassador's not answering his phone. We need to find him. Quickly."

Minutes later, both men, perspiring and out of breath, arrived at the Ambassador's private residence. Ignoring the ornate doorbell, Ramirez banged on the door. A light was on inside and after a few seconds, the Ambassador's wife answered.

"I'm sorry to disturb you, ma'am. Is your husband in?"

The Ambassador's wife knew Ramirez as a contact of her husband and had met him a few times at various functions at the University but she was more concerned about his companion, the dishevelled, unshaven, greasy-haired and bandaged up Kamil Joroev, who stood a couple of steps behind him.

"He….he's not here Joe," she said. "He'll be back soon."

"It's really important I speak with him tonight," insisted Ramirez. "Could you....I have to speak with him. I tried calling but he is not picking up."

"No, he wouldn't. He's at the Hyatt, at the gym and sauna. He always goes there on a Friday but he usually switches his phone off and leaves it in his locker."

Ramirez turned, almost falling back into Joroev.

"Thank, you, thank you, I need to see him urgently," repeated Ramirez as he and Joroev made their way towards the nearest *marshrutka* stop, leaving the startled Ambassador's wife at the door.

Ten minutes later, they were at the hotel. Time was moving on. Ramirez had no idea how the Ambassador might react to what he was about to tell him, but he knew him as a man of principle, with friends in high places. If anyone could do anything, he could. But what? And how quickly?

He burst through the double glass doors of the Hyatt and made for the reception desk. There was no one in attendance. His eyes averted to the large, multi-capital wall clock located behind the concierge desk. He took in the numbers. Bishkek, 1942 hours. London, 1342 hours. Washington, 0942 hours. And the day. Friday.

Ramirez was about to ring the service bell when 'ping', the elevator doors opened. Out stepped the Ambassador, an *Adver Group* holdall, emblazoned with its distinctive red and black AG logo, slung over his shoulder. He was walking with another man, his face flush, and carrying a Fila holdall.

The apologetic Ramirez persuaded the surprised Ambassador to sit down in the lobby area.

"You are a busy man, always in demand," grinned the Ambassador's American gym partner as he exited the hotel. "See you next week."

The three men took a spacious corner seat curved around the window adjacent to the entrance. Ramirez wasted no time. He blurted out the story, a nervous looking Kamil Joroev affirming Ramirez's every word with a vigorous nod of the head. Incredulous as it all sounded, the Ambassador didn't need much persuasion for him to decide to call Washington and interrupt de Layney's Friday morning. He nodded to the concierge before stepping into a side room to make the call.

De Layney sounded shocked. But not convinced. Perhaps, thought the Ambassador, things don't seem so urgent when you are 6,000 miles away. De Layney told him that he wanted something more concrete than a verbal report.

He found it hard to believe that the man he had just spent more than a day with, Feliks Ormanbekov, would stoop so low. But more than that, there was his pride. He didn't want to entertain the idea that he, an American Secretary

293

of State no less, could be duped by a central Asian dictator. That he could conceivably become a major player in an international conspiracy.

"I need more proof and I need it immediately," he told his Ambassador in Bishkek, just as two pieces of overdone toast popped up from the silver appliance in his kitchen.

Whether the information that the Ambassador had just relayed to de Layney across continents was true or not, he had the same dilemma as Ramirez. He couldn't keep it to himself. He had to cover his tracks. Miriam Serenatti had to be told. He picked up the phone and called for his driver, simultaneously grabbing his jacket and brief case. It would be another uncomfortable conversation on an empty stomach.

50

Friday evening, Bishkek Daily News office

Roza arrived at the newspaper office at 7.45pm. Batyrov played the recording on his phone to the two women. They listened in muted silence. He paused the audio before it reached its conclusion.

"We may not be able to stop the killings, but we have proof that they are about to happen, right here, this weekend," said Batyrov, holding up his phone.

"Tomorrow night," said Olga, a helplessness in her voice. "There must be something we can do. What about the police?"

"The new Chief is in Ormanbekov's pocket. And anyway, even if we did go to him how are we going to explain how we came by this information? It would put Joroev and his White House accomplice at risk. And us."

Roza looked at Olga, who was welling up.

"What about Mr Kurkambek?"

Olga spoke under her breath, her head bowed.

"He is away with Ednan. I've tried them repeatedly but there is no signal where they are."

"One of us could drive down there to alert them," Roza said, clutching at straws.

"That would take hours, and then they'd have to get back here," said Batyrov dismissively. "And I'm the only one who knows where Shirin's cabin is, but I haven't been there for a few years. Even if I left now I'm not sure that I could find it in the dark. And they'll be off to the river early tomorrow."

Olga held a tissue to her nose and wiped away a tear. The three journalists, usually so full of ideas, remained silent.

Batyrov stared at his phone. He paused before standing up, his fists clenched, his knuckles placed firmly on the desk, as if in need of support for what he was about to say.

The two women looked up. He spoke quietly.

"I'm afraid to say…." he began, taking time to choose his words carefully…."time is not on our side. These lives may already be beyond our ability to save them. I'm sorry, but we have to be realistic."

Their heads dropped. Batyrov needed to lift them. He shifted gear.

"We have no way of knowing how this is going to play out. But we do know that it's happening tomorrow night. Our responsibility now is to make sure that if some of…."

He breathed in deeply.

"….if some of our fellow citizens are to die, that they don't die in vain. Those who are responsible must be brought to justice. We are journalists. We have a job to do. To expose the perpetrators."

The women knew that Batyrov was right. Roza, her eager mind active, her adrenaline pumping, her desire for instant justice palpable, came up with a suggestion.

"What if we expose Ormanbekov on social media?"

Olga looked at Batyrov. On the face of it, it sounded genius, but Batyrov soon dampened the mood.

"That's good, Roza, but I'm afraid that Ormanbekov would simply pause his plan, deny it ever existed and arrest his accusers, Joroev included, citing treason. We need more proof of his intentions so that we can act accordingly. But sadly, retrospectively."

Batyrov had spoken the last word. The reality of their dilemma had finally kicked in.

"I feel sick," said Olga, hastily taking herself off to the rest room. Another awkward pause.

"How can we sleep tonight?"

"Tonight, Roza, perhaps we don't. But tomorrow, we work to expose this murderous corruption in our midst."

Olga returned, ashen faced. Roza stood up and embraced her colleague. Batyrov spoke.

"Go home and try to get some rest. I have to get back to Joroev. There is nothing more that we can do. For now."

The two women, united in grief, walked briskly, arm in arm, the short distance from the *marshrutka* stop back to Roza's apartment. Roza asked if Olga would spend the night at her apartment again. Neither woman wanted to be alone. Olga took her place on the sofa and stared at the ceiling. Neither said a word. What was there to say?

Eventually, Roza went to bed, checking the news app on her mobile for anything that might offer her fellow Kyrgyz citizens some hope of redemption. It would need a miracle.

Batyrov headed back towards Jash Gvardiya. He was worried about Joroev's state of mind. He would need emotional and physical reassurance. Batyrov certainly didn't want him to do anything that would jeopardise the situation or reveal what he knew.

Exposure of the perpetrators either before, or more likely after the fact, had to be a surprise in order for it to have maximum impact. He couldn't allow Joroev to make a wrong move. He would have to keep him on a tight lead.

51

Friday evening, Jash Gvardiya

Batyrov continued to bang long and hard on Joroev's door. Batyrov called him on his mobile phone. No response.

'Maybe he's on the toilet,' thought Batyrov. Frustrated.

"*Esikti ac, Kamil*. Open the door," shouted Batyrov, frightening an elderly lady who was wearily making her way up to the fourth floor. She dropped her wicker shopping basket, spilling some loose fruit and a rather sad looking lettuce on to the floor. A brown paper bag bounced down the steps, shedding asparagus tips along its way.

"*Keçirim suraym ayım,*" uttered an apologetic Batyrov, wondering why she would be carrying her shopping so late in the day.

The woman gestured her thanks as he bent down to pick up the spilled groceries.

"You won't find him in," she said in her northern territory, *Kipchak* dialect. "I've just seen him with a couple of men outside the Hyatt Hotel."

Batyrov hurriedly put a couple of loose mushrooms back into the elderly lady's bag, thanked her and raced back down the metal staircase. He headed back to the *marshrutka* stop, not for the first time that evening. He waited, feeling out of control. The situation he found himself in saw him rushing from one crisis to another, without knowing where each short journey would lead. Normally, the thoughtful Batyrov would think strategically and plan his course of action. This Friday evening, he was under pressure. He had no time to think. Darkness had set in, and murder was underfoot. Batyrov was unwittingly fearful. He felt the weight of responsibility for the sewer families, for his colleagues, for the newspaper and even, momentarily, for his country.

'What happens now?' he kept asking himself as he made his way to the Hyatt. 'How will this play out over the weekend? Could he really trust Joroev to hold his nerve?'

The questions kept on coming but the answers were evading him. The *marshrutka* pulled up. It was full. Friday night full. Batyrov squeezed himself in and acknowledged the driver, his pass raised above his head.

The *marshrutka* began its slow, bumpy journey up Frunze Streer towards Yusup Abdrahmanov. Next stop the Hyatt.

Batyrov was sweating profusely as he alighted the *marshrutka*. He entered the hotel, looking around for any sign of Joroev but there was none.

"I think the gentleman you describe may have just left, sir," said the concierge to a distraught Batyrov.

Batyrov felt stupid, chasing round Bishkek looking for a man he hardly knew in order to keep him from acting in a way that might endanger even more lives than were currently under threat, including perhaps his own. It seemed like a wild goose chase, but surely, he thought, a worthwhile one.

His problem was, he didn't know what to do next. The players in this saga were disparate and largely uncontactable. He didn't feel a part of it.

Batyrov decided to take himself back to his apartment. He had already sent Roza and Olga home and there was nothing more he could do without Joroev. He called Roza on the way and asked her if she would meet him the following morning, Saturday.

"I'm due at the Kyrgyz Opera House tomorrow lunchtime to interview Ekaterina Stepanchikov," she responded.

Stepanchikov, the lead Russian ballerina for the touring Russian Chamber Ballet, was in the country to perform the female lead, Dulcinea del Toboso, in Don Quixote, which was launching the theatre's autumn season of events. Stepanchikov's agent had agreed only one media interview and it was a coup for the Bishkek Daily News to have been chosen. Batyrov knew of its importance to the paper.

"Yes, I'd forgotten. What time?" he asked.

"I'll be at the Opera House for 12, so we could meet next door in the Hyatt. 11 o'clock? Shall I bring Olga with me? She's staying with me here tonight."

Batyrov knew that he had also given Olga a Saturday assignment, but that wasn't until the afternoon.

"Of course. 11am tomorrow."

Batyrov texted Joroev and told him to come to the Hyatt meeting the following morning.

'Let's hope he gets this,' he thought to himself, as he pressed the *Send* button.

His evening's work was done. It was unproductive, but he could do no more. Exhausted, he went home, took a shower and collapsed into his bed, naked.

52

Saturday morning, Vefa

Rays of early morning sun, permeated with particulate matter, penetrated through the minute cracks between Ormanbekov's window blinds. Daylight lit up the room in straight lines.

His phone was vibrating far too aggressively for the hour, and the President half-heartedly lifted his bulk away from it, hoping it might go away of its own accord. It didn't.

He turned back on to his side, waving his hand in the general direction of the pneumatic noise in the hope of silencing the unwelcome intrusion. No chance. In one wildly disoriented move, he inadvertently knocked it sideways to the edge of his bedside table, its smooth outer casing teetering on the edge. But then, and with a gymnastic dexterity that surprised even him, his index and little finger caught the phone just as it was about to fall. Saved.

The rescue lasted a mere three or four seconds, sufficient time for him to fully awaken from his slumber and identify the caller.

"Kulov, good morning comrade. What a fine morning it is. But why so early?"

Kulov was shocked. He hadn't expected such joviality from his President on such a day. Before he had time to respond, Ormanbekov continued.

"It's going to be a good weekend I think."

Kulov knew what was on Ormanbekov's callous mind, and he didn't like it. It was ok for his President to wax frivolity, but he wasn't the man tasked with giving the order to flush the pipes. Kulov had always been loyal, but Ormanbekov would be testing that loyalty to its limits in just a matter of hours.

"Alexander. Alexander. Are you there?"

"Yes, Feliks. I am here."

"Is everything ready?"

"Yes, the pipes are ready. Our men are just awaiting their orders."

"Do it this evening, Alexander. Tonight. Brief the men and pay them. I want no hitches."

A long pause followed. Ormanbekov allowed it, knowing that the inevitable question would arrive. It did.

"Feliks. Are we sure we want to go through with this?"

Kulov had been awake much of the night, tossing and turning, wondering if he dared to challenge Ormanbekov's authority. Was the

President really that ruthless, heartless enough to drown even his own?

He already knew the answer.

"Tonight. We do it overnight, tonight. Away from prying eyes and ears. After all, darkness is always the best time to suppress the unfortunate but inconvenient necessities of life, don't you agree Alexander?"

In a moment of bold but futile push back, Kulov suggested a delay.

"Monday would be quiet also, Feliks."

Perhaps Kulov hoped that something might happen between now and then which might change the President's mindset. It wouldn't.

"Indeed, it would. But why put off until tomorrow what we can do today. We do it tonight."

Kulov's heart was sinking fast. There would be no reasoning with Ormanbekov. Why would there be? His plan to clear the sewers of its residents had never wavered. Death would be quick, and final. The unstoppable tsunami of water would seal their fate. A mass grave would await them. And once burial had taken place, post genocidal activity would begin, immediately.

Henchman, paid to collect and bury the mountain of bodies that would amass at the southern most tip of the sewer, would do their work. No questions would be asked.

And then, just a few hours later, a group of Bishkek Water Authority engineers, oblivious of preceding events, would gather at the northern end of the pipeline and calmly repeat the flush process, this time with the intention of disinfection. By lunchtime Sunday, the pipes would be operational. And fresh water would be flowing freely within days. The plan was foolproof, detailed, worked out between Ormanbekov, Akayev and Kulov over many weeks. Now, it was finally happening.

Ormanbekov, for his part, was already looking beyond genocide, thinking about how he would announce his new initiative. A blaze of media glory would prevail following the announcement that Kyrgyzstan was ready to become the region's saviour. It would be Kyrgyzstan which would be supplying what the region desperately needed, right now. Water. Fresh water. Millions of gallons of it, direct to the worst affected countries.

Strategic elevation was underway, not only regionally, but geo-politically. And all paid for with American money, two down payments of which had already been banked! Kyrgyzstan's drought ridden neighbours would become beholden to the Republic's new found status. And there was a bonus. Security.

Ormanbekov's actions would help secure his porous borders, something which would see predator raids, particularly from Tajik nationals, cease overnight.

"After all," Ormanbekov had assured his colleagues many weeks before, "with American troops on our soil, no hostile invader would seek to breach our newly established security."

Ormanbekov's plan was underway. And moving at a pace. He was not about to stall it. The secret drowning of hundreds of Kyrgyz nationals would go ahead. Tonight. Overnight.

53

11am Saturday morning, Hyatt Hotel, Bishkek

Roza, Olga and Batyrov arrived at the Hyatt and sat in the bar area. They ordered sparkling water. Joroev, who, much to Batyrov's relief had responded to his text the previous night, joined them just as the lift doors were opening.

Out stepped the elegant Ekaterina Stepanchikov along with two handsome, slimly built cropped haired beaus, both shorter than her. Two of her company dancers, thought Roza. The three of them were bantering, giggling with each other. They were light on their feet as if walking on air, sweeping flamboyantly past Roza, Olga, Batyrov and Joroev and out into the morning sunshine, before turning left towards the Opera House. Their journey from the elevator to the exit doors was like an unplanned mini ballet, spontaneously performed by three of its principal actors, for the enjoyment of those in the lobby.

"Did you sleep?" Batyrov asked Joroev after introducing him to Olga.

"What do you think?"

There was no other place to go with Joroev other than to the point. The events of the last 24 hours had left him vulnerable, a threat even, not only to the scenario that was about to be played out below ground that night, but to himself. Batyrov had to keep him busy.

"You need to contact Ramirez again to find out what the Americans are going to do. The Ambassador has had all night to speak with Washington. We need to know?"

Joroev looked at Roza for the first time since his arrival at the Hyatt.

Batyrov had asked the question, but he nodded the answer back towards Roza, whose eyes always seemed to be drawn to his disfigured hand. The knowledge that it was she who was responsible for his injury was both chilling and satisfying, an unwelcome reminder every time they met.

"We'll wait here for you."

Joroev stepped out of the Hyatt to make the call.

Batyrov was not one to waste time, especially time that he didn't have. Time wasn't his friend. And there was little if anything he could do until he had spoken with Kurmanbek and Askar.

If only they were here. Kurmanbek would know what to do. He had enough dirt stored in the newspaper's basement to at least threaten the President with the publication of one of his many past misdemeanours. Such an immediate course of action might just be enough to force

Ormanbekov into a change of heart, even a temporary one.

And Kurmanbek had immunity. Ormanbekov wouldn't dare to ignore one of Bishkek's most senior and respected, not to mention popular, businessmen.

But Kurmanbek wasn't here. And he wasn't contactable.

Roza had one eye on the international clock which hung behind the concierge's desk.

"I will need to go soon for my interview."

"If you can wait until Joroev gets back….he won't be long."

He wasn't. Joroev came back in and sat down. He looked pale and stumbled over his words.

"I….he….I spoke with Ramirez. He spoke with the Ambassador again early this morning. He wouldn't tell me what was going on. But he did say that the Americans believe that….confirmed that….if mass murder is imminent then their objective now is to disassociate themselves from it."

"What does that mean? How will they do that?"

Joroev looked at Roza, who had asked the question.

"I don't know. Ramirez wouldn't say. But he sounded sort of numb. He said that if the Americans panic, they will act 'decisively'. Whatever that might mean."

Batyrov looked at the clock. Washington time was showing 01.47 hours. He was deep in thought, trying to second guess the Americans.

"What are they up to?"

He had no answer to his own rhetorical question.

Roza looked at the clock again.

"I need to go," she said. And she did.

Roza's exit to meet with Ekaterina was Olga's cue to leave also.

Batyrov had asked her to attend the *'commencement of grieving and viewing'* of one of Bishkek's leading businessmen, Izatbek Alymkulov, the owner of the multi national Goldpro Electrics, who had unexpectedly died on Thursday night, seemingly from cardiac arrest following a week of chest pains. It was news that Batyrov could have done without but, as a loyal supporter of the Bishkek Daily News, not to mention a long time friend of Shirin Kurmanbek, Alymkulov couldn't be ignored, even in his passing.

It was important that the paper would, in the absence of its proprietor, be seen to be sending one of its staff team to pay its respects and write the obituary. Olga was the obvious choice, not least as she had met Mr Alymkulov once at a drinks function for the opening of a new Goldpro factory base in Karakol. More importantly, she had met his wife, and she and Olga had chatted over champagne.

"It was a long time ago," she told Batyrov when he called her on Friday morning. "I doubt she will even remember me."

"I know, Olga, but I'd like you to go. Roza has the Ekaterina Stepanchikov interview to do and I have to deal with the Ormanbekov situation. This is not one for a freelance. If you can just show your face, pay your respects on behalf of Mr Kurmanbek, and write up the obituary and get it to me in time for proofing early Sunday morning, we can get it into the Monday edition."

Olga wasn't best pleased, not least as it was her birthday the following week. She had arranged to call her parents on the Saturday evening and meet a friend on Sunday. The passing of an important business associate of Kurmanbek would not make any headlines. But she was dutiful and loyal. She planned her timetable.

She would arrive around 2pm for the *'commencement of grieving and viewing'* which started around lunchtime. She would leave around 4pm and write the obituary later that afternoon, leaving her free to make the call to her parents in Moscow that evening. Her timetable was set.

Roza concluded her interview by 1.15pm and headed home via the Osh Bazaar, where she picked up some local *kurut* cheese, some wild onions and a watermelon.

Throwing them on to the kitchen table, she went to her bedroom and sat down at her makeshift 'home desk,' her phone recorder at the ready. She began the long, slow process of transcribing Ekaterina Stepanchikov's eloquent words, spoken in a mix of pure, northern Russian and *Balachka*, a dialect Roza struggled to comprehend. It would be a long afternoon, but as by-lines go, it would be worth it. Something for her CV. A real feather in her cap. She had a heavy heart but it was a good distraction from the other events of the day.

54

9.30pm, Friday evening, White House, Washington

Back in Washington, President Serenatti's second day of meetings with central American leaders from Panama, Costa Rica, Nicaragua, Honduras, El Salvador, Guatemala, and Belize was concluding. The day had gone well. Security and drug trafficking had been up for discussion, though recent climate emergencies in south America, not least the widespread floods of 2023 which had devastated Argentinean cattle exports and Brazilian coffee plantations, had seen climate challenges in the region added to the agenda. Her keynote speech over dinner addressed all these issues and was being warmly applauded by the delegates when she was handed a piece of paper by an aide.

"Secretary of State de Layney says it is very urgent, Madam President. He's in your office now."

The President read it, and then re-read it. She went pale.

She apologised to her guests and deferred the hosting of the meeting to the Secretary of the Treasury before striding back down the corridor to the Presidential suite.

"What the heck is going on Robert?" she demanded as she walked through the door, waving the note in the air.

"It is what it says," he responded coyly.

"What? It's impossible. Crazy. Not even he would be so mad as to drown his own people. And for what? A water transportation corridor from the north of the country to the south? It's mad. Our Ambassador must have got it wrong."

"I agree, Miriam, but....he seems pretty sure."

"....and using our money," interrupted Serenatti. "And this weekend...?"

"I've been on the phone all day with the Ambassador, trying to confirm the story. He is adamant that it's planned for this weekend, tomorrow night, overnight Kyrgyz time. That's our lunch time. We don't know exactly when."

"Get Ormanbekov on the phone and stop him. Tell him we'll cancel the deal."

As Serenatti was speaking, an aide knocked on her door. He handed a note to de Layney. It was a follow up message from the Ambassador.

De Layney stared at the message. The President watched him slowly ease himself into a leather bound armchair.

"He confirms that its this weekend. The Kyrgyz General of Armed Forces and the Chief of

Police are Ormanbekov allies, former communists. He's not sure if they are in on the plot, but unlikely, he thinks. But he doesn't feel he can put pressure on them to stop the massacre, especially as Ramirez obtained the intel through a source in the Kyrgyz White House. If the Ambassador went to either the Army or Police, Ormanbekov would think that *we* have someone in the White House, even though we don't. But someone does. Worst case scenario, we could lose the deal we've just signed."

"…and which you have just announced to the world, Robert."

"He says that if this goes ahead, and we expose it, diplomatic ties could be suspended and they'd throw us out of the country. Ramirez could also be in danger. And it would almost certainly threaten our agreement."

"Ormanbekov won't do that. He needs us. He needs our deal," responded Serenatti. "And it's already been signed."

"Yes, but Ormanbekov would want to save his own skin at all costs."

Serenatti took her seat opposite her Secretary of State. She had calmed a little and was gathering her thoughts.

"We don't have anyone in their White House, you say," she asked, wondering how the information had been leaked to the Ambassador.

They stared at each other, neither hiding their differing emotions.

Mass murder on the other side of the world carried out by a rogue dictator would normally only prompt a simple but sternly worded statement from Washington and a referral to the United Nations. But if it got out that it was linked to American money, the US government's options would be greatly reduced. Certainly, it wouldn't be able to claim any moral high ground.

"...and, we'll be a laughing stock the world over."

Serenatti wasn't mincing her words. This was happening on her watch.

"What is the status of the signed agreement, financially, Robert? How much of our money do they already have?"

"Well, you will recall back then, that we were so keen to secure the deal at any cost and get a lead on any other nations the Kyrgyz might be speaking with, that we paid the first two instalments up front. We got it past the Treasury by calling the first one a sweetener, while the second came under the heading of 'goodwill deposit.' Green signed it off."

"So the first two payments are already in Kyrgyz government bank accounts? Great."

Serenatti sounded exasperated.

"There's no way of extracting ourselves from a financial arrangement which is already in process. That would require backward gymnastics that not even a smart financial operator like Green could manage. It would draw ridicule and embarrassment around the world, not to mention the loss of that which we had fought so hard to achieve!"

Another pause.

"Why didn't I see this coming?" a forlorn de Layney asked of his President, not expecting an answer.

The possibility of exposure was slowly dawning on them. International humiliation could remain active for years, perhaps decades, 'a forever threat,' as Serenatti would call it. She had to act, and act now.

"We'll close it all down," she said, determinedly. "This intel cannot be leaked. It mustn't get out, at any cost."

Serenatti looked de Layney in the eye. He was wondering what she had in mind.

"Find out what our secret service presence is in the region and get back to me. I'll inform the CIA. Do we know who else knows about this other than our Ambassador and Ramirez?

De Layney had no answers but was pleased that the President was coming up with the questions.

"I'll call the Ambassador to find out who we have who is active in the region. What do you have in mind, Miriam?"

She ignored him.

"We'll reconvene here in an hour, 10.30pm. Get me answers by then," and with that, the President jumped up

from her chair and headed back to the central American summit dinner. De Layney followed her, two steps behind, still wondering what was on her mind.

55

10.30pm, Friday, White House, Washington

Serenatti was already at her desk when de Layney stepped in, closely followed by Ocean.

"Any update?" she demanded

"Good or bad?"

"Just tell me, Robert," Serenatti replied, tetchily.

De Layney looked grim.

"We've received more detail of Ormanbekov's intentions in the last hour. The Ambassador confirms his intention to murder hundreds of his own people living in the underground sewers. He has heard it from Ramirez's source, who has access to a recording of Ormanbekov."

The room fell silent for a moment before de Layney stated what everyone was thinking.

"They're half a day ahead. For all we know, it may have already taken place."

"Whether today or tomorrow, we can't stop it. But we can suppress it as a story which implicates us."

The President looked away, towards a blank, bland, cream coloured wall, a metaphor for the seemingly hopeless situation that she found herself in. Her mind was considering the damage to the US's reputation around the world should the news ever become public. She also knew that it was happening on her watch. If any hint of complicity was ever suspected, she could be impeached. It would be the end of her Presidency and she would have to live with the consequences of failure for the rest of her life. Worse, the United States would become a laughing stock around the world. Trust in its future negotiating strategies would lie in tatters. Market confidence would see a run on the dollar. The Dow Jones would take a fall causing a 21st century Wall Street crash. The political coup that the agreement was intended to be would be seen for what it was fast turning out to be; expensive, and corrupt.

Serenatti looked back at de Layney.

"How many?"

"Several hundred, maybe as many as six hundred."

Serenatti slumped against the wall. After drawing breath, she looked up at de Layney with a contemptuous look.

"What else?"

"Our Ambassador tells me that Officer Ramirez has at least four operatives he can call on in the region, all special air service personnel.

Two are in Dushanbe and can cross the border into Kyrgyzstan."

"Order them to drop what they are doing and get them there now. I will alert Miller at the CIA. What about the other two?"

"One is in Kazakhstan and will drive, the other is in Bucharest, at our base there. We have a Grey Wolf which was due for relocation to Manas anyway. He'll come over on that, kill two birds with one stone."

Serenatti then asked the question she was avoiding, fearful of the answer. But she needed assurance before ordering a covert and dangerous operation in the region.

"What cast iron proof is there of Ormanbekov's genocide?"

De Layney sighed.

"Our Ambassador hasn't actually heard the audio of Ormanbekov's plan but Ramirez's Kyrgyz contact has. It's on some journalist's phone or another device. We don't know yet."

"That's all we need. Reporters involved. Do we know who they are?"

"Some local media outfit, independent, not government, set up the recording."

"Smart. Maybe we should employ them."

De Layney remained stern faced. Serenatti continued.

"So it may not be Ormanbekov we need to worry about, but the media. If they're anti government they'll have no hesitation in exposing their story. We need to get hold of it and destroy it. And maybe the whole media operation."

Serenatti was demonstrating a ruthlessness that de Layney hadn't seen before. She was thinking on her feet, something de Layney thought she must have learnt when serving with the US Navy in its DSV submarine corps, prior to her moving into politics.

"What else do we know?"

"We believe only two others were in on the recorded conversation, both of them political allies of Ormanbekov, communists and both known to us, Alexander Kulov and…"

De Layney looked at Ocean.

"Kadrjvan Akayev, sir, his Prime Minister."

"We believe that the only others who would know about this whole thing would be the paid henchmen Ormanbekov would have recruited to set this whole thing up and carry it out. Given the immediacy of his planned actions, it seems like they might have been preparing this for a long time."

"So this was all in place before your visit?"

De Layney and Serenatti stood in silence, thoughtful. They could hear the multi-lingual hum of conversation dying away as delegates and officials said their farewells, just a few feet from where they were standing.

At the sound of muted laughter, Serenatti spoke.

"Bring Miller and Powell in to meet with us tonight. Now. We'll reconvene at 11. And get the Ambassador to call in those agents without delay. That's an order.

56

11pm Friday evening, White House, Washington

Robert de Layney, Jim Powell, James Miller, Head of the CIA, and Kendrick Richardson, Director of US government online security and monitoring, met in Serenatti's private office.

De Layney had briefed Powell and Richardson when they arrived at the White House and Serenatti had briefed Miller on his way in. The call had not been cordial. Miller was angry that his department hadn't identified any negative intelligence coming out of Kyrgyzstan during preliminary preparations for de Layney's visit, and he certainly hadn't been alerted to Ormanbekov's subsequent plans. He was also put out that he was being summoned to the office at 11 o'clock on a Friday evening.

"We need to get more bodies in there on the ground. And our Ambassador is useless," he would tell Serenatti in an attempt to distract from his department's own shortcomings.

The President had already agreed that the US needed to review its special services presence in the region. But she also reminded him that the situation had only just been brought to her attention that evening, while she was hosting the summit. She was, she said, acting as quickly as circumstances would allow.'

"I'd appreciate your full co-operation James," she had concluded, by means of an order.

The meeting began in faux accord.

Serenatti opened a leather-bound folder.

"Thank you for coming in at this late hour, gentlemen, but a situation has arisen which we have to deal with, urgently. And as you all know, when we have a situation, we must make bold choices in order to protect the good name, reputation and standing of the United States of America. This meeting is confidential, will not be minuted and is not for outside consumption, even within our departments for now. Maybe for all time."

Nods all round.

"According to our Ambassador in Bishkek, hundreds of Kyrgyz nationals who live underground in old Soviet, cold war pipelines are at risk of being murdered. And this, just days after our agreement signing. I don't have to emphasise how serious this is. The Ambassador says that it is scheduled to take place this weekend. If it's tonight, it's already happened but I'm not sure that's likely. The Kyrgyz aren't that efficient, even in genocide. If it's tomorrow, that would, because of time difference, mean any time after lunch time here. It could be Sunday night. Whenever it is, we can't stop it, but we can, I believe, make sure that

327

there is no link between what Ormanbekov is about to do, and any connection, however tenuous, to the United States.

As I see it, we have two possible courses of action, and only two. Neither of them are pretty but both would have the immediate effect of halting any threat to our international standing in the world which, believe me, is my primary and non-negotiable intention. Option one. We could take out Ormanbekov, Kulov and Akayev.

They thought up the plan and they are the only three who know about it, as far as we know, apart from some local media outfit. We could do that. I'd like to do that, actually. In my experience, though, taking out a central Asian President and two senior government officials, however corrupt they might be, would cause a lot of excess political noise for a long time. The collateral political unrest in the region would be immense. And assassination is a messy business. And of course, time is not on our side. We wouldn't be able to get to him in time to save his people. Our agents are only in transit, currently.

So, we move to option two, which would seem much less divisive and could, according to James here, be done quickly, and without too much local fall out. We destroy the evidence. All of it. We obtain the audio which implicates Ormanbekov and make it disappear. This may appear to be letting Ormanbekov off the hook, but it will only be temporary. We will bring him down at a later date. We also destroy the media operation which seeks to expose his corruption. Taking down the media operation will see the destruction of any files they may have which relate to the genocide and implicate us by association. Kendrick tells me that we can neutralise and destroy all online traffic to and from the media outlet for the last six months. That should cover the timeline. He and his team can do that from here, within 12 hours of my order. There it is, gentlemen. I favour option two; obtain any audio evidence of Ormanbekov's genocidal plan, and decimate all comms activity within the media outlet for the past six months. That would include the raising to the ground of its premises. Operatives in the region are heading to Bishkek as we speak and they will liaise with James to assess the best options at our disposal to bring down the media building. If we decide to go down that route, James favours explosives or we may look at arson. Which ever way we act, our objective is to eliminate all possible links to inadvertent US complicity in any Kyrgyz state corruption, forever. Ormanbekov's plan to illegally trade his way to power on the back of a corrupt but believable message of compassionate environmentalism is bad enough. If that was all it was, we could live with the fact that we were unaware that our money would be used in such a way…."

"….which we were," butted in de Layney, unwisely. "Unaware, I mean."

Serenatti didn't look up.

"But the fact that he is willing to murder his own people puts the whole thing on a different level. We cannot be seen to be in any way

329

complicit in mass slaughter. If that gets out, it won't matter how much we profess our innocence. It would be a forever stain on our history and an indefensible failure of foreign policy, the very same foreign policy which, may I remind you gentlemen, has just delivered a geo-political re-balancing of the world order, some stability in the Middle East and reassurance for Israel. It still can if we act now. Gentlemen, we have been in negotiations with the Kyrgyz for months, and in good faith, to get a deal, dollars for air space. We have achieved that. Our fight against Middle East terrorism continues but it's gotten a whole lot easier, geographically and militarily, now that our feet are firmly established on central Asian soil. Let's be pragmatic and keep in mind the longer picture. We have hit a major bump in the road, but it is not insurmountable. If we deal with it now, quickly and efficiently, we can continue to implement our foreign policy objectives, and secure peace in the Middle East. Comments."

Powell spoke first, offering a steer which would open up the discussion.

"I agree with Miriam. We have to act decisively. Option two is in the best interests of the United States. That takes care of the immediate threat. But Ormanbekov is dangerous. We need to rein him in in the future."

"Agreed," intervened Miller. "As long as he is alive, he carries a threat, not only to his own people, but to us. He needs eliminating. But I concur with you Jim. That's for another day."

"Thank you. Anyone else?"

De Layney spoke up.

"As things stand, no one but Ormanbekov's group and a journalist know what is going down. Whichever option we choose, we have to act now to protect the American brand."

Serenatti gave a small nod in de Layney's direction.

Miller, the man charged with overseeing the execution of either option, spoke again.

"We can deal with Ormanbekov down the line. For now, the quickest and cleanest option is to neutralise all sources of information pertaining to anything that might compromise our position."

They all looked at Richardson.

"Kendrick…?"

"James' operation and mine are separate. For me, it doesn't matter whether the building is up, or down. I can neutralise the media outlet's servers within a couple of hours. Hacking and neutralising their cloud storage may take longer. But I will de-activate them both at the same time."

"OK that's settled, we go for option two. James?"

"I'll get our operatives to convene at the Ambassador's residence for a briefing. The priority will be to get hold of the phone with the recorded conversation on it and then get it to Mira. The Ambassador can arrange diplomatic passage to get it here for analysis. If what we have been led to believe is on it, then we can use it against Ormanbekov in the future, should we need to. We can take down the media offices, tomorrow night, Saturday, if the operatives arrive in Bishkek in time. That will destroy any paper documents that may implicate us. We can't guarantee that there may be documents located elsewhere but it's highly unlikely. As a minimum, destroying their offices will halt their activities. My intel is that the premises host two other businesses on different floors so there may be some collateral damage, but we'll keep it to a minimum."

"Let's hope they are insured," interjected Serenatti.

"We'll do our best, Miriam. But as you know, collateral damage is not something we have any control over. "

Serenatti looked Miller in the eye.

"No casualties," she repeated forcefully. "There are going to be enough deaths by all accounts without us adding to them."

It was fair comment.

"Liaise with Kendrick on timings, and both of you, keep me fully informed, any time. I'll call the Ambassador now."

Serenatti stood up. "Thank you gentlemen. We have a long night ahead of us. Let's get to it."

57

Saturday afternoon, the Alymkulov Estate

Olga arrived back from the Hyatt and made her way to her bedroom to dig out her *jooluk*. She felt ashamed of herself as she searched for the mourning garment at the back of her underwear draw. Surely it deserved more prominence than that. She blushed, as a photograph of her and her late husband on the dressing table caught her attention.

She pulled the *jooluk* out and held it in her hands, observing it closely. Her eyes moistened momentarily as she caressed it with her fingers, remembering the last time she had cause to wear it. Seven years ago. Kylych's funeral. Then, it was personal. Now, she had been asked to attend in a professional capacity, the first of seven days of mourning for a man she didn't know and had only met once in her life. Journalism wasn't the business of offering its workers healing for past hurts.

She wrapped the *jooluk* around her neck and looked at herself in the mirror. It complemented nicely the navy dress that she had chosen to wear. She turned to one side, then the other before smoothing it down from the waist. She was ready.

She wandered over to the northbound *marshrutka* stop located on the opposite side of the road from her apartment. To Olga's relief, it was almost empty when it pulled up. Twenty minutes later, she awoke from a short doze to find it turning into Michurina Street. Olga alighted and made her way towards the Alymkulov estate. She walked up the paved driveway, and around the side of the house to its rear garden which hosted two white *gers,* lit with votive candles from within. The gers had been set up a week earlier at the suggestion of the Mullah when it became obvious that Izatbek Alymkulov's health was diminishing. Today, his body lay at rest, on a warmly decorated table in one of the *gers*, the one on which was placed a white flag. Alymkulov was nothing if not a traditionalist and it was his dying wish that this ancient tradition, announcing his demise in the neighbourhood, be observed.

The other *ger* was full of grieving women, relatives and friends of the deceased who were wailing and singing *koshok* funeral verses. Olga had heard their lamentations from afar, estimating that there must be more than fifty women involved in the ceremony, while even more men, some wearing *ktebetei* hats, others sporting *kalpak* headgear, stood outside.

Despite feeling somewhat an imposter Olga stood in the sunlight, observing from a short distance, listening in reverential silence to the commencement of the formal ceremony of mourning, led by the Mullah from a white sheeted podium situated between the two gers. Alymkulov's widow, Ayana, stood a few steps behind him. After a few minutes of wailing prayer, the Mullah stepped back down, greeted the widow with a short bow, and walked towards the house.

Before Olga could come to a decision about what to do next, Mrs Alymkulov strode towards her and grasped her hands.

"Thank you for coming, Olga."

"Mrs Alymkulov."

"Oh please, call me Ayana."

Olga was surprised, shocked, not only that Mrs Alymkulov would remember her name, but that she would welcome her so warmly, as if she was a family friend or relative. She was a beautiful woman, in her early fifties. She was also, thought Olga, bright, not one to forget, even in the midst of grief, a name or a face.

Olga apologised for her proprietor's absence, explaining that he was away and wouldn't even be aware of her husband's passing, but that she would inform him as soon as he returned on Monday morning. She didn't like to mention he was away on a fishing expedition. It seemed a rather cruel, unnecessarily flippant detail at such a time.

Ayana, though, did not seem to mind Kurmanbek's absence or even his lack of awareness of her husband's passing. Olga was a little taken aback by it all, wondering why Ayana didn't seem to be behaving like the grieving widow that she herself remembered being when Kylich had died.

Perhaps Ayana, twenty years younger than her late husband, was comforting herself in the knowledge that the beautiful, tree bordered estate in which they stood, would now belong to her.

Whatever Olga's speculative excesses during their stroll around the southern perimeter of the garden, Ayana insisted that Olga join her and other invited guests inside the house *'to honour my husband, his life, his death and his memory.'*

Put like that, Olga had little choice but to accept. They strolled, arm in arm towards the house, Olga aware of her time restraints. She thought about her schedule, her desire to get the obituary to Batyrov as soon as possible for his approval. He would send it to design and it would be printed in time for the Monday edition of the paper. Olga knew that newspaper deadlines could be a breathless business. She would first need to swing by the office to pick up the file on Alymkulov which was kept in a cabinet in Askar's office. She would head there as soon as she had a couple of quotes from mourners.

Ayana left Olga at the door and headed towards one of the wine waiters for a whispered word in his ear, before joining a group of three smartly suited men who greeted her formally. Respectfully. She wondered, should she leave, now that she had spoken with the widow? No. Not without a quote from one of the guests. But who?

While she weighed up the options, a glass of a seductively perfumed and extremely expensive Lagyl Arba Saperavi Reserve 2014 was presented to her on a silver tray with such grace that she didn't have the heart to say 'no'.

"It's central Asia's finest, Miss Kola," commented the wine waiter, a pristine white cloth draped over his right arm, "and this particular wine's best year, I believe. 2014."

"Oh," Olga exclaimed with some surprise, "I had no idea. Of course. Thank you."

No sooner had he said it, than he had moved on to the next empty glass, leaving Olga wondering how he would know her name. She decided that it didn't really matter. Right now, she was, apparently, holding a very expensive glass of wine in her hand. She really ought to try it. She put the glass to the rim of her nose, as if a connoisseur judging at an international wine festival.

"Mmmm. Seductively sweet vanilla tones, hints of cherry and almond, a suggestion of tannins and some underlying nutty shades."

She was churning out all of the cliches she could muster in her mind, none of which seemed to resemble the wine she was tasting which in reality had a smooth, rich, glowing taste which warmed her lips.

She stood in the orange hallway and listened to the light hearted hum of conversation and laughter coming from inside the spacious room to her right. She was beginning to wonder whether this was more a celebration than a wake.

She took a second, longer drink. The glass, from being full just seconds earlier, was now half empty. Pleasant as it was, she began to consider her circumstances, actively pondering her journalistic responsibilities. Maybe she would have one more glass of wine and then depart.

As she glanced around the room, pondering her options, the wine waiter appeared from nowhere and replenished her glass. Olga didn't resist.

58

Saturday afternoon, Mira

Two cars pulled up outside the Ambassador's residence simultaneously. Out of the first one stepped Joe Ramirez, who had been to the airport to pick up the agent who had travelled in from Romania. Carrying a dark green holdall, he made his way into the residence, closely followed by Ramirez.

The Ambassador's personal secretary, Michael, was at the door to usher them in. There was no ceremony.

The other car was driven by the Kazakh based agent. He had been held up at the the Ak-Tilek border crossing on his drive from Almaty. What should have been a straightforward four-hour drive had taken nearly six. But he had arrived.

The other two agent had been at the residence for a couple of hours, having made the relatively short journey from Chatyr Tash earlier that afternoon. Ramirez made the introductions, and handshakes were exchanged. The Ambassador, standing at the head of the table in front of two angled stars and stripes flags, wasted no time in setting the assignment.

"Welcome gentlemen. I'm glad you were able to make such good time and I'm sorry for the short notice, but you will appreciate, there are reasons for the urgency. I have been on the phone with Secretary of State Miller in Washington for much of the day and we have full US government authority for your co-ordinated mission, which is to be carried out tonight. I apologise again that you have little time to prepare, but the President herself has expressed to us via Mr Miller how extremely urgent and important these assignments are to protect US interests in this region and beyond. I cannot give any further information at this stage, suffice to say that failure to deliver on the mission to which we have been assigned, is not an option."

The Ambassador slid a beige folder to each of the four officers around the table. His secretary looked on.

"Officers Ryan and Johnson, you will access this man's apartment and relieve him of his mobile phone. His name is Temir Batyrov, a journalist. Here is his address. His photograph is in your folders. Do what you need to do to obtain it but under no circumstances is he to come to any harm. When you have the mobile phone in your possession, you will bring it back here for safe keeping before it makes its diplomatic passage to Washington. Officers Patten and Willock, you are charged with bringing down a floor in this building, the Star Building, without casualties. In your folders is a picture of the building. The address is in your file. It is three storeys and the office you will take down is on the third floor.

The objective is to destroy any paper trail or written content that might relate to that which we are seeking to dismantle. Mr Miller thinks that arson is too risky an option. So he has ordered a controlled, internal explosion, sufficient to decimate the floor, but not enough to bring down the whole building or adversely affect content or activity on the two floors below. I realise of course, that there may be some damage and they will probably be out of commission for a few weeks while any subsequent police investigation is carried out. We can't help that. It's not our problem. Ramirez has done a risk assessment which tells us that the two offices below are rented out we think by an insurance company and real estate. Also, they are open only on weekdays, and in working hours, so they will be empty tonight. The third floor is the one we are interested in. It houses the editorial Bishkek Daily News office, but it tends to use satellite, freelance journalists for its weekend copy and only has four or five full time employees, none of which work at night. The office is manned during the day on Saturdays but only until 5 or 6pm.

So you will enter the building this evening, and set the timed explosives as instructed in your orders. According to Ramirez's profiling of the types of businesses in the area, it is highly unlikely that other employees or members of the public, passers by and so on, will be in the vicinity. But be careful. Our instructions are 'no casualties'. When your mission has been accomplished, and only when it has been accomplished, you will call myself or Michael here, and confirm. At that point, you will destroy your folders by fire. Gentleman, you will have noted that these are Category 1 assignments. I repeat, failure to succeed in carrying them out is not an option. Once accomplished, you will head to Manas region where reservations have been made in two airport hotels as detailed in your folders. Tomorrow afternoon, you will depart from Manas airbase back to the US via RAF Benson in the UK. Are there any questions?"

While the Ambassador was speaking, the men were looking through their folders. Apart from a couple of photographs, there was some written content, a timed itinerary for both assignments and an email confirmation of the two hotel reservations.

"No questions? Thank you, gentlemen. You have your orders. Michael will provide you with the necessary assists from our armoury before you leave. He'll show you out when you are ready."

The four men stood up and placed their hands to their chests. The Ambassador saluted the men.

"God's speed and safety to you all."

The four agents saluted the Ambassador.

"God bless America."

And with that, the room cleared.

59

Saturday early evening, the Alymkulov Estate

Olga was on her third, or possibly fourth, glass of wine when she glanced out of the window of the Alymkulov mansion. The two white *gers* shone brightly in the gathering dusk. Time was moving on. Darkness was beginning to approach and here she was, in deep conversation about her life in journalism with the family's silver haired lawyer, Mr Osmonaliev. Having identified him as someone who might offer a word of tribute to his late friend and client to enhance her obituary, she had introduced herself to him some 40 minutes earlier. It wasn't part of the schedule. And it was a mistake.

Mr Osmonaliev had enjoyed too many glasses of Arak and was in no state to offer condolence or tribute to anyone, preferring to indulge himself in complementing Olga in slurred words on her attire while eyeing her cleavage.

She listened to this man with some contempt for over ten minutes. Why was he even there if he was just going to get drunk? As an aside, Olga was also wondering why, if he was going to consume too much alcohol, he would choose Arak over the much smoother and more expensive Arba wine with which to do it.

When he finally made his drunken move, enquiring about the possibility of them *'making each other's acquaintance a little better after the funeral,'* it was, she thought, time to go.

She searched the room for a clock. Ten past six. She had been at the ceremony for nearly four hours.

Feigning shock at the time, she swallowed the last of the wine in her glass and hurriedly left the room, the house and the estate, jumping on to the nearest *marshrutka*. She hadn't even said goodbye to her host, but with over one hundred people in the house and grounds, Olga gambled that her hurried exit, in the gathering gloom of the evening, wouldn't be noticed, at least not by anyone other than the lecherous Mr Osmonaliev.

Fuelled by time constraints and feeling annoyed for drinking too much wine, she stared out of the window into the darkness, trying to think clearly about how her evening would pan out. This morning, everything had seemed so straightforward. She looked forward to fulfilling her journalistic responsibilities in a measured and orderly way. But as she had often learnt to her cost, media life is never what it seems, especially when a rich, mature red gets in the way.

She contemplated her next move as the bus trundled its way back along Michurina Street. Even though it was later than was planned, she decided she would call her parents. Then she would take a taxi to the office to collect the written file on Mr Alymkulov. She would go home and write the obituary and send the draft to Batyrov before going to bed. All being well, she would be in bed by midnight. She allowed herself a little smile before a bump in the road alerted her to a developing headache. She rested her head against the window, wondering if she was up to writing an obituary at all that evening. Maybe she should get up early and go to the office first thing Sunday morning, write the piece and file it, all before 10am, leaving the rest of the day free for her to meet with her friend. She would see how things went. And then she remembered. Genocide. Imminent genocide. Ashamed of herself, she began to weep, her forehead pressed against the window.

The *marshrutka* made its stop outside her home around 6.45pm. She staggered up the stairs to her first floor apartment and fumbled the key into the lock. Her hand reached inside and stroked the wall, feeling for the light switch. As soon as she clicked it on, the lighting flickered for a moment before going off, leaving her in total darkness. "*Blin…blin!*" she cried out in frustration.

She suspected it was one of Bishkek's regular power cuts which always seemed to happen at the most inconvenient moments!

She managed to switch her mobile torch on and make her way along the short hallway towards the living room, carefully avoiding a small table on which sat a vase of bright orange *Germeras* offset with some white *Edelweiss*, a gift from Roza for helping her with one of her stories during the week. By the time she had successfully negotiated her way to the sofa, she had completely forgotten her agenda for the evening. Removing the *jooluk* from her neck, she slumped down on the sofa, and fell fast asleep.

60

Saturday evening, Bishkek

After they had left the Embassy, Ryan and Johnson went straight to Batyrov's address where they quietly and efficiently installed a powerful sleeping gas pellet into the outside vent of his apartment. Activation would be remote and impact immediate.

They had a good view of his apartment from the window seat of the Bishkek Beer Cellar, often frequented by Batyrov himself after a long day at the office. They were both on their second bottle of mineral water when, at 7.55pm, Batyrov came into view. He was accompanied by a female. The US agents hadn't anticipated that he would have company. There was no mention of Batyrov having a wife or a female companion, in their folders. Not that it would deflect them from their mission though.

They waited for the couple to enter and as soon as the light went on, Johnson activated the tiny remote device without even removing it from his right hand pocket. A masterclass of disablement.

"Sweet dreams," said Ryan.

The two men clinked their glasses together triumphantly and left the bar.

They entered the block and stood outside the door of Batyrov's ground floor apartment. There was no conversation or sound coming from within. Silence.

"Never fails," said Ryan as he took a flimsy looking rubber face mask from his pocket and placed it over his nose and mouth.

Meanwhile, Johnson played around with the lock. Within seconds, Ryan was in the apartment. Batyrov and his female companion were laid out, him on the floor and she sprawled out over the sofa in a rather undignified pose, her legs wide apart, her underwear half hidden, the rest in plain sight. They had at least an hour before the couple would recover their senses, but Ryan didn't waste any time searching for Batyrov's mobile phone, which he found in his jacket pocket. He joined Johnson outside, nodded to him, took his face mask off and closed the door. No one was around. It was all over in a matter of seconds. The first part of their mission was accomplished. All that remained for them to do was deliver the phone to the Ambassador's residence in Mira.

Patten and Willock meanwhile were parked up in Razzakov Street, looking up at the three storey Star Building which, they noted with relief, was in darkness, save for a small security light coming from inside the front entrance. The two men went around the back and climbed the external fire exit stairway, negotiating a narrow balcony which reached halfway around the perimeter. They checked the fire door and skylight, both of which were securely locked, so

349

they ended up breaking the window which they thought would give them the easiest access into building. According to the plans in their folders, there were three main rooms on the top floor, as well as a bathroom, a storeroom, a utility room and a kitchen, all separated from each other by plywood partitions. Patten accessed the office first and switched on his low density torch beam to look around. He calculated that for maximum destruction, he would place explosives under the desks in the three offices and one in the utility area, which was the first room you would come to if you were entering via the office's front entrance. That, he calculated, would be sufficient to destroy the whole floor. Willock watched his colleague in action, admiring his quick, efficient and ordered approach to the task in hand. Patten was a seasoned expert in explosives, a former US marine who had served in Afghanistan. For him, this was a relatively simple job. Except for the safe.

Willock was playing with the dial, wondering whether he would need some explosive help to facilitate access to its contents. He didn't. It was an old safe, a Russian *Pratekt*, one he'd come across several times before. It didn't take him long to crack the code.

Once the explosives were set, connected to each other and placed in position, Patten set a timer for midnight, by which time he and his colleagues would be safely tucked up in bed at their hotels near Manas.

The clock on the timer begun to tick as they climbed out of the window, made their way down the emergency stairs and walked back to their car. Now, all they had to do was inform the Ambassador, head to Manas, and get some sleep.

61

Saturday morning, White House, Washington

Back in Washington, Kendrick Richardson and his pony-tailed colleague high-fived each other. His other hand held a mobile, glued to his ear, awaiting his boss to answer.

"Mr Miller, sir. The elimination of internet and server access, including its history, of the Bishkek News Corporation's IP address and cloud, has been activated. Server de-activation is timed for 14:01 hours in Washington; one minute past midnight, Sunday morning, Bishkek time."

Miller didn't need to ask any further questions. Kendrick was the best of his kind in the business and had never let him down.

"Thank you Kendrick. Are you staying here or are you heading home?"

"I'll be staying, sir. Once it has happened, I will leave."

"Ok, but keep your mobile phone switched on for the rest of today….just in case. And Kendrick. Good work. Thank you."

The two-pronged operation's chronology had been decided by Miller, who knew that timed coordination was the key. Even if by only a minute, the destruction of the Bishkek News office had to happen before its internet was disabled, so as not to draw any attention to the hacking of the newspaper's system.

Now all that Miller needed to hear was that the incriminating audio had been located and secured. He would await the call from his Ambassador in Bishkek.

xxx

Ryan and Johnson arrived back at the Ambassador's residence around 8.20pm, just 20 minutes after they had retrieved the mobile from Batyrov's apartment. Johnson got out of the cab and rang on the doorbell. The Ambassador himself answered the door. No words were spoken as he handed the Ambassador the phone. He nodded his approval and closed the door. Johnson joined Ryan back in the cab, their work complete. The two men headed out of Bishkek towards Manas.

No sooner had the Ambassador placed Batyrov's phone in his study safe than his mobile rang. It was Patten.

"Sorry sir, I tried to call Michael, but he isn't answering. Operation successfully completed. Expect to hear some news at midnight. Heading to Manas now."

"Good work, safe travels," responded the Ambassador, before concluding the call.

353

The Ambassador went to his study to access his Secure 18 communications option.

He informed Miller of the dual success of the operations and advised him to listen out for an alert from the US government's Asian desk a little after 1400 hours, Washington time.

"By then, sir, the Bishkek News Corp will cease to exist."

"Excellent. Get the mobile phone into a diplomatic bag and on the next flight out of Bishkek. Good work."

Miller replaced the handset without awaiting the Ambassador's response, and a red light confirmed the conclusion of the call.

He sat back, a cup of camomile tea in *Washington Redskins* mug, and reflected calmly on the events of the past 24 hours. He allowed himself a moment of self congratulation.

The mobile phone was in American hands, the explosives were in place, ready to bring down the Star Building in Bishkek in a few hours' time, and the newspaper's internet was about to be disabled. Success.

So why did he have mixed feelings about it all?

Maybe exhaustion was catching up with him. And guilt. Working 18 hours solid, catching only a couple of overnight hours sleep in his White

House office along the way, was not conducive to either his physical or emotional wellbeing, let alone the needs of his family.

Not for the first time in his career, he had missed his son's baseball game that morning. His wife would be livid. His son subdued. Both had become used to his absences.

'Where *do* my loyalties lie?' he had often asked himself.

He should have been feeling ecstatic. Instead, he found himself staring at the floor, tired and sad. Once again, duty had triumphed over family. One day, maybe, he would reap the consequences of his choices.

He took a sip of his steaming tea before lifting his heavy frame from the seat to exit Secure 18.

He walked the corridor towards the exit, past the security guard, the same one who had let him in minutes earlier.

"Good day, sir."

"Good day, officer.

62

Late Saturday evening, Olga's apartment; Star Building

Olga awoke with a start, feeling heady. A light had come on in the hallway and the familiar hum of kitchen appliances clicked into life. The electricity was back on.

She looked at the clock on the wall. 11.35pm. She had slept for almost five hours.

She went to the kitchen and filled a glass with water. She felt disappointed with herself. Angry even. She had missed her call with her family and still had to write up the obituary. While most of Bishkek was taking to its bed, Olga knew that any further sleep would be impossible any time soon. She was wide awake albeit with a mild hangover. Glass of water in hand, she stared into the hall mirror but didn't like what she saw.

"Most people have a hangover in the morning," she muttered. "Trust me to get one in the evening."

She needed to retrieve the situation. She decided then and there that she would get a taxi to the office to access the file on Alymkulov, then write up the obituary as soon as she got back, before trying to snatch a few hours sleep. That way she would meet her deadlines. If she went now, she would be there and back within the hour. She slipped out of the tight-fitting dress that she had worn to the wake that afternoon, and into some comfortable grey track suit trousers, a green T Shirt and navy jumper. She picked up a dark brown jacket on her way out and headed down Malikova Kubnychbeka towards the taxi rank on Ammosova. By 11.55pm, she was outside the Star Building. Razzakov Street had never seemed so dark. So quiet. She asked the taxi driver to wait for her while she went inside. All was completely silent, eerie even, as she headed towards the entrance. Olga let herself in and pressed the arrow. She counted the numbers as they changed, one by one. The elevator came to a shuddering halt at 3, and the doors opened. She unlocked the main door to the office, as she had done so many times before, and put the low energy light on. It took its time to light up the reception area, but it was all she needed. She noticed the digital desk clock on Ednan's desk. Its bright white numbers spelled out 11.58. She went to the filing cabinet next to Roza's desk and opened the A-D draw.

"Alymkulov. Alymkulov. Where are you?" she whispered to herself as she ran her fingers across the buff folders. There you are."

She removed the file, feeling good that she was beginning to take back control of her agenda after a wasted evening. She pushed the metal drawer back, a little harder than she intended. A loud, exaggerated clunk, metal on metal, broke the night silence, making her jump. She was ready to leave.

As she turned towards the door she felt something beneath her feet and looked down. She was standing on a cable, which ran from under Roza's desk, along the floor towards the storeroom. She was curious about the cable.

"That wasn't there yesterday," she announced, to no one in particular.

She followed its course around the office, its pathway leading in two directions, one to the storeroom and another to the open plan office.

The desk clock changed its digits. 11.59pm.

Outside, the taxi driver lit up an Apollo-Soyuz and wound down his window. He rested his arm on to the side and stared into the darkness ahead. He breathed a long line of smoke out, which drifted and separated itself into the black of night. It had been a long day.

'I think I'll make this my last fare,' he mused.

63

Saturday night, Sunday morning, Bishkek

Three hours earlier, a disoriented Batyrov woke up. His female companion was still out cold. He carried her to the bedroom, removed her shoes, and lay her on the bed. He looked around the apartment in a vain attempt to work out why they ended up asleep in their clothes, sprawled out on the floor. In the end, all he could think of was the possibility that the oysters that they had consumed earlier in the evening had affected them in some way. Food poisoning, perhaps?

He searched for his phone. He couldn't locate it anywhere.

Maybe his companion had picked it up.

He went back into the bedroom and began to rummage through her coat pockets and loose clothing. Just as he was searching her handbag, she woke up.

"What are you doing?"

She quickly realised however that raising her voice was not making her feel any better. She fell back on to the pillow, her hand to her forehead.

"What are you doing?" she asked again, this time more gently.

Batyrov explained his dilemma and asked if she had picked up his phone in the restaurant. It took Dayana some time to compute his question. She shook her head and closed her eyes again.

"I'll get you some aspirin," he said. "We must both have had some food poisoning. I feel the same way."

A minute later, he was back in the bedroom with a glass of water and two aspirin tablets. He looked at her. She was in the foetal position, soundly asleep.

He picked up her phone from the side table and called his number. No ring tone in the apartment, and no response.

In the living room was his wallet. He emptied the contents on to the coffee table. Four business cards dropped out. Roza's was one of them. He called her.

"Roza. I'm sorry to call you. But I've lost my phone."

Despite the lateness of the hour, she immediately grasped the seriousness of the situation.

"It's ok. I hadn't gone to bed. Did you download the recording?"

He paused, taking in the magnitude of the loss, his stupidity in not downloading the audio file on to an external hard drive. Batyrov was downcast.

"No. No, I didn't. I'll look around here again."

He kicked out at a chair, missing the lower leg and hitting his shin on the cross bar.

"Naalat, men kantip kelesoo boldum. Naalat, naalat."

Roza ignored his angry oral explosion.

"You mustn't blame yourself, Temir. It may turn up. Where did you last see it?"

"I'm sure I had it when I came home."

There was a pause….

"Unless…" ventured Roza.

Batyrov knew what she was about to ask. It had already crossed his own mind.

"What if someone knew about the recording and wanted to obtain it. Is it possible that it's been stolen?"

Batyrov thought about his evening, about how he and Dayana had both passed out together in the apartment; their headaches; his lost phone. Even though there was no obvious indication that his apartment had been broken into he couldn't account for the time that he was out cold, whether drugged or asleep. Batyrov was suspicious, but there was little more he could do at 9.30pm on a Saturday evening.

"OK, let's leave it for now and hope it turns up. I'll have another look now and again in the morning. And I'll call the restaurant just in case. Sorry to have troubled you Roza."

Two and a half hours later they were back on the phone to each other. Roza had been awoken by a loud explosion. She sat up in bed, her ears ringing, her mind numb with fear. She was sure that her building shook a little. An earthquake? A gas explosion? A bomb?

She put on her sidelight and looked at the wall clock. It was just after midnight.

She jumped out of bed and made for the window. Across Bishkek, she could see flashes of light, and smoke, thick black smoke, travelling north across the city skyline, obscuring some of the bright lights of the late night Chuy bars and nightclubs.

She opened the window and leaned out as far as she was able. The noise and smoke were coming from south-east of the city. For a fleeting moment, she allowed herself to think the worst. The Bishkek Daily News offices were located there.

But surely not. Mindful of earlier events in Batyrov's flat and his missing phone she decided to call him on the number he had called her on earlier. He had been awakened by the explosion too.

"I will put Euro News on," he said. "Stay on the line." Neither of them really suspected that the explosion might have been anything to do with the Star Building. They were simply treating it as just another potential news story which would need to be covered by one of them, or Olga, if she could be persuaded at this late hour. Neither suspected that Olga might *be* the story.

Central Asian 24 hour news was on, but there was no mention of an explosion. Maybe it was too soon. Or maybe it was just a gas explosion, not worthy of broadcast.

"I'll go down there, Roza. Probably just a gas leak. You go back to bed. Thanks for the call."

Batyrov got himself dressed, wrote a note for his friend, who was still asleep, and headed down Moskovskaya Street towards Razzakov.

The streets were quiet, save for a few drunken souls in doorways, the odd taxi passing by. It was chilly.

He felt uncomfortable about the mysterious events of the evening and his mind turned to his companion, sound asleep in his bed. He had only been out with her two or three times, and was still getting to know her.

"What must she think?" he wondered as he crossed over Toktogul Street.

Batyrov hadn't enjoyed any female company since his wife died nine years previously, so his recent chance meeting with Dayana, a nurse, seemed timely.

A couple of weeks earlier, he had been out on his early morning jog along Adyshev Street, in the south west of Bishkek. It was his favourite running route, away from the smog of Bishkek life. After about ten minutes, he stumbled and fell, causing abrasions to his hands and knees. He limped around the corner into Ulitsa Ayni, and to the gates of No 4 Hospital where he bumped into Dayana, one of the nurses, arriving for her shift. She helped him inside and dealt with his abrasions.

Two days later, they were enjoying each other's company in the upmarket Vinoteka Bar in Chuy, known for its extensive range of fine wines. Tonight had been only their third date. It would be one that they would both remember for a long time.

64

12.05am Sunday, Vefa

Ormanbekov called Kulov just after midnight.

"What was *that?*" asked the President.

"You heard it then, Feliks? I have called Ergashev and his deputy and the security forces. He is on his way there with the fire services."

"Where?"

"We think it's in Razzakov Street."

"Mmmm…. Isn't that where Kurmanbek has his newspaper office?"

"It could be just gas or an electrical fault," said Akayev.

"Then again," retorted Ormanbekov, "it could be terrorist related or…."

He was thinking aloud, something he had become good at over the years.

"….if it *is* the office of the Daily News, maybe someone is keen to silence an upcoming story."

Akayev considered Ormanbekov's speculative words but didn't comment.

"Keep me informed."

Ormanbekov hung up and returned to his bed.

He woke up at 6am to five missed messages from Akayev and several others from Ergashev, his Chief of Police. He made himself a green tea, went to his study and called his Prime Minister.

"What do we have Kadrjvan?"

Akayev was still in bed, trying to catch a few hours sleep ahead of what he knew was going to be a busy day ahead.

"It *was* the newspaper office," confirmed Akayev. "Ergashev and the fire people think it may have been deliberate. There is only top floor damage, though there is some ceiling damage to the second-floor office and some street debris. They have also found a body, a woman. She has been taken to the district morgue for identification."

Ormanbekov did not react.

"Message me when you know more," he said abruptly, before concluding the call.

65

Sunday morning, Star Building

Batyrov was in shock. It was 1.15am on a Sunday morning. He was standing on the corner of Moskovskaya and Razzakov, surveying the grim scene less than one hundred metres ahead.

As he looked upwards at the smoking building, he wondered what was going on in his life. In one evening, he had lost his phone with incriminating evidence on it; he had passed out in his own flat, a victim of food poisoning or something more sinister, and now, it looked like he had lost his place of work to an electrical fault, arson, or some kind of explosion. What was happening? Who was targeting him, or the newspaper?

Emergency vehicles lit up the scene. Two fire appliances, several police vehicles, an army truck, and an ambulance stood stationary at all angles outside the Star Building.

Why is there an ambulance there, Batyrov wondered?

He had to wait half an hour before he got his answer. Two medics in protective clothing emerged from the ground floor entrance. They were wheeling out a trolley, on which was lying what looked like a body bag. Batyrov's heart missed a beat as he strained his eyes to see more clearly, pressing himself forward into the tape which had been stretched across the junction where he was standing.

He had to find out more. Kurmanbek and Askar would not be returning from their fishing trip until Sunday evening, probably another 18 hours, Roza was at home, asleep, Olga too. He only had Dayana's phone for company.

He slipped beneath the tape and approached the building.

"Daroo toktot, daroo toktot."

A young policeman emerged from the shadows, waving his arms at Batyrov, ordering him to stop immediately.

"I work in that building," said Batyrov, pulling himself together. "Can I be of assistance?"

"Let me see your identification."

Batyrov may have lost his phone, but he still had his wallet. He showed his national identity card to the policeman.

"Come this way."

Batyrov followed him.

"Wait here."

A few minutes later, two men appeared from the interior of the building. One of them was Ergashev.

"Who are you?" he asked abruptly.

"My name is Temir Batyrov, a journalist with the Bishkek Daily News. What has happened here?"

"Take his statement," Ergashev ordered his colleague, before walking back towards the building.

Batyrov, still in shock, was not going to argue. He sat down on a side wall, a police colleague of Ergashev's standing over him.

"Before I give you my statement, can you tell me please, did I see the medics removing a body from the scene?"

"You know her?" enquired the policeman.

"A woman? Who was she?"

"She has gone to the morgue to be identified, what's left of her."

Batyrov looked to the ground. Tears welled up in his eyes. Apart from the owner, who lived in Kochkor in the Naryn region to the south of Bishkek, only six people had access to the office building; the site manager, who only came in when there was a problem, Shirin Kurmanbek, Ednan Askar, Roza Beshimov, himself....and

369

Olga Kola. He knew that Roza was at home and his two male colleagues were away on their fishing trip.

If it was a woman, it had to be Olga.

"Jok, jok, jok, jok," whispered Batyrov to himself. "Please, no."

"You knew this woman?" enquired the policeman for a second time, without emotion.

"I hope not," said Batyrov, solemnly. "But it may be my colleague, Olga."

At the whisper of her name, the policeman turned and walked away, returning a minute later with Ergashev.

"Come with us," he said, and they led him towards one of the police cars. It was 2am and some drops of rain were beginning to fall.

Batyrov remained silent throughout the journey. He was fearful of what lay ahead. The car, its blue lights flashing, headed south on Razzakov, turning right into Bokonbayev Street and left into Yakov Logvinenko Street.

After it passed Bishkek Railway station, it turned right into Lev Tolstoy Street before turning into Dooronbek Sadyrbayev. By this time, Batyorv was realising that the car was heading towards the junction of Gagarin Street and Adyshev Street, and its destination, No 4 hospital.

Of course. Dayana had told him that the hospital where she worked had a morgue. That is where they must have taken the body.

The police car arrived at the front entrance. It was raining heavily now.

The three men walked into the almost deserted hospital. Ergashev, showing his credentials, commanded a nurse who was sat in a tiny, glass walled office.

"Take me to the morgue."

The four of them walked the length of three corridors before arriving at a double swing door above which was a sign *'Ollukana'*.

An attendant sat at a small desk.

"She's in cubicle two. She will be attended to in the morning, maybe Monday morning," he said blandly.

Batyrov was shocked by the callousness of the attendant. He knew that the Kyrgyz health service had its challenges, but to leave a body unattended for 36 hours was not what he was expecting. Despite his anticipated grief, he allowed his journalistic antennae, just for a second or two, to consider the possibilities of an exposure story.

Ergashov spoke.

"Would you mind trying to identify the body? Let us know if it is your colleague? I am sorry to ask you this."

It was the first compassionate thing that the Chief of Police had said to Batyrov since they had been acquainted forty-five minutes earlier.

The attendant, dressed in white overalls, gave white face masks to the three men and they entered the morgue. It was dimly lit and cold.

Batyrov was scared. He walked in with his head bowed. He had no desire to lift his eyes to the form that was lying on a trolley. But he knew that he must.

The attendant removed a sheet from the body. The remnant of what had been a beautiful woman lay motionless on the trolley before Batyrov's moistened eyes. Her hands had been placed together and were laid on her burned torso. Her face, arms and legs were part exposed, covered only by remnants of scorched clothing.

Batyrov looked at them, one by one. Loose fitting grey track suit trousers, a green T Shirt and a navy jumper. Some unidentifiable belongings were lying idle in a plastic tray to the side of the trolley. The remains of a dark brown jacket hung from one corner of the trolley. A simple beige card with some numbers on it was attached to her bloodied ankle.

It was Olga.

Batyrov was driven back home. He was numb with grief. Twenty minutes after leaving the mortuary, he was released into the damp street outside his apartment. He mumbled his thanks to Ergashov and his driver.

The car drove away but Batyrov stood outside his door, not knowing what to do, what to say, and even how to say it, even if there was someone there to say it to. He had no mobile phone, a woman he barely knew was in his bed, and his editor and the proprietor were out of contact. And then there was Roza, his friend; Olga's best friend. How would he break the news to her?

He wasn't even thinking about the atrocity that was taking place below ground. Perhaps it had already happened. All that his mind could compute was the loss of his colleague.

He looked at his watch. It was 3.15am.

He walked away from the door back towards the main road. There was very little traffic. A taxi would be a forlorn hope at that time of the morning. He wanted to get to Roza. He was not going to give her the tragic news over the phone. But walking to her flat and waking her up in the middle of the night to tell her that her work colleague was dead was perhaps not his best option. He would wait until morning. He turned and slowly walked the few metres back to his apartment.

Dayana was still in bed, asleep. He removed his clothes, put on some nightwear, got into bed and held her, tightly.

66

Sunday morning, Batyrov's apartment

Dayana, feeling much better after a long sleep, brought a cup of hibiscus tea to Batyrov. It was 7.15am. He had managed a few hours sleep but even she could see that he was exhausted.

He opened his eyes and looked at his watch.

"I need to get up."

"You need a cup of tea."

They sat on the bed together, revisiting the strange and tragic events of the evening before. Resting his head upon Dayana's warm chest, he allowed a few tears to emerge as he shared the moment he realised that Olga Kola was dead.

Then he spoke out a slow apology for his behaviour and for everything that had happened.

"It's ok Temir. It's ok....It's not your fault. I am so, so sorry."

"I worked with her for ten years. She still had her life ahead of her."

Dayana held him tightly. Even in his grief, Batyrov's journalistic mind was working overtime.

"But what was she doing there? Why? And at midnight? Something's not right."

Dayana stroked his cheek. He began to weep, uncontrollably, his body shaking as his tears emerged. The last time he had cried like this was a decade ago. It was in Osh Municipal hospital, after he had said his final goodbye to his wife.

Ten years on, Dayana didn't try to stop him. Working in a hospital, she had observed too often the grieving process. She knew that it took place in different ways, and that it needed to. This was Temir's time to grieve. Tears. Better now than later. After all, he would be the one to tell all of his colleagues, and possibly even make the call to Olga's family in Russia, later that day. He needed to be strong.

As his weeping slowed, Dayana got showered and dressed.

"It's going to be a long day ahead, Temir," she had said as she headed out of the door of the apartment to the baker's across the road. "Wait here."

Half an hour later they were dipping their fresh *kattamas* into sour cream. Batyrov didn't have much of an appetite but Dayana insisted that he eat something.

"My shift begins at lunchtime but I'll come with you to Roza's flat if you would like me to."

They arrived shortly before 10.30am. Roza was still in her pyjamas and was clutching a coffee cup when she opened the door. She had tears in her eyes. She put the cup down on the hall table and gave Batyrov a long, long hug.

"I know," she whispered in his ear. "I know."

The pair separated but held hands for a time, saying nothing. Batyrov wondered what she knew. Did she only know about the explosion? That it was their workplace? Or was there more that he would have to tell her?

"This is a friend of mine, Dayana. Dayana, this is my work colleague Roza Beshimov."

Dayana had a kindly face, a caring demeanour, a nurse's empathy. Roza offered her hand, but Dayana drew her in for a warm embrace.

"Come in, please. Sorry about the mess. I've been up since five, glued to the news. It's so frustrating. They only mentioned it a couple of times at midnight and then moved on to some stupid movie."

Dayana looked at Batyrov. He returned her stare. He would have to tell her.

"So it's true, Temir? The office is gone, blown to smithereens?"

"It's true," he said. "I saw it with my own eyes. The office is gone."

"But why? How? Was it deliberate do you think?"

"I don't know Roza. I don't know. It's too early to say."

Roza looked into her half empty coffee cup.

"Does Olga know?"

Batyrov drew breath. Dayana took his hand and squeezed it firmly. It was time. "Roza. I'm afraid...I'm afraid there's something I need to tell you.

67

Early morning, Sunday, Jalalabad, south Kyrgyzstan

The early morning mist had disappeared completely from the top of the Tien Shan mountains and by 11am, the light was almost Sorolla-esque in its beauty. Another hot day was underway.

In the Jalalabad region of the country, a motley group of farm workers, all known to the government, were gathered at a cutting which overlooked an exposed part of the pipeline. They would soon be getting on a truck for the short journey to the Fergana. All seemed calm.

The unstoppable torrent of water unleashed overnight along the 400 kilometres of pipe, from north to south, would have done its job. Now it was time for them to do theirs.

They had been paid handsomely and were awaiting instructions about locating and transporting the stacked up bodies from the exit of the underground pipeline to their final resting place, a large, newly dug mass grave hidden deep in one of the established walnut fruit forests. Thereafter, the grave diggers would remain silent for life. They knew their fate should they deviate from their orders and anyway, why would they when they each had a year's wages, in *som*, in their pockets?

Once their work was done, a second wave of disinfected, purifying water would follow during the day, cleansing the pipe in readiness for its primary function, the clean water transportation from the north of the country to Batken. There, aquifers and the newly renovated Alay Valley dam were set to store millions of litres of fresh water, ready to use as barter in trade deals with south Asian countries, '*Aid to Trade,*' as Ormanbekov liked to call it. Akayev's agreement with the President of Tajikistan would see a withdrawal of Kyrgyz troops from one of the disputed parts of the border in return for Tajik support in creating a safe land corridor for the water to pass through in tankers.

Ormanbekov had no qualms about unofficially sacrificing some Kyrgyz land in order to achieve ongoing safe passage for his water carrying vehicles. The violent skirmishes between the two countries, which had resulted in dozens of deaths on both sides of the border over many years, was put to bed. Tajikistan and countries to the south of it needed what Kyrgyzstan was offering and were willing to accept political compromise to get it. Endless supplies of water for hydro-electric power and agricultural needs, not to mention fresh drinking water for their populations, was a dangled carrot worth holding on to. The drought had only exacerbated those needs. Ormanbekov was meeting them. For a cost. It was exploitation, pure and simple.

Once again, the President had thought of everything. His power grab was set to succeed. The geo-political landscape of central Asia would be changed overnight.

Political turmoil would be released in the region's capitals. But there would be no comeback against Ormanbekov's masterplan.

He had gone to bed on Saturday night a satisfied man. This Sunday morning, he had awoken to a greater Kyrgyzstan.

68

Sunday lunchtime, Roza's flat

Roza was lying on her bed, having cried herself back to sleep, when her mobile phone rang.

She was shocked to see Kurmanbek's name come up on her screen. She didn't even realise that he knew of her existence, forgetting that it had been at her father's initiative that she had been brought to his attention. But he had never called her before or even met her. She sat up abruptly.

"Mr Kurmanbek!"

"Sorry to be calling you on a Sunday lunchtime, Miss Beshimov. I have tried calling Temir and Olga but they are not responding. My wife got word to me about the explosion via a local friend early this morning, so I am on my way back now with Ednan. I take it you are aware of everything?"

"Yes, I heard the explosion in the night. Temir has lost his phone or had it stolen. And Olga…."

"Anyway," interrupted Kurmanbek, "I am on my way back now with Ednan. We should be back around 6pm this evening. Would you be able to meet at my home at 7pm this evening to talk about what we will do? Temir has my address."

"Yes, of course, Mr Kurmanbek."

"And tell the others please. See you at 7. And don't worry, Roza. We will work something out."

Before Roza could say anything further, the solemn sounding Kurmanbek ended the call. He obviously hadn't heard about Olga and she hadn't been given the opportunity to tell him.

Roza fell back into her pillow. Grabbing a second pillow, she rammed it into her face to absorb more tears.

Just an hour earlier, Batyrov and Dayana had left Roza's apartment, giving her some space of her own to grieve. He accompanied Dayana to her workplace in time for her 10 hour shift. He asked her if she would like to return to his apartment after her shift ended, but she declined. She needed some time alone after the heavy night and frankly, she suggested, so did he. Her wisdom prevailed and anyway, she reminded him, he had things to sort out; a new mobile phone and getting in touch with his editor and proprietor. He would also have to continue to deal with the grief of losing a close friend.

"Of course, my phone."

He knew of a friend who ran a refurbished mobile phone kiosk on Zelenaya, but Batyrov figured it would be closed on Sunday. He headed for the Bright Lights Lounge, a down market bar on Bokonbayev, in the hope of finding him there.

"Red Sun please."

The bartender poured out the rich, ruby beer. Batyrov followed the beer on its short journey from bottle to glass. He was ready for a drink.

"Has Jyral been in?" Batyrov enquired. The bartender didn't say anything but pointed back over Batyrov's shoulder at a man sitting at a round table. He was reading Saturday's edition of the Bishkek Daily News.

Batyrov took a sip of his beer, pausing to look at Jyral, his head buried deep in the paper's sports pages. Batyrov wondered for a moment whether his friend might unknowingly be reading the newspaper's very last issue.

"Temir, greetings my friend. Long time. How are you today?"

Batyrov sat down next to him, placed his beer on the table and they exchanged pleasantries. He was not going into the detail of what had just taken place. And it didn't seem as if Jyral knew anything about the explosion at the newspaper's premises. So he got to the point.

"I need to ask you a big favour, Jyral."

An hour later, the two men were walking away from Jyral's kiosk on Zelenaya Street, Batyrov the proud owner of a newly refurbished, pay as you go Huawei mobile phone.

"I owe you, Jyral. Thank you."

"Ah, until next time," responded the jovial Jyral, before heading back to the Bright Lights Lounge, his copy of the Bishkek Daily news tucked firmly under his arm.

It was early afternoon. Batyrov dug Roza's card out of his wallet and called her on his new phone.

Roza picked up immediately. She was able to update him on Kurmanbek's call, and their proposed meeting at 7pm.

"We'll go together," offered Batyrov. "I will pick you up in a taxi at 6.45pm."

"One thing Temir. He doesn't know about Olga yet."

Batyrov paused. His mind went back to the morgue. Olga's body would still be lying there, covered up but unattended. He closed his eyes for a moment.

"I'll try to call him. He'll be on his way back now. Text me over his number on this phone."

69

Sunday morning, White House, Washington

Back in Washington, President Serenatti switched on CBN's Sunday morning *'Early Show'*. The programme's guests were reviewing the newspapers. The deal struck with the Kyrgyz government during the week for regional airspace featured as the lead in most of them, and was being generally well received by the commentators, who focused on its geo-political impact in the region and beyond. The overnight explosion in a central Asian capital was not attracting much attention, much to the relief of James Miller, the *Early Show's* political guest. It had happened too late for most of the newspapers laid out on the table in front of the panel. Apart from one, held up by one of the reviewers. A fireball picture lit up the page.

"Could it be a terrorist response to the deal?" she enquired of the host.

"Well, let's ask the man himself. Welcome, Secretary of Defence, James Miller."

The camera switched to Miller, already seated in his chair.

"Thank you for being with us this morning James. Shall we start with Lena's question about the explosion at a media office in the Kyrgyz capital. Gas explosion or terrorism? After all, Secretary of State de Layney was only there a few days ago. Coincidence? Do you have any information?"

Miller was well prepared, a polished response at the ready.

"Thank you Dan, for having me on. Lena, Brad. As far as the explosion is concerned, we have no information at this stage. Whatever the cause of the incident, which is for the Kyrgyz security authorities to deal with, we deeply regret the loss of life of a local journalist, as we understand it to be. It goes without saying that the US government deplores terrorism wherever it occurs, and, if this proves to be an act of terror, the Kyrgyz authorities can be assured of our full support in tackling any future threat in the region."

Serenatti stared at her TV monitor, staring right back at her from high up in her kitchen.

"I said, 'no casualties.'"

She paused the chewing of her croissant, mid-bite and picked up the phone.

"Ocean?"

De Layney's Press Secretary was taken aback.

"Madame President."

"It's ok Stoski. Call me Miriam. It's Sunday. Are you planning on going to church this morning?"

She already knew the answer. Ocean always tried to attend church on Sundays, wherever he was in the world.

"Affirmative, Miriam."

"I know it's short notice but I would like to come with you if I may. Can you let Pastor John know and make the security arrangements. My car will come by yours at 10.45am."

Ocean wondered why the President would choose today, and at such short notice, to advise of her intentions, but he was pleased nevertheless. He had extended an open invitation to several of his colleagues, including the President on numerous occasions, but few had taken him up on it. Until now. Perhaps she wanted to give thanks for the success of the joint operation which Miller had informed her about at 6.30am that morning. Perhaps.

Right on schedule, a motorcade, headed up by two police Electra Glide motorbikes, followed closely by the President's Cadillac and an unmarked police car to the rear, drew up outside Ocean's plush apartment on 9th Street NW in the Penn Quarter of DC.

He got in the back seat of the Stellar Black Metallic limousine, a career first for him. The car's interior was more spacious than it seemed from the outside. He sat back on the comfortable, ruby coloured leather seat, stretched out his long legs and placed his forearm on the large rest that separated him from the President.

As the convoy started up its journey again, Ocean continued to wonder why the President, his President, would want to travel with him to church. After all, he was just a humble press officer. But he managed a smile, which the President acknowledged with her own cautious greeting.

"Thank you, Stoski, for arranging everything this morning at such short notice."

Ocean stuttered out a response.

"It's fine, Madame President. I was attending anyway. It's good, I mean it's lovely, to have your company, this morning. It's fine. An honour."

Serenatti admired Ocean's faith which manifested itself in compassion and integrity. It was something that challenged her in her own role, in her own life. She thought of herself as a good person who knew right from wrong. She justified her more questionable actions as 'working for the greater good'. Today, she felt challenged.

An awkward silence followed as the Presidential car headed north up 9th Street, before Serenatti spoke again.

"Did you hear about the explosion in Bishkek overnight?"

"Yes. I did Madame President. I saw Mr Miller on *The Early Show'* this morning. And someone was killed. It's a tragic…."

"Oh please, Stoski. As I said, Miriam will suffice today."

" Yes Ma'am. It's, it's a tragedy….Miriam."

"That was us. We had to close the media operation down. They were asking too many questions. But we did it overnight in an effort to avoid any casualties. So I'm not happy."

Ocean stared ahead. De Layney, defying Serenatti's orders, had told him about the operation late on Saturday evening. He felt that he needed to know in case there was any fallout.

"But there won't be," de Layney assured his Press Secretary. "It's just something we need to do."

Ocean didn't know what he meant, but on this Sunday morning, he knew about the explosion, and the death. Even if the latter was unintended, it was down to the United States. Down to the woman sitting next to him.

He observed her out of the corner of his eye. Guilt. He had expected her to be triumphant, but instead he was seeing a side of her that he hadn't previously encountered. Compassion for an unknown, central Asian journalist.

As the convoy headed up 16th Street towards Lafayette Square, she suddenly leaned forward and switched off the in-car microphone below the sealed glass panel, denying the driver access to all back seat conversation.

She spoke softly.

"Find out what happened, who she was, if you can?"

"I will Ma'am."

"….who her family is, what hopes and dreams she had. Why was she at work at such a late hour?"

"Maybe she was one of the journos working on exposing Ormanbekov."

"And we might have killed her. We only wanted to destroy the evidence, not those who had dug it up."

Ocean was surprised by her candour but was beginning to realise why Serenatti had called him that morning. Guilt. Shame. She wanted….she needed to seek forgiveness. God's forgiveness. He looked over at her. Her head was turned away from his. Her hands were firmly gripping her knees. Here was a woman with repentance on her mind.

Lafayette was coming into view.

Worshippers were gathering at the steps and a few tourists and onlookers caught his eye before anyone began to take notice of the convoy in their midst.

"I want life for me to be as normal as possible this morning, Stoski. No frills. No fanfare. Just me. And God. My entrance will be from the front. I'll let Adams know that I want a light security presence."

Serenatti knew that it was good for her to be seen in church, indeed, her role required it. Often. And when that happened, her own Press Secretary would ensure that there was a media presence, often requisitioning the vestry to the east of the huge 19th century, Greek revival structure and turning it into a makeshift press room. But not today. No press. This was not official state business. This was Miriam Serenatti's own decision to do business with God. It was He who had convicted her that morning.

As the car drew up at the steps, Ocean observed her orders being carried out. A loose, human corridor of the President's security detail lined the upward steps towards the oak panelled door, the same entrance used by worshippers for over 300 years.

This Sunday, all seemed normal.

"Yesterday was the Saturday from hell," Serenatti told Ocean as the car stopped at the steps of St John's Church. "Now I need a little glimpse of heaven. I want to feel better about myself, Stoski, if only for an hour."

Ocean listened to her not as a President, not as his President, but as a person, a human being, and in that moment, a friend.

"Seeking God's forgiveness for our sins is what is required of us, Miriam. It's the only way that we can make sense of our lives. You're doing a good thing. This is a safe place."

Serenatti placed a gloved hand on Ocean's.

"Here we are."

70

Sunday evening, Vefa

Ormanbekov was keeping a low profile. Apart from taking a short stroll in Togolok Moldo Park with his security guard, he had spent most of Sunday at his home, reflecting on the overnight events in Razzakov Street. He did so in the company of Rachmaninoff and Prokofiev.

The destruction of the Bishkek Daily News, a shock to most normal thinking people, wasn't totally unwelcome news to the President. He was aware of the formidable Shirin Kurmanbek, who had never been afraid to post anti-government perspectives in his newspaper. He tended to blank him at functions but that didn't mean that he underestimated him.

"He could cause some trouble for us," Ormanbekov had once told Akayev. "Keep an eye on him."

Although it had been reported on some radio outlets, the explosion had not been the lead story on TV bulletins. Ormanbekov was relieved, concluding that it would simply turn out to be one of Bishkek's regular infrastructure failings. The less said about the affair, the better, unless some terrorist organisation claimed responsibility, of course. That would be a different matter.

Privately, Ormanbekov did have his suspicions, and had summoned the American Ambassador to the White House to find out whether the yanks knew anything about the explosion, and if they did, why they might have an interest in the Bishkek Daily News? The Ambassador would, of course, deny all knowledge of any interference by American Security Personnel on sovereign Kyrgyz territory, and refer the President to the statement issued by *his* President, Miriam Serennati, offering the US government's condolences for the loss of a Kyrgyz national in an unexplained explosion. But at least Ormanbekov could reassure his fellow parliamentarians that he was exploring all possibilities.

In parliament, his political opponents would ask questions about national and media security to which he could, with rare honesty, respond by saying that he had no idea who was behind the explosion.

If the explosion and murder was proven to be the work of a hostile presence, he would issue a statement denouncing the perpetrators, promising that *'those responsible for the death of the journalist, a Kyrgyz national, would be hunted down and brought to justice.'* Other than that, he would simply defer all other questions on the matter to his Prime Minister, Kadrjvan Akayev.

Ormanbekov had even instructed his press office to put out a statement suggesting that, while nothing untoward had yet been proven, media proprietors might consider reviewing their security arrangements in light of Saturday night's events. He liked to be seen to be doing something, everything, covering all bases, even if he was merely going through procedural motions.

71

Sunday evening, Kurmanbek's home

Shirin Kurmanbek opened his front door. His face was pale. Always the upbeat, shrewd businessman, respected, admired, and strong, he now looked deflated.

"Thank you for coming."

"Mr Kurmanbek. It's good to meet you."

Roza offered her hand. He took it.

"It's a pity that it is under such circumstances, Miss Beshimov."

They stepped into the marble floored hallway, brightly lit by a 24 bulb crystal chandelier which hung majestically from the ceiling. A vase of wild pink tulips adorned a carved wooden table beside the banister rail.

Askar was already in the living room, a large, open plan area with two sofas and what looked to Batyrov like a Grotrian-Steinwegg grand piano in one corner. On the wall above the fire place, on either side of a large mirror, hung two traditional folk lyres.

Batyrov had managed to call Askar and he had let Kurmanbek know about Olga.

‹

Askar got up and kissed Batyrov on both cheeks before shaking Roza's hand warmly. This was no time for hierarchical formalities. Or small talk.

Kurmanbek gestured them to their seats but remained standing. On the table in front of them was a carafe of water.

Kurmanbek spoke softly.

"Thank you all for coming this evening. Today is a tragic day in the life of the Bishkek News Corporation, and in our lives. We are all in shock. I am devastated, as you are. We have lost one of our own. Olga Kola has been a good and loyal servant to the newspaper. More importantly, she has been a good friend to each one of us. We will all miss her, each in our own way, and more than we can imagine. But let it be known that we will get to the bottom of how this tragedy happened, and if, as we suspect, Olga has been the victim of foul play, we will bring her murderers to justice, with or without police help."

Kurmanbek walked to a large, antique wooden dresser on which sat a tray. On it were four cut glasses. He poured four drinks.

"Please stand."

The four of them stood. He handed each of them a glass.

"We know that Olga enjoyed a good brandy. This is the best. For the best. Please join me in toast. Olga Kola."

"Olga Kola," they echoed in suppressed unison.

One, seamless swig and the glasses were empty, even Askar's who, despite having given up alcohol after his heart attack in 2020, decided that the extenuating circumstances surrounding this occasion warranted his participation.

He sat down, followed by Batyrov and Roza. Kurmanbek remained on his feet, his empty glass in his hand.

"The Bishkek News Corporation was started by my grandfather in the late 1920s against much opposition. He was a brave man, a fearless man. My father took it over when my grandfather passed, in the 1960s. I took it over in 1999. Friends, I have no intention of letting the tragic events of the past weekend threaten the future of the newspaper I love. I also believe that to close the title which Olga gave ten years of her life to would dishonour her memory. I do not believe that would be her desired wish and I will not let it happen. I intend to begin the process of resurrecting the newspaper from the ashes, immediately. Indeed, I have already begun."

Askar reached for his glass of water.

Kurmanbek put his glass on to the mantlepiece.

"I have spoken with colleagues in the media and also some trusted police contacts and they all agree that we have been targeted. Apart from the loss of our colleague in suspicious circumstances, we have also lost our premises. And overnight, it would seem that our IP address has been hacked and closed down. Temir's mobile phone with evidence of Ormanbekov's criminality on it has likely been stolen. It all leads me to believe that someone is trying to sabotage our work, our investigation into the Kyrgyz US deal, but as yet, we don't know who. Temir, please use your sources on the ground to find out more. I will speak with the American Ambassador and try to set up a meeting with Kadrjvan Akayev tomorrow, if he'll see me. It comes to something when it's easier for a Kyrgyz newspaper proprietor to arrange a meeting with the US Ambassador in the region than with his own country's Prime Minister!"

Batyrov offered a limp smile. Kurmanbek looked at Roza.

"Miss Beshimov. I want to ask. How are you feeling about all of this?"

Roza was thoughtful.

"I think we all feel a sense of loss, sir. What with Olga and everything, the explosion, Mr Batyrov's stolen phone....it just seems as if we have had the rug pulled from beneath our feet."

"Indeed, Miss Beshimov. It's a murky business. But I have to ask you. Do you feel able....are you willing to assist Temir in our investigations?"

Roza looked Kurmanbek in the eye.

"Olga was my friend. She helped me from my first day at the newspaper. I want justice for her. I would like to be a part of bringing that justice about."

Kurmanbek stared at the impressive young woman before him and gave the smallest of nods in her direction.

"Your father will be proud of you, Miss Beshimov. OK. We move forward as a team. We will rebuild when it feels appropriate. Meanwhile, Ednan will mobilise some extra freelance cover to help with the workload, freeing you, Roza, under Temir's guidance, to work on the aftermath of last night's...."

Kurmanbek's words tailed off as his wife Maryem entered the room. He introduced her to the guests.

"Would anyone like some tea or something else, some mineral water perhaps?" she asked.

They all politely declined her offer.

As the door closed behind her, Kurmanbek sat down in his chair, not an easy feat for such a large man. Once installed, he continued.

"OK. Logistics. As you may know, I own several satellite offices in and around Bishkek. One of them, located in Mederova Street, in the south east of the city has been empty for a while. It is just a five minute *marshrutka* ride from Razzakov Street. Carpenters have been there all afternoon, putting up shelves and storage. An IT team will set up a new computer network, with server and laptops first thing tomorrow morning. At 7am they tell me. All being well, by mid-morning, we should be looking at a modern, secure, firewalled internet system, the latest Chinese technology. I suggest that we all convene at the new premises at 10am. Number 25, Mederova Street. Second floor. Ednan will brief you on security going forward, but for the time being, I don't want anyone to know where we are operating from, until we know more about the circumstances of Olga's passing, and how the explosion occurred. Is that understood?"

He sat back in his chair, indicating that he had said all that he wanted to say for now.

"Ednan, any comments?"

The editor looked towards Temir and Roza, sat at the two ends of one of the large sofas, like book-ends on a mantlepiece with no books in-between.

"Temir, Roza. Shirin and I were discussing matters in the car on our way back to Bishkek this morning. We are very sorry that you have had to go through the traumatic events of this weekend alone. We considered whether to acknowledge

Olga's passing by closing down operations for a day or two, but as you know, the newspaper industry doesn't work like that. And we don't believe that Olga would have wanted us to do that. We also sensed that you would both want to avoid any delay in seeking out justice for Olga. If you need some time, please take it, but if you feel able to continue, then we will proceed at 10am tomorrow."

Temir and Roza acknowledged Askar with a nod.

"Good. Thank you."

He stood and faced Shirin, who began the process of getting himself out of the chair he was so comfortably sitting in. Roza and Temir took Askar's lead and stood up.

"Thank you for your hospitality, Shirin," said Askar shaking his proprietor's hand.

The three of them exited the house. Outside was a BMW. Kurmanbek's driver opened the rear door and ushered Batyrov and Roza in.

"Go home to bed and get a good night's sleep, if you can," Askar called out. "I will see you both in the morning. *Tunc uktoo.*"

He got into his car and drove off in the same direction as Kurmanbek's BMW. It was ten past eight. Tomorrow would be another day.

403

72

Monday morning, Jash Gvardiya

Batyrov felt rested and refreshed after a good night's sleep and was up early on Monday morning. He had made good use of his new phone, entering data on to it, including contact details of all the key people he would need to be in touch with.

One of those was Joroev who he had arranged to meet at 9am at his apartment, together with Roza. They both wanted to know if he knew anything about the explosion.

Roza was stood at the intersection of Jibek Jolu and Mahatma Gandi Street at 8.55am, when she spotted Batyrov. They greeted each other warmly, giving each other a brief hug.

Roza sighed.

"The morning after the weekend before," she said, as they walked down Jash Gvardiya Boulevard towards Joroev's apartment.

Joroev opened his door with caution. After the events of Saturday night, he didn't know who he was expecting to see. He had no idea why Batyrov and Roza would want to see him so early on a Monday morning. He looked scared.

"I don't know," Joroev would keep insisting in response to Batyrov's persistent questions.

"If you don't know anything, then your friend Ramirez might," said Roza, who had grown increasingly confident in her dealings with Joroev over time. "Find him and ask what's going on."

Batyrov and Roza, feeling frustrated by any lack of information forthcoming from their only accessible source, got up to leave. Batyrov had been particularly hostile in his questioning of Joroev, even though he couldn't come up with any reason why Joroev might know anything about the blowing up the offices of the Bishkek News Corporation. He had no motive for killing Olga either. He had only met her once, a few days earlier, at the Hyatt. No, the only possible explanation for Joroev's involvement might be linked to a fear of him being exposed as the man who had organised the leaking of the agreement to the newspaper. But even that was unlikely.

Before they exited the apartment to head to their new offices, Batyrov turned to face Joroev in one final, conciliatory effort at eliciting any information that he may be keeping to himself about the events of Saturday night.

"Look, Kamil. We have lost a colleague, and we have lost our evidence against Ormanbekov. We have also lost our working premises."

"Have you forgotten about our fellow nationals? Underground? responded Joroev."

Batyrov looked ashamed but Roza noted an unusual calm in Joroev's challenge to her colleague, a quiet calm which didn't make much sense. Where was the grief of the weekend? Maybe he had already come to terms with the demise of his patriots. Or maybe, just maybe, he knew something about their plight that he was keeping from them. Before she could compute a conclusion, Batyrov spoke.

"Of course Kamil. I understand. I'm sorry. But so much has happened over the weekend. It's all very confusing. All we can do now is to try to make some sense of it all. But we are starting with nothing. If you can find out anything, anything at all, then…."

Batyrov suddenly stopped in mid sentence.

"Wait, wait," he shouted out, so loudly that it made Roza jump.

He turned away in deep thought, one hand to his temple.

"We may not have lost everything."

"What do you mean?"

The listening device….in Ormanbekov's 7th floor meeting room."

"What about it?"

Batyrov was thinking out loud, a realisation of something that had suddenly come to mind. He looked Roza directly in the eye.

"The device."

"What about it?"

"It's not only a listening device."

"What," exclaimed Roza.

"I'm sure I gave you one of the newest models," he said, addressing Joroev, who was looking bewildered. "The listening device I gave you is one of the new batch we had in the office, an X11 I think. Chinese. I'm sure it is one of the new ones. We need to get it back."

"Why, what good is it?"

"The X11 doesn't only listen and transmit. If I am not mistaken, it also records what it transmits, up to 36 hours worth. How could I have been so stupid?"

He slapped his brow with his fist, twice, admonishing himself in Kyrgyz.

Batyrov turned to Roza, placing his hands firmly on her shoulders.

"Don't you see, Roza. I am sure it's one of the new devices. If I'm right, then we may still have the evidence. All may not be lost."

They offered each other a cautious smile, Batyrov more in hope and Roza in encouragement. Then they turned to look at Joroev. He knew what was coming.

"Today, Kamil. Today. You will be well rewarded."

"This morning," interrupted Roza loudly as she followed Batyrov out of the apartment.

In all of their encounters, including their first one at the hospital, Roza had found it almost impossible to look Joroev in the eye. Today, she didn't hesitate. There was more at stake now than there had been previously, and she wasn't afraid to put to one side her own sense of fear and awkwardness that she had felt towards her historic adversary, in order to get to the truth.

And, she still had the evidence of his wrong-doing in her possession, something he was reminded of every time they met.

"This morning," she repeated sternly, before taking the stair rail.

73

10am, Monday, 25, Mederova Street

Batyrov and Roza headed for Mederova Street with a spring in their steps. If Batyrov was right, and the evidence that they had heard *was* also recorded, then all was not lost. It may not tell them how Olga died, or why someone might be trying to shut down the newspaper, but at least they would be in a position to bring about some justice into the corrupt world that passed for Kyrgyz politics.

They turned into Mederova. It wasn't hard for them to spot their new office. Number 25. A couple of vans were lined up at the side of the road a short distance away, one of them being unloaded by two men carrying bulky boxes. Batyrov and Roza followed them in.

Askar was already in the second floor room with a couple of overalled workers, one of whom was fixing some shelves to the wall. An electrician was tightening a screw into a plug socket on the floor. Another man, wearing his cap back to front, was installing computer terminals into floorboards under desks. His companion was playing around on two laptops. A new coffee maker, with its wires and plug coiled around it and held with a knotted piece of black ribbing, was on the floor, Its opened, brown cardboard box beside it.

Roza stood at the door and looked around in admiration.

"I'll say this for Mr Kurmanbek. He knows how to mobilise a workforce at short notice."

Batyrov leaned in towards Roza.

"Money talks. And he has a lot of it, Roza."

The floor space was less than what they had at their previous office, but it was open plan. It was also bright and clean, save for the smell of dust that permeated the air. The absence of any filing cabinets, cupboards, white board, even files and folders on desks, was a stark reminder of what had been lost.

Roza looked at the desk count. There were three. She didn't need reminding about Olga's demise, but the absence of what would have been a new desk for her late friend, grieved her. She walked across the room, stepping over loose cables, ignoring Askar and Batyrov who had begun a quiet conversation.

The larger window of three looked out over Bishkek and Roza immediately identified the nearby Garden Hotel, where she and her parents had eaten once in celebration of their 20th wedding anniversary. In the distance, Roza could see the University of Engineering and further on the horizon, she spotted what she thought must be the roof of the Birinchi District Police Headquarters on Panfilov Street. This was certainly a new and largely unexplored part of the city for her, a new beginning, thought Roza, even if she wasn't ready to let go of the old.

Although it was another sunny day, a dull haze rested over Bishkek's skyline. Roza admired its ugliness. She had grown used to it and while it wasn't pretty, it was *her* 'ugly' city. She had come to know and love it. She was a proud Kyrgyz, like so many of her contemporaries. She had no desire to escape to the US or Europe to further her studies. Kyrgyzstan was rebuilding itself after communism, and she was determined to be part of the process. Lofty ambitions held no fear for the educated alumni of the AUCA.

Right now though, her only ambition was to help bring Olga's murderer to justice.

"Roza...Roza?"

It was Askar. She heard her name being called but was allowing herself to dream. The shock of what had happened to her colleague was still sinking in. It may be 36 hours on, but Roza remained in mourning.

"Roza."

"Yes, I'm sorry, I was miles away."

Askar ushered her and Batyrov into a side room. A circular table sat in the centre, with five chairs around it. The three of them sat down. Askar exhaled, slowly.

"Well, here we are. When we left our office in Razzakov Street on Friday, no one could have predicted that three days later, we would be sitting here, in this new office. Thank you both for being willing to continue our journey for journalistic truth and campaigning. Never has it been more important."

He looked at Batyrov.

"Temir, thank you for continuing with us. You could be relaxing at home, writing your memoirs, walking, taking in the mountain air, but here you are. Such loyalty and devotion are rare in this day and age."

Roza looked admiringly at the slightly embarrassed Batyrov, wondering if he would respond. He did.

"There is more for me here than in retirement, Ednan."

A week before the tragic events of the weekend just passed, he couldn't deny that the thought of retirement hadn't crossed his mind. But then Sidarov happened. And his new, unexpected relationship with Dayana had given him another reason to put any thoughts of leaving the capital for the lake on hold.

Mostly though, following Olga's death, he knew that it would not be right to desert Askar, Roza, or Shirin Kurmanbek. He was nothing If not loyal.

Retirement would have to wait.

"And Roza, I have to ask you also. Having slept on it, are you willing to carry on with our ongoing investigation into Ormanbekov as well as Olga's passing? I know it will be hard for you, as it will for all of us. But you are under no obligation."

Askar knew what the answer to his question would be and Roza confirmed it with a nod of her head.

"OK. OK. Thank you. Now, Temir has told me about the possibility that we may still have the recording of Ormanbekov that will implicate him in genocide and corruption. It is not absolute proof and probably would not be permissible in a court of law, if it ever got that far. But if it is as damming as Temir says it is, the court of public opinion will condemn him and he will have to resign and be charged with murder of his own people. And then he *will* come to trial. It's unprecedented. It will embarrass the US too, hugely."

"That may not be such a bad thing," interjected Batyrov.

"With regard to Olga, we are very much in the hands of the police I am afraid. Shirin….Mr Kurmanbek, is in touch with the Chief of Police as the explosion, and Olga's passing, happened on his property. That said, Roza, do you know why Olga would have been at the office around midnight on Saturday? Did you speak with her on the day?"

"Temir and I saw her at the Hyatt before I went to interview Ekaterina Stepanchikov, the ballerina. As I was on that assignment, which had been in the diary for a couple of weeks, Temir...sorry, Mr Batyrov, had asked Olga to attend the *'commencement of grieving and mourning'* for Mr Alymkulov. Apparently, Olga had met his wife once and in Mr Kurmanbek's absence, we had to improvise. I know that Olga had some plans as it is her...."

Roza checked herself.

"....it would have been her thirty-third birthday on Thursday. She was so, so young...."

Askar and Batyrov didn't say a word. They gave her time to gather herself.

"I think she was planning on speaking with her family, as she always did on Saturday evening. She was going to Mr Alymkulov's wake in the afternoon and then planned to write up the obituary after that. The only thing that I can surmise is that she needed to collect the file on Mr Alymkulov. That is the only reason I can think of that she would go to the office on a Saturday. Why she would wait until midnight, I have no idea."

Roza's voice faded away. She had said enough, which was all she knew. And yet, she knew that there was more.

One of the workmen put his head round the door.

"All finished, Mr Askar. I'll need to come back later to replace some bulbs which are faulty, but your computers are all set up. You will need to set your own passwords when you log in for the first time. Any questions, you have my number."

With the workmen gone, Askar took Batyrov and Roza into their new office.

Roza headed for the desk next to the window.

"Is this one ok for me?

Askar had already stationed himself at the far corner of the office, away from the window.

Batyrov put his bag down on the remaining desk.

"I suggest we open two new internal online folders for our investigations, one for Ormanbekov and the other…."

He paused.

"Shall we call it 'Justice for Olga'?"

Roza smiled. She liked that.

"Roza can you set that up and let us have the password access. From today, we transfer any document that we have put online into our folders but also on to this external hard drive. I will keep it in the safe, which is coming on Wednesday. Roza, could you visit with Ayana Alymkulov and ask her about the events of Saturday. She

415

probably won't even know about Olga's passing but she would have seen her there. And she may even have been the last person to see her alive. Find out when she left, who she spoke with and so on. Temir says that Olga…" Askar paused to dignify what he was about to say. "…Olga was dressed casually when she died, so we can assume that she didn't go straight from the wake to the office. In any case, that would be a long time lapse between the afternoon and midnight. Find out what you can, Roza. Temir will follow up on Joroev."

As she listened to Askar, Roza's anger at Olga's death was boiling up inside her. She was personally involved, but she had to separate out her emotions. She had to be professional. This is what she came into journalism for, to be investigative and to bring about justice. Her mission was ahead of her.

"I will go there now," she said, a steely determination in her eyes.

"And Roza….be sensitive. Don't forget, Mrs Alymkulov is grieving too."

74

Late morning, Monday, Alymkulov Estate

Roza walked up Mederova, breaking into a run when she saw a *marshrutka* approaching. She sat at the back, rehearsing what she might say to Mrs Alymkulov. They were two grieving women coming together, for different people, different reasons, as Ednan Askar had reminded her. And Mrs Alymkulov would probably not even know about the explosion at the Star Building, let alone Olga's passing as a result of it.

She pondered these things as the *marshrutka* began is bumpy ride along Panfilov Street, passing Bishkek Railway Station on the left, turning right into the familiar territory of Chuy, into Ala Too Square and left into Frunze Street before rejoining Panfilov and the peace and calm of the quieter, residential streets heading north out of the capital.

By the time it reached Michurina, with its leafy sidewalks and large houses, she was the only person left on the *marshrutka*. All she had to do now was to identify Mrs Alymkulov's house. It didn't prove difficult. No one could possibly miss the two large gers whose canopies dominated the low skyline of gardens along the spacious suburban freeway. Affixed to one of the canopies was a white flag. This was the place. Roza alighted the *marshrutka*.

She walked up the curved driveway a little tentatively, approaching what looked to her like wooden period doors, possibly 19th century, the same doors Olga had entered just two days earlier. Today they were closed. Roza stood on the steps leading up to them for a moment, admiring their teak finish, the detailed workmanship, the craftmanship.

Without warning, one of the doors opened and a woman, wearing a black gown and high *elechek*, stepped out. Roza immediately recognised the person standing in front of her as Mrs Alymkulov. As the wife of an immensely powerful and wealthy Bishkek businessman, she would attend functions with him, often being photographed alongside him. She had also become something of a socialite in her own right, known for managing her husband's charitable foundation, something which he only allowed because it suited his image.

But today, it was the poised and upright Mrs Alymkulov, widow, who stood in the doorway.

"Mrs Alymkulov," exclaimed Roza, feeling immediately ashamed not to have thought to wear more formal, dark attire.

"My name is Roza Beshimov, I'm from the Bishkek Daily News. I work for Mr Kurmanbek, who knew your late husband."

"Have you come for an interview?" Mrs Alymkulov asked, somewhat sternly.

Mrs Alymkulov's response confirmed Roza's suspicions that she hadn't heard anything about the events of Saturday night, or the death of one of her Saturday afternoon guests.

"I know that this can't be a good time for you, Mrs Alymkulov, but please may I come in? I have something very important to tell you, something to ask you. It will only take a few moments of your time."

Roza's pleading innocence and seductive smile served her well when she needed it. This was one such time.

Mrs Alymkulov looked intrigued. She called back into the house.

"Karima, some green tea please, for two, in the garden. And bring me my shawl, the *Orenburg*. Let's walk around here, Miss Beshimov. We can sit outside. It's chilly but we can sit in the late morning sun before it disappears behind the house for the afternoon."

Roza sensed Mrs Alymkulov warming towards her. A bonding of two women, who didn't know each other, brought together by grief, now perhaps with the opportunity to speak about things they wouldn't normally share with each other even if they had been friends. They sat down.

"I am so sorry for your loss Mrs Alymkulov."

"Are you, Miss Beshimov? Did you know him?"

Roza was taken aback by her tone. Maybe she had misinterpreted her host's welcome.

"Only by reputation, Mrs Alymkulov."

"Ah, his reputation. That mattered to him Roza. No one knew him like I knew him. Like so many, he was one man in public, with a reputation to protect, and another one in private. Do you have a young man, Miss Beshimov?"

Roza was surprised by Mrs Alymkulov's directness.

"No, no, I don't."

"Choose wisely my dear. Choose wisely. The only blessing to come out of my twenty-nine years of marriage to Izatbek, is this."

She swept her arms flamboyantly around her in grand gesture, looking adoringly at the estate. "I am now a very wealthy woman in my own right. I never had that luxury when he was alive."

Roza sat there listening, open mouthed. She didn't know what to say.

"I'm sorry," was the best that she could come up with.

Karima brought the tea to the garden table and set it out. Mrs Alymkulov put her *Orenburg* around her shoulders and waited for him to leave before pouring two cups.

"I have often wondered, would I have preferred another life? Maybe if I had chosen differently all those years ago, I could have avoided *this*."

She rolled up the sleeve of her gown to reveal the remains of some bruising around her biceps.

"Or this."

More bruising was revealed as she pulled down a diaphanous strap from the brightly themed organza dress she was wearing, revealing black and blue blotches on her lower shoulder.

Roza looked away, shocked by what she was seeing.

"He was a dying man and yet he still couldn't keep his hands to himself, even as his health deteriorated…."

She spoke without a hint of misandry in her voice. Maybe she loved him despite his indiscretions.

The two women sat in silence for a few moments, listening to the sounds of the sparrowhawks and goldfinches which nested in the fruit and spruce trees around the perimeter fence.

Mrs Aymkulov picked up her cup. In just a few moments, she had been able to unburden herself of years of pain. A few simple disclosures, and all to a stranger.

Roza felt a sense of unease for this stunningly beautiful woman who had hinted at so much fear in her life. Unease for her situation was soon replaced by anger, though.

Roza knew about domestic violence. Conversations in the yard at break times at school were often about what her friends had observed in their homes. Maybe one day there would be a newspaper campaign to run about violence against women in the family home. One day, thought Roza, thankful that her own parents were kindly and loving.

"Now then Miss Beshimov. What can I do for you?"

Roza tried to stay calm and unemotional as she shared what had happened to Olga and the office premises.

A shocked Mrs Aymkulov put her cup down.

"My dear, I am so sorry to hear this news. I spoke with her, yes. She was most charming. Oh, Miss Beshimov, this is such a shock. Please pass on my condolences to her family and to Shirin. Is he back from his trip?"

"Yes. I will, of course."

Another pause.

"Mrs Aymkulov, did you see Miss Kola leave on Saturday?"

"I didn't see her leave, but I do know that she was still here around six. Quite late. We concluded the first day of mourning at 7pm, so she may have been one of the last to leave. Quite a few people stayed until the end."

"So she didn't say where she was going. No, of course not. Why would she?"

Roza admonished herself and asked a different question.

"Did she leave with anyone, do you know?"

"I'm not her guardian, Miss Beshimov. I am a grieving widow. Saturday was all a bit of a daze."

"Yes, I'm sorry. That was insensitive of me."

Roza finished her tea and got up.

"Thank you for seeing me, Mrs Aymkulov."

Mrs Aymkulov sat in her chair, staring up at Roza. "Please, don't tell Shirin about what we spoke about. That's between you and I. For now, I am happy for him to think of Izatbek as he knew him, the jovial, generous donor to good causes."

She rubbed her bruised arm and shoulder as she got out of her chair.

"Sadly, I wasn't one of them."

She smiled as she led Roza to the front of the house.

"Thank you for coming, Miss Beshimov. I hope to see Shirin at the burial next Saturday, if he can make it. And I am sorry for the loss of your colleague."

"I am sure that Mr Kurmanbek will be in touch. Thank you for the tea."

75

Monday, late morning, Metro Bar

Batyrov had tried calling Joroev several times since his early morning visit to his flat with Roza. If he couldn't get through by midday, he would go back there. In the event, Joroev answered Batyrov's call just before half past eleven. It was good news.

"I've got it. I had to wait for Taalay to come on duty at 11. But he has it. I will need another 2,000 *som* for his trouble."

"Have you checked the device? Does it have a recording option on it?" Batyrov was impatient but no reply was forthcoming. "Never mind, I'll meet you in the usual place at 12. Don't be late."

Batyrov nodded enthusiastically towards Askar, who was gazing into his laptop from his new workstation, before rushing out of the office to head for the Metro Bar. Not for the first time in recent days, he was a man in a hurry.

He sat in his usual seat awaiting Joroev. Only a handful of people were in the bar.

The clock struck 12.15pm. Surely Joroev should be here by now. Batyrov began to get anxious. He picked up his mobile phone and searched for Joroev's contact details, one of nine that he had managed to re-enter on to his new device. Just as it was connecting, Joroev walked in.

He sat down and took out a brown paper bag from his pocket, sliding it across the table towards a relieved Batyrov.

"Have you checked it?"

Joroev shook his head.

Batyrov looked around the bar. It was still quiet, just the usual clientele in, office workers, a few couples and a group of three girls in one of the alcoves.

He opened the package. He was not wholly familiar with the device, given that it was a new model, but he identified three tiny slide buttons to its side. One had a speaker emblem on it. Batyrov's thumb hovered over it. Eventually, he pressed it, hoping that the volume wouldn't be set too loud if and when it played back. A green light came on. Batyrov put the device to his ear, just as Joroev's mobile phone rang.

Batyrov continued to listen intently to the device. Nothing.

Then, after a few seconds, he suddenly moved the device away from his ear and stared at it. He heard a small noise, a click of some kind and the sound of glasses clinking. Drinks being poured. Then came what he had been waiting for, Ormanbekov's voice.

"Gentlemen, it has been a long week, an historic week for our beloved Kyrgyzstan…."

He closed his eyes. "Yes," he whispered. "Yes."

Batyrov's heart was pumping. He was ecstatic and so engrossed in his own discovery that he had failed to notice Joroev in sombre conversation on his mobile. After a few seconds, the call ended, and Joroev looked blankly at his phone, before welling up with tears.

"What is it? What has happened?"

"That was a colleague of Taalay, my friend at the White House, the one who has been helping us, the one who got this device for us just an hour ago. He has been taken away for questioning by the secret police."

The two men sat in stunned silence.

Joroev knew that he would never see his friend again. Batyrov immediately calculated that if Taalay talked, probably under torturous conditions, that could implicate Joroev. And if they linked the bugging device to the newspaper, the police would come after it, and its personnel. From there, there would only be one outcome. Closure. Prosecution.

What did this all mean? What might it mean going forward? Batyrov was thinking quickly, his heart rate escalating.

Perhaps it was Ormanbekov who was behind the explosion after all. But how could he have known about the intelligence that they had obtained, sitting here on the table in front of them? And now Taalay had been arrested. Nothing was making sense to Batyrov. He had to act on impulse.

"Kamil, you and I need to separate. You need to lie low. Does Taalay know where you live?"

"No, I don't think so. We always met at the bar."

Joroev was beginning to realise the seriousness of his situation. This was not only about Taalay, his friend, being arrested. It was about how loyal he could be in the face of the hostile questioning that would inevitably be coming his way. Joroev could soon become a wanted man. "You have to go back to your apartment and stay there. I will call you."

Joroev jumped up, walked quickly to the door, leaving a bewildered Batyrov at the table, device in hand.

Batyrov called Askar, who called Kurmanbek.

Kurmanbek summoned Askar and Batyrov to his home for 3pm.

"…and bring Miss Beshimov with you."

76

Monday afternoon, Jash Gvardiya

Joroev was shaking as he walked to his apartment. He looked around him, behind, to the other side of the road, suspicious of anyone who might be following.

He arrived at his door. From three floors up, he had a good view of the street below. It was all quiet.

As he put the key in his lock, his mobile phone rang. It was Joe Ramirez.

"What does he want," he mouthed to himself as he wrestled with the lock.

"Listen, I don't know why I am telling you this, but the explosion…."

"What about it," interrupted Joroev.

"I…I…I feel so ashamed." Ramirez was struggling to get his words out, unusual for a lecturer, an orator. Joroev realised by his tone that it was something serious.

"The Ambassador. I went to see him last night. He was intoxicated and he let it slip."

"Let what slip. What did he tell you? What is it Joe?"

"It was US agents who blew up the offices and immobilised the newspaper's online presence. They are worried about Ormanbekov's motives going forward and they got word that the newspaper may be on to it. So they wiped it out."

Joroev entered his apartment slowly, kicking the door shut behind him, his phone to his ear. He was trying hard not to believe what he was hearing. And what it all meant.

"One of the journalists was killed. That's murd...."

"I know, I know, Kamil. I shouldn't be telling you any of this, but I had to tell someone. And it just confirms my decision."

Joroev shuddered.

"Decision. What decision?"

"The reason I went to see the Ambassador yesterday evening was to tell him I want out. I've been here too long. I'm tired. I need to go home. My family need me. My son needs me."

Joroev's heart sunk. This was more bad news. Taalay had been arrested, and now his confidante and friend was heading back to America. He was beginning to feel abandoned.

"When do you leave?"

"I have to give notice at the University and get a leaving visa but within the month hopefully."

Joroev was still standing in his hallway. He was surprised by Ramirez's news. He had known him for many years and he was a trusted friend, even though he had always felt his subordinate. Suddenly Joroev's head was filled with thoughts of his own future. Maybe he should be thinking of getting away from Ormanbekov's men. But what could he do? He had no desire to return to the nomadic life he once lived. Maybe he could work undercover for the newspaper. He liked Batyrov, and he wanted to make amends with Roza. But how? If he became a wanted man, he would have to go into hiding. But to where?

"Kamil? Kamil, are you still there?"

"Yes, I'm here."

"I'll get back to you with any further news. I would keep your head down if I was you, until things die down a little."

"Yes, yes, that's good. I will….and Joe, thanks for telling me."

Joroev ended the call and sat down. It was a lot to take in. He felt guilty that his actions had led to his friend Taalay's arrest, and was confused about the chain of events that were happening in quick time, not least this latest one, an act of terrorism by the Americans, on foreign soil. Joroev put his head in his hands. He was in deep, much deeper than he wanted to be. And he was frightened. It was time to get out. And quickly.

He called Batyrov, who was walking towards Kurmanbek's house.

"I know who was behind the explosion; who murdered your journalist friend."

Batyrov stopped in his tracks. The sun disappeared for a brief moment. A dark cloud hovered overhead. A few spots of rain began to fall.

Monday afternoon. Kurmanbek's home

The autumn shower had passed by the time Batyrov rang on the doorbell, the White House recording implicating Ormanbekov safely tucked away in the inside pocket of his jacket. That evidence was damning enough. But this latest revelation he had just heard about from Joroev was equally incriminating. The Americans committing murder in a country it had just signed an agreement with was global dynamite. Kurmanbek's wife ushered him into the drawing room.

This time, there was no tea. Instead of sitting on a sofa, they were invited to sit around a hardwood table. The light rain cloud was heading south out of Bishkek. Sunlight was streaming in through the windows once again, reflecting brightly across the polished table.

Batyrov was desperate to share the devastating information he had just received with Kurmanbek, Askar and Roza, who were all sitting down when he arrived.

But he waited for the host to start the meeting.

"As we know. today's edition of the paper was printed overnight but not distributed. This is fast moving and we need more facts. We don't want to muddy the waters of our investigation."

"Sir, if I may," interrupted Batyrov.

Kurmnbekov was not used to being interrupted, but he conceded.

"I've just received further information. I have just been on the phone to my contact. Ramirez called him in the past hour to say that....to say that it was US agents who were behind the explosion at the Star Building...."

The two men looked aghast at Batyrov. Roza put her hand to her mouth, suppressing her shock.

Kurmanbek sat back in his chair. It creaked.

"That probably means they were also behind the closure of our online operation," continued Batyrov.

"The Americans...." Kurmanbek said, staring out of the window. "That means...."

"....yes...," interjected Askar. "The Americans murdered Olga."

The room fell into eerie silence. Batyrov broke it.

"It's only come to light in the past half hour, as I was coming here."

Kurmanbek and Askar had discussed at length about who might be behind the explosion, always suspecting Ormanbekov. It had to be him. He would be the only one who would go to such lengths if he thought that the newspaper was on to him. He had motive. If exposed, Ormanbekov would be finished, trialled in the Hague and probably jailed for life by the International Criminal Court, who never look kindly on genocidal dictators. His dream, years in the making, would be in tatters.

But they were going after the wrong target, at least as far as the explosion was concerned.

"So it's not the White House, Bishkek where the blame lies," said Kurmanbek after a long pause.

He stared out of the window again, taking in the post-shower greenery of his garden lawn, glistening in the sunlight.

"It's the White House, Washington. It seems we have been wrong all along, Ednan. Our suspicions have been laid at the wrong door. But how reliable is this new intel, Temir?"

"It's from the Ambassador himself, via Ramirez and my contact."

"The Americans. This is huge."

"And now we know who killed Olga," interceded Roza, up until now a quiet observer at the table.

"Indeed. Indeed."

"And that's not all," continued Batyrov. "My contact's man in the White House has been arrested."

Roza gasped.

Kurmanbek was trying to take it all in. His eyes stared at the straight lines of dust coming through the large panelled windows, their passage driven by the sun's rays. He knew and understood Kyrgyz politics. He knew how the system worked. He had been in political journalism, first as a reporter for his father, and then as owner of the newspaper that his grand-father had started, for all his working life. He understood the culture, the backgrounds, the motives. He knew Bishkek inside out. He could – and often had – taken on the Kyrgyz establishment, with confidence. But this was the Americans. They were a different, and more deadly opponent. After a short pause, he spoke, with authority.

"The Americans weren't even on my radar until this afternoon. This changes everything. Tomorrow's edition of the newspaper was going to be our tribute to Olga Kola. We will delay that until Wednesday. Tomorrow, we expose the Americans."

"But…."

Batyrov placed a firm hand on Roza's arm.

She looked downcast. It was a tough call, but the publisher had made it. There was no debating his decision. She rested back in her chair, staring blankly at a painting on the wall on the far side of the room.

But she did have one other thing on her mind.

"Mr Kurmanbek, if the Kyrgyz secret service have arrested someone in the White House who has helped us, they will go after our contact, Kamil Joroev."

"Joroev," interrupted Kurmanbek. "Is he the same man who abducted you all those years ago?"

"He is, sir. Mr Batyrov thought that we could use my evidence against him for *Ala Kachuu* as leverage in our quest for information from within the White House. And he has come good but his source has now been arrested. So we need to protect him, get him to a safe location. If they get to him first, they could torture and even ….."

She stopped in mid-sentence. Even as she spoke, she was surprising herself. Why, she wondered, was she advocating for a man who perpetrated an illegal act against her when she was a teenager? Was it for her own safety, and the safety of her own colleagues? Or could it be that her animosity towards him was waning? Batyrov had already shared with Roza about Joroev's regret at what he had done, what he had put her through. And Roza had seen Joroev's willingness to help Batyrov and her in their mission to expose Ormanbekov's corruption. Now he could be in danger of paying for that support with his life.

Kurmanbek was writing down something on his A4 pad as Roza was talking.

"Temir, can you move him to this address today?"

He slid the paper over to Batyrov.

"And make sure he stays there. Thank you Roza. It would seem that very soon, we might all go on to the Kyrgyz secret service wanted list, so we will have to take further precautions. I haven't registered the new newspaper address with the Ministry of Economy yet and I don't intend to, for the time being at any rate. But all my premises are known about by the Ministry of Justice land registry, so unless they want to visit each one, we will be safe and able to operate at Mederova. I have many properties so it's unlikely they will come sniffing around. But I think I can expect a call, which I will deal with. They have been looking for a reason to silence the paper for many years, to bring us into their fold, but they wouldn't dare exacerbate this situation further, especially now. And of course, they don't know what we now know about what we have on them, or the Americans. We can use that to our advantage. If we play this right, we will be able to kill two birds with one stone."

Roza was thankful for Kurmanbek's immediate action on Joroev's behalf, even if it was partly in his own interests. She continued to wonder why she was suddenly seeking to protect the man who, just two weeks earlier, had walked back into her life, the man who she was determined to make an example of in her wishful campaign against *Ala Kachuu*.

Batyrov sat forward, creating a welcome shadow on the increasingly hot table surface on which Roza's lower arms rested. He put the listening device on the table.

"So, how do we move forward?"

All eyes were on Kurmanbek, but it was Askar who spoke.

"Mr Kurmanbek and I have conferred today and we believe that we have no option but to expose the evidence of corruption that is on this device, a copy of which will be made and then placed in our new safe when it arrives on Wednesday. Shirin and I both agree that we have to move very quickly on this. It's now Monday. Our original plan, before we recovered the Ormanbekov tape, was for us to alert regional and international media tomorrow morning of our concerns through our editorials and follow it up with a global internet broadcast to the international media from a secret location. But this new information about American involvement changes everything. We will run our tribute piece for Olga on Wednesday. I have Jamilya writing it."

Roza looked at Batyrov inquisitively. But it was Kurmanbek who responded.

"Jamilya used to work with us, Roza, but left a couple of years ago to look after her sick father. She worked closely with Olga on several campaigns."

Roza nodded, pleased that her proprietor had, for the first time, used her Christian name to address her. Askar looked back at some notes he had made.

"Shirin, in light of the information that Temir has brought today, we need to change the focus about who is behind the explosion and the sabotaging of our online presence. We will divert our allegations towards the Americans. But we need proof. Evidence. At the moment, it's just hearsay. We can still implicate Ormanbekov about the genocide by what's on this recording, but we can't accuse the Americans unless we hear what Ramirez has passed on to Temir's lead, from the US Ambassador himself. Temir, can you get back to your contact and find out exactly what the American Ambassador said to Ramirez. Get him to write up a transcript if you can."

"That may be difficult, but I will speak with Joroev when I move him."

"When will that be?" interjected Roza.

"I've just alerted him by text that, for his own safety, the newspaper will be moving him to a safe house. I stressed to him that it has to be immediate. He's gathering his belongings and I'll pick him up at 5.30pm."

"I'll put a call in to the Ambassador to hear what he has to say," added Kurmanbek. "I won't be able to get him to implicate his own side, I am sure, but I know him well enough to be direct with him. If he'll speak with me, that is."

"Thank you," concluded Askar. "If we can firm up the circumstantial evidence and get something on the record from someone, we can aim to go live internationally at 6pm on Wednesday on both stories."

"That'll give the American voters something to think about over their midweek hash browns," said Batyrov, unapologetically.

"So that's settled then," concluded Askar. "Tomorrow's edition of the newspaper will ask questions of the Kyrgyz and American governments, suggesting their collaboration in political misdemeanour. That should set heads spinning. I'll work on it this afternoon and evening. We'll run Roza's interview with Ekaterina Stepanchikov and Shirin, would you be able to write Izatbek Alymkulov's obitu….?

His voiced trailed away. The implication of what he was asking suddenly dawned on him. He looked at Batyrov, whose head dropped slightly.

"It was the last thing I asked her to do," he said, a valedictory gentleness in his voice.

Shirin leaned towards his longest serving employee.

"Come now, Temir, you must not blame yourself. This was the work of American government terrorists, murderers. You could not possibly have known."

Askar continued his request to Kurmanbek.

"You knew him best, Shirin, so if you would be willing, I will allocate space. I have sport covered and can carry over today's regional issues, which means that we will be back on the news stands tomorrow morning. No one will expect it, but we will do it."

"It will be a powerful statement of intent to our own government, and to the Americans," added Kurmanbek. "Neither will be happy. But if all goes to plan, we will expose them before they have time to act further."

There was a short pause. The meeting was about to come to its natural conclusion. Except for Roza, who offered the final word.

"Olga would expect no less of us."

The three turned their heads towards her and nodded their agreement.

Kurmanbek and his wife bade farewell to the departing group at the door. He had instructed his driver to take Askar, whose car was in for its annual service, Batyrov and Roza to Mederova. They all stood on the steps awaiting the car's imminent arrival, Kurmanbek waited with them. Roza felt a drop of rain on her forehead. Another passing cloud under a forever blue sky. Something was on her mind. It would need courage to ask. She turned to face Askar.

"If there is to be an online media statement on Wednesday, could I be the one to make it?"

The three men turned their heads and looked straight at her, causing her to blush a little. The rain came down a little harder as Kurmanbek's BMW pulled up in front of the house.

"It's just that, I feel responsible for so much that has happened. I brought the *Ala Kachuu* story to you all, and that started a chain reaction with Joroev which led to the information leak and that led to Olga's death, and the persecution of the newspaper. I feel I owe it to you all, owe it to Olga and her family, to be the one to front up and expose this particular wrongdoing."

Kurmanbek looked at her sternly and then raised an eyebrow towards Askar. It was always assumed that he or Askar, as editor, would lead any press conference. It had always been that way. Not even Batyrov had been let loose in front of a camera. Roza was a junior. It was a bold question for her to ask.

"Well. What do you think Ednan?"

Askar sensed that she would be more than capable of delivering the information, the case for the prosecution, in a compelling way. It had come up in her interview for the job that her university degree included a termly module on broadcast journalism and she had been seconded for a short time to TVM, the TV Monitor programme, a Friday staple for late night, central Asian news buffs. But this story wasn't merely about alcoholism amongst Kyrgyz youth; or the allocation of government funds to the regions. This was the uncovering of murder, genocide, corruption. It was bigger than anything that the newspaper had previously tackled.

In the absence of any response to Roza's request from Askar, Kurmanbek spoke up.

"Let me think about it, Miss Beshimov. I'll speak with Mr Askar and let you know our decision tomorrow."

Roza could tell that Mr Kurmanbek was taken aback by her request. He was not used to being asked such questions by a junior, let alone a female. His deferring back to surnames was evidence that Roza may have overstepped the mark. She would have to wait until tomorrow to find out if that was true, or not.

78

Monday afternoon, Jash Gvardiya

Batyrov turned up at Joroev's at 5.15pm. He checked for any police activity, covert or otherwise, before knocking on his door, announcing himself in a low voice. Joroev stood in the hallway, holding a tattered, black suitcase in one hand and three carrier bags on one finger on the other. On his back was a rucksack and over his shoulder was a laptop bag.

"Come," said Batyrov, taking the suitcase from Joroev.

The waiting taxi drove them south along Jash Gvardiya Boulevard, past Young Guards corner towards Fuchick Street, before taking the M39 motorway. Joroev didn't know where he was going but he had enough geographical nous to know he wasn't staying in Bishkek. The taxi travelled for an hour before taking the Sadovaya turn off and the sign, Kara Balta. Batyrov knew it as one of the places where Kurmanbek still had some mining interests. Joroev had never been to this part of Kyrgyzstan. In fact, as he looked out of the window of the taxi, he was beginning to realise that he didn't know Kyrgyzstan at all, other than where he had been brought up, and the capital.

The driver took a couple of rights on coming into Kara Balta city, and pulled up on Uchitelskaya

Street, outside what looked like a modest shack, square, detached from other properties, pale green in blistered colour and in need of a lick of paint. A few children were kicking a ball around at the end of the road and a black and white *Taigan* was sniffing around at the front of the shack.

Batyrov ushered Joroev through the overgrown, unkempt garden space and opened the front door, using the key which, Kurmanbek had informed him, was located under a rock in between the wild apple and walnut trees. There was a room to the left which had a cupboard and single bed in it. The kitchen, which offered a good view of the road on which the taxi was parked, was basic. It had a small refrigerator and storage unit, a portable electric hob which looked as if it had seen better days, a table and two chairs. To the rear of the small property there was a flushing toilet and a small metal tub, both items that represented luxury in this part of the world. A bulb dangled at the end of a wire cable which protruded down from the ceiling. A double electrical point hung from a fractured hole on the wall.

Batyrov exited the abode, closely followed by Joroev.

"Stay here until I contact you. Here's the key. Don't lose it. There is a small daytime market stall at the end of the road and a Turkish supermarket store in town. I will call you. By the way, there's no internet access here."

"What am I meant to do all day without internet or TV?" protested Joroev.

"Would you rather be alive without a TV, or dead with one?" barked Batyrov a little too loudly for his own liking, causing the taxi driver to look round at what was going on. "Anyway, there may be some signal in town, nearer the supermarket perhaps."

Joroev looked glum.

"Look, it's only for a few days until things settle. Look on it as a sort of free holiday."

Joroev didn't look convinced.

"Trust me. I will call you. You will be back in Bishkek before you know it."

Batyrov got into the taxi, leaving a forlorn Joroev at the front door.

"Bishkek. Let's get back."

With Joroev safely out of the way, Batyrov's thoughts turned to the pursuance of hard evidence of murder. American murder. The Ambassador was the key, or at least his sidekick, Ramirez. But would Joe Ramirez repeat the allegations told to him by Joroev? He was about to find out. He scrolled down to find the latest addition to his contact list, reluctantly given to him by Joroev.

His finger paused. Ramirez.

Mira, 10 hours earlier

Back in Mira, the Ambassador had woken up late that morning with a throbbing headache. The digital clock on his bedside table, its shiny green numbers causing him to screw his eyes a little, told its story. 8.35am. His first meeting was at 9.15am. He sat up, disoriented and tried to recount his steps of the previous evening.

Ramirez. Resignation. And several large glasses of Colonel EH Taylor whiskey.

On his way to the lounge, he looked at the bottle on the table. More than half of it had been drunk, much of it still resting in his stomach. He took a couple of aspirin, had a quick shower, and dressed himself for the day ahead. He chose an open necked, white shirt and his favourite, 'almost-black' suit. It was his 'go to' suit when he was feeling ill, or worse, hungover!

He swallowed some water and went to his office across the hallway, declining the continental breakfast laid out for him with military precision by Michael, his trusted assistant of seven years.

He sat at his desk and thought for a moment. It was all slowly coming back to him. Ramirez. Ramirez. And then he remembered. 'He wants to resign. We conversed. What did he say? What did *I* say?'

His heart was pumping, his head pounding. Panic was setting in. He needed to pull himself together. He was being summoned to the White

House, Bishkek. A knock came at the door. "Your car is outside, sir."

The five-minute journey to the Ministry of Foreign Affairs was one that the Ambassador had travelled many times. Usually it was made in more cordial circumstances. But after the events of the weekend, even the Americans would not be immune from scrutiny. And rightly so. They were guilty of murder, not that Kulov suspected anything. Even if he did, Ormanbekov was not going to rock the boat. The agreement just signed was too important. But he did order Kulov to go through the motions, making sure that his government was seen to be investigating all possibilities in the hunt for the perpetrators of the attack on the Star Building on Saturday night. To emphasise the point, Kulov had arranged for a government photographer to be on hand to mark the Ambassador's arrival on the White House steps. The Ambassador, looking pale, was not best pleased.

"This is a bit over the top, isn't it, Minister?"

"It's just routine, Mr Ambassador. Just routine."

Twenty minutes later, the Ambassador was heading back to Mira, his denial of any knowledge about the events of Saturday night duly noted.

Kulov had done his job. There would be no need to bother the Americans again.

79

7.55am Tuesday morning, Bishkek

A greyish van, with rusted paintwork above its rear wheels, pulled into Mederova. Chyngyz, Kurmanbek's weighty delivery man, heaved a batch of newspapers into the lobby, where the new part-time receptionist, Dinara, who Kurmanbek had offered a job to after the explosion, was waiting. She stared at the unmissable headline which took up half the front page.

BISHKEK'S MEDIA MURDER

Five Questions for the American Administration to Answer

Droplets of blood, scarlet on black, began their journey down the right hand side of the page. An image to tell a story. It was powerful stuff.

Dinara's eyes moistened. Olga had been her friend too.

She cut the black tape that secured the bundle, wondering to herself why the paper would have questions for the Americans?

Batyrov was heading towards Mederova but stopped at the newspaper stall located on the corner of Maxim Gorky Street and Mukay Elebayev. Like Dinara, he was impacted by his first view of the newspaper's front page and paused for reflection. His contemplation didn't last long though.

An angry Kyrgyz voice coming towards him from behind broke the silence.

"Oşol kızdı kim öltürsö uyat. Al öz işin gana atkarıp jatkan."

Batyrov turned round to see a man waving his arms furiously before pointing to the picture of Olga.

"You're not wrong, sir. Such an innocent life lost. And for what?"

The street vendor, with what looked like a Russian *Belomorkanal* hanging from his bottom lip, smoke exhaling from his mouth, joined the conversation with a small nod.

The angry passer by stabbed at the paper in Batyrov's hands.

"Kılmışkerdi tabışat dep ümüt kılalı, işeneli. Naalat amerikalıktar."

"I'm sure that the newspaper will do all that it can to help bring about justice for the journalist," replied Batyrov, calmly. The man went on his way, muttering to himself.

In the exchange, Batyrov hadn't noticed Roza, solemn faced, sidling up to him.

"Sympathy for the victim, anger at the murder and a desire for the perpetrators to be caught all wrapped up in one man's response."

"Ah Roza. You heard him?"

"I did. And if that's a measure of public opinion, the newspaper has done it's job. Well done whoever came up with it."

"That was Ednan. And it will anger Ormanbekov. His agreement's been knocked off the front pages by a media tragedy."

"Yes, but I guess he'll be happy that the focus of attention is on the Americans and not him, for once!"

Batyrov paid the vendor before they continued their journey to Mederova. Roza's inquisitive mind was working overtime as she quickly absorbed all of the newspaper's content.

"How did we get proof about all of this? About American involvement, I mean."

"I got Joroev to give me Ramirez's phone details when we drove over to the safe house. I called Ramirez on my way back to Bishkek. He wasn't happy to hear from me but I guaranteed him anonymity and he talked. It's quite a story."

The two journalists turned into Ulitsa Skryabina.

"Mederova is next on the right, I think."

Roza was happy that Batyrov was taking the lead on directions. Her mind was on the newspaper Batyrov was carrying. She made it obvious that she wanted to know more.

"So, tell me."

"Ramirez told me that on Sunday evening he visited the US Ambassador to tell him he would be leaving his long term placement at the University and would be heading back to the USA. The Ambassador was surprised but invited Ramirez to sit and have a drink with him, producing an unopened bottle of Colonel EH Taylor, apparently. That's a strong one, Roza. Anyway, the Ambassador had a few too many and became a bit loose with his tongue. He admitted....get this....that the Americans were behind the Saturday night bombing."

Roza stopped in her tracks. Dumbfounded.

"He didn't deny it?"

"I gave him too much detail about what was said for him to deny it. And anyway, he knew the source of my information was authentic."

Batyrov slowed his pace, pulled out his notebook and began to flip its pages.

"Here it is."

They both stopped just yards from their destination.

"The Ambassador said to Ramirez something along the lines of '.... we have some of the best intelligence and the finest agents in the world. And they can be ruthless when required. As they demonstrated last night.'

Ramirez went on to tell me that he was aware of some American agents who had arrived in the city on the Saturday but he had no intel on why they had come until he put two and two together. He told me that he been working for the Ambassador for 10 years, but he was shocked by what he was hearing especially when...." Batyrov flipped a page on his notebook before continuing.

"You don't need to hear any more, Roza."

She was having none of it, though.

"No, please, tell me what he said."

Maybe she deserved to know. They looked each other in the eye.

Batyrov re-opened his notebook.

"According to Ramirez, the Ambassador called   Olga's death '*collateral damage*'. I'm sorry Roza, that's what he said."

Roza looked blankly ahead of her, before hastily crossing the road to No 25, followed closely by Batyrov. The callousness of the Ambassador's words were unforgiveable and she had been shaken by them. Batyrov suddenly felt guilty for sharing them with her. He needed to reassure her.

"Roza. Roza."

She stopped outside the entrance.

"Ramirez did the right thing. *And* he told Joroev, which is what put us on to the Americans in the first place. And now, because of his evidence, we can seek justice. Let's stay focused. For Olga."

Roza looked up at her mentor and sealed her lips, before nodding her agreement.

Ramirez picked up his own copy of the newspaper on the way to the AUCA. He stared at its front page which made him feel sick to his stomach, even a little fearful? His innocent visit to offer his resignation to his Ambassador on Sunday evening had not gone as expected. And now the content of their conversation was emblazoned on all of the billboards of Bishkek's news vendors. In the public domain. And all because of him.

He had gone to Mira on Sunday evening in good faith, simply to convey his decision to resign his post. He couldn't possibly have expected the Ambassador, his Ambassador, his boss, to get drunk and reveal American complicity in murder. And having then become the recipient of such a deadly piece of information, how could he possibly live with his conscience if he didn't share that information with the media, even if it might serve to bring down the government he had so faithfully served for decades.

Why he felt so obliged to pass on the information told him by his intoxicated Ambassador, he would never know. If he had known it would end up so prominently on the front page of the Bishkek Daily News, he might have thought twice about it. At least he was only named as 'a reliable source.'

By the time he had arrived at page six, he was feeling a little more content. He reassured himself that he had done the right thing in succumbing to Batyrov's persistent questions of the previous evening. And now it was out there in black and white. And because it was out there, he determined that his decision to resign his post was the right one. He definitely wanted out. Especially now. Maybe this unedifying and unexpected exit strategy was his way of getting his wish. And if he was going to go out, he was going to go out with a bang.

His mind suddenly switched to the Ambassador. What would his reaction be to such headlines? Now sober, he would surely have no difficulty linking this editorial to their Sunday night meeting over a bottle of whiskey. Would he remember his drunken excesses, he wondered?

As he stepped into the AUCA, a colleague called out. "Good morning Joe. I see you've got the paper. Sounds like your man at Mira might be in a bit of trouble."

Ramirez shuddered, but knew that his colleague was only generalising. No one at the University knew about his Sunday evening conversation with the Ambassador. He wanted it to stay that way.

80

Tuesday evening, Bishkek

"I think we should let her do it."

Kurmanbek sounded surprised by Askar's enthusiasm.

"Are you sure, Ednan?"

"I am," continued Askar. "I've been thinking. We're behind the times here in Asia. Way behind. The West love women reporters. They're all over the Western media. We can pioneer change here in Kyrgyzstan. Us, the Bishkek Daily News. And we can do it with Roza. She's young, attractive and articulate. And she'll be making the case against two governments. It doesn't get much better than that…."

"I don't know, Ednan…."

"….and, it will be dynamite for our sales figures. We know that we have more voting women in the country than men. They all want an end to corruption. Let's give them what they want."

Askar switched his mobile phone from one hand to another and continued apace. He was on a roll.

"And she has a good face for the camera."

Askar was correct. She could fill a screen with her smile. Her presentation was good. Kurmanbek liked the reference to sales figures but was still concerned about Roza's standing and experience for such a huge task.

"Yes, she is presentable. Where is the gravitas though?" asked Shirin. "It's a press conference for Bishkek News Corp. People will expect me, or you, especially on such an important issue. We have accused our government of corruption on many occasions. But never have we accused it of the killing of its own citizens *and* provided proof to back it up."

Askar could sense Kurmanbek beginning to engage with the possibility of Roza fronting the news broadcast but the proprietor continued to express doubt.

"And then there's the American side of it. I don't even know which story is bigger, genocide or American terrorism. But what I do know, whoever tells it, it's going to create a storm."

"Let's not forget Olga in this," Askar chipped in after a few seconds. "Roza wants to do it for her, not for herself."

Kurmanbek shuddered. How easily his publishing instincts got the better of him.

"Of course, of course, Ednan." he corrected himself, with a slightly embarrassed tone.

Askar had little else to say. He had made his case for Roza. It was up to Kurmbanbek now.

"We may be setting a precedent here, Ednan."

"We may be, Shirin. But it is a precedent people want. We have lost Olga, a woman. Putting a woman up to accuse the Americans of killing her is about as radical as it gets. This is the biggest political story for decades, since the breakup of the Soviet Union. Ukraine. Since Watergate from the American side, or Trump. Accusing our government of corruption is not a story anymore. But genocide against its own people, with a woman making the case to the mothers of sons and daughters, is. It will get a lot of traction, especially internationally. She wants to do it, Shirin. I think we should let her."

Askar could be very persuasive when he needed to be.

"OK, but I will stand behind her. We need the gravitas of the owner beside her. And our banner. We need our banner, our brand telling this story. This isn't the Roza show."

Adnan identified reluctance in Kurmanbek's decision, but his case was won. Roza would deliver the evidence as they had it, live, online, to the world's media.

"Leave it with me. I'll go through the statement with her tomorrow. I'll rehearse her in the afternoon. And I'll alert all the agencies and news broadcasters here and in the US."

"You'd better be right on this one, Ednan. We only get one shot doing this." "I am, Shirin. She won't let you down."

81

6am Wednesday, White House, Washington

Washington was getting itself out of bed. Stoski Ocean was an early riser. He was brushing his teeth when his phone pinged. Toothbrush in his right hand, phone in the other, he read the text from one of his team alerting him to the *Bishkek Daily News* conference at 8am. There was nothing to suggest what it was about.

Ocean calculated that, despite the hostile questions posed by the Bishkek Daily News on its front page yesterday, they could not possibly have uncovered any evidence of foul play by the Americans in the downing of their offices. Or the murder of one of their journalists. There simply had not been enough time.

The newspaper's questions had initially unsettled the Administration, especially Miriam Serenatti, but after a late evening call between the President, Miller, and the President's press officer, the White House consensus was that they should adopt a 'no response' strategy, play it down and let the Ambassador deal with it locally.

"It's hardly registered with the American news media, and those who have picked it up haven't reacted adversely, so why should we comment and make it into a story over here," Serenatti's

Press Officer had advised. "Let it die a death over there."

It was fair comment. Logical.

And this Wednesday morning, after a night's sleep, the White House view hadn't altered.

'A local issue. Nothing to see here,' Ocean told his deputy on his mobile. "Whatever they're about to announce will probably be negligible. Maybe they just want to capitalise on their questions of yesterday. It's a sales ploy at best. But keep an eye on it for me. I don't want it getting out of hand."

He tossed the phone back on to his bed and rinsed his mouth. Despite his bravura, he couldn't help but feel a little uneasy as he bent down over the sink to spit out the mint flavoured residue.

As he made his way back to his bedroom to dress, he began to wonder about the unusually short notice given for the conference. And the questions posed by the newspaper were alarming, even if they only resonated locally in the region where they had been posed.

By the time he had straightened his tie, his curiosity was further aroused.

He alerted the President by text and called Robert de Layney, waking him from his sleep. He felt a little embarrassed to be calling them both for what might well turn out to be an irrelevance, but he sensed he needed to.

"I'm sorry Robert. I genuinely don't know what it could be about, unless they're about to internationalise their questions."

"Ok. Let's watch it together. Prepare an immediate response if that's what it's about. Again, downplay it. Let them know we'll look into their allegations. But deny them strongly. Publicly. Maybe we should have done that yesterday."

"It's only a newspaper making them Robert. Not the Kyrgyz government. I can't see that we have anything to fear."

And with that, he made his way to the underground car park to head to his White House. Another Wednesday on Pennsylvania Avenue was about to begin.

xxx

It was approaching 5pm Kyrgyz time; 7am in Washington. Global clock hands were on the move. Time never stands still in international politics.

A Kyrgyz television camera stood on a tripod in front of a brown patterned office sofa. Its lens faced two bookcases, full of cultural, historical and political titles. A protruding sound mic lurked overhead. The whole set was lit by a spotlight which was positioned in a corner of the room, behind the camera.

At 5.15pm, Roza, followed by Askar and a moustached man holding a clipboard under his arm, entered the room. They were followed by a technician, who took his place on a stool behind the camera. Shirin Kurmanbek came in and watched proceedings. Askar chatted with Roza, who was positioning herself in front of the camera. A make up artist was putting some touches of blush to her cheeks.

The technician, who looked as if he ought still to be in school, was dipping a discreet lapel microphone to her shirt, positioning it to the side of her mouth. He asked her to say some words so that he could monitor the sound quality. Red, green and yellow lights travelled speedily across the mini sound desk, a laptop to its side absorbing the data.

At 5.45 pm the director brought up the screen visuals, those that would shortly be beamed around the world.

Kurmanbek was nothing if not thorough. He knew how to put on a show because he knew the right people, and he paid well. More to the point, he paid. Everyone wanted a Kurmanbek gig, whether they agreed with what his newspaper had to say, or not. Political leanings were put to one side when a pay day was to hand. As a businessman, a property developer and a newspaper owner, the broadcast media was not really his scene, but this story was huge, and international. He had paid for a good team, some of the best broadcast brains in the country, and he was getting it.

"Five minutes everyone," someone shouted out.

Batyrov stood in the corner of the room, observing the activity. As a newspaper man, he too, like Kurmanbek, was out of his comfort zone. He felt it strange to be involved in a press conference without any press present. Like Kurmanbek, he was of a generation which had to adapt to the modern ways of doing things; social media, broadcast media, live media. He was thankful that he lived in a country whose population still relied heavily on news print for its information. But he understood the importance of what was about to happen. He knew that the very nature of this conference was to relay serious charges across the internet against two governments in real time. The need to impart international revelations well and instantaneously was paramount. It would at best serve to bring down both governments, at worse, lead to resignations and impeachments. Such huge global implications over-rode any communications preferences Batyrov might favour.

"Thirty seconds."

Roza, dressed in a tan two-piece suit, settled herself in front of the camera. Behind her head was a striking red and yellow banner, the words *Bishkek News Corporation* to the fore. Its subheading, *'Truth and Justice'* prominent in red type below the title, was about to be realised.

"15 seconds. Live feed being activated."

Shirin Kurmanbek stood alongside her, composed and statesmanlike as ever, but wondering why he had let himself be talked into

allowing a subordinate, a junior in his employ, to make such an important announcement. He felt uncomfortable. But there was nothing that he could do about it now.

"We're going live, in 5, 4, 3, 2, and go."

82

6pm Wednesday, Vefa

Ormanbekov poured himself a drink. Vodka. This evening, he would drink alone. Akayev had alerted him to the online news conference, but, like the rest of the world, he had no idea what was about to take place. When Tuesday's edition of the Bishkek Daily News hit the news stands, Ormanbekov had contacted de Layney and reassured him that there was nothing for him to be concerned about. Kulov's meeting with the Ambassador had confirmed that there was no American involvement in the events of Saturday night. Kulov had no reason to doubt the Ambassador's assurance, even if it was a false one. Neither did Ormanbekov.

"Don't worry about a rogue report from one of our independent newspapers, Robert. I will get my people to have a word with them. It will all be forgotten about by the end of the week."

De Layney had reported his conversation to Serenatti. Both were reassured.

36 hours later, Ormanbekov was sat in his lounge, logging on. He clicked on the link to see Roza, standing alongside Shirin Kurmanbek. Kurmanbek was holding a copy of the updated agreement, its maroon outer evidence of its status

as the amended document that Ormanbekov had just signed with the Americans.

He swallowed his vodka, down in one. And froze.

"What is this," he asked himself, out loud. He turned up the volume on his laptop. Roza cleared her throat.

"Good evening from Bishkek, Kyrgyzstan. Thank you for joining with us from around the world for this important press briefing. My name is Roza Beshimov. I am a Kyrgyz journalist working with the Bishkek News Corporation here in central Asia. I stand here with my publisher and owner of the Bishkek Daily News, Mr Shirin Kurmanbek and other colleagues.

This online news conference is brought to you from a secret location. There are two reasons for this. Firstly, many of you will know that our premises were destroyed on Saturday night by an explosive device activated by agents working, we believe, for the United States government. One of our colleagues, Olga Kola, aged 32, died during that incident. We have evidence that links the US administration to that atrocity. Secondly, we are in hiding from our own government, led, we believe, by a corrupt and murderous leader, Mr Feliks Ormanbekov who, had he known the location for this press briefing, would undoubtedly, have sought to close it down."

Ormanbekov launched his crystal tumbler at the wall, shattering it into pieces.

"Treason. Treason. What is she talking about? I will kill Kurmanbek!"

He got up from his chair and paced the room, his heart racing. Was this to be the exposure that he feared?

"I regret to inform the international media listening and other interested parties, that my own government, the government of the Kyrgyz Republic, together with the government of the United States, have, contrary to the UN agreement on climate change, the EU agreement on fair water distribution, Central Asian protocols on shared water protection, and ignoring previously signed agreements with the campaign group Fair Water, collaborated in a plot to exploit our regional, drought-ridden neighbours, by taking control of the primary resource in the region, water, for commercial gain.

Exploitation of thirsty people for gain is abhorrent enough, but we can reveal that just this past weekend, President Ormanbekov has carried out genocide against his own people by drowning, in order to achieve his objectives. We believe that as many as 600 people, men, women and children, as well as some animals, have drowned and their bodies washed up underground in Songkol region. The motive to drown these precious nationals, who have lived below ground for many years and were therefore reluctant to leave, was to clear and cleanse the pipeline so that fresh water could be transported from north to south of the country and then sold across borders to our drought ridden neighbours, at a price. This goes against our regional agreement on the sharing of natural resources between former Soviet republics. None of this, of course, is referenced in the agreement signed by our President and the Americans one week ago. We have evidence that President Ormanbekov planned and authorised this dreadful act. We do not have evidence that the American government knew about this atrocity, but we question whether it asked enough questions before handing out a further 250 million dollars to our government, supposedly for environmental benefits in the region.

In addition, we have proof that the agreement that was signed by the Kyrgyz and American governments was different to the one that journalists were given on the day of the announcement. This in itself is a breach of international media and political protocols and lends itself to the lie that President Ormanbekov's aims, as stated in the revised agreement, are simply ecological and humanitarian. In fact they are the opposite. For your own scrutiny, a copy of that part of the revised agreement, which we have obtained, will be among documents that will be available to view on our website immediately following this press conference.

We now move on to the explosion at the Bishkek Daily News office on Saturday night, which resulted in the death of our friend and colleague, Olga Kola...."

83

8.05am Wednesday, White House, Washington

De Layney and Ocean sat in the Secretary of State's office, numb. Two morning coffees were on the table. De Layney sat up in his chair at the start of the online proceedings. He looked at Ocean. As Roza Beshimov began to speak, they twigged.

"They know," said Ocean.

De Layney's stomach turned.

"But how?"

The two men listened in grim silence, fearful of what might be coming their way.

Along the corridor, President Serenatti was fearful too. What, she wondered, was about to be exposed to the US media and beyond? Would Americans in their kitchens, in their cars, in their work places, at school gates, be about to hear accusations of corruption and murder against their own Administration? Surely not. How?

The White House fell silent. It seemed that every Secretary of State had heard about the press conference and was listening in. Never had the American administration felt so impotent as it did that moment.

"On Saturday night at midnight, an explosion devastated the offices of the Bishkek News Corporation. I am sorry to say that it had tragic consequences for one of our own. It killed one of our most valued and dearly loved colleagues. This press conference...."

Roza's head dropped down from the camera. Her voice cracked in the emotion of the moment. Was she about to fold, live online? Kurmanbek placed a soothing hand on her shoulder until she was ready to re-commence.

"....this press conference is dedicated to Olga Kola, our friend and colleague. Let me, if I may, address our colleagues in the United States of America at this point. We have uncovered evidence from a reliable source that it was the United States government which ordered the destruction of the top floor of the Star Building in Razzakov Street, Bishkek on Saturday night. We believe that American agents working in Bishkek planted and set off the device, its purpose to destroy any evidential link that this newspaper might have about the substantial additional payment made by the Americans to the Kyrgzs, in return for Mr Ormanbekov's signature on the agreement. We believe that subsequent to the signing of the agreement, the Americans discovered that we had evidence about their collaboration with the Kyrgyz government, and decided to close down our operation.

But it wasn't enough simply to destroy our office. There was our online presence to contend with. And so, at the exact same time that our premises were being decimated, our media operation, our server, our online communication network and our current and historic files were also being destroyed by rogue intervention.

Coincidence? We think not. It was, we believe, an act of hostile aggression by the United States government. And we intend to prove it. We have anecdotal and recorded evidence as well as a witness statement to back up our claims. That the Bishkek Daily News was able to relocate and start up a new, online presence, from scratch, within 48 hours of being wiped out will no doubt be a shock to those who sought its destruction.

To you, including those listening right now in the White House, Washington, we say this. Your mission has failed. Here is the front cover of yesterday's edition of the Bishkek Daily News. You can see, the headline. It reads: 'BISHKEK'S MEDIA MURDER' - five questions for the American administration to answer.' Those five questions that we pose inside the newspaper and which are on our website, relate to American involvement in the terrorist act which we believe destroyed our offices, and killed our colleague. American media colleagues, we urge you to ask these and other questions of your own President and Secretary of State, today.

In conclusion, this has been a difficult and emotional time for all who are associated with the Bishkek Daily News. But as people in our capital,

Bishkek, have seen, we are not going away. We will continue the fight for truth and justice, both here in Kyrgyzstan, and worldwide, where it impacts us. Ladies and gentlemen of the international media, we urge you to do the same.

Thank you."

A black and white portrait of the deceased, the words *Olga Kola 1993-2025* filled the screen.

"Cut."

Silence. The small, disparate group of journalists and technicians looked around at each other in disbelief at what had just been shared around the world. No one moved.

After several seconds, the young sound technician walked slowly towards Roza. She bowed slightly to allow him to remove the microphone. But he didn't. Instead, he put his arms around her and hugged her, warmly.

It was the cue for the cameraman to clap his hands, slowly. A ripple of applause flowed around the room. The sound technician stepped back.

Roza, overwhelmed, turned towards Shirin Kurmanbek, standing behind her.

"Thank you," she said, softly.

She offered her hand to her employer.

Ignoring it, he stepped forward and embraced her.

Head on his chest, she burst into tears.

84

6.30pm, White House, Bishkek

Ala-Too Square had seen its fair share of demonstrations over the years. They had never ended well for governments, or their Presidents. Even as Ormanbekov was hurriedly commencing his journey into exile, crowds were gathering in the gardens to the front of the White House.

In front of its greying steps, Kyrgyz troops were lining up. Whether they were convening to protect the President or arrest him, no one knew. But as he viewed the growing commotion outside his office window, Ormanbekov was in no mood to hang around to find out.

Abandoning his two loyal colleagues without any thought of their years of political omerta in the face of hostile investigations into his many scandals, he took the elevator down to the lower basement level. He knew all of the underground exits that previous Presidents had prepared in readiness for times such as these. All had failed in their escape attempts. Ormanbekov was about to attempt to become the first to succeed.

He was activating his escape plan with urgency. He hadn't even waited for the conclusion of the press conference before making his move.

As the elevator made its way downwards; 6, 5, 4, 3, 2, 1, G, LG, B, he tried calling Ankara. Weeks earlier, as a precaution, he had spoken to the Turkish President to ask for temporary political asylum in the unlikely event of a coup. Suspicious of events which had taken place in Bishkek over the weekend, he had followed up with the Turkish President on Sunday afternoon to confirm that the pre-agreed terms on which he could seek political asylum, still stood.

The Turkish President had become cautious, however. Rumours of serious wrongdoing in Kyrgyzstan were circulating as much in Ankara as they were in Bishkek. Mindful of its continued efforts to seek full EU membership, Turkey would have to think long and hard before welcoming in someone who was suspected of collaborating with the United States in questionable political practices.

But things had moved quickly since their weekend call and time was not on Ormanbekov's side. As he made his way along the secret underground passage that lay beneath the White House and its northerly facing gardens, he could only hope that his pleas would find favour in Ankara.

After 20 minutes of walking, he exited the passageway at the north east corner of the estate at Veselaya. The car he had hurriedly arranged to take him the four hour drive to Issyk-Kul's satellite airfield was waiting for him. The first part of his escape into exile was underway. But it was the second part which concerned him. Would he be able to get hold of the Turkish President en-route to the airport to beg him for safe passage into Turkish airspace? And if he did manage to contact him, would he say 'yes'?

Seeking diplomatic immunity and exile from another country was never part of Ormanbekov's grand plan for the region. But now, he needed them more than anything else. His life depended on it.

85

8.30am, White House, Washington

California was asleep, but on the east coast, Americans were wide awake, stunned at the news they were hearing. The American media had mobilised quickly. News channels broke into their normal programming as soon as they realised the scale of the breaking story. Broadcast agendas were re-hashed and anchors mobilised. Pre-planned news agenda scripts were ripped up. Journalists speculated, politicians were readied, political commentators and representatives of the environmental lobby, *Fair Water*, were put on call.

CBN's Jane Morley was in her element. Impeachment is not a word used lightly in American politics, but suddenly, on this otherwise ordinary Wednesday morning, she was using it liberally. She knew how to create interest in what could often turn out to be a non-story. This was not, and she knew it.

On two continents, rumours of a deadly scandal was rife. Downfall in some shape or form was imminent. For de Layney, as with Ormanbekov, there were limited options. There was nowhere to run. Head in hands, he sought comfort in the isolation of his office.

Ocean watched him from the window. He was anticipating the turmoil about to be unleashed on the government he served, the man he served. Even as a respected a media veteran, there was little that he would be able to do to protect his Secretary of State on this one.

His mind went back a week to Bishkek, to the manhole cover and the decoy girl who had disappeared into it. In his momentary silence, he wondered whether God had answered the prayer that he had prayed. Was she rescued, he wondered, or had she, along with the 600 or so others that the Bishkek media were alleging had perished, been miraculously rescued? It would surely have needed a miracle. As he lost himself in prayerful thought, there was a knock at the door.

"Mr de Layney. President Serenatti would like to see you in her office."

De Layney didn't move.

"Now, sir."

Epilogue

Five days earlier – Redemption

Few things in life unite the human spirit more than a crisis.

Late on the Friday, 24 hours before Ormanbekov's atrocity was due to take place, the phone rang at Nurdeen Askarov's home in Chauvai, a good 300 kilometres south of Bishkek as the crow flies.

"Good evening Nurdeen. It's Kamil here. Kamil Joroev. I hope you remember me. I'm so sorry to call you after so long, and so late, but I didn't know where else to turn."

Nurdeen Askarov had been a trading partner of the Joroev family for many years, horses mainly. Joroev knew him as a good and trustworthy man. He had stables and a large barn. More importantly, he knew many of the 300 or so sewer families, those who had given up living their lives above ground in preference to occupying the pipelines below it.

Joroev hadn't spoken to Askarov for over a decade. He didn't even know if he was still alive. But he did have his number, which the arthritic farmer, now in his 80s, answered, much to Joroev's relief.

"Kamil, my dear boy. Is that really you? It's been so long. How is that father of yours, and your family?"

Kamil explained that his father had died, and that he himself had left the family home and was now living in Bishkek. He explained how he had gained some work with the government and how his life had moved on. And then he came out with it.

"Nurdeen. I need your help please. It's extremely urgent."

"It must be urgent if you need my help after all these years," responded Nurdeen. "And so late in the day."

Kamil went on to explain the dilemma that he found himself in. How he had overheard the President give the order to kill by water the sewer people living in the Songkol to Fergana pipeline; to clear it so that he could deliver fresh water resource from north to the south of the country.

"It's a long story Nurdeen, but the water is gong to be released tomorrow night, overnight we think. We must do something, alert our sewer friends somehow. But how?"

"Are you sure about this, Kamil?"

"I have heard it with my own ears, in the company of journalists. It's true Nurdeen. Why would I be calling you after all of this time, and so late, if it wasn't? I need your help to rescue our friends below ground. I didn't know who else to turn to. Please…."

There was a long silence. Kamil could hear Nurdeen's chesty breathing down the phone line.

"Our President is not a man worthy of his position."

"He is a despot. I have come to know of his indiscretions over many years. But this is the worst. You are my only hope Nurdeen. My last hope. Can you help me, please. Please!"

The old man paused once again. Joroev didn't hurry him. It was enough that he was speaking with him. After a few moments, Nurdeen spoke.

"I am an old man now, Kamil, who walks with a stick. My arthritis has taken hold of me. I walk from one room to another in the day, and then to my bed at night. I cannot help."

There was another long pause.

"But my son Mirgul….maybe he can help you. Do you remember him? He lives the other side of Fergana now, in Kara-Kyshtak. It's about two hours drive away from here. He farms a small holding, but visits me every week, usually on a Saturday."

"So he'll be calling on you tomorrow?"

"Yes, he will, around 10 in the morning."

"We have so little time. We need to alert everyone we can tonight to help get everyone out of the pipeline tomorrow, first thing if possible."

"You are asking much, Kamil….but your heart is on the right side of justice. I will speak with Mirgul right now. It's late in the day for me Kamil, and I am not used to too much activity any more, but if I can help you to save even one of my fellow countrymen, I will do so. And then I will be able to die a happy man."

After he had concluded his call with Joroev, Nurdeen decided to call Kuban Zhumaliev, an old horse milk wholesaler he knew who lived in Baetov, 60 kilometres south of Song-Kol lake. If his memory served him well, it was in that region that one of the entrances to the pipeline was located. Kuban and Nurdeen went back years. Like Nurdeen, Kuban was also retired, though more active. He would know what to do. He had a large network of contacts in Baetev region. He was not familiar with the geography south of Song-Kol. But he might be able to co-ordinate a rescue mission with Mirgul.

"To move that many people such a distance in such a short space of time will require planning," Kuban said. "The further north they are located, the more danger they are in, but…." said Kuban, determinedly, "….I will try. I will call Mirgul now. What is his number?"

Despite not knowing each other, Kuban and Mirgul understood the importance of the mission that they had unexpectedly been asked to undertake, not least as it was now close to midnight. They agreed to try to mobilise groups in their areas to drive to where they thought entrances to the underground pipelines might be located. Used by Russian troops as a secret transportation route for military vehicles and personnel during the war, the entrances had been sealed, some of them camouflaged.

"Since 1951," chipped in Kuban's older brother from his armchair. "They won't be easy to locate, let alone open."

"But we will try. We must try."

Kuban and Mirgul agreed that the they would mobilise friends, family and neighbours that night. The rescue operation would begin at 6am on Saturday morning. Mirgul's group would meet at his father's small holding while Kuban would meet with his group at Ak-Tal on the main road and head eastbound towards Song-Kol. Both groups would try to locate access points which, according to Kuban's brother, had been built into the pipes every 30 kilometres or so. Mirgul's group would search in the south. Both had agreed that if they could just find one entry point each, they would access it and send men and women into the pipeline to alert the sewer families to their plight.

With only a handful of farm workers, working up to 400 kilometres apart, the likelihood of success was thought to be minimal, but Kuban and Mirgul weren't saying anything like that out loud. Morale was essential. And these were

Kyrgyz people. Their people. They didn't deserve to die like this. They had to believe.

Kuban and Mirgul ended their call just after midnight. Whatever was about to happen later that morning, they had agreed that they would conclude the rescue operation by 10 pm, maximising their efforts until darkness prevailed. That would give them all of the Saturday's daylight hours to locate any exits and open them, even though they hadn't been opened for 80 years. They would then send teams into the pipes to run north and south in search of sewer communities, and persuade them to come out of the only life that many of them, especially the children, had known. It was a tall order, but, as one farm worker would put it, *'God is on the side of justice. He won't let us down."*

North

Finding an entrance at the north end of the pipeline would prove difficult, but when word spread around Baetev that a search and rescue operation was underway, distant memories revived themselves. One ninety-four year old resident had, as a teenager, worked to secure the pipeline back in 1947. He knew exactly where it was located and by 6.30am, he was sat in the front of an old Gaz 66 Russian farm truck alongside six men, two women and three young children. At his direction, it negotiated its way down a grassy bank towards a cutting between some overgrown hedgerows. The elderly man, a veteran of Kyrgyz struggle, a man with history etched into every pore of his body, suddenly pointed ahead.

"Al oşol jerde jaygaşkan."

Everyone began to speak excitedly, pointing and asking questions. Behind a large tree trunk which had fallen across the pathway, separating Kuban's team from the entrance, was a huge, circular, metal doorway.

All but the old man jumped from the vehicle and went up to it. It was huge, much bigger than they had anticipated and large enough to take military lorries, tanks and service vehicles. Even their Gaz 66 could negotiate its way through.

Kuban and his team stood perfectly still in the silence of the morning, staring at it. A piece of history before their eyes. Nature had been its only companion over decades. It may be sealed with rust, covered in soil and almost fully hidden beneath bracken, but it was visible.

Now, all they had to do was to prize it open.

"Get me the tools," said Kuban. "We will have to wrench it open."

Even as he said it, he was not confident. Using old farm tools would never move this 20th century icon.

The old man looked through the windscreen as the tools were brought from the vehicle; old forks, spades, pick axes, sledge hammers, in fact, anything that might help them to move the door.

"Right, let's get to work."

The group, men women and children hacked away at the grass, trying to get a foothold near to the entrance. If they could only get closer, they could get a pick axe between the door and its outer perimeter and lever it open.

The old man looked on in frustration. He banged on the windscreen as hard as his weak hands and ailing strength would allow. He tried to hoot the horn, but that didn't work. He couldn't get out of the truck and he couldn't attract attention. The vehicle was on the roadway, looking down on the doorway, and too far away from all of the noisy activity that was taking place below.

After a few minutes of gruelling straining and effort, no progress had been made. Sweat was building up on the men's bodies, as the early sun took its first deep breaths of the morning. It was going to be a long day.

xxx

"*Umütsüz, umutsuz"* said the old man as one of the women brought him some hot broth from a canister they had brought along for sustenance.

"What do you mean, *hopeless*?" she asked.

"Tell them, not the sides, but the ground. Go to the base of the door. There is a lever which will release the door towards them. Once they release the lever, the door will open outwards from the bottom."

The woman jumped down from the van, spilling some of the broth on the vehicle floor. She excitedly relayed the message to Kuban, who asked everyone to stop for a moment. He knelt down on one knee and pushed some grass and moss to the side. And there it was. A handle attached to an exterior zip mechanism.

Kuban looked at the old man in the van. A smile crossed his face. The old man was gesturing. Kuban didn't need any further prompting.

"Pass me the pickaxe."

He locked its blade into the handle, turned it sideways to the ground in order to get some traction, and began to pull. It didn't move. It hadn't been opened for decades. Why would it?

He stood up and looked around him. It was a strange, but melancholy sight, this disparate group, standing in this remote valley, a few kilometres from Song Kul lake and surrounded by some of Kyrgyzstan's finest mountains. They were all looking at Kuban. He looked back at them. Apart from the birdsong which was welcoming in the morning, there was silence. Then he lifted his eyes to the truck, and through the filthy, mud splattered windscreen, he could see the ancient man, waving his hands, urging him on.

It was all the encouragement he needed.

"Nurlan, Sukhrab, Nurbek. Come. Come."

They came. Nurbek brought another pick axe with him and placed it next to Kuban's. They were in parallel. The four of them grasped the pick axe handles as best they could.

"After three, one, two, three, pull."

"Pull."

"Pull."

On the third pull Sukhrab fell backwards into the grass, hitting the side of his head on a tree stump.

A sweating Kuban picked him up and Sukhrab, rubbing his head with one hand, grabbed the pick axe handle with the other.

"Pull," shouted Kuban.

"Pu…."

Sukhrab fell backwards once again only this time, he was holding the splintered handle of one of the pick axes which had separated itself from its iron head.

"Do we have another?" asked Kuban.

"Here, try this."

Aziz, one of the older members in the group who had driven the truck down, handed Kuban a heavy metal bar.

Kuban secured the pickaxes together at an angle, taut against the thick door handle. He asked Nurbek to hold it in place and lean away.

Kuban lifted the metal bar up behind his ears and brought it down with such a thud on the join of the axe head and handles that Nurbek was forced to let go and fall back. None of the watching group followed Nurbek's journey to the ground. Their eyes were transfixed on something else.

Movement. Kuban saw it, Nurlan saw it and Sukhrab saw it. Even the old man in the truck saw it. The handle had twisted itself a few inches.

Kuban grabbed hold of it and tried to force it further to the right. Sweat was pouring from his brow. Nurlan joined him in the effort and after a few seconds, the handle began to turn. The two men, now re-joined by Nurbek, were moving the handle to a greater degree with each turn, easing its grip on the mechanics that held it. A few minutes and a lot of perspiration later, it was free from its coil. The door was separated from its locking mechanism. It was ready to be opened. It was 8.45 am.

South

250 kilometres south, a similar operation was in progress. A convoy of two open topped farm trucks and a tractor edged its way towards an exposed area of pipe. The group of hill dwellers, led by Mirgul, had met at Nurdeen's farm at 6am,

493

loaded a few rusty tools on to the back of one of the trucks and began the slow journey westwards out of Chauvai. The group was larger than the one in the north, but didn't include a 96 year old!

Finding the pipe proved difficult. Mirgul went with the tractor and one of the trucks north and sent the other truck south in an effort to locate an access point but it wasn't until two hours later, around 8.25am that he received a call from the southbound group, which included Mirgul's brother, of an access point. That in itself was a miracle, given the lack of signal either side of the mountains.

Mirgul noted the location and began the journey southbound, keeping as close as possible to the likely pipeline pathway. By 10am, Mirgul's group, bumping along on the back of his truck, had located the other truck and they all began preparing the area. Twenty minutes later, while the group was clearing the overgrown grass and weeds from the front of the pipe's access door, the tractor arrived, smoke pouring from its exhaust. Kuban had messaged Mirgul the information about the location of the door's handle and Mirgul tied ropes to it, before attaching them to the back of the tractor. If the tractor couldn't shift it, nothing could, he thought.

While the farm workers watched on in silent hope, the tractor driver sought to distance himself, and his vehicle, from the door, inch by inch. The tractor had manoeuvred itself backwards towards the door, settling at an angle, facing the road. Its back tyres, huge as they were, would struggle to gain a firm grip on the dewy grass verge. The engine was revving itself to a standstill. The ropes looked as if they were about to snap.

"Get the oil," shouted Mirgul.

A large barrel was rolled towards the door, and he poured it generously over the handle's mechanism. The tractor continued to strain forwards, but edged backwards. One movement forward, one back.

Mirgul asked two of the teenage boys to bring planks of wood, the thickest ones, from one of the trucks. He placed them between the access point and the back tyres and asked the driver to ease back on to the parallel planks, slackening the rope. A couple of the men were drying the tyres with rags, and clearing out the tread of clogged soil, with screwdrivers, wrenches, anything solid metal that they could get their hands on.

After a few minutes of maintenance, Mirgul told the driver to make his way slowly forward. Time was not on their side. More importantly it wasn't on the side of those living inside the pipe who had no idea of the operation going on outside to try to free them. This could well be the group's final hope of moving the stubborn door.

The noise of the tractor engine drowned out the men's shouts, but they kept at it, encouraging the driver in his task. As the tractor continued its slow, painful journey, the ropes behind it became firm and taut once again. Suddenly, a creaking noise could be heard, followed by a lurch forward by the tractor. All eyes went to the handle. It had pulled away from the door, and lay on the ground, exposing its inner workings. Mirgul motioned to the tractor driver to pause. Stillness.

He approached the handle, looking closely at the mechanism that lay in one piece on the grass verge. Amazingly, it still had some of its shine. 70 years hiding behind the handle casing had protected it from the worst of the elements. He scooped oil into it, took a screwdriver and began to dismantle first the outer casing, and then the bigger components behind it. Another hour passed but each piece of metal discarded on to the grass verge brought increased hope to a weary Mirgul.

By mid-morning, Mirgul had created a hole big enough for four men to access the sides. He called them over. They gripped the sides of the depleted locking system and, as one, they pulled. With each pull the men released shouts that echoed around the valley. But no discernible movement. Until….

On the fifth, or was it the sixth pull, there was a sound. Metal on metal. The slightest shift. They couldn't see it, but they could feel it. The door had loosened, very slightly.

One of the men lay on his back, tears forming in his eyes. It was 11.15am.

North

Having broken the door from its hinges using cutters, Kuban, using all of the manpower he could muster, pulled it ajar, exposing the dark inner of the pipeline. He looked inside before turning his head to observe the old man, his face peering attentively out from the truck's windscreen.

The sun shone brightly back over Kuban's shoulder and into the darkened tunnel that awaited his entrance. He could tell it was large, huge in fact, like one of central Asia's motorway tunnels, big enough to take in a vehicle if they could prize the door open a bit more. As he peered further into the spacious area, he spotted a sign of life, a soft light reflection on the wall cavity, about 50 metres from where he was standing. As his eyes continued to adjust to the dim light, he could just about make out several large, grey rocks in the distance. On one of them were lain some strips of linen. Alongside, on a flat stone, was some white cloth, folded and laid carefully to the side.

Kuban's heart skipped a beat.

"This is not a place of death," he said to himself. "Not any more."

He stepped back and turned round to face the expectant group.

"My friends, we have access."

Joyful applause followed Kuban's announcement and a couple of the men embraced. But they all knew that there was plenty of work still to be done.

It took them another hour of digging under the door before it could be fully opened. Once accessible, the empty truck edged its way slowly towards the entrance, inch by inch. It lurched from side to side, and at one stage, it seemed almost vertical, its metal side flaps scraping against the fast drying ground. A journey of five metres took 20 minutes. Finally, it entered in. When it was inside, headlamps on, it turned northbound, its job to locate as many sewer families as it could, explain the immediate danger they were in, and bring them out to a place of safety. He told the driver that he needed to emphasise to anyone he met along the way the urgency of the situation. Everyone needed to come out now. Shelter and food would be provided for them on the farm.

Kuban had calculated that while the residents underground might not have believed the government's message about using the pipes they were living in for water transportation, they would believe their fellow citizens.

With the truck on its way, Kuban sent the rest of the group, men, women and children southbound. Realistically, they could only cover a few hundred metres on foot, but if they could alert one family, it would be worth it.

It was 12.20pm. The search was on.

South

As the afternoon wore on, and silence reigned above ground, Mirgul was beginning to wonder if the whole operation might prove to be futile. He looked at his watch, not for the first time that day. 3.10pm. Then he looked at the entrance. Then he looked around him, at the landscape, the mountains that sat above all that was going on below. What secrets were they hiding under the ground, he wondered?

For the first time that day, he felt alone. He *was* alone. His team were working hard, searching for the unsearchable. What could he do, but wait? And he did. The minutes ticked by. Every sound, every bird song brought him a flicker of hope. But it was false hope.

And then, at 3.22pm, something new.

It doesn't take much to hear a pin drop in the echoey silence of a Kyrgyz mountain slope. But Mirgul heard something. He lifted his gaze towards the entrance, as he had done so many times that day. He was attempting to be as quiet as he could be, but was failing badly. The bracken he was standing on saw to that.

But then, noise. A tiny audible imprint coming from inside the entrance, growing louder, nearer. Footsteps. Life. Breath. And suddenly, recognition. One of Mirgul's brothers, Damire, emerged from the darkened entrance. As he exited into the sunset, breathless, he shielded his eyes from the light before stuttering out his words.

"They are coming…."

He bent over, his hands resting on his knees.

"They are coming."

Before Mirgul could step down to grasp the weary messenger's hand, more life followed.

An older man, his face bathed in hope, stepped out. He was followed by stragglers, sewer dwellers, strangers, refugees as if from another country, all journeying into freedom, together.

They were nearly all on foot, though some had bicycles on which their possessions were piled high.

Mirgul's other brother Aibek emerged among the throng, and he and Damire took their places at the exit, welcoming the sewer people into the light.

Mirgul had arranged for some of his father's friends to provide transport to the two farms, should their mission be successful. The first truck would arrive at 4.00pm. Mirgul's cousin Usen and his wife Lillian had set up straw bedding and some hot soup at their farm in Kara-Kyshtak, while Nurdeen's 76 year old wife did the same at Chauvay. None of them knew precisely how many families would be coming, if any. It didn't matter. Mirgul and his family, his community, would be there for them, come what may. And now, their efforts would not be in vain. Soon, the sewer families would be safe. They would find a home, somewhere to recover, somewhere to adjust, somewhere to dwell, somewhere they could restore their dignity and plan a new beginning. Kyrgyz citizens, in adversity, would look after their own.

At the top of the bank, Mirgul offered each one, male or female, young or old, who made their way out of the pipeline a warm smile and handshake. The rescue mission would continue until 10pm, but by that time, he hoped, every sewer family along the 400 kilometres of pipeline would be saved from death, death by drowning.

North

Kuban and the group rested, drinking green tea and chewing *lepyoshka*. If there was no word back from the search teams, one in a truck and the others on foot, by 3.00pm, Kuban would send in the rest of the group to help, even though they would merely be following in their footsteps.

3.00pm came and went, with no word from Mirgul in the south. Kuban was fearing the worst, but hoping for the best. But with hardly any mobile signal between the two, and none in the pipeline itself, there was very little he could do but wait. And hope.

He looked at his watch again. 3.05pm. He picked up a small stone and threw it at the pipe in frustration.

"Bolsoηçu. Ötünömün. Emnege söz jok, Emnege söz jok," he cried out, angrily.

He stood up, ready to clamber up the bank to the road to alert the second group of his intention to despatch them into the tunnel. But as he made his way up, firmly grabbing a tree stump to help him along the way, he heard something. Despite his awkward stance, he froze his position, motionless. What he heard, in the hidden distance behind him, was an echo. A sign of life.

"E*mnege unchukpaisyng*," he ordered.

The group fell silent.

First, there were voices, Russian voices. Then Kyrgyz and Tajik voices. And then, into the sunlight

stepped a woman, pushing an old perambulator. There was no baby, just belongings. Kuban and the group watched her in silence. One of the men clambered downwards and took her by the hand. Kuban lifted the perambulator up to the road.

She was followed by a steady stream of frightened men and women, some holding the hands of children. Their clothing was colourful, their shoes worn. All of them carried meagre possessions on their backs. Many held their arms to their faces, fending off the brightness of the afternoon sun.

Most seemed bewildered. But none looked reluctant. They knew, in their hearts, that they were making the journey from hopelessness to hopefulness; from darkness to light.

Kuban continued to watch in wonder, a steady stream of nationals streaming out into the sunshine. 150. 200. Maybe more. He looked each one in the eye, in awe of their courage.

A few dogs accompanied the exodus, excitedly running past the flow of humans and jumping up on to the roadside.

Then a pause. A long pause before, stepping out of the darkness, a man.

He was pushing a three wheeled child's buggy, loaded with blankets and towels. He shielded his eyes before being helped up on to the road. And then there were no more….except….

"*Dagi biroo kelet. Jakshy. Kyzyngyzby?*"

Kuban smiled, and looked eagerly over the man's shoulder.

"One more to come. That is good. Your daughter?"

"My daughter. My miracle girl. My wife died during childbirth, sending us into the sewers. My daughter is 13 now. This was her pushchair when she was a baby. She deserves better than I have been able to give her. Thank you for saving us. Thank you. Thank you."

He embraced Kuban, and began to weep into his shoulder.

Kuban, his eyes welling up, watched over the man's shoulder as a child emerged from the darkness; a young, dark haired girl, dressed in grubby, knee length khaki shorts and sporting a white T shirt with a red, star logo on the chest.

On the high slope, overlooking the scene below, sat the 96 year old man observing the exodus, both of his hands clasped together, pressing down firmly on the top of his walking stick. His tired eyes had seen a lot of conflict in his life. And yet, here was good in his midst. He allowed himself a smile. His eyes began to moisten.

Saturday morning, White House, Washington

6,000 miles away, in Washington's White House, Stoski Ocean stared out of the window of his Secretary of State's office, wondering whether his faith allowed him to believe in miracles.

"What are you thinking, Stos?"

Ocean looked back over his shoulder at de Layney.

"I was just thinking about the sewer girl, sir. In Bishkek."

This time it was de Layney's turn to pay attention.

"You're too good for politics, Stos. Let her be. There's nothing you can do for her now."

"No sir. I guess you're right."

He turned back to the window, still wondering whether God answered prayers. His prayers. He would have to wait until he reached the heavenlies to find out.

Saturday evening, Kara Balta

Joroev, isolated in his Kara Balta bolt hole, was lying on his bed, playing a game on his phone.

He hadn't been anticipating any good news, so when his Russian ringtone, *'Straight Jeans and Fitted'* gate-crashed his game, his heart skipped a beat. He clicked on the green icon with trepidation. The ringtone stopped, mid beat. The game disappeared from the screen, and was replaced by two words: *Nurdeen Askarov.*

"Nurdeen. What news?"

There was silence. After a short pause, Nurdeen spoke, with gentleness. This was a moment.

"The mission has been accomplished, Kamil."

Thereafter followed an elongated sound of silence. It never tasted sweeter.

Eventually, it was broken by Kamil whose tears began to flow, softly, and again, softly.

Nurdeen listened in silence for a minute or two.

"All 600?"

"More than 700, men, women, children and even some dogs. Cats. Rats."

"It's a miracle, a miracle. Thank you, Nurdeen. Thank you."

"A miracle indeed. But if it wasn't for you calling me last evening, it would never have taken place. Your father would be so proud of you."

Joroev choked back more tears. No one, not even his father, especially not his father, had complimented him as Nurdeen had in that moment. He took a deep breath in.

"Yes. Maybe, Nurdeen. Thank you, thank you, for what you have done today. This rescue may not make the history books, but someone will have been watching."

"We didn't do it to claim our place in the history books, Kamil. We did it to rescue our people. No one needs to live in darkness all of their lives, and no one deserves to die in it either."

Joroev paused, pondering the authority by which the old man was speaking.

"You are right Nurdeen. I am corrected."

"And now, Kamil, by the grace of God, you have the news we wanted. Now, you need to get some sleep. Go to bed. This has been a momentous day in your life. A defining day. Remember it for what it is and wonder why. I will, certainly, in the days I have left."

"I don't understand Nurdeen. A momentous day; a defining day?"

"You have seen God's love in action today. Everything exposed to the light becomes visible. And everyone. There is nothing hidden that will not be revealed. That is your testimony."

Joroev didn't fully understand what Nurdeen was alluding to but he knew enough to know that he was listening to a man of learning.

"That is wisdom, sir. Wise words indeed."

"Ha, they are not mine, Kamil. Being a good Muslim, such truths will have been hidden from you. But I have discovered the words of Jesus, and his follower, the apostle Paul, in *ıyık Bibliya*. They belong to him. Now, take this victory to your bed and ponder it."

Joroev fell silent, breathing in all that Nurdeen had said to him. How he wished that he had known the old man when he was growing up. His mind was bursting with thankfulness. It was all becoming a bit much.

"I'm sorry," he spluttered down the phone, his emotions evident to Nurdeen, who listened in silence. "I am just so happy."

"No, no Kamil. Don't be apologetic. You have every right to be joyful. Tears of joy are good. It's all good. Our people are redeemed. But now, it is late. It's been such a long day. Let me leave you to your joy. Tomorrow is another day and we will speak then. *Tününör beypil bolsun, Kamil.*"

"Good night to you also, Nurdeen. Allahu Akbar." "And may God bless you too, Kamil. In Jesus' precious name."

Acknowledgements

Thank you to my structural editor, Greer Glover; my cultural adviser, Zoya Belmesova; authors Sarah Lawton and Clare Swatman; Beta readers; Carys Thomas Steer, Hilary White, Richard O'Dair, Jane Barrett and Melissa Cuddihy; my pre-publishing reading group, Stephen Avery, Carol Rigby, Anne McFarlane, David Worthington and Becky Stevens. I would also like to thank those who have journeyed with me in prayer, in particular my prayer companion, Peter Hyatt. Thanks go to Melissa Briggs for advising me on the validity of using Pidyon as a publishing footprint. Special thanks too to my writing group kindly led by Rich Roberts.

Last but not least, special thanks to Sally McIver for her dedication in helping to publish this novel.

Don't miss Alastair McIver's next novel.

Subscribe at alastairmciver.com for updates.

Scan me!

First published by Pidyon Press 2024

Pidyon Press – *Pidyon is a conventional Hebrew word meaning: 'a price that must be paid to redeem, rescue or to deliver someone.'*

Printed in Great Britain
by Amazon